Ascension

BOOK 1 IN THE OF BRIMSTONE & HALOS SAGA

THE OF BRIMSTONE & HALOS SAGA
BOOK ONE

ISADORA BROWN

CHAPTER 1

Everly

The Sanctum of Glyphs was dimly lit, shadows dancing along the stone walls as flickering torches struggled to keep the darkness at bay. The air smelled faintly of incense and aged parchment, a scent that always made me feel like I was on the brink of uncovering some ancient secret. The room itself was circular, with intricate symbols carved into the floor and walls, each one holding a specific purpose in our training.

Elise stood in the center, her auburn hair pulled back into a tight braid. She radiated a calm confidence that I always envied. She was the Seraphim Bride, chosen by God to bear Archangel Michael's children. It made her a figure of awe and reverence within the bunker, but to me, she was just my older sister.

"Elise, do you think we'll be able to practice the Binding Rune today?" I asked, my excitement barely contained.

Elise glanced at me, her green eyes—the same green eyes I had—sparkling with a mix of amusement and affection. "We'll see, Everly. First, let's make sure you've mastered the basics."

She knelt beside one of the runes carved into the floor,

motioning for me to join her. "This is the Protection Rune," she began, tracing the symbol with her fingers. "It's fundamental to everything else you'll learn."

I nodded eagerly and mirrored her movements, feeling the rough grooves of the stone beneath my fingertips. Elise's presence always had a calming effect on me, and today was no different.

I knelt beside Elise, my fingers grazing the rune she had traced. The stone was cool and slightly rough under my touch, its surface worn from years of use. Tiny flecks of mica caught the torchlight, making the symbol seem almost alive as it glimmered faintly. Each line and curve of the rune felt deliberate, imbued with purpose and history.

Elise's voice brought me back to the present. "Feel the energy in the stone," she instructed, her tone gentle but firm. "It's more than just a symbol; it's a conduit for power."

I closed my eyes and let my senses focus on the stone beneath me. It was as if I could feel a subtle hum, a vibration that connected me to something larger than myself. The air seemed to thicken, charged with an invisible force.

"Elise," I murmured, opening my eyes to meet her gaze, "I can feel it."

A smile tugged at the corners of her mouth. "Good. Now, channel that energy into the rune."

Taking a deep breath, I concentrated on the symbol beneath my hand. I imagined drawing power from the earth itself, funneling it through my body and into the carved lines of the rune. The stone seemed to warm under my touch, a faint glow emanating from the symbol.

Elise watched intently, her eyes never leaving mine. "Keep going," she urged softly. "You're doing well."

The glow grew brighter, illuminating the surrounding symbols with a soft, ethereal light. I felt a surge of pride and excitement. For a moment, I forgot about everything else.

Then, abruptly, the light flickered and died.

I gasped, pulling my hand back as if burned. The rune returned to its dormant state, lifeless and cold once more.

"It's okay," Elise reassured me, placing a comforting hand on my shoulder. "You did well for your first attempt."

I nodded, though frustration gnawed at me. I wanted so badly to master these skills, to be useful like Elise.

"Elise," I began hesitantly, "how long did it take you to learn this?"

She chuckled softly, brushing a stray lock of hair from her face. "Longer than you might think," she admitted. "But remember, Everly—patience is just as important as skill."

Her words settled over me like a warm blanket. I knew she was right; mastery wouldn't come overnight. Still, I couldn't shake the feeling that time was slipping through our fingers.

"Let's try again," Elise said gently, guiding my hand back to the rune.

I held out my fingers again, determined to get it right. Determined not to give up.

"Good," she said softly. "Now focus your energy here." She placed her hand over mine, guiding me through the motions.

The room seemed to hum with energy as we worked together. Elise rarely had time for these sessions anymore, consumed by her duties as the Seraphim Bride. It made these moments all the more precious to me.

"Elise," I said as we paused between runes, "do you ever wish things were different?"

She looked at me thoughtfully before answering. "Sometimes," she admitted. "But we all have our roles to play in God's plan."

Her words hung in the air as we continued our training. The weight of our responsibilities pressed down on us, but in that moment, it felt like nothing else mattered except the two of us and the ancient symbols we traced together.

"Let's try something more advanced," Elise suggested after a while. "How about the Healing Rune?"

I nodded eagerly again, grateful for every minute spent with her. We continued our practice in silence, each movement bringing us closer to mastering the sacred art of runes.

Elise's eyes sparkled with anticipation as she led me to another part of the Sanctum. The floor here bore a different kind of symbol, one that seemed more intricate and delicate.

"This is the Healing Rune," Elise said, her voice soft but commanding. "It's more complex than the Protection Rune. It requires a deeper connection with both the earth and your own inner strength."

I knelt beside her, my gaze fixed on the rune. It spiraled outward from a central point, like the petals of a blooming flower. Tiny lines crisscrossed its surface, forming an intricate web of energy pathways. Unlike the bold strokes of the Protection Rune, this one felt almost fragile, like it could shatter under too much pressure.

Elise placed her hand over the central point of the rune, and I followed suit. "You'll need to focus your energy here," she instructed, pressing down gently. "Imagine it flowing outward through each line and curve, filling the entire symbol with your intent. But be careful. This will drain your energy."

I closed my eyes and took a deep breath, letting my mind clear. I visualized my energy as a warm, golden light pooling in my chest before radiating down my arm and into the rune beneath my palm.

"Elise," I whispered, "when would we use this? It's not like the Bunker is ever in danger. Not with the Seraphim guarding us."

She paused for a moment, her hand still steady over mine. "The Healing Rune is used in times of great need," she explained. "When someone is injured or sick, it can help mend their wounds and restore their strength."

"Can you heal a demon with it?" I asked.

"Demons are men who made deals with the devil," she replied. "The only one who can revert a demon back into its original form, back into a human, is the devil himself. And it's only after a demon has paid his penance to him. Remember, they were once humans. It's not our job to judge why they sought the devil—"

"They could have gone to God," I said. "It makes no sense why anyone would even want to go to the devil when we have God."

"Everly, you must mind your privilege," she said. "You were born into a blessed life, where God was worshipped, as He should be. You already have an advantage. These demons... Some have been around before the fall. We cannot change their decisions. We haven't been in their positions. All we can do is pray they find God again."

"Isn't it too late for them?" I whispered.

"It's never too late for God."

I nodded slowly, trying to absorb the gravity of her words. The idea of being able to heal someone was both exhilarating and daunting.

"Think about someone you care about," Elise continued softly. "Imagine them hurt or in pain and let that drive your intent."

My thoughts immediately went to Elise herself. I pictured her strong but weary form after a long day of training or fulfilling her duties as the Seraphim Bride. The image fueled my determination, and I felt a surge of warmth flow through me.

The rune beneath our hands began to glow faintly, its lines lighting up like tiny veins filled with golden light.

"Good," Elise murmured encouragingly. "Keep going."

I focused harder, feeling the energy spread through every line and curve of the symbol. The glow grew stronger, casting a soft light on our faces.

After what felt like an eternity but was probably only minutes, Elise gently lifted her hand from the rune.

"You did well," she said, her voice filled with pride.

I opened my eyes to see the Healing Rune still glowing faintly beneath us. It felt like a small victory—a step closer to mastering these ancient skills, despite the slight dizziness.

"Thank you," I whispered, looking up at Elise with gratitude.

She smiled warmly at me, brushing a stray lock of hair from my face. "Remember this feeling," she said softly. "It will guide you when you need it most."

She straightened, her eyes narrowing with a sense of purpose. "Everly," she said, her voice taking on a serious tone. "I want to teach you the Rune of Flames."

I blinked, taken aback. "But we don't need that in the Bunker," I protested, confusion lacing my words.

"You don't always know if you'll be in the Bunker," she pointed out, her gaze unwavering. "And you need to be prepared. If something happens to me... you need to learn how to protect yourself."

"What could possibly happen to you?" I asked.

"You never know what's in the outside," she replied.

Her words sent a shiver down my spine. My eyes widened, darting around the room even though it was empty save for us. "Elise, discussing the Outside... that's close to treason," I whispered, lowering my voice as if someone might overhear. "We need to be grateful we're even here, and to even discuss the Outside is acting against God."

Elise cupped my face gently, her touch warm and reassuring. "Everly," she murmured before letting out a sigh. She looked away. "Perhaps you're right. But may I teach it to you?

Just in case? You know demons run free up there. Maybe they use their trickery and their savagery to get in. I want you capable; I want you to be able to defend yourself and our bunker."

I bit my lip, considering her words. The thought of learning something so powerful both thrilled and terrified me. But Elise's earnest eyes held a determination that was hard to refuse.

"All right," I agreed, nodding slowly.

Elise's face softened with relief. She took my hand and guided me to a new section of the Sanctum where the Rune of Flames was etched into the stone floor. The symbol was unlike any other—sharp lines and jagged edges radiated outward like tongues of fire.

"This rune harnesses the power of fire," she explained, kneeling beside it. "It can be used for both offense and defense, but it requires immense focus and control."

I knelt beside her. Elise placed her hand over the central point of the rune, motioning for me to do the same.

"Feel the energy within you," she instructed softly. "Imagine it as a spark that you can ignite into a flame."

I closed my eyes and took a deep breath, visualizing a tiny spark in my core. I focused on that spark, willing it to grow into a flickering flame.

"Elise," I murmured, opening my eyes slightly to meet hers.

She nodded encouragingly. "Now channel that flame into the rune."

With her guidance, I concentrated on transferring the fiery energy from within me into the symbol beneath our hands. The lines of the rune began to glow with an intense heat, illuminating our faces with a warm light.

"Good," Elise said. "Keep going."

I focused harder, feeling the power surge through me as the rune's glow intensified.

"That's it," Elise whispered.

As the rune's glow intensified, I felt a sudden surge of fear. The lines blazed with an intense heat, and for a moment, it felt like the flames might leap from the stone and engulf us both. Panic seized me, and the glow snuffed out as quickly as it had appeared. I pulled my hand back, heart pounding.

"Elise, I—" I stammered, looking at her with wide eyes.

She placed a calming hand on my shoulder. "It's okay, Everly. You did well on your first try. The Rune of Flames is powerful and requires immense control. It's natural to be afraid."

I nodded, swallowing hard. "But what if I can't control it? What if I hurt someone?"

Elise's eyes softened with understanding. "That's why we practice," she said gently. "So you can learn to harness its power without letting fear take over." Her expression grew serious. "Against a demon, you need to channel all your intent into the rune," she explained. "Imagine the flame growing larger and more intense, burning away the darkness. Demons thrive on fear and chaos, so your resolve must be stronger than theirs."

I nodded slowly, trying to absorb her words. The idea of facing a demon was terrifying, but Elise's calm demeanor gave me some comfort.

Her gaze held mine steadily. "Against a man, you must use restraint," she said firmly. "The flame should be controlled, enough to deter but not destroy. Imagine it as a shield rather than a weapon—something that protects you without causing unnecessary harm. However..." She let her voice trail off. "Sometimes, it's easy to assume the line between a man and a monster is clear. But the truth is, men can be just as evil as monsters. Demons were men once. But with the devil's influence, their debauched sensibilities are free to run rampant."

"Are you saying... to use this against men as well?" I

paused. "I don't understand, Elise. You tell me demons must be shown grace and that men are monsters."

Elise sighed. "Just... forget about it, okay?" She smiled. "Trust your intuition. That's God. And I know you trust Him."

I took another deep breath, letting her words sink in. The idea of wielding such power was daunting, but Elise's guidance made me feel like it was possible.

"You speak as if something's going to happen," I said quietly, searching her face for any hint of what she might be thinking.

Elise smiled faintly, but didn't meet my gaze directly. "You never know," she replied softly.

Her words lingered in the air between us as we continued our practice in silence. Each movement brought me closer to mastering the Rune of Flames and understanding the delicate balance of power and control that it required. With Elise by my side, I felt more determined than ever to learn and protect those I cared about.

"I'm surprised Archangel Michael allowed you to learn this," I said, my voice barely above a whisper as I traced the fading lines of the Rune of Flames.

Elise's expression tightened. "I didn't ask."

My eyes widened in shock. "But—"

"I wanted to surprise him," she cut me off, a hint of defiance in her tone. "Being promised to someone like him has... humbled me. I needed to show him I could be useful in more than just...bearing children."

I nodded slowly, trying to process her words. "Of course," I murmured. "Do you think I'll be as happy as you are with my intended?"

Elise chuckled softly, shaking her head. "You don't have an intended."

"Yet," I pointed out.

"There's no rush," Elise said. "You're only twenty-three."

"Practically a hag," I retorted, rolling my eyes dramatically.

"Please." She scoffed, but there was a playful glint in her eye. "At the Reaping, you'll be Matched and you'll be able to start your family. It's only a few months away. You'll do your duty to the bunker and to God Himself, and you'll be rewarded for eternity. Just like you want. Just like we're all supposed to want."

A smile tugged at my lips despite myself. "I know it's vain, but do you think he'll be handsome?" I asked. "Do you think he'll be kind?"

"He'll probably be scarred and mangled and broken," Elise teased, a mischievous grin spreading across her face. "Maybe he'll even be a demon."

"Don't joke about that," I said, though I couldn't help but smile at her jest. The thought of demons still sent a shiver down my spine.

Elise's expression grew more serious as she nodded. "Well, once they complete their job, Lucifer either keeps them or turns them back to their human form. It could work out for you."

"That sounds like an awful life," I said, frowning at the thought. "Who would choose such a thing?"

"You'd be surprised," Elise murmured, her eyes distant as if recalling some painful memory. "Life on the surface isn't easy, Everly. And when you're desperate, you'd do just about anything to survive."

"I don't think I could ever be that desperate," I said firmly, shaking my head.

Elise gave me a long look, her green eyes searching mine. "I hope you'll never be faced with such a thing," she said.

Her words lingered in the air between us until she smiled, the kind that was forced, that wrinkled her smooth complexion. "Come on," she said. "I'm hungry. Let's get something to eat. I'm sure the dinner bell is going to ring any second."

I smiled, following her out of the Sanctum of Glyphs. I was willing to follow her anywhere.

Elise was this Bunker's great hope. Archangel Michael chose her, and for good reason. Anything she chose to do was for the good of the bunker, for our safety. I would do anything for her. And I knew she'd do the same for me.

CHAPTER 2

Walton

The dim, smoky interior of The Seraph's Embrace buzzed with the hum of whispered conversations and clinking glasses. Shadows danced on the walls, cast by the flickering candlelight, creating an atmosphere that was both intimate and foreboding. I sat at a table near the back, a half-empty glass of whiskey in front of me and a cigarette smoldering between my fingers.

Lyra perched on my lap, her body warm and pliant against mine. Her black hair fell in soft waves around her shoulders, brushing against my skin as she leaned in close.

"Can you see him?" she whispered, her breath hot against my ear.

I took a slow drag from the cigarette, letting the smoke curl out of my mouth before answering. "As clear as day."

Across the room, my target sat between two whores, a devilish smirk on his angular face. His cold blue eyes were focused on the cards in his hand, calculating and ruthless even in leisure. The black military-style uniform he wore stood out starkly against the worn, muted tones of the brothel's interior.

Insignias of Magnus's regime adorned his chest like medals of dishonor.

Everyone in here knew who he was.

Everyone knew better than to fuck with him. Even Seraph.

The two women flanking him giggled and leaned into him, their laughter high-pitched and false. Decimus barely acknowledged them, his attention fixated on the poker game before him. He held his cards with a confidence born of countless battles won, both on and off the field. A small pile of chips grew steadily in front of him as he played with methodical precision.

Around the table, his opponents—rough-looking men with hard faces and tired eyes—watched him warily. They were no match for Decimus's strategic mind; they knew it as well as I did. Each move he made was calculated to intimidate and dominate.

Lyra's fingers traced idle patterns on my chest as she watched me watching him. "He's dangerous," she murmured.

"That's why I'm here," I replied, my voice gravelly and rough from years of smoke and vengeance.

I lifted my glass to my lips, letting the whiskey burn its way down my throat. My eyes never left Decimus's face, every fiber of my being attuned to his slightest movement.

This was a hunt, and I was ready to bring down my prey.

Lyra fiddled with my hair, her fingers gentle and probing. "Are you sure it's him?" she asked, her voice a soft murmur in the noisy room.

I stiffened at the touch, every nerve ending flaring. Intimacy was a forgotten concept to me. I hadn't been touched like this in a hundred years. Sex was one thing. Caressing? That was something else entirely. It reminded me too much of my life before all this.

Before The Divine Collapse.

A life I didn't want to remember.

"You sure it's him?" Lyra asked again, her voice breaking through my thoughts.

I flicked my eyes to hers, catching the concern there. "You ever know me to be wrong?" My voice came out low and gravelly, a reflection of the rage simmering just beneath the surface.

Lyra pouted, her emerald eyes searching my face for something I couldn't give her. "You know," she purred, her tone shifting to something more seductive, "we can always go upstairs... I can do that thing you like, the one with my tongue? Forget all about it. This. Him."

"Lyra," I breathed out, narrowing my eyes. "I asked you here for a reason."

She arched her back and rolled her hips against mine, trying to draw me away from the task at hand. It was tempting, too tempting. But I had a mission.

"Not that one."

She sighed dramatically but settled back against me, her fingers still playing with my hair absentmindedly. We both returned our gaze to Decimus across the room, his cold eyes locked on his cards as he continued to dominate the game.

Every move he made brought him closer to his inevitable fall, and I wasn't about to let some fleeting pleasure distract me from that moment of retribution.

"I don't like this," Lyra murmured, her voice barely audible over the din of the room. "You know he's dangerous, D. You know he's—"

"I know who he is," I replied between clenched teeth. "He's the job."

"But why would Lucifer want him?" Lyra asked, her fingers still tracing lazy circles on my chest.

"How the hell should I know?" I snapped, my patience wearing thin. "Quite frankly, I don't care. I do my damn job."

And then I'd be one tally closer to my freedom.

One step nearer to being released from this demonic state.

One breath closer to being human again.

When I could finally find my family and get some fucking answers.

Lyra's touch became more insistent, her fingers pressing into my skin as if trying to ground me in the present moment. "But what if it's a trap?" she pressed, her voice tinged with genuine worry.

"Every job's a trap," I said, my voice low and dangerous. "But this one's mine to spring."

Across the room, Decimus laughed, a harsh sound that grated on my nerves. His opponents shifted uncomfortably in their seats, aware that they were being toyed with, but powerless to do anything about it.

I took another drag from my cigarette, letting the smoke fill my lungs before exhaling slowly.

My eyes never left Decimus. Each flicker of his fingers, each smirk and cold calculation—they all told me one thing: he was a man who thought he was untouchable.

He was wrong.

Lyra shifted on my lap, her movements growing restless. "Just be careful," she whispered, her voice almost lost in the noise. "I don't want to lose you too."

"I ain't yours to lose, darling," I said. "Everything out here's lost. But me? I've got too much left to do."

Decimus tossed his cards onto the table with a triumphant grin, collecting his winnings with casual arrogance. His gaze flickered briefly in my direction, a spark of recognition lighting his eyes before he dismissed me as just another patron in the crowded room.

Big mistake.

Lyra's hand stilled on my chest as she followed my gaze. "What's the plan?" she asked softly.

"The plan is simple," I said, crushing the cigarette into the ashtray with deliberate force. "We wait until he's good and drunk. Then we take him out back and have a little chat."

Lyra's eyes widened slightly at the implication of my words, but she nodded in understanding. This was a game we both knew well—a deadly dance of shadows and whispers where only the strongest survived.

And tonight, Decimus would learn just how strong I really was.

Decimus stood up from his table, his eyes locked on mine with a predatory gleam. The room seemed to hush, the weight of his presence causing a ripple of tension. He strode over, ignoring the curious glances thrown his way. Without invitation, he plopped himself down in the chair across from me, a smug grin spreading across his angular face.

"Demon," he said, leaning back with an air of disdain. "I'm surprised they let you in an establishment like this. Don't your kind feed on the blood of women?"

I smirked and leaned back in my chair, the whiskey glass cool against my fingertips. "You're in a whorehouse," I replied, letting my eyes sweep over the room. "Do you see an innocent woman in this place?"

"Oh, right," Decimus said with a smirk that didn't reach his eyes. "I forgot the innocent part."

"Darling," I said without looking at Lyra, "why don't you get me another drink, hmm?"

Lyra slid off my lap with practiced grace, her movements smooth and fluid.

As she walked away, Decimus's eyes followed her, a cruel smile playing on his lips. "She doesn't flinch around you anymore, does she? I bet it took a while before she got used to you."

"Hmm," I drawled, moving a rare coin between my fingers with practiced ease. "Took a while before she got used to some things about me, certainly."

Decimus's gaze shifted to the coin, his interest piqued by the gleam of metal and its fluid motion. He leaned forward slightly, curiosity etched into his hard features.

"Why are you here, demon?" he asked, his voice low and dangerous.

I kept my expression neutral, the coin dancing across my knuckles as I considered how much to reveal. "Same reason anyone comes here," I replied evenly. "To relax. To forget."

Decimus snorted, clearly unimpressed with my answer. His eyes narrowed as he studied me, searching for any hint of weakness or deception.

"Relax?" he echoed skeptically. "You don't strike me as the type to relax."

"Appearances can be deceiving," I said with a shrug.

Lyra returned with another glass of whiskey and set it down in front of me before stepping back respectfully.

Decimus's eyes flickered briefly to her before returning to mine. "So what's your real reason for being here?" he pressed.

I took a slow sip of the whiskey, savoring the burn as it slid down my throat. The game had only just begun, and I wasn't about to tip my hand too soon.

I leaned back in my chair, the weight of the whiskey glass in my hand grounding me. I gave Decimus a hard stare, letting the silence stretch before finally speaking. "What if I told you I was here to cut off your head and hand it to Lucifer on a silver platter?"

Decimus threw his head back and laughed, the sound echoing through the dim room. His eyes sparkled with amusement as he leaned forward, his grin widening. "Why, you're actually funny," he said, his voice dripping with sarcasm. "I didn't think demons could be funny. I thought you were all pathetic humans too lazy and too scared to take matters into your hands after The Divine Collapse, so you sold your pitiful soul to the devil himself to make your life easier." He leaned even closer, his breath hot and taunting. "Was it worth it?"

I chuckled, swirling the amber liquid in my glass before taking another sip. "I'm glad you think I'm funny," I said evenly. "Not many people do. But I can promise you, son, every word that comes out of my pretty mouth, I mean."

Decimus's eyes flicked over my face, a sneer curling his lips. "I don't think I've seen something as ugly as you," he spat. "How they can stand to look at you, I don't know."

"Oh no," I replied with mock concern. "Let's not be cruel. It's not about what I look like, anyway; it's about how I make 'em feel." I smirked, letting my words sink in. "And I can assure you, I've gotten no complaints. Did you need some tips? I recommend taking 'em, especially since you may need to compensate for something else, huh?"

Decimus's face twisted with anger for a brief moment before he masked it with a cold smile. He leaned back in his chair, crossing his arms over his chest as he studied me.

"Compensate?" he echoed softly, the word hanging in the air like a challenge.

I held his gaze steadily, unflinching under his scrutiny. The tension between us crackled like static electricity, an unspoken understanding passing between predator and prey.

"Listen here," Decimus said finally, his voice low and menacing. "You may think you're clever with your little quips and insults, but you're out of your league. I don't think you know who I am... and who I work for."

I raised an eyebrow and took another leisurely sip of my drink. "Out of my league?" I repeated slowly.

"You have no idea who you're dealing with," Decimus continued, his tone deadly serious.

"And you have no idea who you're dealing with," I countered smoothly.

The room seemed to hold its breath as our gazes locked in a silent battle of wills.

"Now, now." Seraph herself set a drink down in front of me, her movements graceful and deliberate. She was striking, an enigmatic presence with long, silver hair that cascaded down her back like liquid mercury. Her eyes were an otherworldly shade of violet, piercing through the smoky haze and seeming to see right through a person. She carried herself with an air of calm authority, each step purposeful and commanding respect.

"You both know the rules, boys," she said, her voice smooth yet firm. "There's a reason we stay in business. Everyone's welcome, but grievances and everything else need to be taken outside."

I tipped my hat to her, acknowledging her presence. "Seraph," I greeted.

She narrowed her eyes at me, a silent warning in their depths. "I'm not kidding," she added, her tone brooking no argument.

"Well," I said, turning to look at Decimus, who was watching us with a smirk playing on his lips. "Should we take this—"

Without warning, a sharp pain exploded in my shoulder as a bullet lodged itself deep into the muscle. I wrinkled my nose in irritation rather than pain. This wasn't the first time I'd been shot, and it sure as hell wouldn't be the last.

"Sorry, Seraph," I said as I stood up, my voice calm despite the throbbing wound. "He shot me."

"Hey, you're supposed to be dead," Decimus said, disbelief coloring his voice.

I snorted, more amused than angry. "From a shot in the shoulder? No wonder your older brother is the right-hand. You're a fucking fool, boy."

Reaching for my mare's leg with one swift motion, I aimed

it at Decimus. But before I could pull the trigger, one of his men came up behind me and smashed a beer bottle against the back of my head.

"Christ," I muttered, thrown off balance but still standing. Annoyance flickered across my features as I shook off the dizziness.

As the bottle shattered against my skull, I staggered but didn't fall. A century of brawling and bounty hunting had hardened me, making my reflexes sharp and instincts deadly.

The first man lunged at me with a knife, but I was quicker. My mare's leg flashed out, and I fired a shot point-blank into his chest. The force of the bullet sent him sprawling backward, his knife clattering to the floor.

Decimus's men hesitated for a split second, their eyes wide with shock. It was all the opening I needed. With a smooth motion, I swung my gun around and fired again, hitting another attacker squarely between the eyes. Blood sprayed as he crumpled to the ground.

The third man charged me from the left, trying to tackle me to the floor. I sidestepped his clumsy attack and brought my gun down on the back of his head with a sickening crunch. He dropped like a sack of potatoes, unconscious before he hit the ground.

Two more men closed in on me from either side, their fists raised and ready to strike. I ducked under a wild punch from one and drove my elbow into his gut, feeling the air rush out of him as he doubled over in pain. Before he could recover, I grabbed his head and smashed it against the bar counter, leaving him dazed and bleeding.

The last man swung a broken bottle at me, aiming for my throat. I caught his wrist in mid-air and twisted it sharply, forcing him to drop the weapon with a yelp of pain. With my free hand, I brought my mare's leg up and fired once more, the bullet tearing through his shoulder and rendering him useless.

Decimus watched all this unfold with a mixture of anger and fear etched across his face. He reached for his own weapon, but I was already moving, pulling bullets and loading six more.

In one fluid motion, I leveled my gun at him and pulled the trigger. The shot rang out in the smoky haze of *The Seraph's Embrace*, echoing through the room like a death knell.

Decimus staggered back as the bullet hit his chest. He blinked, blood dripping from his lips before he collapsed. I watched him fall, his eyes wide with shock and pain. No one got up from that.

I moved back to the men I'd left unconscious. They were sprawled on the floor, breathing, but unaware of the world around them. One by one, I finished the job, my blade swift and merciless. I couldn't risk them coming after me later.

"D!" Seraph's voice cut through the haze of smoke and blood. "The rules!"

I shrugged, wiping the blood from my knife onto a rag. "He fired first," I said simply.

Seraph's violet eyes bore into me, but she didn't argue. The rules were clear, but exceptions always existed in this place.

I went over to Decimus's body and pulled out a box cutter. With practiced precision, I severed his head from his shoulders. Blood pooled around his lifeless form as I stood up, holding the head by its hair.

With one hand, I reached into my coat and pulled out a couple of angel feathers. They glowed faintly in the dim light of the bar. I placed them on the surface of my table, a way to attempt at some kind of recompense at the destruction to Seraph's establishment. They were rare and worth more than a house.

I downed the second glass of whiskey in one gulp, wishing

it could numb me, even just a little. The burn was satisfying but ultimately hollow. No drink could drown my demons— not the ones inside or out.

When I finished, I tipped my hat to Seraph in acknowledgment. She watched me with a mixture of resignation and something like respect.

I stepped out of *The Seraph's Embrace* and into the night, Decimus's head still clutched in my hand. Bounty 665 was ready to be turned in.

CHAPTER 3

Everly

Elise and I made our way down the narrow, dimly lit corridor that led to the mess hall. The bunker was a maze of steel and concrete, with pipes snaking along the ceilings and walls. The hum of generators filled the air, mingling with the distant chatter of our community members. It was a familiar sound, one that had been a constant backdrop to our lives.

"Remember, Ev," Elise said, her voice steady and firm. "You can't expect that everything will go the way you think. You have to prepare for the worst. Why do you think we have combat training? Why do you think we have weapons training? Because sometimes, God tests us. And we need to show Him we can handle anything."

I nodded, absorbing her words. "Of course."

We passed by several doors labeled with numbers and symbols, each one leading to different sections of the bunker. Some were storage rooms, others housed sleeping quarters or workspaces. The air was cool and slightly musty, carrying the scent of metal and earth.

As we turned a corner, the hallway widened, and we could

hear the clinking of utensils and the murmur of conversation growing louder. The mess hall was up ahead, its entrance marked by a simple wooden sign hanging above the doorway.

We stepped inside and were greeted by a bustling scene. Long tables filled the room, each one crowded with people eating, talking, and laughing. The walls were adorned with faded posters and hand-drawn maps, remnants of a world that once existed above ground. In one corner, a small group was playing cards, their laughter punctuating the steady drone of conversation.

The aroma of freshly baked bread and simmering stew wafted through the air, making my stomach rumble in anticipation. We joined the line at the serving counter, where volunteers ladled out portions of food onto trays.

The mess hall had always been a place of solace for me—a reminder that even in this confined space, we still had a sense of community. Elise nudged me as we moved forward in line.

"Don't forget to grab some extra bread," she said with a grin. "You never know the last time you're going to eat something you love. Take the time to enjoy it."

I smiled back at her, grateful for this moment of simplicity during our complex lives. As I picked up an extra roll for myself, I couldn't help but feel a flicker of hope—hope that despite the tests from God and everything yet to come, we could still find strength in each other.

The line moved quickly, and soon we had our trays loaded with steaming bowls of stew and warm bread rolls. We found an empty spot at one of the long tables and sat down side by side.

We sat down at one of the long tables, and I took a deep breath, savoring the aroma of the stew in front of me. The steam curled upwards, mingling with the warm, comforting scent of bread. We quickly said a soft prayer before turning to our food. Elise tore off a piece of her roll and dipped it into her bowl, her movements practiced and precise.

"Have you seen Archangel Michael yet?" I asked, breaking the silence between us. "Have you met him?"

Elise shook her head, taking a bite of her stew. She glanced towards the door as if expecting someone to walk in at any moment. "No."

"I hear he's handsome," I continued, unable to contain my curiosity. "A prince, straight out of a fairytale."

Elise nearly choked on her roll, coughing slightly before managing to swallow. "I'm not sure about that. Handsome, yes. I've seen paintings of him. But no, I haven't met him. He's supposed to come during The Reaping."

"Are you excited?" I asked, leaning forward. "You're so lucky, you know. I heard Fiona and Zoey talking about it, and Archangel Michael specifically selected you. Out of a century of potential mates, you were chosen."

Elise didn't respond immediately. She stared into her bowl as if searching for answers in the depths of the stew.

At that moment, High Priestess Dolores and Elder Jonas walked into the mess hall. High Priestess Dolores was an imposing figure with sharp features and piercing blue eyes that seemed to see through everything and everyone. Her long silver hair was braided intricately, adorned with small charms that clinked softly as she moved. She wore flowing robes of deep indigo embroidered with golden runes that shimmered under the dim lighting.

Elder Jonas followed closely behind her, his kind face weathered by years of experience and wisdom. His long white beard brushed against his chest as he walked with the aid of a staff carved from dark wood. He wore simple yet practical clothing—brown trousers and a linen shirt—with a leather belt cinched around his waist.

As they approached our table, the room fell silent. Everyone stopped eating and bowed their heads in unison.

"Bless us, O Lord," we all murmured together.

"Amen," Dolores intoned with authority.

The room remained hushed for a few more moments before people resumed their conversations and meals; the spell broken but not forgotten.

Elise finally looked up from her bowl, meeting my gaze with a mixture of resolve and something else—something I couldn't quite place but felt deeply within my own heart, too.

"What about you?" Elise asked, her eyes twinkling with curiosity. "Are you looking forward to your Selection?"

"Of course," I replied, setting my spoon down for a moment. "To repopulate the earth as children of God? That's a duty I take very seriously."

She chuckled, shaking her head slightly. "You take all your duties seriously, Ev. I don't know... one of these days, you're going to have to break the rules." She cleared her throat and leaned in closer. "Hey. I think I forgot my butterfly clip back in the Sanctum of Glyphs. Can you grab it for me?"

"Oh," I said, glancing down at my half-eaten stew. "Of course."

I stood up; the bench scraping softly against the floor as I pushed it back. With a nod to Elise, I made my way out of the mess hall and into the quieter corridors of the bunker.

The Sanctum of Glyphs was located in one of the more secluded areas, a place where we trained in runes and studied ancient symbols. The walk there was familiar, yet always held an air of reverence; it was a place steeped in history and mystery.

As I approached the door, the hum of activity from the mess hall faded into silence. The quiet was almost eerie, amplifying each footstep and breath. I pushed open the heavy door and stepped inside.

The room was dimly lit by a few strategically placed lanterns, casting flickering shadows on the walls adorned with runic inscriptions. The scent of old parchment and herbs filled the air, mingling with the faint metallic tang of our training weapons.

I scanned the room for Elise's butterfly clip but couldn't see it on any of the tables or shelves. My brow furrowed in concentration as I moved through the room, checking every possible hiding spot.

Just as I was about to give up and head back, I turned towards the door and froze. A man stood there, someone I didn't recognize. He had a rugged appearance with dark hair and piercing blue eyes that seemed to drill into me.

"Hello," I said cautiously, trying to keep my voice steady. "My name is Everly."

He gave me a long look, his expression unreadable. Something inside me churned uneasily—but what exactly felt off eluded me.

The man's silence stretched on, and my pulse quickened in response.

"Can I help you with something?" I asked, trying to keep my voice steady.

The man didn't respond, just continued to stare at me with those piercing blue eyes. His appearance was unsettling —his bunker uniform, which should have been pristine and white, was stained and disheveled. The jacket hung loosely on his frame, the high collar creased and smudged with dirt. His pants were frayed at the hems, and his boots were scuffed and muddy.

But there was something else, something off about him that made my skin crawl.

"Sir?" I asked again, my voice firmer this time.

Without warning, he lunged forward and grabbed my

throat, slamming me against the wall. Pain shot through my back as I gasped for air, his grip tightening around my neck.

"I haven't seen no one like you before," he growled, his breath hot against my face. "I want a taste."

Fear surged through me, but I forced myself to stay calm. "Please," I choked out, struggling to breathe. "You don't have to do this."

He ignored me, his eyes filled with a twisted hunger. His free hand moved to the zipper of my uniform jacket, fumbling to pull it down. Panic flared in my chest as I realized what he intended to do.

"Stop," I pleaded, trying to keep my voice steady despite the terror coursing through me. "Think about what you're doing. This isn't you. This isn't what God wants from you."

"God is dead. He forgot about us." His grip didn't waver; if anything, it tightened. The zipper slid down slowly, exposing the pale skin of my collarbone. Desperation took hold as I realized words alone wouldn't stop him.

I wished I had my runes, but they were back in the mess hall. And Elise had the ones I practiced with earlier.

I knew I had to fight. It wasn't my strength, but I had to do something. Surely God would want me to protect myself.

Drawing on everything I learned in combat training sessions, I summoned every ounce of strength left in me. With a swift motion, I brought my knee up hard into his groin.

He grunted in pain and loosened his grip just enough for me to break free. I twisted out of his grasp and landed a sharp elbow strike to his face, sending him stumbling back.

He recovered quickly, eyes blazing with fury now. He lunged at me again, but this time I was ready. I sidestepped his attack and delivered a powerful kick to his midsection.

He doubled over in pain but didn't fall; instead, he staggered backward towards the door.

The man's expression twisted with frustration as he stumbled backward. "More trouble than you're worth," he muttered, wiping blood from his split lip.

Before I could respond, screams echoed through the halls outside. My eyes widened in alarm. What was happening out there? Panic gripped me, but I couldn't afford to lose focus now.

He took advantage of my distraction, lunging forward and knocking me to the ground. The impact sent a jolt of pain through my back as I hit the cold, hard floor. Before I could react, he straddled me, his weight pinning me down.

His hand clamped over my mouth, muffling my cries. His other hand pawed at my breasts, making nausea rise in my throat.

Where was God? Why wasn't He protecting me?

I struggled beneath him, desperate to free myself from his grasp. My mind raced for a way out, any way to escape this nightmare. Gathering all the strength I had left, I bit down hard on his finger.

He yelped in pain and yanked his hand back, giving me a momentary reprieve. But then he pulled out a dagger—an old, rusty blade that looked nothing like the weapons we had in the bunker.

"Caleb," a voice called from the doorway. "Let's go. We have the target."

"I just want—" Caleb began, but the urgency in the other man's voice cut him off.

"We're not here for her," the man insisted. "Hurry up. We have to leave."

Caleb glared down at me, his eyes filled with a hatred I didn't understand. Before I could react or plead for mercy, he drove the dagger into my side with brutal force.

Agony exploded through my body as the blade pierced my flesh. A scream died in my throat as he left the knife embedded in me and stood up, rushing towards the door to join his companion.

Pain radiated from the wound in waves, each breath sending fresh jolts of agony through my body. I pressed my hand against the injury, trying to stem the flow of blood even as darkness threatened to consume me.

I lay on the cold, hard floor, my vision blurring as I stared up at the ceiling. The intricate patterns above me seemed almost surreal in their beauty. The ceiling was a masterpiece of craftsmanship, adorned with elaborate carvings of vines and celestial symbols that seemed to dance in the flickering lantern light. Each curve and swirl told a story, a testament to the artisans who had poured their souls into creating this sanctuary.

Truly, a place for God.

But where was He?

The pain radiated from the wound in my side, sharp and relentless. It felt like a hot iron had been plunged into my flesh, searing everything in its path. Every breath sent fresh waves of torment through me, each exhale more labored than the last. I continued to press my hand against the injury, trying to stem the flow of blood, but it felt like trying to hold back a river with a single pebble.

My mind raced, struggling to make sense of what had just happened. Who was that man? Why had he attacked me? The questions swirled in my head, but no answers came. Only the raw, unrelenting pain remained.

I forced myself to focus on the ceiling again, desperate for anything to distract me from the agony. The carved vines intertwined with depictions of angels and runes, their wings outstretched as if offering protection. It was ironic, really—this place was supposed to be a sanctuary, a haven from the horrors of the outside world. But here I was, bleeding and broken on its sacred floor.

The pain intensified with each passing moment, spreading

from my side and radiating outward until it felt like my entire body was engulfed in flames. My vision dimmed further, dark spots dancing at the edges as consciousness threatened to slip away. I fought to stay awake, to hold on just a little longer.

But it was getting harder. So much harder.

The beautiful ceiling blurred and wavered above me as if mocking my suffering with its serene elegance. The carved angels seemed distant now, their outstretched wings offering no comfort or solace. Only cold indifference.

My hand trembled as I tried to keep pressure on the wound, but I could feel my strength waning. Blood seeped between my fingers despite my efforts—a warm, sticky reminder of my fragility in this brutal world.

I closed my eyes for a moment, trying to gather whatever reserves of strength I had left.

Stop it.

I had to get up. I had to keep moving. No one was going to come for me. I needed to see what happened. I needed to help... I needed help.

Forcing myself to stand was like trying to lift a mountain. My entire body screamed in protest, pain radiating from the wound in my side with every tiny movement. I bit down hard on my lip, tasting blood as I struggled to push myself up. My vision blurred, but I kept my focus on the goal—getting out of this room, finding Elise, helping the others, and figuring out what was happening.

Each step was agony. The pain was a searing, relentless fire that spread from my side and threatened to consume me entirely. I leaned against the wall for support, using it as a crutch as I stumbled down the hallway. The dim lighting cast long shadows that seemed to mock my every faltering step.

It felt like forever, each second stretching into an eternity of suffering. But eventually, I reached the mess hall.

Chaos greeted me. Bodies lay scattered across the floor,

lifeless and still, while a few others tried to apply CPR or press against bloodied wounds. The metallic scent of blood filled the air, mingling with the lingering aroma of stew and bread. My heart clenched painfully in my chest as I scanned the room.

The High Priestess Dolores lay sprawled near one of the long tables, her once-imposing figure now bloody and motionless. Her piercing blue eyes were closed, and her chest didn't rise or fall with breath.

Elder Jonas was slumped against a wall, his staff lying beside him. He looked unconscious, his kind face marred by bruises and cuts.

But where was Elise?

I tried to call out, but my throat was too dry and raspy. "El —" I managed to croak before my voice failed me again. "El... Elise?"

There was no response. My eyes frantically searched the room for any sign of her, but she wasn't there.

My head spun, dizziness overtaking me as my strength waned further. The room seemed to tilt and sway around me as if mocking my desperate efforts.

"Elise..." I whispered one last time before my legs gave out beneath me.

The world went dark as I collapsed onto the cold floor, consciousness slipping away like sand through my fingers.

CHAPTER 4

Walton

The Hellgate Citadel loomed ahead, a twisted monument to despair. Once a grand city, now it was a fortress of nightmares. Jagged black spires pierced the sky like malevolent teeth, and the stench of sulfur clung to the air, choking out any remnants of purity. Fires burned eternally within its heart, casting an eerie glow that danced on the stone walls.

These walls weren't just barriers; they were statements of power. Built from a dark, almost obsidian material, they pulsed with an unnatural heat. Spiked fortifications jutted out at irregular intervals, designed to deter any who dared approach without permission.

As I neared the front gate, two demons barred my path. I recognized them instantly: Gorak and Thalza. Gorak's hulking frame and serrated horns made him hard to forget, while Thalza's lithe, serpentine form coiled with a dangerous grace.

"You've got no business here," Gorak growled, his eyes narrowing into crimson slits.

"I've got business," I replied, my voice gravelly as ever. "Lucifer expects me."

33

Thalza hissed softly. "Doesn't matter. Orders are orders."

Frustration bubbled up inside me, but I kept it in check. Instead, I tugged at my shirt collar and exposed the tattoo over my heart. The mark of Lucifer's ownership was intricate—a demonic sigil intertwined with barbed vines, glowing faintly with an inner fire.

Gorak's scowl deepened, but he stepped aside grudgingly. "Fine. But don't cause trouble."

"Trouble finds me," I muttered as I moved past them and into the dark palace that awaited within the Citadel's walls.

The air inside felt heavier, thick with malevolence and the whispers of damned souls. Lucifer's throne room lay ahead, its entrance flanked by more of his loyal enforcers. Each step I took echoed with a hollow finality, leading me deeper into the heart of darkness itself.

As I moved deeper into the Citadel, the oppressive heat and sulfuric stench grew more intense. My thoughts were scattered like leaves in the fall, but the sound of heavy footsteps interrupted my focus. A figure emerged from the shadows ahead, his presence immediately recognizable.

Malak.

He towered over me, even more imposing than usual. His skin was a dark, ashen gray with cracks that glowed faintly red, like molten lava. Eyes burning amber flickered with an inner fire, and his long black hair flowed wildly around his face, giving him a feral appearance. Jagged, ritualistic scars marked his allegiance to dark forces, and his own tattoo peeked out of his shirt that dipped low over his chest.

"D," Malak's voice rumbled, filled with contempt. "Didn't expect to see you here."

"Malak," I replied, keeping my tone steady. "Not surprised you're skulking around."

He sneered, exposing teeth that looked more like fangs. "Skulking? No, just enjoying my latest kill." He motioned to a grotesque trophy hanging from his belt—a severed head, still dripping with blood.

Malak's sneer was a thorn in my side, but I wouldn't give him the satisfaction of seeing me flinch. I glanced at the grotesque trophy hanging from his belt, feeling a mix of disgust and indifference.

"Another bounty?" I asked, my voice steady despite the gravelly edge. "Must be scraping the bottom of the barrel if you're parading that around."

He laughed, a deep, guttural sound that echoed through the stone corridor. "Jealous, D? Heard you've been having trouble keeping up lately."

I shrugged, leaning casually against the wall. "I've been busy. Got bigger fish to fry than whatever poor soul you've managed to drag in."

His eyes narrowed, flickering with anger. "You think you're better than me? Always did have that high and mighty attitude. But look where it got you—working for Lucifer, just like the rest of us."

"Difference is," I said, pushing off the wall and stepping closer, "I've got a plan. You're just a lapdog looking for scraps."

Malak's wings twitched, and for a moment, I thought he might lash out. But he held back, perhaps sensing that a fight here would be unwise.

"Plan or no plan," he growled, "you're still stuck here like the rest of us. And if you're not careful, I'll make sure you stay that way permanently."

"Big talk," I replied with a smirk. "But last I checked, you were trailing behind on bounties. Must be tough knowing you'll always be second best."

His face twisted in fury, and he raised his double-bladed axe slightly before lowering it again with visible effort.

"I've got my eye on you, D," he spat. "One wrong move, and I'll be there to collect."

"I'm counting on it," I said.

For a moment, we stood there in a tense standoff, eyes locked in a silent battle of wills. The ambient noise of the Citadel faded away; all I could hear was the sound of my own heartbeat and Malak's heavy breathing.

"You think you can waltz in here and get special treatment because you have Lucifer's mark?" Malak spat on the ground between us. "You're still just another pawn. And one day, you're going to turn into me. You think he'll release you after you've completed your last bounty?" He scoffed. "Lucifer collects souls like hags collect rings. He won't let you go, and soon, you'll have horns in your head and wings in your back. You'll be condemned to this Hell for the rest of eternity."

"Maybe," I agreed. "But if I'm a pawn, what does that make you?"

Malak's wings flared slightly at my words, their edges sharp and intimidating. "I embrace what I am," he hissed. "You? You're just fooling yourself."

"Believe what you want," I said coldly. "Just stay out of my way."

He laughed again, a harsh sound that echoed through the corridor. "Oh, I'll be watching you closely, D. Don't slip up. Anything I can do to keep you from scoring that final bounty, I will. Mark my words."

With that parting shot, he stepped aside reluctantly but not before giving me one last burning glare.

I continued forward without looking back, knowing full well this wouldn't be our last encounter.

Inside Lucifer's throne room awaited another kind of hell altogether.

The door to Lucifer's throne room creaked open, and a wave of oppressive heat washed over me. Stepping inside felt like crossing into a furnace. The room itself was a cavernous expanse, its high ceilings lost in shadows. Blackened stone walls were adorned with twisted, grotesque sculptures, each one depicting scenes of torment and despair. The air crackled with dark energy, making my skin crawl.

At the center of the room stood Lucifer's throne. It was an abomination of iron and bone, a macabre masterpiece that seemed to pulsate with malevolent life. Jagged spikes jutted from its frame, and demonic runes glowed faintly along its surface, casting eerie shadows that danced in the flickering firelight.

Lucifer himself lounged upon this ghastly seat of power. His appearance was as regal as it was terrifying—a tall figure draped in flowing black robes that seemed to absorb all light. His skin was pale, almost luminescent, contrasting sharply with the darkness. Horns curled back from his forehead like those of a ram, and his eyes glowed with a cold, calculating fire.

At first, he appeared bored, one hand resting lazily on the armrest while the other twirled a goblet filled with some dark liquid. But as I entered, those glowing eyes flicked up and focused on me with unsettling intensity.

"D," he greeted, a slow smile spreading across his face. "I wondered when you'd be back."

I stood my ground, meeting his gaze without flinching. "I'm here to report," I said simply.

I reached into my sack, feeling the weight of my latest bounty. The rough fabric scraped against my fingers as I pulled out the severed head of Decimus. With a quick, deliberate motion, I tossed it at Lucifer's feet.

Lucifer's eyes, cold and calculating, locked onto the head. He stared at it for a moment before leaning forward and picking it up. He turned it in his hands, examining the lifeless face with a mixture of amusement and curiosity.

"You succeeded," he finally said, his voice a slow drawl.

"You sound surprised," I replied, my tone flat but edged with defiance.

Lucifer glanced up at me, his gaze piercing. "You know who he is." It wasn't a question. "You would think you'd be worried about the repercussions when you're so close to getting your soul back."

I met his gaze head-on, my expression unyielding. "Well now, Prince of Darkness, you underestimate me," I drawled. "Repercussions don't much scare me when I've come this far."

A smirk tugged at Lucifer's lips as he tossed Decimus's head behind him like discarded trash.

"I am surprised," I continued. "The devil himself concerned over a pithy group of humans that you'd need to kill some pathetic piece of shit."

"Suffering is something I endeavor," Lucifer said, his lips pursing slightly. "The Dominion is too powerful for their own good. Collecting women, selling them as slaves, keeping men to work the Abyssal Sprawl. They're trying to mine our magic, and crucifying those that won't give them what they want."

That caught me off guard. I raised an eyebrow. "Then why go for some stupid shit and not Magnus Rex himself? Cut the head off the snake, as it were."

Lucifer's eyes flickered over to me with a gleam of interest. "You sound like you're actually intrigued," he observed. "Tell me. Are you interested in gathering information for a hefty sum?"

I stared back at him, unblinking. "I'm here to find my last bounty," I said firmly. "And then I'll be back to collect my soul."

"Would you really want it if it means The Dominion is after you?" he asked, his voice softening just enough to hint at genuine curiosity. "You won't have healing abilities."

"Yeah, well." I shrugged, unperturbed. "They fire a shot between my eyes, I'm dead either way, demon or not. Or they use runes on me, and I highly doubt they have the mental capacity to learn that."

"Besides the angels, no one knows runes," Lucifer said, his tone casual but laced with something darker. "Not even most demons." He glanced at me, eyes narrowing slightly. "But you do?"

I took out a cigarette and lit it before taking a deep drag; the ember flaring bright in the dim light of the throne room. The smoke curled lazily upwards, filling the space between us with a haze that smelled faintly of sulfur and ash.

"I've been around a while," I replied, letting the smoke trail out slowly from between my lips.

Lucifer's eyes narrowed further, and he wrinkled his nose in obvious distaste. "Did I give you leave to smoke in here?"

I held his gaze, unflinching. "Now, my Prince," I began, my voice smooth and dripping with that southern charm that masked my steel resolve. "In all the years I've known you—and trust me, it's been a few—I never did take you for one to stand on ceremony."

Lucifer's lips twitched into what might have been a smile or a snarl; it was hard to tell with him sometimes. His eyes bore into mine, as if trying to peel back the layers of my defiance and find something more pliable underneath.

"Now," I continued, tapping the ash from my cigarette onto the cold stone floor with deliberate nonchalance. "My final bounty?"

He gave me another long look, as if weighing something in his mind. The tension between us hung heavy in the air, like an unspoken challenge.

Finally, Lucifer leaned back on his throne, his fingers drumming against the armrest. "You really think you're ready for this?" he asked softly, almost as if speaking to himself.

I met his gaze without hesitation. "You know I am."

"Elise Harrington," Lucifer said, his eyes never leaving mine.

"Who?" I asked, taking a drag of my cigarette, letting the smoke curl lazily upwards.

"Elise Harrington," he repeated, leaning forward slightly. "How do you know runes and not Elise Harrington?"

I exhaled slowly; the smoke hanging in the air between us. "Now, Prince of Darkness, you underestimate me again. I've been around this hellhole long enough to know plenty of things most folks don't. But a name like that? Can't say it rings any bells."

Lucifer looked away for a moment, an edge in his eyes. "Elise is the Seraph Bride," he said. "She was born to be sacrificed to Archangel Michael. In exchange, he's supposed to take God's Nephilim Army and eradicate demons from Earth."

"Nephilim?" I asked. "I thought they were crossbreeds between humans and angels."

"They are," Lucifer said. "And Elise Harrington is the most important of them all."

I chuckled, the sound echoing in the oppressive silence of the throne room. "He requires a human sacrifice in order to protect God's creatures?" I drawled. "How Pagan of him."

"Quite," Lucifer replied with a hint of amusement. "But our friend Mikey isn't pleased at the notion of it, either. And by sacrifice, she's to wed him and give him bountiful little half-breeds. God thinks once the angels have skin in the game, they'll actually touch down on Earth and purify it again."

"Why doesn't God do it Himself?" I asked.

"Probably because He's fucking tired," Lucifer said with a weary sigh. "He's already had to restart the earth a few times because His children refused to cooperate. Trust me, I understand the feeling."

"Why can't He just order the angels to do His bidding?" I asked, genuinely curious.

"You ever hear of a thing called free will?" Lucifer countered. "Angels have that, too."

"And yet, Michael's going to marry the girl even if he doesn't want to?" I pressed.

"My brother is an arrogant fool," Lucifer said, his voice tinged with bitterness. "In exchange for the reign of God's army, he agreed to marry one of the Purifiers—one he selected himself—and only when she turned thirty. Now that she's thirty, he has to follow through on his promise to God."

"All for control over God's army?" I asked.

"Power," Lucifer said simply. "That's what it is. Power. And Michael has always craved power."

I took another drag from my cigarette, considering his words carefully. The smoke mingled with the heavy air of the throne room, creating an almost tangible fog between us.

"A girl, then?" I asked, my voice betraying a hint of skepticism. "That's it?"

"Alive, D. You bring her directly to me," Lucifer replied, his tone leaving no room for negotiation.

"And how am I to get to her?" I pressed.

"She's in a bunker," Lucifer said, and the words set my teeth on edge. Bunkers were the bane of my existence—fortresses of paranoia and zealotry, filled with fanatics ready to die for their cause.

"I'll give you the coordinates," he continued. "But you won't be the only one after her, I assure you. Hell, The Dominion, The Marauders, even demons—they'll all want their hands on her. Controlling her controls Michael."

"Unless he can just pick another," I said, stomping out my cigarette on the cold stone floor.

"No." Lucifer shook his head. "He picked her for a reason."

I knew there was more he wasn't telling me. There always was.

"I find her, get her to you, and I'm done?" I asked.

"Done," he confirmed, extending his hand.

ISADORA BROWN

I looked at it for a long moment before finally shaking it. His grip was cold and unyielding, like a steel trap.

When we pulled away, Lucifer waved his hands, and a bag appeared at my feet. "Your payment," he said. "For Decimus. You'll get three times that for Elise."

I picked up the bag. It clinked with the unmistakable sound of demon shards—probably more than I'd ever seen in one place.

"Do I have a room for the night?" I asked.

"And access to food and drink," Lucifer said, leaning back on his throne. "But leave soon, D. Because if you don't, someone else will grab her. And I will not get you another bounty if that happens. Your freedom will be in limbo. You'll never get your soul back."

"She's in a bunker," I repeated, the frustration evident in my voice.

"You think they care?" he asked with a dismissive wave of his hand. "They're much more resourceful than you give them credit for. If you know where to look, you can find anything up here. And now that she's thirty, they're all going for her. You need to get to her first." He paused. "Oh, and D? If anything happens to her, if she's dead, your long life will be Hell. Do you understand?"

I looked at the bag in my hand, weighing my options one last time, before nodding. "Consider it done," I said.

Lucifer's smile widened as he reclined further into his grotesque throne. "I knew you'd see it my way."

42

CHAPTER 5

Everly

I woke to the soft blinking of lights and the persistent beep of medical monitors. The sterile smell hit me first, followed by a dull, throbbing pain in my stomach. I tried to sit up but quickly abandoned the effort with a groan.

"Everly," a voice murmured.

I squinted through the haze and saw Zoey leaning over me. Her dark eyes were full of worry, her skin a warm shade of brown that reminded me of caramel. She was a sharp beauty, with high cheekbones and an intense gaze.

"You can't move," she said, her voice steady but tinged with concern.

"What happened?" My throat felt raw, and the words scraped out like sandpaper.

Zoey sighed, brushing a strand of hair from her face. "Where to start?" She glanced away for a moment, gathering her thoughts. "Ev, we were attacked. Scavengers."

My eyes snapped open as the memories rushed back—the chaos, the shouting, the searing pain. "Elise?" I asked, panic edging into my voice.

Before Zoey could respond, Mother Margaret approached.

The head MedNurse was a stern woman in her fifties with graying hair pulled into a tight bun and eyes that seemed to pierce right through you. Her presence always commanded attention.

"Everly," Mother Margaret said, her tone as firm as ever but with an underlying softness reserved for moments like these.

I furrowed my brow, staring at my hands. Was that traces of blood under my fingernails?

"Everly," Mother Margaret began, her voice firm but with a softness that wasn't often there. "You were injured during the attack. A deep laceration to your abdomen. We had to perform surgery to stop the bleeding and repair the damage."

I tried to process her words, but everything felt like it was moving through molasses. "How bad was it?" My voice sounded distant, even to me.

"It was serious," she replied, her eyes steady on mine. "We did what we had to do to save you."

I swallowed hard, the pain in my throat matching the ache in my stomach. "What day is it?"

"Monday," Mother Margaret said.

"Monday," I repeated, the word echoing in my mind like a foreign concept.

"Three days?" I asked, struggling to wrap my head around it. "I've been out for... for three days?"

"It was important," she said, her tone unwavering.

"Why?" I pressed, needing to understand.

"The pain was too much," she explained. "You needed... rest."

I lay back against the pillows, letting the information sink in. Three days lost in a fog of unconsciousness while everything around me moved forward. My mind drifted to Elise—where she could be, what might have happened to her in those three days.

"What's being done to find her?" I asked.

Mother Margaret and Zoey exchanged a look before turning back to me.

Mother Margaret placed a reassuring hand on my shoulder. "Focus on healing, Everly. We'll need you strong."

I wanted to argue, wanted to insist on being involved in every step of the search, but exhaustion weighed me down like lead. Instead, I closed my eyes and let myself drift back into the darkness, hoping that when I woke again, there would be good news about Elise.

* * *

The next time I woke up, the room was dimly lit. A figure sat in the chair by my bed, head bowed. As my vision cleared, I recognized her fiery red hair.

"Fey?" I croaked, my voice barely a whisper.

Fiona's head snapped up, and she rushed to my side. Her freckles stood out against her pale skin, and worry etched lines into her usually cheerful face.

"You're okay," Fiona said, relief flooding her voice. "Golly, Everly, you had us so worried."

"What happened?" I asked, struggling to piece together the fragments of my memory. "I tried asking Zoey—"

Fiona glanced around nervously before leaning in closer. "She can't tell," she whispered, her breath warm against my ear. "Not with Mother Margaret hovering."

Her eyes darted around the room as if expecting Mother Margaret to materialize out of thin air. "Everly," she continued in a hurried whisper, "Elise was taken by scavengers."

"I know," I murmured, trying to keep the panic from rising in my chest.

Fiona's words tumbled out quickly, almost too fast for me to follow. "I've heard they think it was a targeted attack to kidnap Elise and ransom her to Archangel Michael."

I blinked at her, trying to make sense of what she was saying. The pain in my abdomen flared again, reminding me of how helpless I felt.

"Ransom?" The word felt foreign on my tongue.

Fiona nodded, her expression grave. "With her being thirty, everyone on the surface must be aware that he's going to claim her and set the prophecy into motion?"

"Prophecy?" Everly asks.

"Oh, no, I've said too much," Fiona muttered. "There have been whispers, a prophecy that once Michael marries his Seraph Bride, he'll take God's army to the surface and purify it with his children, as well as all of us. The world will be new."

My mind raced as I tried to process the information. Elise being used as a pawn in some larger game—it made my blood boil.

"Why would they—" I began, but stopped myself short. "Why would they take her?"

"To control Michael," Fiona said. "If they have her, he can't claim her. There are bad people up there, Ev."

"We're not supposed to judge others —"

"Fudge all of that," she said, frantic. "Everly, they got into our Bunker. The High Priestess is dead. Her blood still stains the tile. Elder Jonas barely survived. Half of our numbers are either dead or injured. Everything is... everything is wrong. Where is God, Everly? I thought He was supposed to protect us. I thought we were chosen for a reason. And with Elise gone... We don't know what's going to happen."

I sucked in a breath, steadying myself. Fiona's panic was palpable, and I knew I needed to be the rock she could cling to.

"We can't question God's plan now," I said, my voice firm yet gentle. "We can't judge those on top for their actions, either. That's for God to do. We need to trust in God."

Fiona's eyes were wide, brimming with unshed tears. "But

why would God let High Priestess Dolores die? Like that? So brutal... choking on her own blood? I... I don't know. Where is He, Everly?"

"He's here," I said, feeling the weight of her question settle in my chest. "We have to be strong, Fiona. We can't give into our fear. That's what the devil wants."

Her eyes narrowed, a mix of disbelief and anger flashing across her face. "How can you say that? They took your sister. Don't you care—"

"Of course I care," I snapped, feeling defensive. The words stung more than I'd expected.

"I'm sorry," Fiona murmured, running her fingers through her hair in a gesture of frustration and helplessness. She pulled something from her pocket and held it out to me. "Here. I snuck you something from the cafeteria. I know it's your favorite."

I glanced down at the small bundle wrapped in cloth. When I unwrapped it, the familiar scent of chocolate-covered almonds wafted up to me—a rare treat, usually saved for The Reaping.

"Fiona, you shouldn't have," I said, my voice softening.

"You were stabbed, Ev," she replied, her eyes earnest and filled with concern. "If anyone deserves that, it's you."

She glanced at the door, worry creasing her brow again. "I've gotta go. They're going to do bed checks. I'll visit tomorrow. Or today. I don't even know what time it is."

With that, she slipped out of the room as quietly as she'd entered, leaving me alone with my thoughts and the small comfort of chocolate-covered almonds.

The room felt colder without her presence, and the silence pressed in on me like a tangible weight. My mind swirled with questions and fears—about Elise, about Michael's plans, about our very survival.

But for now, all I could do was wait and hope that our faith would be enough to guide us through this darkness.

* * *

When I woke up again, the dim light filtering through the makeshift curtains from the lanterns positioned throughout the bunker told me it was morning. Mother Margaret stood beside my bed, her face a mask of professional concern. Zoey hovered nearby, her hands gentle as she pulled back the blankets covering me.

"We need to check on your wound," Mother Margaret announced, her voice firm.

I sat up slowly, wincing as pain shot through my abdomen. Zoey peeled away the gown I was in, exposing the injury. The gash ran diagonally across my stomach, the edges angry and red. Stitches crisscrossed over the wound like a grotesque lattice.

"It'll scar," Mother Margaret muttered under her breath. "He won't be happy."

I scrunched my nose in confusion. "He?" I asked.

Mother Margaret ignored me and turned to Zoey. "Let's put on the balm."

Zoey nodded and moved to a nearby cabinet, retrieving something from one of the shelves.

"Elder Jonas is going to discuss something of great import with you," Mother Margaret continued, still not meeting my eyes. "I'm going to have Fiona bring you breakfast, and then he'll be sent in. How are you feeling?"

"Good," I replied automatically, though it was far from the truth. "Do we have any word on Elise?"

Zoey returned with a mason jar filled with a pure white balm that seemed to glow softly in the low light.

"What's that?" I asked, curiosity getting the better of me.

Mother Margaret sighed, a trace of exasperation in her expression. "You've always been curious, Everly. I hope you learn how to quell your questions. Your husband will not like to be questioned."

Her words sent a shiver down my spine, but I bit back any retort that might get me into more trouble.

Mother Margaret took the jar from Zoey and dipped her fingers into the balm. She began applying it to my wound, her touch surprisingly gentle. The cool substance spread over my skin, and I felt an immediate tingling sensation. It wasn't like any balm I'd experienced before; it felt almost alive, settling into my skin with a strange, comforting warmth.

"That should make everything better," Mother Margaret said, her voice void of emotion. She straightened up and handed the jar back to Zoey. "Everly, I'll send in Fiona with your breakfast. Please eat quickly. It's important Elder Jonas speak to you. Let's go, Zoey."

Zoey gave me a sympathetic smile as she turned to leave.

I opened my mouth to say something—anything—but they were already gone; the door clicking shut behind them. Their footsteps echoed faintly in the corridor before silence reclaimed the room.

Alone, I shifted slightly, testing the balm's effects on my wound. The tingling persisted, but it wasn't unpleasant. It was almost... soothing. I couldn't shake the feeling that something was different about it, something I couldn't quite put my finger on.

Moments later, Fiona appeared with a tray of food. She placed it on the small table beside my bed and gave me a nod before leaving just as quickly as she'd arrived.

I looked at the food—bread, some kind of oatmeal, and a cup of what smelled like herbal tea. My stomach growled in response. Despite everything going on, I realized how hungry I was. I picked up the spoon and began to eat.

The oatmeal was hearty and warm, filling me with a sense of temporary comfort. As I ate, I couldn't help but wonder what Elder Jonas wanted to discuss with me so urgently.

I finished the last spoonful of oatmeal and reached under my pillow for a small tin. Inside, I kept my chocolate-covered almonds. Popping one into my mouth, I savored the smooth, sweet chocolate coating that gave way to the crunchy, slightly bitter almond inside. The flavors mingled perfectly, creating a momentary escape from my thoughts.

As I chewed, the door creaked open again. Elder Jonas stepped in, leaning on his staff for support. He was an elderly man with a kind, weathered face and a long, white beard that gave him an air of wisdom. His simple, practical clothing spoke of a life dedicated to service and hard work. His eyes, though clouded with age, held a spark of determination.

As he got closer, I noticed a fresh wound on his forehead, a gash that looked like it had been hastily bandaged. Blood had seeped through the makeshift dressing, forming dark patches that contrasted sharply with his white beard.

"Elder Jonas," I said, rising from the bed. "What happened to you?"

He waved a dismissive hand. "A minor inconvenience," he replied, though his eyes betrayed a flicker of pain. "We've more pressing matters to discuss."

I straightened up instinctively, bracing for the familiar pain in my stomach. To my surprise, there was none. The balm must have worked its magic already.

"I hope you're feeling better." Elder Jonas greeted me with a nod.

"Better than I expected," I admitted, still marveling at the lack of pain.

He moved closer and took a seat on the wooden chair beside my bed. "That'll be the Angel Dust."

"Angel Dust?" I repeated, my voice barely a whisper.

The name alone sent a chill down my spine. I knew the legends, the whispered stories of its potency. It was said to heal anything short of death itself. But it wasn't just its miraculous properties that made it legendary; it was also tied to the darkest tales of Lucifer's fall.

Elder Jonas leaned forward, his eyes narrowing as if gauging my reaction. "Yes, Angel Dust," he confirmed. "It's rare, precious."

"Why use it on me?" I asked, unable to mask the suspicion in my voice. "I thought it was reserved for Elise. Just in case."

Elder Jonas sighed heavily, a sound laden with unspoken burdens. "Circumstances have changed," he said, choosing his words carefully. "Elise is... gone. Taken."

I clenched my fists, nails digging into my palms. I knew this. But I couldn't show it. I didn't want Fiona to get in trouble for telling me.

He studied me for a moment, then nodded as if making a decision. "You are crucial to our plans now, Everly."

"Plans?" I asked. "What plans? We need Elise back and —"

"Elise is gone," Elder Jonas said.

I blinked, trying to process the words. "Have we sent anyone after her?" My voice trembled, each word a struggle.

He remained silent, the weight of his unspoken answer settling heavily between us.

"Elder Jonas," I said, my voice cracking with desperation.

"Elise is gone," he repeated, his tone devoid of any hope or comfort.

Tears filled my eyes, blurring my vision. "But she's... she's the Seraph Bride. She's my sister."

"The needs of the few cannot and will not outweigh the needs of the many," he replied. "We cannot forget why we're doing this."

"I don't understand," I said, shaking my head. "Wouldn't Archangel Michael want his bride back?"

"The second she was taken from the bunker, she was of no use to him," Elder Jonas said. "She's tainted. Impure."

"What?" I felt a sharp pang in my chest. "That's not true. God can purify anything—"

"We aren't talking about God," Elder Jonas pointed out, his gaze hardening. "We're discussing Archangel Michael."

"He knows Elise has been taken?" I asked, dreading the answer.

"He does."

"And?"

"And he's decided she is not worth the trouble when his responsibility is to our bunker, to purifying the world again," he said with a finality that left no room for argument. "Nothing can come between him and that goal."

My heart pounded in my chest as I struggled to understand the implications of his words.

"Which means," he continued, his eyes pinning me in place, "he requires another Seraph Bride." His gaze bore into me, unyielding and resolute. "And he's requested you."

CHAPTER 6

Walton

Lucifer's castle loomed like a blackened wound against the blood-red sky. I trudged through the twisted halls, the echoes of my footsteps swallowed by the stone walls. The wing for bounty hunters lay deep within, away from Lucifer's ever-watchful gaze.

As I approached the counter, a gaunt demon with hollow eyes glanced up from a ledger. "D," I grunted.

The demon's bony fingers flipped through the pages with an eerie precision. "Room 13," he rasped, sliding a tarnished key across the counter. I grabbed it, feeling its cold weight against my palm.

With a nod, I turned and headed down the narrow corridor. Shadows danced on the walls, cast by flickering torches that lined the passage. Each step felt heavier than the last, burdened by the weight of another bounty completed and another night spent in this forsaken place.

Reaching Room 13, I pushed the key into the lock and turned it. The door creaked open, revealing a dimly lit room that smelled of sulfur and despair. The bed was nothing more than a slab of stone with a thin mattress thrown on top, but it would do.

I closed the door behind me and dropped my bag onto the floor. The room offered no comfort, only a brief respite from the chaos outside. I sat on the edge of the bed, running my fingers over my scarred skin, feeling every bump and ridge.

The room was sparse and utilitarian, like every other I'd been given in this place. Gray stone walls with no windows, lit by a single flickering bulb hanging from the ceiling. A small table with a chair, both made of rough-hewn wood, sat in one corner. On the opposite side, a door led to a cramped bathroom. The mattress on the stone slab looked barely thicker than my own hide.

I dropped my sack on the floor; the contents clinking and thudding softly. Kicking off my boots, I began to strip, peeling off layers of worn leather and fabric that clung to my skin like a second, less forgiving layer. I moved toward the bathroom, eager to wash away the grime of the day.

Finding running water was like finding a needle in a haystack. Most places had dry pipes or water tainted with sulfur. But here, if you were lucky enough to get assigned a room with working plumbing, you took full advantage.

I turned the shower knob and waited. A moment later, water sputtered out before settling into a steady stream. Steam filled the small space as I finished stripping off the last of my clothes.

Stepping into the bathroom, I caught sight of myself in the cracked mirror above the sink. The face staring back at me was a ghoul's nightmare—scarred, blistered skin stretched taut over an angular skull. Hollow eyes glowed faintly red, like embers dying in a firepit. Patches of skin were missing entirely, exposing raw muscle and sinew underneath.

I didn't remember what it felt like to look human anymore. That face was long gone, replaced by this grotesque mask forged from radiation and demonic transformation. I ran my fingers through my dark hair.

The shower's warmth beckoned me. I stepped under the spray, feeling it cascade over my ruined skin. For a brief moment, it felt almost cleansing.

Water poured over me in rivulets, carving temporary paths through the grime and blood. It was one of the few small comforts left in this twisted existence—this brief illusion of normalcy.

I closed my eyes and let the water wash away more than just dirt; it washed away fragments of memory and pain, if only for a moment.

I was so close, so damn close to ending this. To being done. To getting my soul back.

And then what?

I'd find my family... find Betty, demand answers. The thought alone twisted something deep inside me. After discovering her part in The Divine Collapse, the anger flared hot and immediate. I could still picture the look on her face when I told her what I'd done for her, for them. Her rejection. Her... everything.

My fist connected with the shower tile wall before I realized it, cracking it. Pain flared up my arm, but it was a distant thing, already dulling as my body began to heal itself. The shattered tiles fell into the drain, swirling away with the water.

The water turned colder, but I didn't move. Couldn't move. Anger mixed with despair in a toxic brew that left me feeling hollowed out and raw.

I'd done everything for them—sacrificed everything. Yet she cast me aside like I was nothing more than a mistake, an aberration.

I could still see the way her eyes had hardened when she learned of my deal with Lucifer. The way her lips had pressed into a thin line of disgust and disappointment. That look haunted me more than any nightmare.

The showerhead sputtered and hissed as the pressure fluctuated, pulling me from my thoughts. My knuckles were healing fast, the skin knitting itself back together over the bruised bone beneath.

With a heavy sigh, I shut off the water and stepped out of the shower. Grabbing a rough towel from the hook on the wall, I dried myself off, each movement mechanical and automatic.

The reflection in the cracked mirror caught my eye again —a demon masquerading as a man who once had a family and dreams of a peaceful life.

As I dressed in fresh clothes from my sack, I tried to focus on what needed to be done next. One more bounty—just one more—and I'd be free from Lucifer's grasp.

Then I'd find Betty and make her face what she'd done.

But for now, all that mattered was completing this final task.

I wrapped the towel around my hips and walked back into the room, the chill of the stone floor seeping into my feet. Droplets of water dripped from my hair, tracing cold paths down my back. The sack lay where I'd dropped it, a tattered reminder of countless battles and bounties.

Kneeling beside it, I reached in and pulled out a dagger. Its blade was long and slender, forged from obsidian-black metal that seemed to absorb light rather than reflect it. Runes etched into the blade's surface glowed faintly with a demonic red hue, remnants of the celestial war's chaotic magic. The hilt was wrapped in worn leather, fitted perfectly to my grip, its weight familiar and reassuring.

I turned the dagger over in my hands, feeling the balance of it. This blade had seen more blood than I cared to remember, its edge honed to a razor-sharp finish capable of slicing through flesh and bone with ease. It was both a tool and a weapon, an extension of my own wrath.

Returning to the bathroom, I grabbed a bottle of antiseptic from the small shelf above the sink. The liquid sloshed inside as I unscrewed the cap, its pungent scent filling the air.

Carefully, I began to clean the dagger. The antiseptic hissed as it touched the blade, sizzling against unseen impurities. Using a piece of cloth torn from an old shirt, I wiped away the residue, watching as the metal regained its dark luster.

Each stroke of the cloth felt like a ritual—meticulous and deliberate. This was how I kept my tools sharp and ready; how I maintained some semblance of control in this chaotic world.

With every pass over the runes, they pulsed brighter for a moment before settling back into their dim glow. It was as if they acknowledged my efforts, whispering promises of power and vengeance.

I finished cleaning the blade and inspected it one last time under the harsh bathroom light.

I turned so my back faced the mirror. The jagged cracks in the glass distorted the reflection, but I could still make out the latticework of scars covering my skin. Each mark represented a life taken, a debt collected. I raised the dagger and took a deep breath, steeling myself.

Carefully, I pressed the blade against my flesh and made a tally.

The cut was precise, just deep enough to leave a permanent mark, but not so deep as to cause unnecessary damage. Pain flared briefly before dulling into an ache, blending with the countless other wounds that had healed over time.

My entire back was littered with these tallies, each one a testament to the path I'd chosen. Or perhaps the path forced upon me. The one I chose, regardless. The skin there was a roadmap of my sins and sacrifices, a scarred canvas chronicling every bounty I'd ever done.

When I finished, I reached for the antiseptic again. The liquid stung as it touched the fresh wound, cleaning away any lingering traces of blood or infection. I watched in the mirror as it bubbled and fizzed, cleansing both skin and conscience in its own small way.

I wiped the dagger clean once more, ensuring it was ready for whatever lay ahead. The ritual was methodical—almost comforting in its familiarity. It reminded me that despite everything I'd lost, I still had control over this one aspect of my existence.

I grunted, satisfied. The wound would heal soon enough, blending into the tapestry of scars that already adorned my back.

I slipped on a clean shirt and took one last look in the mirror before turning away. The face staring back at me was still monstrous—still scarred and blistered—but beneath that grotesque mask lay a man driven by purpose and fueled by vengeance.

665 tallies. One more to go.

I headed back to the room and dropped onto the bed, leaning against the headboard. The stone slab beneath me was unforgiving, but I had grown used to discomfort. My eyes landed on a laminated menu resting on the nightstand. I picked it up, flipping through its worn pages.

The offerings were varied and repulsive—girls, boys, drinks, food. Each option was more grotesque than the last, catering to every depraved desire a demon could have.

I sneered, tossing the menu aside.

Would I ever succumb to my demonic nature and crave flesh the way others did? The way Malak did?

I clenched my fists, feeling my claws dig into my palms. No. I'd kill myself before I ever let myself get that way.

Reaching for the rotary phone beside the bed, I dialed the number for room service. The receiver crackled as a voice answered on the other end.

"Room service," it droned.

"A steak," I growled into the phone. "With mashed potatoes."

The voice acknowledged my order with a bored grunt before hanging up. I replaced the receiver and kicked my feet up on the bed, allowing myself a moment of relaxation.

The room's oppressive atmosphere pressed in around me, but for now, I could afford to let my guard down just a bit. The mattress was thin and lumpy beneath me, but it was a far cry from the hard ground I'd slept on countless times before.

I closed my eyes, feeling the tension slowly seep out of my muscles. The fight wasn't over—far from it—but for now, I could take this small respite.

I leaned back against the stone wall, trying to find a semblance of comfort on the hard mattress. The dim light cast long shadows across the room, and for a moment, I let my eyes close, hoping for just a second of reprieve. But then, from the room next door, I heard it—moaning.

My eyes snapped open, and I frowned. The moaning grew louder, mingling with muffled voices and the rhythmic creaking of a bed. I ground my teeth together, irritation bubbling up inside me.

Silence. Was that too much to ask for? Peace?

A bitter laugh threatened to escape my lips. Peace was a luxury I could no longer afford. Not in this place. Not in this life.

I pushed myself off the bed and reached for my gun—a MTS255 revolver shotgun. Its sleek design resembled the OTs-62, but it was far more efficient and deadly in my hands. The barrel was matte black, with a smooth wooden grip that felt familiar and reassuring beneath my fingers.

I placed it on the table and began disassembling it with practiced ease. The metal parts clicked softly as I laid them out in order, each piece gleaming faintly in the dim light. Reaching for a cloth and a small bottle of oil, I started cleaning the gun, making sure every part was free of grime and debris.

As I worked, my mind wandered back to simpler times—days spent tinkering with engines in my garage, teaching Emma how to hold a wrench properly while Betty watched with that warm smile of hers. Those memories felt like another lifetime, belonging to someone else entirely.

I shook off the nostalgia and focused on my task. The rhythmic motion of cleaning the gun was almost meditative, each stroke of the cloth grounding me in the present moment. Once every part gleamed under the light, I began reassembling it with precision.

Finally, I checked the cylinder to ensure it was loaded—five shells nestled snugly within their chambers. Satisfied, I snapped it shut and set the gun down on the table.

A knock on the door pulled me from my thoughts. My stomach growled in anticipation as I crossed the room and opened it to find a demon server holding a tray.

"Your steak," he grunted, shoving it into my hands before disappearing down the hallway.

I closed the door behind him and set the tray on the table beside my gun. The scent of cooked meat filled the room, momentarily overpowering the stench of sulfur and decay.

I picked up the fork and knife, slicing into the steak with deliberate precision. The scent of cooked meat mingled with the ever-present sulfur, but for a moment, I let myself get lost in the aroma. I took a bite, savoring the rich, tender flesh as it melted on my tongue. Each chew was a reminder of simpler times, when meals were shared around a family table rather than devoured in isolation.

I poured myself a glass of whiskey from the bottle I'd

found earlier. The amber liquid sloshed into the glass, catching the dim light and casting flickering shadows on the walls. I lifted it to my lips and took a long sip, feeling the burn as it traveled down my throat and settled warmly in my chest.

Despite everything—despite the demon I'd become—my senses had only sharpened over time. My eyesight was keener, my hearing more acute. And my sense of smell? It was almost supernatural. I could pick up scents from miles away, distinguish individual aromas in a crowded room. It was both a blessing and a curse.

As I ate, I became aware of another scent drifting in from next door—a woman's arousal. It mingled with the other smells in the air but stood out like a beacon to my heightened senses. My jaw tightened as I focused back on my meal, willing myself to ignore it.

The steak was cooked perfectly—medium rare, just how I liked it. The mashed potatoes were creamy and smooth, each bite a comforting reminder of what real food tasted like. In this wasteland, meals like this were few and far between. You never knew when you'd get another chance to eat something decent.

I made sure to savor every bite, taking my time despite the hunger gnawing at me. The whiskey complemented the meal perfectly, its warmth spreading through me and dulling some of the edge that constant vigilance had carved into my bones.

When I finished, I set the fork and knife down with a clatter that echoed in the silence of the room. I wiped my mouth with a napkin before reaching for my Stetson resting on the table. The hat was worn and weathered, much like myself, but it still held its shape—a testament to resilience.

Placing it on my head, I adjusted the brim until it felt right. With a weary sigh, I sank back onto the bed, feeling the lumpy mattress beneath me give way under my weight.

Sleep claimed me quickly, pulling me into its dark embrace where memories couldn't haunt me—for now.

CHAPTER 7

Everly

Dinner was a quiet affair, the kind that made every clink of cutlery and murmur of conversation feel amplified. Elder Jonas stood at the head of the table, his staff tapping lightly against the floor as he cleared his throat. His weathered face held a solemn expression, one that made my stomach twist even before he spoke.

"Tonight," Jonas began, his voice carrying through the hall, "we have an announcement to make. Everly Harrington has been selected to replace Elise as the Seraph Bride."

A murmur spread through the room like wildfire. I glanced down at my plate, feeling every eye turn towards me. The food before me had lost all appeal; it might as well have been dust.

Someone raised a glass in my direction. "To Everly!" they cheered.

The room erupted in applause and congratulations, but it all felt distant, like an echo in a cavern. Faces blurred into a sea of nods and smiles. Each word of praise hit me like a blow I couldn't feel.

Elise's absence hung heavy around us. Her kidnapping

had left a void that no amount of congratulations could fill. Even the food now felt tasteless and foreign in my mouth.

"You've earned this," another voice chimed in from across the table. "We're proud of you."

Except, I had done nothing to earn this.

Archangel Michael picked me.

Why, I didn't know, and I wasn't allowed to question it.

I nodded politely, my mind far from their words. It felt like ash on my tongue, dry and empty. The praise was meant to be a blessing, but to me, it was anything but.

The numbness had settled deep within me. I almost wished for the pain in my side to return just so I could feel something again—anything besides this emptiness.

The night wore on with more cheers and raised glasses, but none of it penetrated the haze. I was there in body but absent in spirit, adrift in a sea of hollow accolades and tasteless food.

When dinner finally ended, I excused myself quietly and slipped away from the hall, seeking solace somewhere outside the circle of forced celebration.

I burst into my room; the door slamming shut behind me with a force that rattled the walls. My breath came in ragged gasps as I grabbed my pillow and buried my face in it. A scream tore from my throat, muffled by the fabric, but the raw emotion still surged through me. It felt like a release, but only just. The tension coiled tighter within me, refusing to let go.

Why was I acting this way? I knew it wasn't right. I should be grateful. This was supposed to be an honor. But how could I feel anything but rage and sorrow when Elise had been taken? People had died, and now they expected us to forget and move on like nothing had happened?

I dropped the pillow, sinking to my knees on the cold floor. My hands clenched into fists as I looked up at the ceiling, eyes stinging with unshed tears.

"God," I whispered, my voice trembling with desperation. "Why? Why would You allow this? How can this be Your plan?"

My fists pounded against the floor, each thud resonating through the room.

"Answer me!" I cried out. "Please, I need to understand!"

Silence greeted me, heavy and oppressive. The room seemed to close in around me; the shadows growing longer and darker. I felt so small, so insignificant in the grand scheme of things.

Tears streamed down my cheeks as I bowed my head, fingers digging into the wooden floorboards.

"Please," I begged again, my voice breaking. "Give me a sign. Anything. Help me understand why Elise had to be taken... why people had to die."

I stayed there on my knees, waiting for an answer that never came.

I took a breath, trying to control my emotions.

One breath, then another.

I sat up, leaning against my bed. What would Elise do? If I had been taken, what would Elise do?

She would come after me, I realized. She wouldn't hesitate. And she wouldn't wait for permission. She'd come after me.

But... but now I was bound to Michael. I had a responsibility to the bunker. They could only be saved, the world could only be saved, through me.

The needs of the many outweigh the needs of the few, Elder Jonas said.

And it made sense.

But even so, Elise was my whole world.

I knew I wasn't more important than the bunker, even with the honor of Michael's Selection. But Elise...

I couldn't just accept that Elise had been taken and no one would do anything about it. When I was three, scavengers raided our bunker, leaving casualties, including our parents. Elise took care of me.

No. I couldn't let this go.

I wouldn't.

I stood up, determination flooding through my veins. My hands shook slightly as I gathered a few essential items: a knife from under my mattress — the same one that had stabbed me — and some dried food from my stash. I made sure to grab the chocolate almonds.

But I needed water.

Which meant I needed to take my canteen to the kitchen and fill it without anyone being suspicious.

I stared at my canteen, debating how best to fill it without being noticed. My mind raced with possible scenarios. Could I sneak into the kitchen? Would someone question why I needed water so late? Each possibility tangled with another until my head throbbed.

I had to be smart about this. Hiding the canteen in my jacket seemed like the best option. Hopefully Fiona was there. If she was, maybe I could get in and out without any issues.

Taking a deep breath, I slipped the canteen into the inner pocket of my jacket. The weight felt oddly comforting.

When I stepped back into the mess hall, it was empty and eerily quiet. The tables stood abandoned, all freshly washed. The scent of lemon lingered in the air, the floor mopped. I sucked in a breath, letting the silence fortify my resolve.

Heading towards the kitchen, each step felt heavier than the last. The door creaked as I pushed it open, revealing Fiona bustling around with a dishcloth in hand.

I exhaled a sigh of relief. "Hey, Fiona."

She looked up; her face breaking into a warm smile. "Everly! What brings you here?"

I hesitated at the threshold of the kitchen, my heart hammering in my chest. Should I tell Fiona the truth? Would she try to stop me? The doubt gnawed at me, making me hate myself for even questioning her loyalty.

"I'm... I'm just thirsty," I managed to say, my voice sounding weak even to my own ears.

Fiona nodded, seemingly oblivious to my inner turmoil. "Let me get you a cup," she said, turning her back to me as she headed toward a cabinet.

The moment she turned away, I pulled out my canteen from my jacket. My hands moved quickly, unscrewing the cap and positioning it under the faucet. The sound of water rushing into the container was almost deafening in the silent kitchen.

Just as I finished filling it and screwed the cap back on, Fiona turned around, catching sight of me with the canteen.

Her eyes widened in surprise. "What are you doing?"

I opened my mouth. I was tempted to lie. In fact, I would have. But I also knew I wasn't good at it. The truth spilled out before I could stop it. "I'm going after her."

Her face turned pale, and she set the cup down with a shaky hand. "What? No! Everly, if they catch you—"

"They won't," I interrupted, my voice firmer than I felt inside.

She shook her head, looking around as if expecting someone to burst through the door any moment. "Everly, you've lived in a shelter your entire life. How are you going to survive on the surface where actual demons roam?"

"The scavengers were humans," I pointed out.

"And look what they did to us!" Fiona snapped, her eyes flashing with a mix of fear and anger. "You think you're ready for that? For worse?"

"Elise is out there," I said, my voice softening but losing none of its resolve. "I can't just leave her."

She took a step closer, her expression pleading. "Do you even have a plan? Supplies? Weapons?"

I held up the knife from under my mattress, feeling its weight in my hand. "I've got this and some food. And I'll find more if I need to."

She reached out and grabbed my arm, her grip surprisingly strong. "You're not thinking straight. This isn't like managing the hydroponics or fixing a broken pipe. This isn't runes in a sanctum or combat with a partner. This is life and death."

"I know," I replied, meeting her gaze with all the determination I could muster. "But I can't stay here and do nothing."

"You're throwing your life away!" Fiona's voice cracked, desperation seeping into every word.

"Maybe," I admitted, my throat tightening. "But Elise would do the same for me."

She blew out a breath, her shoulders sagging. "And what about Michael?" she asked, her voice strained. "He picked *you*, Everly. *You*. Are you seriously going to take that for granted?"

"You're the one who asked where God was," I replied, my voice trembling but steady.

"And you told me to trust Him," she fired back, eyes flashing with frustration. "Do you? Trust Him?"

"I trust that He knows more than me," I said, swallowing hard. "And I trust Elise would come after me."

"You don't owe her anything," Fiona insisted, her grip tightening on my arm.

"I owe her *everything*," I whispered, my voice breaking. "Please, Fey. I just... I need your help leaving."

"I can't," Fiona said, shaking her head, her eyes filled with sorrow. "If they catch me..." She let her voice trail off, the unspoken consequences hanging heavy in the air. "I'm sorry, I can't."

"But... it's Elise," I said, my chest tightening with desperation. "If it was me, would you just..." My voice trailed off as the realization hit me harder than I expected. The truth settled in my chest like a weight, pressing down until it hurt to breathe.

Fiona's eyes softened with regret. She didn't need to say anything; her silence spoke volumes.

I turned away from Fiona. My mind raced with thoughts of Elise—her laughter, her strength, and the way she had always been there for me.

I couldn't abandon her now.

I took a deep breath and steadied myself. This wasn't the end of the road; it was just another obstacle to overcome. Elise had taught me that much.

With or without Fiona's help, I was going after her.

"Thank you," I said quietly, turning back to Fiona one last time. Her eyes were filled with tears she refused to let fall.

"Stay safe," she whispered, barely audible.

I nodded and slipped out of the kitchen into the darkened hallway. The silence felt different now—no longer oppressive, but charged with purpose.

Elise needed me.

And I wouldn't let anything stand in my way.

I sucked in a breath, clutching the canteen. At least I had water. But then what? How could I get out?

The scavengers had breached from the top. No way the technicians had fixed everything. Maybe I could escape that way.

But demons roamed above... and scavengers. And all I had was a knife. Was there anything else I could take?

I fixed my pack, tightening the straps as I thought. The armory was too dangerous; I'd be caught.

Runes.

The runes. I could grab some.

Steal? a voice questioned. *That's against God.*

But... what if I'm doing it for the right reason?

And who decides what the right reason is? the voice countered. *God.*

Yeah, well, I thought, trying to quell my rising frustration, *I asked God, and He didn't respond.*

Decision made, I slipped out of the kitchen and made my way toward the Sanctum of Glyphs, my footsteps as silent as possible on the worn stone floor.

The hallway felt longer than usual, shadows stretching and twisting around me. My heart pounded in my chest like a war drum, each beat echoing in my ears. The Sanctum loomed ahead, its door slightly ajar.

Good—it meant someone had been careless or confident enough to leave it unlocked.

I glanced around one last time before slipping inside. The room greeted me with its familiar scent of old parchment and ink, shelves lined with books and scrolls containing runes of every kind.

Glancing down, I saw it—a dark crimson stain marring the otherwise pristine floor.

My blood.

The sight stopped me cold, and for a moment, I just stared at it, feeling a strange detachment.

That was my blood.

From my body.

But I had survived.

I shook off the eerie feeling and moved towards the shelves lined with runes. The weight of what I was about to do settled heavily on my shoulders. Stealing from the Sanctum went against everything I had been taught, yet here I was, driven by desperation and love for Elise.

Did that make it okay?

I didn't know.

My fingers traced over the spines of several tomes until they landed on one with protective glyphs. Carefully, I pulled it off the shelf and opened it to find a collection of small wooden talismans etched with runes.

I hesitated for a moment, the voice of doubt whispering again in my mind. But Elise's face flashed before me—her smile, her strength—and any remaining hesitation melted away.

I grabbed a handful of talismans and stuffed them into my pack before closing the book and returning it to its place on the shelf. The weight of the stolen runes settled heavily in my pack, but also gave me a small sense of reassurance.

As I turned to leave, a soft creak from behind made me freeze. My heart leapt into my throat as I slowly turned to see if someone had followed me or if it was just the old wood settling.

Nothing but shadows greeted me.

Letting out a shaky breath, I carefully exited the Sanctum and made my way back through the dimly lit corridors. Each step brought me closer to my escape—and closer to Elise.

I moved cautiously, every step calculated and deliberate. The faint hum of machinery grew louder as I approached the upper levels. My heart pounded in my chest, but determination pushed me forward. Elise was out there, and I had to find her.

As I neared the top, I heard voices. Panic surged through me, and I quickly ducked behind a stack of old crates.

"...won't be able to finish this until at least two days," the first voice said, frustration lacing his words.

"Yes, yes," Elder Jonas responded, his tone placating. "As long as it's fixed before he arrives. He will not be pleased we've been infiltrated again."

"But I don't understand how it's possible," the first voice continued. "Unless someone here has maintained contact—"

"Now, now," Elder Jonas interrupted. "You can't possibly assume one of us would betray the bunker. Doing so is akin to betraying God—"

Their footsteps grew louder, coming dangerously close to

my hiding spot. I held my breath, heart racing as I pressed myself further into the shadows.

The voices passed by without noticing me, their conversation fading into the distance.

When I was sure they were gone, I slipped out of my hiding spot and made my way to the ladder that led to the top. My hands trembled as I grasped the rungs, the cold metal biting into my skin.

I hesitated, doubt gnawing at me. Was this really the right thing to do? What if I failed? What if Elise—

No. I couldn't afford to think like that. Elise needed me.

I closed my eyes and sent a quick prayer to God, hoping for guidance and strength. Then, with a deep breath, I began to climb.

Each rung brought me closer to the surface and further from the safety of the bunker. When I finally reached the top, I paused for a moment, taking in another deep breath before stepping onto the surface.

With one final glance back at the hatch, I steeled myself for what lay ahead. Elise was out there somewhere, and I would find her no matter what it took.

CHAPTER 8

Walton

The thin light of dawn seeped through the cracks in the boarded-up windows. Sleep had once again been an elusive ghost, haunting the edges of my consciousness but never fully settling in. I lay on the worn mattress, staring at the ceiling, trying to recall the last time I truly rested.

With a groan, I pushed myself up. My body ached, not from fatigue, but from the unending weight of my existence. The boots went on first, heavy and well-worn, followed by thick pants that had seen countless miles and fights. My shirt, though threadbare, clung to me like a second skin.

I strapped on my belt, laden with pouches and holsters for weapons and tools. The weight was familiar, grounding me in the present moment. I draped my long duster over my shoulders. It was tattered at the edges, but still sturdy enough to ward off both physical and emotional blows. Finally, my Stetson.

The sky outside was just beginning to lighten as I stepped out into the desolate street. The sun barely touched the horizon, casting long shadows that seemed to reach out like grasping hands. The world was silent save for the distant rustle of wind through abandoned buildings.

Each step I took felt deliberate, purposeful. The early morning air bit at my exposed skin, but it did little to rouse me from my somber thoughts. The city lay before me, a labyrinth of ruins and broken dreams. It mirrored my own internal landscape—fractured and scarred, but still standing.

I moved through alleys and side streets with practiced ease, avoiding any potential encounters this early in the day. My destination loomed ahead, another contract waiting to be fulfilled. Another name to cross off my list in this endless pursuit of vengeance.

By the time the sun had fully risen, painting the sky with hues of orange and pink, I had already covered several blocks. My thoughts remained locked on my mission—another step toward a resolution that always seemed just out of reach.

The day awaited me with its usual trials and tribulations. And so I continued onward, driven by a purpose that had become both my curse and my salvation.

Leaving Hellgate's jagged black spires behind, I stepped into a wasteland that stretched endlessly in all directions. The ground beneath my boots was cracked and dry, a spiderweb of desolation that seemed to suck the very life out of everything it touched. The air was thick with the stench of sulfur, and fires burned eternally in the heart of the citadel, casting an eerie glow that barely reached the outer edges of this forsaken place.

The landscape was a bleak canvas of decay. Twisted remnants of once-grand structures jutted out like skeletal fingers clawing at the sky. Ash and dust swirled in the wind, biting at my skin and stinging my eyes. There were no signs of life, only the echoing silence of abandonment. It was as if Hell itself had vomited out this forsaken land.

Lucifer's coordinates burned a hole in my pocket. According to them, the bunker was a day and a half away—a tantalizingly short distance for someone so important. It made me uneasy. Why would they hide someone of value so close to Hellgate? The thought gnawed at me as I trudged forward.

To the east lay a settlement, a small dot on the horizon where humans still clung to some semblance of normalcy. Supplies would be needed for the journey ahead; I couldn't afford to be caught unprepared. This settlement had earned a reputation for its tolerance—or rather, its pragmatic indiffer-ence—towards demons. That didn't mean I could stroll in without caution; trust was a luxury neither side could afford.

As I moved closer to the settlement, I kept my eyes peeled for other hunters. In this line of work, competition was deadly serious. If others were seeking the same prize, things could get complicated fast. The girl wasn't just another bounty; she held importance I couldn't yet fathom but couldn't ignore either.

With each step, I weighed my options: head straight to the bunker or make a pit stop for supplies and information? The latter seemed more prudent but carried its own risks. My mind raced through scenarios, each more precarious than the last.

The settlement grew nearer, its outlines becoming sharper against the wasteland's bleak backdrop. Buildings that once thrived now stood like weary sentinels, their walls scarred by time and conflict.

I pulled my duster tighter around me as I approached, readying myself for whatever lay ahead. The wasteland hadn't beaten me yet, and neither would this task—no matter how close or far it took me from Hellgate's shadows.

I decided to head straight for the bunker. Supplies could wait; I needed to find this girl first. As I walked, my mind churned through possible infiltration tactics. Bunkers like these were fortresses, built to withstand assaults from demons and humans alike.

Would they have guards posted outside? Likely. Auto-mated defenses? Definitely. The challenge wasn't just getting in; it was doing so without setting off alarms that would bring a world of hurt down on me.

I imagined the layout: narrow corridors, steel-reinforced doors, and choke points designed to trap invaders. I could try a frontal assault—brute force had its merits—but that would alert everyone inside. A more subtle approach might be better. Maybe find a ventilation shaft or a maintenance tunnel. Those often got overlooked in security protocols.

Still, whatever awaited me inside didn't worry me much. Bunker rats were typically ill-prepared for someone like me. They relied too heavily on their walls and tech, never expecting a demon with my skills to breach their sanctum.

But first, I needed to get clear on Elise. Piercing green eyes, auburn hair usually pulled back in a ponytail, and freckles dotting her cheeks like stars scattered across the night sky— that's how Lucifer described her. The details felt etched into my mind.

Lucifer's description of her lingered uncomfortably in my thoughts. It was too knowing, too... intimate. His voice had carried a strange edge when he spoke of her, something beyond mere instruction or casual mention. It unsettled me.

Lucifer rarely showed his hand unless he had an ace up his sleeve. What was it about Elise that warranted such personal attention? Was she just another pawn in his game or something more? The uncertainty gnawed at me as I pressed on through the wasteland.

Whatever secrets Elise held or whatever role she played in Lucifer's grand design, I would find out soon enough. The bunker lay ahead, hidden beneath layers of rock and metal. Each step brought me closer to answers—and perhaps more questions.

For now, I focused on the mission: locate Elise. Everything else didn't matter.

Hours passed as I trudged through the wasteland, the

barren landscape stretching endlessly before me. The sun hung high in the sky, its unforgiving rays baking the cracked earth beneath my boots. The wind picked up, dry and relentless, carrying with it the stench of sulfur and decay.

I stopped for a moment, pulling out my canteen. The water inside was warm, but it quenched my parched throat, nonetheless. Every drop was precious out here; there were no guarantees of finding another source anytime soon. I screwed the cap back on tightly and returned it to my belt.

Reaching into one of my pouches, I pulled out a strip of jerky. The meat was tough and salty, but it provided the sustenance I needed to keep going. Chewing slowly, I scanned the horizon. Nothing but desolation greeted my eyes—a sea of emptiness punctuated by jagged rocks and twisted remnants of what once might have been buildings.

Rationing what little I had left became second nature out here. There was no room for indulgence or carelessness. Each sip of water, each bite of food had to be measured and deliberate. I couldn't afford to waste anything.

I drank from my canteen again before stowing it away securely and pressed on through the barren expanse before me.

The silence was oppressive, broken only by the sound of my own footsteps and the occasional gust of wind.

Then, a whine pierced the stillness. My eyes snapped in the direction of the sound, my hand instinctively going for my gun. I paused, muscles tensed, ears straining for any further noise.

Another whine, followed by a low growl. The hairs on the back of my neck stood on end. Suddenly, an animal darted across the road ahead of me, moving with a speed and grace that was almost unnatural.

I narrowed my eyes, trying to make out its form. Was that... a Hellhound?

The creature was massive, easily the size of a wolf but with an otherworldly aura that set it apart from any natural beast. Its matted fur was as dark as night, patches missing to reveal raw, scarred skin underneath. Its eyes glowed an eerie red, like embers smoldering in a fire pit. Every movement seemed fluid yet deliberate, muscles rippling beneath its hide as it sprinted across the wasteland.

But what caught my attention most was its behavior. It wasn't hunting or stalking prey; it was running—fleeing from something. The Hellhound's head darted back repeatedly as if it expected to be overtaken at any moment.

What the hell was a Hellhound doing in the waste? These creatures usually prowled closer to Hellgate Citadel or areas teeming with demonic energy. Seeing one this far out made no sense.

I kept my grip firm on my gun and watched as the Hellhound disappeared into the distance. Whatever had spooked it must be something formidable—Hellhounds didn't scare easily.

I waited for several minutes, senses on high alert for any sign of what might have chased it. But nothing followed; no shadows loomed or roars echoed across the barren landscape.

Releasing a breath I didn't realize I'd been holding, I holstered my weapon but stayed vigilant. If something could drive a Hellhound into a panicked run, I needed to be prepared for anything.

With renewed caution, I resumed my trek toward the bunker. The wasteland had just become even more dangerous than I had anticipated.

The Hellhound's frantic retreat had barely left my sight when another creature slithered into view. Its scales shimmered with an iridescent glow, catching the sparse sunlight and refracting it into a kaleidoscope of colors. The Radiant Serpent moved with a fluid grace, its body coiling and uncoiling like liquid mercury. Each scale seemed to pulse with its own light, making the serpent appear almost ethereal.

It was a stark contrast to the Hellhound—where the hound was all raw power and ferocity; the serpent embodied elegance and lethal precision. I watched, transfixed, as it glided across the cracked earth in the same direction the Hellhound had fled.

Then, out of nowhere, the Hellhound reappeared. It had circled around and now charged at the serpent from the side. The Radiant Serpent reared up, fangs bared and ready to strike, but the Hellhound was faster. It lunged, sinking its venomous teeth into the serpent's shimmering body.

The Radiant Serpent thrashed violently, its scales flashing in a frenzy of light. The Hellhound held firm, growling low and deep as it clamped down harder. The serpent coiled around its attacker, trying to squeeze the life out of it, but the Hellhound's sheer strength seemed to overwhelm even this predator.

I couldn't help but feel a grudging respect for the Hellhound. It had used its instincts and intelligence to flank an opponent that should have been out of its league. This was no mindless beast; it was a cunning hunter.

I stayed back, watching as the two creatures battled fiercely on the barren ground. The Hellhound's glowing eyes locked onto mine for a brief moment before it returned its focus to the serpent. There was something almost human in that gaze —a flicker of understanding or recognition.

The Radiant Serpent lashed out with its tail, catching the Hellhound square in the side. The impact sent the beast sprawling, a whimper escaping its maw. It tried to scramble to its feet, but the serpent loomed over it, fangs bared and poised to strike.

Instinct took over. I didn't even think—my hand flew to my gun. Two quick shots rang out, echoing across the desolate landscape. The bullets found their mark, tearing into the serpent's iridescent head. It hissed in pain, its body convulsing as it collapsed to the ground.

The Radiant Serpent twitched once, then twice. Its glowing scales dimmed as life drained from its form. Finally, it lay still, defeated and dead.

I holstered my gun and took a moment to catch my breath. The Hellhound remained on the ground, panting heavily but alive. It looked at me with those eerie red eyes.

"You're welcome," I muttered, more to myself than to the beast.

The wasteland was silent once more, save for the faint rustle of wind through the desolate terrain. The immediate threat had passed, but my journey was far from over.

The Hellhound stood, its eyes still locked onto mine. It approached cautiously, dragging the limp body of the Radiant Serpent with its powerful jaws. It dropped the serpent at my feet, looking up at me with an expression that could only be described as hopeful.

I hesitated. This was a wild creature, untamed and feral. Hellhounds didn't form bonds with anyone, and if they did, it was a lifelong commitment. I couldn't afford to have anyone depend on me, not when I couldn't guarantee my own survival from one day to the next.

But damn it, I'd been alone for so long. The thought of having some kind of companion, even one as wild as this Hellhound, was tempting. And this beast was smart—smarter than any Hellhound I'd ever encountered, and I had only encountered two since turning.

I crouched down, inspecting the serpent. Its scales still shimmered faintly in the dying light.

The Hellhound watched me intently, its ears perked up and tail wagging slightly.

"All right," I said finally, picking up the serpent. "Don't make me regret this."

The Hellhound let out a happy bark, its eyes gleaming with what looked like gratitude.

"We still got some miles to cover before we make camp," I continued, standing up and slinging the serpent over my shoulder. "But when we do, we'll have serpent for dinner."

The hound barked again, clearly pleased with itself.

"Fuck me," I muttered under my breath. "One hundred years and I'm going soft."

We set off again, the Hellhound trotting alongside me with newfound energy. Its presence was strangely comforting —a reminder that maybe I wasn't entirely alone in this godforsaken wasteland.

At least my bounty should be easy enough to handle compared to taming a Hellhound.

CHAPTER 9

Everly

The air outside the bunker felt different. Stale, metallic, with a hint of something burnt. The Forsaken stretched before me, an endless expanse of barren earth and twisted remnants of what once was.

I took a deep breath, feeling the grit in my lungs, and let it out slowly. My eyes scanned the horizon, adjusting to the harsh light after years underground. The sun hung low, casting long shadows that danced across the cracked ground.

Under my boots, the earth crunched with every step, a far cry from the soft, fertile soil of our hydroponic gardens. I bent down, scooping up a handful of dust. It slipped through my fingers like fine sand, gritty and lifeless. A faint smell of decay lingered in the air, mixed with the sharp tang of rusted metal.

The wind whipped around me, tugging at my hair and clothes, carrying with it the faint scent of something rotten. I paused, the weight of my decision pressing down on me. Was I really doing the right thing? The safety of the bunker, its familiar routines and walls, suddenly seemed like a paradise compared to this desolate wasteland.

Fear gnawed at my insides, a relentless beast that whispered of dangers I couldn't yet see. I looked down at my hands, soft and clean. What I even survive out here? Did I have what it took? Every step felt like a gamble with fate.

But then I thought of Elise. My sister, taken away to some unknown fate. If there was even a chance I could find her, how could I turn back now? My heart ached with the memory of her laugh, her smile—both now distant echoes in this harsh reality.

God is with you, Everly.

The words echoed in my mind, not in the stern voice of the Purifiers' teachings, but in a gentle whisper that felt more personal, more real. Maybe He wouldn't agree with what I was doing. The Ascension Rite was supposed to be an honor, after all. But out here, away from their dogma and rituals, I felt a different kind of faith stirring within me. One that was less about rules and more about love and justice.

I adjusted the pack on my shoulders and took another step forward. Each step felt like defiance of everything I had been taught to accept without question. The sun beat down on me mercilessly, but there was a strange comfort in its warmth—a reminder that life existed beyond the bunker's cold embrace.

My heart pounded in my chest as I walked further into The Forsaken. Each rusted piece of metal and charred piece of earth told stories of a world long gone, a world we had been taught to fear and forget. But standing here now, it wasn't just fear that filled me; it was also a fierce determination.

"Elise," I whispered into the wind. "I'm coming for you."

With that resolve burning brighter than my fears, I continued forward into the unknown.

As I walked further from the bunker's entrance, the wind picked up, whipping my hair into my face and carrying with it the distant howl of some unknown creature. The sound sent a shiver down my spine. My hands instinctively tightened around the straps of my pack, every muscle in my body tensed and ready.

The Forsaken's silence was oppressive, broken only by the occasional creak of old structures and the distant echo of falling debris. I spotted a dilapidated building in the distance and made my way towards it, hoping for some semblance of shelter while I figured out what way I needed to go. As I approached, I noticed faded graffiti on its walls—messages from those who had passed through before me. *Survive* one read in bold red letters; another simply said *Hope.*

I reached out to touch the rough surface of the wall, feeling its warmth from hours under the sun. It was strange to be here after all the stories we were told in the bunker about this place—stories meant to scare us into staying below ground. Now that I was here, it was both more terrifying and less so than I imagined.

A rustle caught my attention. My heart raced as I turned towards the sound. A small animal darted across my path—quick as lightning—and disappeared into a pile of rubble. My breath came out in short gasps as I tried to calm myself.

In this desolate place, everything seemed magnified—the colors duller yet sharper at once; every sound a potential threat; every smell a reminder of decay and survival. This was no longer just a concept or a cautionary tale—it was real life now.

And I had to find Elise.

I pressed on, each step taking me deeper into this new reality, senses on high alert for whatever lay ahead in this unforgiving land.

I stepped into the building, seeking refuge from the relentless sun. The temperature inside dropped a few degrees, offering a small reprieve. I wiped sweat from my brow, my skin sticky and uncomfortable. This heat wasn't like anything I had ever envisioned. In the bunker, we had controlled temperatures, a predictable environment. Out here, everything felt like it was trying to drain the life out of me.

I took a moment to get my bearings. The room was cluttered with debris—broken furniture, shattered glass, and remnants of lives long abandoned. My eyes adjusted to the dim light filtering through the cracks in the walls. I needed to figure out where the scavengers might have taken Elise.

Scanning the room, I searched for any clues—anything that could point me in the right direction. The floor was dusty, and if there had been footsteps, the wind had already shifted them. I knelt down, hoping to find some trace, but it was futile. The dust swirled around me as if mocking my efforts.

I moved deeper into the building, looking for signs—anything that might help me understand where they went. Would they come here? It was the closest shelter, but that didn't mean anything if they were familiar with the terrain.

My hands ran over surfaces, feeling for something that could give me a lead. But there was nothing concrete. Just fragments of a world that had moved on.

A wave of frustration washed over me. Tears sprang into my eyes, blurring my vision. What was I even doing out here? Who did I think I was? My heart ached with the weight of doubt and fear.

I sank to the floor, letting my pack slide off my shoulders. It landed with a thud beside me. For a moment, I just sat there, feeling utterly lost and overwhelmed. The reality of my situation hit me hard—this wasn't a mission I had been trained for; it wasn't even something I fully understood.

Elise's face flashed in my mind, and it fueled a flicker of determination within me. But that flicker felt so small against the vastness of this desolate world.

I wiped my tears away with the back of my hand and forced myself to stand up again. This wasn't about being a hero or proving something; it was about finding Elise and bringing her back safely.

With renewed resolve, I took another look around the room, hoping against hope that something would stand out this time.

A whimper reached my ears, faint and trembling.

I froze, heart pounding.

"Help," a small voice whispered, barely audible. "Please. Help!"

Without thinking, I raced up the stairs, my legs propelling me faster than I thought possible. Halfway up, the old wood gave way beneath my weight. My leg crashed through, splintering the step and trapping me in its jagged embrace.

Panic surged through me as I struggled to pull my leg free. It was stuck tight, the rough wood scraping against my skin. I gritted my teeth, fighting back the rising tide of fear.

"Hey!" I called out, trying to keep my voice steady despite the pain. "Are you all right? I'm a little incapacitated, but I'm going to get you some help."

Silence answered me.

"What's your name?" I asked, hoping to coax a response. "My name is Everly."

Again, only silence greeted me. My gut twisted with worry, but I pushed it aside. This wasn't the time for doubt or fear.

"Are you hurt?" I continued, shifting my weight to ease the pressure on my trapped leg. "It might be easier to help if you spoke to me, if you're comfortable with that."

Still nothing.

I tried to focus on freeing myself, using my hands to push against the unyielding wood. My fingers dug into the rough surface, splinters embedding themselves in my skin. The pain was sharp but distant compared to the urgency of finding whoever had called for help.

At that moment, I heard footsteps. Two figures emerged at the top of the stairs. Relief washed over me.

"Hello," I said, my voice filled with hope. "Are you all right? Did you hear the... I think she was a girl. She needed help. Is that you?"

I took in their appearances. They were two of the Forgotten. The man had a wild, unkempt beard, his face smudged with dirt. His clothes were tattered, hanging off his lean frame in rags, but he couldn't be that much older than me. The woman beside him was equally disheveled, her hair matted and tangled. Her eyes, sharp and wary, flicked over me.

"Is that a Bunker Rat?" the man asked, his voice gruff and suspicious.

"She's too clean to be a Forgotten," the girl replied, her tone filled with disdain. "Look at that uniform. I'd say she is."

"What's she doing up here?" he asked.

"I am from a Bunker," I admitted, trying to keep my voice steady. "Actually, I'm looking for my sister. Maybe you could help me out and we can go search for her together."

The girl's eyes narrowed further. "She'd fetch quite a price."

"I still think we should kill her and be done with it," the guy said, his hand reaching for something at his waist. "She might have some valuable shit in that pack."

"There's no need for that language — Wait, kill me?" I asked, panic rising in my chest. "Why would you do that?"

Their expressions remained hard and unforgiving as they stared down at me.

"No," the woman said, shaking her head. "Magnus Rex is looking for Bunker Rats. Says they'd fetch a high sum, especially the virgins. You think she's a virgin?"

My cheeks burned, though I knew I had nothing to be ashamed of.

"Well, girl?" the male asked, eyes narrowing as he leaned closer. "You a virgin?"

"It means you haven't—"

"I know what it is," I snapped, trying to mask my embarrassment with indignation. "And my sexual history is private, thank you very much. That's something I'll discuss with my husband when I get married."

The couple exchanged a knowing look.

"Definitely a virgin," they both said in unison.

"Which means," the woman continued, eyes gleaming with a greedy light, "we'll be paid so well we can afford to live permanently in a settlement. Hell, maybe Magnus Rex will let us live in the Iron Citadel."

"No way in fuck am I going to live there," the man shot back, his voice filled with revulsion. "I heard you can smell the rotted flesh on those crucifixes out front."

"We ain't gonna be crucified," she countered, rolling her eyes. "We're going to be worshiped."

I couldn't keep quiet any longer. The talk of crucifixion and worship gnawed at me in ways they couldn't understand.

"Crucifixion isn't something to be taken lightly or spoken about so callously," I said, my voice trembling with emotion. "It's a symbol of sacrifice and redemption, not some grotesque display for power and fear. Worship should be about reverence and respect, not idolatry and coercion."

The woman's eyes narrowed at me again, this time with an edge of curiosity mixed with her greed.

"Listen to this one preach," she said, almost laughing. "Maybe we'll fetch an even higher price for her piety."

Their words stung, but they only reinforced my resolve. This world was twisted beyond recognition from the teachings and values I held dear.

My leg throbbed where it was trapped in the broken step,

but I forced myself to focus on their faces—searching for any sign of empathy or doubt that I could exploit.

"Help me out," I urged softly. "There are better ways to survive out here than selling each other out. Please?"

They stared at me for a moment before bursting into laughter. The sound echoed off the crumbling walls around us.

"Dream on," the woman said finally. "We do what we have to do."

"What about the girl upstairs?" I asked, hoping against hope that there was some chance of reason with these people.

"What girl?" the woman asked, her eyes narrowing in confusion.

The man laughed, a harsh sound that grated against my nerves. "She thinks there's a girl," he said. "Oh no. That was a setup. Try to trap mice and turn them over for a few shards. That would buy us some food. But you? You're something else. I don't like turning you over to Magnus Rex—"

"Think of all the demon shards we're going to get for her, baby," the woman interrupted, her eyes gleaming with greed.

"Demon shards?" I asked, genuinely confused.

"This Bunker Rat don't know currency!" the woman said, shaking her head in disbelief. "She's more of an idiot than I thought."

They both laughed, the sound echoing around the decrepit building like a cruel mockery.

"Go get her, Bruce," the woman said, her voice dripping with anticipation. "Maybe knock her out if you have to."

I tensed, my muscles coiling like springs ready to snap. How was I going to get out of this? My leg was still trapped in the broken step, and my options were running thin. But I knew one thing for certain: I wasn't going down without a fight.

Bruce moved towards me, his movements slow and deliberate, as if savoring his impending victory. My mind raced, searching for any possible way to gain an advantage.

"Wait," I said quickly, trying to buy myself some time. "You don't have to do this. There has to be another way."

Bruce ignored me, his focus entirely on closing the distance between us. Desperation clawed at me as I struggled harder against the splintered wood trapping my leg.

"Please," I pleaded, my voice trembling but firm. "This isn't who you are."

He stopped for a brief moment, something flickering in his eyes—doubt maybe? But it vanished as quickly as it appeared.

"Sorry," he said, his voice devoid of any real apology. "Gotta eat."

He lunged at me then, and I reacted on pure instinct. With all my strength, I kicked out with my free leg, aiming for his knee. The impact threw him off balance just enough to give me a moment's reprieve.

My heart pounded as I frantically worked to free my trapped leg, each movement sending jolts of pain up my body. But there was no time to dwell on that now.

Bruce recovered quickly and came at me again, this time more determined than before. I swung my pack at him with all my might, hitting him square in the chest and forcing him back a few steps.

But it wasn't enough; he shook off the blow like it was nothing and advanced once more.

"Hold still," he growled.

Panic surged through me as he closed in again, leaving me with only one choice: fight with everything I had or face whatever fate awaited me at the hands of Magnus Rex.

With renewed determination, I prepared myself for one final stand against Bruce's relentless assault.

And that was when his head exploded into pieces, coating me in brain matter and blood.

CHAPTER 10

Walton

The Forsaken stretched out before me, a wasteland of twisted metal and scorched earth. The sky hung low, choked with ash and the remnants of once-thriving cities. Each step I took left a print in the dust, echoing the silent desolation around me. Ruined structures jutted from the ground like skeletal fingers reaching for something long lost.

A low growl rumbled beside me. The Hellhound had been shadowing me since I left Hellgate Citadel. Its glowing red eyes kept sight ahead, keeping close but always aware.

Ahead, the bunker loomed like a forgotten tomb. It was nestled against a craggy hill, partially hidden by debris and overgrown with thorny vines. The steel door was reinforced, a stark contrast to the decay. Piles of rubble formed makeshift barricades, like someone was desperate to get in.

I scanned the ground near the bunker entrance. Footprints caught my eye, heading west. They were fresh, cutting through the layer of grime like a wound in the earth. My mind raced with possibilities; someone had been here recently.

The Hellhound let out a soft whine, breaking my concentration. It sniffed the air and turned its head towards the foot-prints, its instincts sharper than mine. I couldn't afford to ignore it.

Another bounty hunter?

I crouched, examining the footprints more closely. Small feet. A woman, perhaps. Not that a woman couldn't be a bounty hunter, but they wouldn't leave their tracks so care-lessly in the dirt and sand. Bounty hunters worth their salt knew to act like ghosts, to move without a trace. These prints practically shouted their presence.

I let my eyes drift back to the bunker. The footprints led away from it, not toward it. Someone from inside going out? It didn't add up. Why leave the safety of the bunker to wander this forsaken land?

"Huh," I grunted, rising to my full height.

The Hellhound sniffed the ground again, eager and restless.

"All right," I muttered. "Let's see where this goes." I turned to the hound. "Track."

The Hellhound shot forward, nose to the ground, following the trail with a single-minded determination. I kept pace beside it, my senses heightened. The air grew colder as we moved further from the bunker; the landscape shifting from ruins to barren wasteland.

Each step felt heavier, like wading through thick fog of unease and questions. Why had they left? What were they running from? My mind raced through scenarios, each one more troubling than the last. The Hellhound paused occasion-ally, ensuring it was still on track before pressing forward again.

The footprints led us to a building barely half a mile away. It stood crooked, like a weary giant, its concrete walls marred by time and violence. Broken windows gaped like empty eye sockets, and rusted metal beams jutted out from the structure, twisted into unnatural shapes.

I noticed a word spray-painted in vibrant red across the crumbling facade: *Hope*.

The irony wasn't lost on me.

I scoffed, the sound barely audible over the soft crunch of debris underfoot. Hope had no place here.

The footprints vanished near the entrance, swallowed by the shadows of the building. The person had likely taken cover inside. I eyed the structure warily. It was the perfect place to set a trap, every corner offering concealment, every broken wall a potential ambush point.

The Hellhound continued to sniff, nose leading it towards the building's entrance. Its glowing red eyes flickered with anticipation.

"Easy," I murmured to it, pulling out my gun. The cold metal felt reassuring in my hand. Ready for anything, I followed the Hellhound inside.

The interior was dim, light filtering through gaps in the ceiling and walls. Dust particles floated in the air, disturbed by our presence. The Hellhound moved cautiously, sniffing at every shadow and crevice. My grip tightened on the gun as I scanned our surroundings.

The Hellhound's ears flattened as I crept closer to the voices echoing through the decayed building. Each step felt like a dance with the shadows, careful and deliberate. I gave the Hellhound a look, signaling it to stay alert but quiet. It complied, muscles tense under its matted fur.

"Think of all the demon shards we're going to get for her, baby," a woman's voice said, rough and jagged like broken glass. I knew that tone anywhere—Forgotten.

"Demon shards?" a girl replied, confusion evident in her voice. She must have come straight from the bunker. Green as grass.

"This Bunker Rat don't know currency!" The woman laughed harshly. "She's more of an idiot than I thought."

It didn't take much to piece it together. The girl had fallen into a trap. But was she my bounty? No. If she were, these scumbags would be swarming her like flies on rotten meat.

But then who...?

I stayed hidden, letting the shadows cloak me while I waited for more information. No point in revealing myself if this wasn't going to benefit me.

"Go get her, Bruce," the woman ordered, her voice dripping with anticipation. "Maybe knock her out if you have to."

"Wait," the girl pleaded. "You don't have to do this. There has to be another way."

I almost laughed. Did she seriously think she could negotiate with these Forgotten pieces of shit?

From my vantage point, I saw her still struggling. Her leg was caught in some splintered wood.

"Please," she continued, desperation coloring her words. "This isn't who you are."

I scoffed but then my eyes widened when I noticed Bruce hesitated. No fucking way.

"Sorry," he said, his voice devoid of any real apology. "Gotta eat."

He lunged at her then, and the girl reacted fast. She kicked at his knee, throwing off his balance.

She kept struggling to free her leg, but it was no good. Her long blonde hair shone under the sparse light filtering through the ceiling. The pristine Purifier uniform she wore made my blood boil. Part of me wanted to see her killed just for what she represented. Another part was curious to see how this played out.

Bruce recovered quickly and came at her again. She swung her pack with surprising speed, connecting with his head.

I had to hand it to her... the girl was quick on her feet.

95

Well, maybe not quick enough, but still.

The impact knocked Bruce back, but he shook it off with a growl.

"Hold still," the man growled, his grip tightening around the girl's arm.

I sighed, the weight of my gun familiar and cold in my hand. A waste of ammo, but necessary. I lifted the gun, sighted down the barrel, and squeezed the trigger.

The man's head exploded in a spray of blood and bone fragments. The girl flinched, eyes wide with shock and terror. I could see her trying to process what just happened, her breaths coming in short gasps.

"Sick," I commanded the Hellhound.

The beast lunged forward, muscles rippling under its matted fur. It raced towards the stairs where the woman stood frozen in shock. She barely had time to scream before the Hellhound's jaws clamped down on her throat. Blood sprayed in a crimson arc, splattering across the Bunker girl's face and clothes.

I smirked, reholstering my gun.

I slowly walked up the steps, each creak of the wood echoing in the silence. The girl was still struggling, her back to me, unaware of my approach. Her long hair hung in tangled strands, and her uniform was smeared with dirt and blood.

"Looks like you're in a bit of a stitch," I said.

She flinched but didn't turn around. "Um, yes, it appears so," she stammered. "My leg is stuck, and I can't... I can't seem to pull it out."

Her voice trembled like a leaf in a storm. Pathetic.

"Bunker rat," I muttered under my breath.

I knelt beside her and examined the situation. Her leg was wedged between two splintered beams, the wood digging into her flesh. I could see where she'd tried to free herself, but it only made things worse.

"Hold still," I barked, grabbing the beams with both hands. "This ain't gonna be gentle."

She whimpered but obeyed, her body tensing as I applied pressure. The wood groaned and cracked as I pried it apart. She let out a small cry as her leg finally came free, collapsing onto the floor.

I stood up, wiping my hands on my pants. "There you go. Now get up and quit whining."

The girl turned around, and my breath caught in my throat. Her face was a stark contrast to the ruin—smooth skin, delicate features, and those eyes. They were a brilliant green, flecked with gold, and they seemed to pierce right through me. I hated myself for noticing. She was stunning, a beacon of beauty in this hellscape.

And so damn young.

Despite living in a bunker all her life, she had freckles on her upturned nose, on her high cheeks.

Her bunker uniform, once pristine and white, was now smeared with dirt and blood. The fitted white jacket with its high collar hugged her athletic frame. The golden halo with wings emblem on her left breast glinted in the dim light, a mockery of purity and order in this forsaken place.

I liked the sight of blood on it.

It made her look less like the untouchable purity she represented and more like just another soul struggling to survive in this hellhole. The red stains clashed with the uniform's intended symbolism, adding an edge of raw reality to her otherwise polished appearance.

"Get up," I growled.

She struggled to her feet, wincing as she put weight on her injured leg. Her movements were slow and unsteady, but there was a determination in her eyes that caught me off guard.

"Thank you," she said again, her voice trembling yet earnest.

Her gaze met mine, and I waited for the usual reaction: disgust, fear, maybe even revulsion. Instead, her eyes scanned my face with a calm intensity. There was no hint of terror or repulsion in them, only curiosity and something else I couldn't quite place.

I clenched my jaw, anger bubbling up inside me. She had no right to look at me like that—not after everything I'd been through, not with what I had become. My demonic appearance had repelled countless others; why should she be any different?

"Thank you," she said softly, her voice trembling but sincere.

I didn't respond. Instead, I motioned for the Hellhound to come closer. The beast padded over obediently, its eyes still glowing with an eerie red light. It sniffed at the girl briefly before losing interest.

"You got a name?" I asked gruffly.

"Everly," she replied. "Everly Harrington."

The name struck a chord. Harrington—the same as Elise. This girl was more than just another bunker rat; she was my lead.

"Long way from the bunker," I drawled.

"I'm looking for my sister," she said earnestly. "She was taken by... by some scavengers a few days ago. You don't understand. She's important. So important. I... I need to get her back."

Her sister.

Like a gift from God Himself.

"Will you help me?" she asked. "Help me find her? I... I don't have money. I think they said demon shards? I don't even know what that is, but... but I can..." She let her voice trail off.

"Your sister's been taken," I said flatly. "You're not gonna find her by wandering around aimlessly, little girl."

Her eyes widened slightly but still held no fear. "Do you know where she is?" she asked.

"I might," I replied evasively. "But it's gonna cost you."

She straightened up, determination replacing the earlier vulnerability in her gaze. "I'll do whatever it takes."

For a moment, I almost admired her resolve. Almost.

"You tell me everything you know about these scavengers that took your sister," I said, keeping my voice low but firm. "Everything you can think of, you got that?"

Everly nodded, opening her mouth to speak. Before she could get a word out, the Hellhound growled, its eyes fixed on the doorway.

I slapped a hand over her mouth, my eyes narrowing as I listened intently. Footsteps echoed through the decrepit building.

"Bruce? Linda?" a voice called out. "You get the girl that wandered in here? Come on, we've gotta go. It's going to be night soon, and I don't wanna be out here... What's that noise? Is that growling?"

The moment he stepped into the room, I fired. The shot echoed in the confined space, and Everly let out a muffled squeal against my hand. The man collapsed with a thud, lifeless eyes staring at the ceiling.

I removed my hand from her mouth and moved swiftly to loot the body. A quick search revealed some food and trinkets —nothing too valuable, but useful enough in this wasteland.

"You killed him," she said, her voice trembling. "You just... what if he could have helped us find Elise?"

"No one's here to help, angel," I replied, pocketing the food and trinkets. "People like him? They'd sell you for a scrap of metal."

"There must have been some other way," she insisted, walking over to me with a determined look in her eyes. "*Thou shalt not kill*. It's one of God's commandments."

I glanced at her, irritation flaring up inside me. "You think quoting scripture's gonna change how things work out here? God ain't gonna save you from people like them—or from me." I glared at her. "Look around, sweetheart. You see God anywhere here? Wanna know why? He doesn't care about you, about me, about any of us."

She bit her lip, eyes wide but unwavering. "We can't lose our humanity," she said softly. "Even out here."

"Humanity," I scoffed. "Out here, it's kill or be killed, a lesson I got a feeling you'll have to learn the hard way."

Everly fell silent for a moment, then muttered a prayer under her breath. She was clinging to her faith like it was a life raft in this sea of despair.

"Come on," I said gruffly, standing up and motioning for the Hellhound to follow. "Unless you don't wanna find your sister, then?"

She hesitated but followed closely behind me as we stepped back into the Forsaken's grim embrace.

We didn't have time for second-guessing or moral debates —every second counted if we were going to find Elise alive. Though something told me I was going to regret setting eyes on this slip of a girl in the first place.

CHAPTER 11

Everly

I brushed the dirt off my clothes, looking up at the man who had just saved me. His silhouette was rough against the dying light. The world beyond the bunker was still so new, so terrifyingly open. There was so much space.

"Thank you," I said, my voice a bit shaky. "I'm Everly. Everly Harrington."

He didn't reply right away, just kept walking ahead, the dog—no, the creature—at his side. I hurried to keep pace with them, trying to make sense of everything. His legs were so long, I had to double-hop just to try to walk by him.

"You... you saved me back there. I don't know how to repay you," I continued, hoping to get more than silence this time.

He finally glanced down at me, his eyes cold and calculating. "Tell me what happened to your sister."

I sucked in a breath, remembering the chaos and fear that had filled the bunker that night. "Scavengers raided our bunker and took her. They broke through our security somehow—You see, our security system was... is... state-of-the-art. It was designed to be impenetrable. We had biometric scanners, motion sensors, even thermal imaging. The entrances were fortified with steel doors that could withstand a blast. The entire perimeter was monitored 24/7 by surveillance drones."

I paused, recalling the alarm blaring, the red lights flashing as people scrambled in every direction. "When they broke through, it wasn't just about brute force. They had inside information, knew exactly where to hit and how to bypass the systems. It was like they had the keys to the castle."

"Who were these scavengers?" he asked.

"I don't know," I admitted, frustration bubbling up inside me. "They moved like they knew exactly what they were doing. Like they had a-a purpose. Well, one didn't."

He nodded slowly, absorbing my words. The dog at his side sniffed the air, sensing the tension between us.

"Did they take anyone else?" he demanded gruffly, cutting me off.

"I don't know," I stammered. "I... I wasn't there—"

"'Course not." He sneered. "Hiding, then?"

I shook my head vehemently. "No! I don't think they took anyone else. They killed our High Priestess and a few others. But besides Elise, everyone was accounted for."

His expression remained unreadable as he processed my words.

"Huh," he said finally.

"Does that mean anything to you?" I asked, hoping for some insight or reassurance.

He didn't respond, just kept walking ahead as if my story meant nothing to him.

Silence stretched between us as we moved forward through the desolate landscape. The sky darkened further, shadows growing longer around us. My thoughts spun with worry for Elise and questions about this enigmatic man who had saved me yet seemed so detached from it all.

But I knew one thing for certain—I needed him if I had any hope of finding her again up here.

I quickened my pace to catch up with him. The dog—or whatever it was—trotted along beside us, its eyes reflecting the last slivers of daylight.

"Well, what's your name?" I asked, trying to keep my voice steady.

He grunted again, not even glancing in my direction.

"You have a name, don't you? Everyone has a name," I pressed, hoping to crack his stoic exterior. "Back in the bunker, there was this kid who insisted he didn't have a name. Turns out, he was just trying to get attention because he thought his name was boring. His name was Jeremy. We called him Jer." I looked up at him. "Well? Do you have a name, or do you think —"

"Do you ever shut up?" he asked roughly, stopping abruptly to look at me.

I frowned, feeling the sting of his words. "That's rude," I said firmly. "You don't just go around telling people to shut up when they're trying to have a conversation with you."

He glared at me, his eyes hard and unyielding.

"I just want to know what to call you," I continued, softening my tone but maintaining my stance. "Can't you give me something?"

"Will you stop talking for the rest of the night?" he asked.

"Oh, I don't know," I replied, pondering it for a moment.

The silence between us stretched as I weighed my options.

He waited, his eyes locked on mine. The air between us felt thick, like it could snap at any moment.

"You're serious, aren't you?" I asked, my voice barely above a whisper. "Fine."

"D," he said flatly.

"D?" I echoed, trying to wrap my head around it. "Is that your name or—"

He placed a gloved finger over my lips, his eyes glaring at me. The pressure of his finger was firm, almost uncomfortable.

"I'm just clarifying," I began, but he pressed harder against my lips.

"You asked for something to call me," he said, his voice low and controlled. "I gave it to you."

"Can you at least tell me—"

"Do you honor your word or not?" he interrupted, his eyes narrowing. "Doesn't your God have something to say about that?"

I jerked away from his hand, feeling a surge of defiance. "For one," I said, straightening up, "He's not just my God. He's everyone's. Yours too."

He scoffed in response.

"Secondly," I continued, reciting the words I'd learned so well in the bunker, "The Lord detests lying lips, but He delights in people who are trustworthy." I paused to let the weight of the words sink in. "So yes, I do honor my word. I'm going to be quiet now. But if you need anything—"

"Shut it, Bunker Rat," he snapped, cutting me off. "Let me enjoy my silence in peace."

I closed my mouth and nodded silently, swallowing the rest of my thoughts. As we walked on through the desolate landscape, I tried to focus on the rhythm of our steps and the occasional rustle of leaves in the wind. The world outside the bunker was still a mystery to me, filled with unknown dangers and unexpected allies—or enemies.

D's presence was imposing and enigmatic; every step he took seemed purposeful yet shrouded in secrecy. I couldn't help but wonder what kind of life he'd led out here and what had shaped him into this hardened figure before me.

Despite the rough start to our partnership, I knew I needed him if I was going to survive out here and find Elise. For now, silence would have to be enough.

The surface stretched out before us, an expanse of desolation and decay. A cool breeze swept over the land. For once, I welcomed the chill. The heat of the day had been oppressive, suffocating in its intensity.

I looked around, taking in the broken remnants of what must have once been a thriving world. Crumbling buildings stood like skeletal sentinels, their windows gaping like empty eye sockets. The ground was cracked and dry, patches of withered vegetation struggling to survive in the harsh environment.

"How far until we find a settlement?" I asked, my voice breaking the silence.

D didn't answer. He just kept walking, his long strides eating up the distance effortlessly. The dog trotted along beside him, seemingly unaffected by the Foresaken.

"Oh, sorry, I didn't mean to talk," I said quickly before biting my tongue.

I sighed and focused on putting one foot in front of the other. My legs ached, and my muscles screamed for relief. The idea of finding a settlement, of having a bed to sleep on, was a distant but tantalizing hope. I could almost feel the softness of a mattress beneath me, could almost hear the creak of wooden floorboards under my weight as I climbed into bed.

The sky above turned from blue to a palette of oranges and purples as the sun dipped lower. Shadows lengthened across the landscape, giving everything an eerie, otherworldly feel. It was beautiful in its own haunting way, but it only served to remind me how far from home I was.

I stumbled over a piece of rubble and caught myself just in time.

"You need to watch your step," D said without looking back.

"Sorry, I was distracted," I admitted, pointing to the sky. "Is that a sunset?"

D gave me a long, incredulous look. "You telling me you've never seen a sunset before?"

I shook my head. "I've read about it in a variety of books."

"Why does that not surprise me?" he muttered under his breath.

"But I've never seen one before," I continued, ignoring his tone. My voice softened as I looked back at the sky. "This is... I've never seen anything like it. I don't think the words did it justice."

"They rarely do," he replied.

For a moment, we both paused and watched the sky together. The colors were unlike anything I'd ever seen within the confines of the bunker—vibrant oranges bleeding into soft purples and deep blues. The fading light painted the world in hues that felt almost magical.

I felt a strange mix of emotions. There was awe, yes, but also a deep sense of loss for all the sunsets I'd missed while locked away underground. Each streak of color seemed to tell a story, whispering secrets of the world outside that I'd never known.

The air grew cooler as the sun continued its descent, and I could feel the weight of its beauty settling in my chest. It was both humbling and exhilarating to witness something so simple yet so profound. The sight made me realize how much more there was to this world than I'd ever imagined—how much more there was to experience and understand.

For that brief moment, standing there with D in silence, I felt connected to something greater than myself. It was as if the sunset had bridged the gap between my past life in the bunker and this new reality on the surface.

As we stood there, sharing this quiet moment of wonder, I realized that even in this harsh place, there were still moments of beauty to be found.

He didn't respond. His silence was infuriating, but also

oddly comforting; it meant he wasn't wasting energy on unnecessary words.

"Let's go," he said. "We can't sit around and gawk."

We continued walking as night began to fall in earnest. The temperature dropped further, and I wrapped my arms around myself for warmth. My clothes felt inadequate against the cold that seeped into my bones.

In the growing darkness, every noise seemed amplified— the rustle of leaves in the wind, the distant howl of some unseen creature. My heart raced at each sound, but I forced myself to keep moving.

I couldn't ignore the gnawing hunger in my stomach any longer. "Um, excuse me?" I asked tentatively, breaking my promise to stay silent. "I know I promised to be quiet, but when are we getting dinner?"

"Dinner?" he echoed, almost incredulous.

"Yes, dinner," I said, reciting the definition automatically. "Dinner is the main meal of the day, usually eaten in the evening."

He scowled at me. "I know what dinner is. Unfortunately for you, we don't have a fancy mess hall where your whims are taken care of. You wanna eat? You gotta catch your meal."

"You mean hunt?" I asked, a spark of hope igniting. "We were taught to hunt. I'm actually a good shot—"

He stopped in his tracks and turned to face me, disbelief written all over his face. "You know how to use a gun?"

"Of course," I replied with confidence. "The bunker thought it was important that we were self-sufficient when we were released onto the surface."

He raised an eyebrow. "Self-sufficient?"

"Yes," I continued, my mind wandering back to one of our hunting lessons. "There was this one time when we were out on a training exercise in the simulated environment section of the bunker. We had to track and hunt these mechanical animals they set loose. They were designed to mimic real prey —quick, agile, and unpredictable."

"And?" he prompted.

"I managed to hit one right between the eyes," I said proudly. "It was a mechanical deer, and it went down instantly. The instructors were impressed; they even called me their star pupil for that session."

He seemed to consider this for a moment before giving a slight nod. "Interesting."

"There doesn't look like there's much game up here," I murmured, looking around.

"Oh, there's game," he replied. "Just not the kind you're used to." He paused. "I thought your God frowned on killing."

I wrinkled my nose at his comment, but quickly composed myself. "God teaches us the value of life and compassion, yes. But He also understands that survival sometimes necessitates difficult choices." I paused, searching for the right words. "In the bunker, hunting wasn't about sport or cruelty; it was about ensuring we had the skills to survive when we faced real threats out here, doing His work."

"So you're saying it's justified as long as it's in His name?"

"I'm saying it's complicated," I replied earnestly. "We were taught that every life has value, but sometimes taking one life can mean preserving many others."

He smirked, revealing yellow teeth and sharp canines. "The many outweigh the few and all that?" he asked, his voice dripping with sarcasm.

"Yes, exactly."

"Bullshit," he said, the word hanging in the air like a challenge.

I felt my cheeks flush with indignation. "It's not bullpoop, sir," I retorted. "It's the truth."

He spun around, towering over me, his shadow swallowing me whole. "If that's the case, why are you out here searching for your sister, hmm? Seems like she's just one in comparison to all those other rats in your bunker, hmm? What makes her so special?"

I opened my mouth to answer, but found no words. I closed it again and looked away, feeling a sting of shame.

"She's my sister," I murmured, the words tasting bitter on my tongue.

"So, all those bunker rats," he continued relentlessly, "they don't mean that much to you for you to give them up for your sister?"

I wanted to argue, but couldn't find the strength. His words cut deep because they held a grain of truth I didn't want to acknowledge. The silence between us grew heavier with each passing second.

He leaned in closer, his breath hot against my face. "You're just like the rest of us." He sneered. "Selfish when it comes down to it."

I looked up at him, trying to muster some defiance. "It's not the same," I said weakly.

"Keep telling yourself that," he replied with a cruel smile. "You're no better than any of us out here."

The dog at his side let out a low growl as if agreeing with him. I felt a wave of helplessness wash over me. The world outside the bunker was harsh and unforgiving—far more so than anything I had ever imagined.

"You're just another rat trying to survive," he continued.

His words stung more than I cared to admit.

CHAPTER 12

Walton

I glanced over at the girl trudging beside me, her feet dragging through the dust. She had this annoying habit of humming under her breath, a tuneless murmur that grated on my nerves like nails on a chalkboard. Barely been a few hours, and I already questioned my sanity. Why the hell had I taken her along with me?

Sure, logically it made sense. Elise Harrington would be more likely to come with me if she recognized her sister. Hell, I could use the girl as bait to draw her out, maybe even have her trade in the settlements that wouldn't deal with demons. But with the way she talked, I wondered if it was even worth it.

She caught me staring and smiled, oblivious or maybe just too stubborn to care. "What's your story, anyway?" she asked, kicking a pebble ahead of her.

"My story's none of your business."

"Fair enough," she said, not missing a beat. "But if we're going to be traveling together, might as well get to know each other, right?"

I ignored her and kept walking. My stomach growled, reminding me that the serpent the Hellhound caught only lasted for one meal. It was getting late, and we needed to find something to hunt soon.

There was a faint scent of something alive on the wind—maybe a deer or one of those mutant rabbits that tasted like ash but filled your belly for a while.

Everly's humming grew louder as we walked deeper into the forested area. The trees here were twisted and gnarled, blackened by whatever celestial curse had scorched the earth. I scanned the shadows for movement, hoping we'd run into something edible soon.

"Are you always this cheerful?" I asked finally, unable to stand her relentless optimism any longer.

She shrugged. "Beats being miserable."

"Misery's more honest."

"Maybe," she said softly, eyes scanning the horizon just like mine. "But it doesn't get you very far."

A rustle in the underbrush caught my attention. I raised a hand to stop her and peered through the tangled branches. A pair of glowing eyes stared back at me—Bats.

Damn it. Not what I hoped for dinner, but they would suit.

I looked at the Hellhound, her eyes locked on the luminescent bats flitting through the branches. "Think you can catch one in that maw?" I asked, half-expecting her to ignore me.

She snuffed, almost as if she were offended by the question, and her glowing eyes narrowed.

"Sick," I commanded, pointing towards the bats.

She bolted off without a second glance, her dark form blending into the shadows as she pursued our glowing prey. I watched her go, knowing she'd make quick work of them.

"Is that a dog?" Everly asked beside me, her big, doe eyes wide with curiosity as she looked up at me.

I scowled down at her. "Does that look like a dog to you, sweetheart?"

She shrugged, looking a bit embarrassed but not deterred. "I don't know," she said. "I've only seen them in books. I'm sure God made so many, it's not possible to catalog them all."

I rolled my eyes. "Books won't save your life out here, sweetheart. Best learn to tell a Hellhound from a house pet if you want to keep breathing."

Her expression didn't change—still curious, still annoyingly unbothered by my gruffness. It grated on me even more.

"You always this dense?" I shot back, hoping to shake that serene look off her face.

She just smiled that same infuriatingly calm smile. "You always this pleasant?"

Before I could answer, she stepped toward where the Hellhound had vanished. "So, that's a Hellhound?" she asked, her voice tinged with curiosity. "Why hasn't she attacked us?"

I raised an eyebrow. "What?"

"I mean," she began, ticking off on her fingers, "Hellhounds are supposed to be ferocious. They hunt in packs, have glowing red eyes, emit a fear-inducing howl, and their bites are venomous. They eat people like snacks. None of this makes sense."

I grunted. "She submitted."

"What?" She cocked her head to the side, an innocent gesture that made me look away. Her naivety was almost painful to witness.

"A Hellhound is a natural pack animal," I explained, keeping my eyes on the park's edge. "If they're separated from their pack, they'll seek to join another by choosing to submit."

"And she submitted to you?" Her eyes widened in surprise.

"You sound surprised," I said, though I couldn't help the smirk tugging at my lips.

"No, of course not," she said quickly, her cheeks flushing slightly. "I just assumed she'd submit to, like, a demon or something."

I gave her an incredulous look. Did she not realize what a demon was?

"What do you think a demon is?"

She straightened up, ready to recite like she was back in school. "A demon has glowing red eyes, sharp claws, elongated teeth, a terrifying presence. They're soulless, evil beings that prey on humans, whether to sell them, to corrupt them, or to claim them. The most wicked ones eat them. They're rotted and ugly, wearing their sins like skin."

My smirk widened. She noticed.

"What?" she asked. "What is it?"

"What do you think I am?"

"A man," she said without hesitation.

"You think a man looks like me?"

She gave me a long, assessing look. Her eyes traveled over my scarred, red skin and my eyes. "Are you saying...?"

My smile widened further, flashing my teeth. "Why do you think they call me D?"

"You're a demon?" she asked, tapping her chin thoughtfully. "But where's your tail? You're supposed to be disgustingly ugly. And you're..." She let her voice trail off.

"They didn't teach you shit in that bunker, did they?"

She frowned, clearly offended. "They taught us a ton."

"Clearly," I bit back. "I'm a demon, little girl. Is that going to be a problem?"

She pursed her lips, considering this new information. "I suppose that depends."

"Depends?" I couldn't believe what I was hearing. "On what?"

"Well, are you going to eat me, corrupt me, claim me, or sell me?" she asked, her voice carrying a blend of curiosity and challenge.

I snorted. "Darling, I couldn't possibly pay anyone to take

you from me, what with the way you can't seem to shut the fuck up."

This was a lie. The girl was as beautiful as she was annoying, in an otherworldly way, rare for the Forsaken. And she was human, not an angel. People would pay a premium for her. Probably why those scavengers were so keen to sell her to Magnus Rex.

"That's not an answer," she pointed out.

"And you'll just, what, take my word?" I asked, eyebrow raised.

"I think so," she said. "You haven't lied to me yet."

"You're a fucking idiot," I muttered.

"You don't want me to trust you?" she asked, genuine confusion coloring her tone.

"Not this easily," I said. "Not up here. This is the real world, or have you forgotten you had your leg in a staircase with people trying to sell you?"

"And you saved me," she pointed out.

I clenched my jaw, biting back a retort. Her logic was infuriatingly sound in its simplicity. She saw things in black and white—a dangerous perspective in this hellscape.

"You don't get it," I said finally, frustration seeping into my voice. "Out here, trust gets you killed."

"But isn't there someone you trust?" she asked, eyes wide and innocent, like a child asking why the sky is blue.

For a moment, an image of my daughter flickered in my mind before I shoved it away. Trust had cost me everything once; it wouldn't happen again.

"Not anymore," I said curtly.

Her face softened with pity—an emotion I didn't need from anyone, least of all her. Before she could say anything else that would make me want to punch something or someone— preferably the latter—the Hellhound returned with one of those glowing bats clamped between its jaws.

"Dinner's here," I announced gruffly, eager to change the subject.

"We're going to eat that?" Everly asked, her nose wrinkling in distaste.

"Watch me," I replied, pulling out my knife. "Pay attention. You're going to carry your weight around here, you hear me? Which means you're going to learn how to skin a bat."

The Hellhound took off, probably on the hunt for another one.

Everly's eyes followed the creature as it disappeared into the shadows. "Aren't you worried she's running away?"

"She'll come back," I said, my focus on the task at hand. "You paying attention?"

She tore her gaze away from the darkness and nodded, though she still looked a bit skeptical. I laid the luminescent bat on a flat rock and positioned my knife at its belly.

"First thing you do," I began, "is make an incision here." I sliced through the soft glow of its underbelly with a steady hand. "Keep your cuts shallow; you don't want to puncture any organs."

She leaned in closer, watching with wide eyes as I worked. I peeled back the thin membrane of skin, exposing the meat beneath. It wasn't much, but it would keep us alive.

"See this?" I pointed with the tip of my knife. "You separate the skin from the muscle by running your blade just underneath. Don't rush it."

She nodded again, her expression shifting from skepticism to concentration.

Good. She was learning.

I handed her the knife. "Your turn."

Her hands shook slightly as she took it, but she knelt beside me and positioned the blade where I'd shown her. With tentative movements, she began to peel back the skin.

"Steady," I instructed, keeping my voice low and calm.

She glanced up at me briefly before returning to her task. She continued to work slowly, methodically—her focus unwavering despite the unfamiliarity of the chore.

Minutes passed before she finished. The bat lay skinned and ready for roasting on the rock between us.

"I guess it's better than having skin on it," I said grudgingly, taking back the knife. The truth was, she wasn't bad. "Now we'll spit it and roast it over a fire."

"We don't have a fire," she pointed out, her voice cutting through the evening silence.

I grunted, stepping back onto the flat terrain. "Come on," I said, moving towards the park. "We'll make one off the road."

"But why—"

"Can you stop asking your fucking questions for one goddamn second?" I snapped, turning to glare at her.

She bristled, crossing her arms over her chest. "You know, sir," she said, her voice taking on a prim tone that made my blood boil, "that language isn't necessary, and I'd like to request you don't take the Lord's name in vain."

I let out a harsh laugh. "The Lord? In case you haven't noticed, sweetheart, He ain't doing us any favors out here. Now shut your mouth and follow me."

Her lips pressed into a thin line, but she didn't argue further. We moved off the main road and into the park, the remnants of civilization crumbling around us. Broken benches and rusted playground equipment stood as silent sentinels to a world long gone.

I scanned the area for a suitable spot—somewhere that wouldn't draw unwanted attention. The last thing we needed was to light up like a beacon for every scavenger and beast within miles.

We walked deeper into the park until I found a small clearing surrounded by tall, overgrown bushes and trees with twisted branches reaching out like skeletal fingers. The ground here was relatively flat, and there was enough natural cover to keep our fire hidden from prying eyes.

"This'll do," I said, dropping my pack onto the ground.

Everly looked around skeptically, but didn't say anything this time. Maybe she was learning after all.

I gathered some dry twigs and branches scattered nearby while Everly watched silently, awkwardly holding the skinned bat in her hands. It didn't take long to assemble a small pile of kindling in the center of the clearing. I pulled out my flint and steel, striking them together until sparks caught on the dry wood.

The fire crackled to life slowly at first before growing into a steady flame. The glow cast eerie shadows on Everly's face as she knelt beside me, her expression contemplative.

"Better get used to this," I said gruffly. "This is how it's going to be from now on."

She nodded slowly, her eyes reflecting the dancing flames as if trying to find answers in their depths. For now, at least, she seemed willing to follow my lead—and that was good enough for me.

"What?" I asked, grabbing the bat from her so I could use a stick and start roasting it. "You never seen a fire before?"

"Of course I have," she replied, her voice softening. "When Fiona turned five, we had a cake with candles. She blew them out so fast, we barely got to sing *Happy Birthday*."

I snorted. "A cake?"

"Yes," she continued, a faraway look in her eyes. "But I've never seen fire like this—wild and untamed. It's beautiful."

I watched the flames dance in her green eyes, catching myself staring longer than I should have. Something about the way she looked at the fire—like it was some kind of magic— stirred something buried deep inside me.

Thrusting the stick back to Everly, I said, "Cook this. I'm going to take a piss."

She wrinkled her nose but didn't comment.

Good. She needed to toughen up if she was going to survive out here.

I walked behind some rocks, putting distance between us and giving myself a moment to breathe. The girl's naivety grated on my nerves, but there was something oddly refreshing about it too—like seeing the world through new eyes.

Focus, D. Don't get caught up in this girl's stupidity.

I unzipped my pants and relieved myself against the rough stone, trying to push thoughts of Everly out of my mind. The flames had brought back memories of another time—a simpler time when birthday candles were our biggest worry.

But that world was gone now, replaced by this harsh reality where trust was a liability and survival meant making hard choices every day.

I zipped up and headed back to the fire, determined to keep my distance from her optimism. The Forsaken didn't allow for such luxuries.

Returning to our makeshift camp, I found Everly diligently turning the bat over the flames. She glanced up as I approached, offering a tentative smile that didn't quite reach her eyes.

"It's almost ready," she said, her voice hesitant but hopeful.

"Good," I grunted, settling down across from her.

I watched the flames flicker and dance, feeling the weight of exhaustion settle into my bones.

The Hellhound returned silently, her red eyes glowing softly in the dim light. She trotted over to Everly and sat down beside her, dropping another bat at her feet before settling in to chew on it.

Everly glanced at the creature, her initial wariness giving way to a hesitant smile. The Hellhound, unfazed by her presence, gnawed contentedly on its catch. For a moment, there was an almost peaceful stillness around our small campfire—a brief respite in the chaos that had become our lives.

We ate in silence, each lost in our own thoughts as the fire crackled between us. The taste of roasted bat wasn't much better than raw meat, but it filled our bellies and kept us warm.

Everly reached out, her hand trembling slightly as it neared the Hellhound's matted fur. The creature's glowing red eyes flicked up to meet hers, and for a moment, I thought she might snap at her. But then, almost gently, the Hellhound leaned into her touch.

Everly's face lit up, a wide smile spreading across her lips as she ran her fingers through the coarse fur. "She's... softer than I expected," she whispered, awe coloring her voice.

That smile hit me like a punch to the gut. It was bright, almost blinding, like the fucking sun piercing through storm clouds.

I had to look away, my jaw tightening. How could anyone still smile like that in this world?

I busied myself with the fire, stirring the embers with a stick, trying to ignore the warmth spreading through my chest. In this forsaken land, such purity felt like a cruel joke—a reminder of everything we'd lost.

CHAPTER 13

Everly

The luminescent bat's body crackled over the fire, its bioluminescent glow fading as the heat did its work. I turned the makeshift spit, ensuring even roasting. The soft light of the flames cast flickering shadows around us, mingling with the eerie luminescence of the bat's flesh. Its wings had shriveled to leathery crisps, and the meat beneath its thin hide had taken on a dark, rich color. The smell was oddly enticing, a mix of gamey and something sweeter, almost floral.

A chill in the air reminded me of the night closing in. I shivered slightly, more from exhaustion than cold. The Hellhound beside me radiated warmth. Its glowing red eyes reflected the firelight, making them seem almost gentle instead of terrifying. For a creature I'd once feared, its presence now felt strangely comforting.

I tore off a piece of the bat's roasted flesh and handed it to D. His fingers were gnarled and pale, resembling something dead brought back to life—like a ghoul from those old stories. His face was gaunt, with hollow cheeks and skin that looked like it had been left too long in the sun. Yet his eyes held an unexpected depth, an intelligence that belied his monstrous appearance.

He took the meat without a word, pulling at it with sharp teeth that glinted briefly in the firelight. He chewed methodically, savoring each bite as though it were a delicacy rather than scavenged survival food. It was hard to reconcile him with everything I'd been taught about demons—vicious, mindless beasts driven by nothing but malice.

As he ate, I couldn't help but study him more closely. His movements were deliberate but lacked any real aggression. He didn't fit into the stories from my childhood or the fearsome images painted by the Purifiers. Instead, he seemed almost... human in his mannerisms.

Watching him gnaw at another piece of meat, I wondered how much of what I'd learned was truth and how much was constructed to keep us compliant and fearful.

"How is it?" I asked.

He glanced up briefly before returning his focus to his meal. "Edible," he grunted between bites.

I tore off a piece of the bat's roasted flesh for myself, hesitating only a moment before taking a bite. The texture hit me first—rubbery and stringy, like chewing on an old boot. The taste followed, an overwhelming bitterness mixed with a rancid, metallic tang that coated my tongue and clung to my throat. My stomach churned, and I fought the instinct to spit it out, swallowing with great effort.

The bile rose in my throat as I gagged, coughing into my hand. "Golly, that's awful," I managed to rasp out, wiping at my mouth. The taste lingered, refusing to be ignored.

D's eyes glinted with amusement as he watched me struggle. He pulled another piece from the bat's carcass and chewed it thoughtfully.

"Do demons have a different palette than humans?" I asked, trying to mask my revulsion with curiosity.

A smirk curled at the corner of his lips, a ghastly semblance of a smile on his cadaverous face. "Heh, you could say that," he drawled in a gravelly voice that reminded me of broken glass scraping against stone. "We don't exactly have gourmet options down here." He picked at the meat again, seemingly unbothered by its repulsive taste. "You get used to it." He shrugged, like he was sharing an inside joke only he found funny.

I tried to focus on anything but the lingering bitterness in my mouth—the way the firelight danced on the cave walls, the rhythmic sound of D's chewing, even the faint rustle of leaves outside. Anything to distract me from the fact that I might have to rely on such disgusting fare for survival out here.

"Well," I said, trying to force some levity into my tone, "I guess it's an acquired taste."

D chuckled—a dry, raspy sound that carried no real mirth. "You'll learn," he said simply. "Or you won't last long enough for it to matter."

His words hung in the air like smoke from the fire, mingling with the bitter aftertaste still coating my mouth. It was a harsh truth, but one I couldn't afford to ignore. Surviving out here meant adapting quickly or facing an end far worse than mere discomfort.

I nodded slowly, letting his words sink in as I took another tentative bite.

I heaved again, my stomach twisting violently as I fought to keep the vile meat down. This time, D laughed—a deep, resonant sound. It caught me off guard, almost beautiful in its unexpectedness. I didn't know a sound like that could come from a demon.

I wanted to be mad, but his laugh was so surprising that I stopped and looked at him. "Your face looks different when you smile," I said without thinking.

His expression shifted immediately, eyes narrowing into a

glare. The warmth of his laughter evaporated like mist. "Time to put out the fire," he growled. "We don't want to attract any unwanted attention."

"Where are we going?" I asked, forcing myself to swallow another piece of the disgusting food. My stomach rebelled, but I held it down. "You never even told me how you know where you're going. Are you using black magic? Some kind of voodoo?"

He snorted as he stood up to extinguish the fire. "Voodoo? It's something you bunker rats don't have too much of, angel —common sense." He kicked dirt onto the flames, snuffing them out one by one. "The nearest settlement is two days north. Unless they want to go to Hellgate—and if they have your sister, they sure as shit don't want that—then they'll go to Ironedge to resupply."

"Ironedge?" I opened my mouth again, the questions tumbling out faster than I could control them. "How do you know that? Besides common sense? What do you mean if they have my sister? And is... is Heckgate where the devil lives?"

D gave me a long, measuring look before answering.

"Do me a favor and shut the fuck up," he groused, glaring at me. "You want to get to your sister? Sleep. I'll take first watch."

"Watch?" I asked, confusion lacing my voice.

"What'd you think was up here, little girl?" His voice dripped with sarcasm. "You think there're no serpents, no wolves, none of those giant ants that came out of the fucking brimstone? And that's not even touching the scavengers. There's always danger up here."

I sighed, the weight of his words pressing down on me. "Okay," I said softly. "Where do we sleep?"

"On your back, I s'ppose," he replied, pulling out a cigarette and lighting it with a practiced flick. The orange glow momentarily lit his gaunt features. "Maybe fetal position. Stomach? How the hell should I know?"

"I... I didn't bring..." My voice trailed off, embarrassed by my lack of preparation.

He clicked his tongue in annoyance. "My point exactly," he said. "'Bout common sense."

I pulled out my toothbrush and toothpaste from my pack, using a bit of water from my canteen to wet the brush. As I scrubbed away the foul taste of the bat meat, I felt a small sense of normalcy return. The familiar minty freshness helped to clear my mind, washing away the lingering bitterness. When I finished, I put everything back in its place, tucking the toothbrush into a side pocket for easy access.

Unzipping my jacket, I was left in just a plain white t-shirt. The fabric clung to me, damp with sweat from the day's journey. I started stretching the way I used to in the bunker, reaching my arms up high above my head and then bending down to touch my toes. Each stretch brought a sense of release, as though I was shedding layers of tension and fatigue.

I happened to glance at D and noticed him watching me with an intensity that caught me off guard. His eyes were sharp, piercing through the dim light like a predator studying its prey.

He sneered, flicking ash from his cigarette. "What the fuck are you doing?"

Tilting my chin up, I met his gaze head-on. "My routine before bed," I said firmly. "It's important to take care of yourself."

He snorted but said nothing more, his eyes never leaving me as I continued my stretches. After finishing my routine, I got down on my knees and closed my eyes. The weight of everything pressed down on me—the betrayal, the uncertainty of our journey, and the fear for my sister's safety.

"Dear Lord," I began softly, clasping my hands together.

"Thank you for keeping us safe today. Please guide us on this journey and protect those we love. Help us find Elise and bring her back safely." My voice wavered slightly but grew steadier with each word.

D watched me with that same intense look, but didn't interrupt. The act of praying brought a small measure of peace, grounding me amidst the chaos.

"Amen," I finished quietly, opening my eyes again.

The fire was nothing more than embers, casting a warm glow around us. D's expression was unreadable now, his earlier sneer replaced by something more contemplative.

I took in a breath, then another, trying to steady my nerves. My hands fumbled in my pack until they found the thin blanket I had packed—more an afterthought than anything else. It wouldn't offer much warmth against the night's chill, but it was something.

Spreading it on the ground, I lay down carefully, every muscle in my body tense and alert despite my exhaustion. The ground was hard and unyielding beneath me, each pebble pressing into my back like a reminder of how far from home I truly was.

The Hellhound curled up nearby, its presence both comforting and unnerving at the same time. Its red eyes glowed faintly in the darkness as it watched me with an inscrutable expression.

I pulled the blanket tighter around myself, trying to find some semblance of comfort in its thin fabric. The night sounds were foreign—rustling leaves, distant howls, the occasional snap of a twig that sent my heart racing.

D stood by the fire's remnants, cigarette smoke curling around him like a ghostly shroud. His eyes scanned our surroundings with an intensity that made it clear he wasn't taking any chances.

I nodded weakly, closing my eyes and willing myself to

relax. Sleep didn't come easily; every creak and whisper of the night kept me on edge. But eventually, exhaustion won out over fear, and I drifted into a restless slumber filled with dreams of serpents and wolves lurking just beyond the firelight.

* * *

A sharp pain jolted me awake. D's boot pressed into my hip.

"Didn't know angels drooled like you do," he muttered, his voice dripping with sarcasm.

I wiped my mouth hastily, my cheeks burning with embarrassment. "I do not drool," I insisted, sitting up.

"Thought you weren't supposed to lie," he said, cocking a brow. He had this annoying way of assuming he was right about everything.

The night was still heavy around us, the darkness unbroken by any hint of dawn. D crouched beside me, eyes gleaming in the faint light of the dying embers. He thrust a gun into my hands, its cold weight unfamiliar and unsettling.

"Your turn, bunker rat," he said, his tone mocking. "You say you're a good shot?"

"With a rifle," I replied, gripping the gun tightly. The metal felt strange and heavy in my hand, its contours foreign to me. It wasn't like the farming tools or hydroponic equipment I was used to handling.

"Just point at the threat and shoot it," he instructed, as if it were the simplest thing in the world.

I looked at him, feeling a knot tighten in my stomach. "What if it's a person?" I asked, my voice barely above a whisper.

D blinked, then shrugged as if the question was irrelevant. "Point at the person and shoot," he repeated with a cold finality.

"But what if—"

"What ifs get you killed, little girl," he drawled, cutting me off sharply. "You aren't stupid, are you?"

"No," I said quietly, taking the gun more firmly. It felt alien and menacing in my hands, each curve and edge a reminder of what it could do. The grip was rough against my skin, a stark contrast to the smooth tools I was accustomed to in the bunker. The weight of it pulled at my arms, making them ache slightly with its unfamiliarity. "But I'm not a killer either."

"You best be," D said without looking at me, leaning back against a rock and tilting his head down so the brim of his hat covered his face. "Or else you're dead."

I swallowed hard, my fingers trembling slightly as they wrapped around the trigger guard. The reality of our situation pressed down on me like an oppressive weight. This wasn't about ideals or morals anymore; it was about survival.

The darkness pressed in on me from all sides, a suffocating blanket that left me feeling vulnerable and exposed. I couldn't see a thing beyond the faint glow of the embers, which only seemed to deepen the shadows. The vastness of the space outside the bunker was overwhelming. It felt like the world could swallow me whole, leaving nothing behind.

I clenched the gun tighter, my knuckles whitening under the strain. The unfamiliar weight of it made my arms ache, and my heart pounded in my chest, loud enough that I feared D might hear it. I couldn't let him down. He was counting on me, even if he'd never admit it out loud.

I took a deep breath, trying to steady myself. The air was different out here—crisp and wild, filled with scents I couldn't identify. In the bunker, everything had been controlled and predictable. Here, it was as if the world itself was alive and watching me.

I shifted my position slightly, feeling the cold ground

beneath me. It was hard to push my fear and doubts aside when every sound seemed amplified in the quiet night. The rustle of leaves, the distant call of an animal—all of it sent my nerves on edge.

"Focus," I whispered to myself, barely audible even in the silence. I had to be strong. For D, for Elise, for myself. My mind raced with thoughts of my sister, wondering if she was somewhere out there in this vast darkness. If she was scared like I was.

I glanced at D's silhouette against the faint glow of the fire. His presence was a strange comfort in my fear. He might be gruff and unyielding, a demon, but he knew this world in a way I didn't yet understand. If he believed I could do this, then maybe I could.

Another deep breath. I had to believe that, too.

The silence stretched on, broken only by the occasional crackle from the embers or a distant rustling in the brush. Each minute felt like an eternity as I fought to keep my mind from spiraling into panic.

"I can do this," I told myself again, more firmly this time. My voice sounded more confident than I felt.

With every passing second, I forced myself to stay alert, scanning the darkness for any sign of movement. The world outside might be vast and overwhelming, but I had to find my place in it.

I had to survive.

For Elise.

For myself.

For whatever came next.

CHAPTER 14
Walton

I didn't sleep much. The girl was supposed to keep watch, but I couldn't trust her to do it right. I could smell her fear. It hung in the air like a thick fog, clinging to her every move.

Good. She should be afraid.

I watched as the horizon began to change colors, shifting from the deep blues of night to the first hints of dawn. The sky bled into oranges and purples, a stark contrast to the cold ground beneath us. The light crept over the landscape slowly, painting the world in shades of gold and pink. Each moment felt like a brushstroke on an infinite canvas, each color fighting for dominance before surrendering to the inevitable brightness of day.

"I don't know what's more beautiful," she murmured, her voice barely breaking the silence. "Watching the sun rise or watching it fall."

I grunted, not bothering to respond. Her words were pointless drivel. The sunrise meant nothing more than another day of hunting, another day closer to my goal.

She shifted uneasily beside me, probably waiting for some

acknowledgment or maybe hoping for a conversation. I kept my eyes on the horizon, focusing on the task ahead.

The sunlight grew stronger, revealing the barren landscape around us. Twisted trees stood as silent witnesses to our presence, their gnarled branches reaching out like skeletal fingers. The ground was cracked and dry, a reminder of the world's broken state.

From the corner of my eye, I watched as she grabbed her pack and pulled out some packaged food. It looked like some kind of jerky. She tore it open with a quick flick of her wrist and took a bite, chewing thoughtfully.

"This is my favorite," she said, her voice breaking the silence. "It's teriyaki. Nelson tried to tell me the jalapeño flavor was better, but—"

"Jesus Christ," I bellowed, unable to contain my irritation. "Do you ever shut up, even at the fucking crack of dawn?"

She scowled at me, her eyes narrowing. "You're pretty grumpy," she said, her tone defiant. "And I'll ask you again not to take the Lord's name in vain."

I turned to face her fully, letting the anger simmer in my gaze. "Blondie, do I look like I give a single damn about your precious Lord?"

Her scowl deepened, but she didn't respond right away. Instead, she took another bite of her jerky, chewing with a deliberate slowness that grated on my nerves. The silence stretched between us, heavy and uncomfortable.

"Well," she finally said, swallowing the last of her bite. "You might not care now, but you used to."

I snorted, turning back to the horizon. The sun was climbing higher now, casting long shadows across the ground. "Used to doesn't mean shit anymore," I muttered.

She didn't say anything after that, just sat there munching on her jerky. I could still feel her eyes on me, though, watching me like I was some kind of puzzle she needed to solve.

The morning air was crisp and cold, but it did nothing to cool the fire burning inside me. Every word out of her mouth was a reminder of what I'd lost—what I'd become. And no amount of sunrise beauty or teriyaki jerky was going to change that.

I clenched my fists and focused on the day ahead. There were bounties to hunt and scores to settle. This girl might be useful for now, but once she served her purpose... well, she'd learn that the world had no place for idealistic chatterboxes.

Not anymore.

"Here," she said, holding out a piece of jerky. "It might make your grumpiness simmer. For however long."

I kept the scowl on my face, but her unpredictability grated on me. I had expected fear when she found out I was a demon. Instead, she offered me food after I was an ass. Was she a glutton for punishment?

I snatched the jerky from her hand, refusing to deny myself a meal. The taste of teriyaki hit my tongue, savory and sweet.

"A thank you would be nice," she said.

"So much for the goodness of your heart, hmm, angel?" I smirked. "You only offered me something in exchange for something."

"What? No, I—"

"Then," I interrupted, "it shouldn't matter whether I thank you or not."

She frowned, crossing her arms. "You're a butt," she said.

I snorted, amused by her choice of words. This girl had more spine than I gave her credit for. She stood there, pouting like a child denied a treat, and it almost made me laugh.

"Call me whatever you want," I said between bites of jerky. "Names don't mean much to me."

She huffed and turned away, focusing on the horizon

again. Her shoulders were tense, but she didn't storm off or throw another insult my way. Maybe she was learning.

The sun climbed higher, warming the air. The light cast long shadows across the ground, illuminating the scars of the land. It was a broken world we navigated, but it was ours to survive in.

I finished the jerky and tossed the empty package aside. "All right," I said finally. "Let's move out. We're burning daylight."

The girl's sharp intake of breath caused me to look at her as the Hellhound finally stood up to stretch.

"What do you think you're doing?" she snapped, her voice rising.

I raised an eyebrow, genuinely puzzled. "Eating breakfast. What does it look like?"

"No," she said, marching over and picking up the discarded wrapper. "This. Littering."

She shoved the wrapper into her backpack, her eyes flashing with anger. It was almost amusing how seriously she took it.

"You think that's going to matter?" I asked, my tone dripping with disdain. "Look around, little girl. The Forsaken is just that—a dead land forsaken by the God that created this place. What the hell does it matter if I litter?"

Her eyes met mine, wide and earnest, and I felt an irrational surge of hatred for those goddamn doe eyes. "Of course it matters," she said firmly.

I let out a derisive laugh.

"Every action, no matter how inconsequential, matters," she insisted.

Her conviction was almost impressive, if not entirely misplaced. This world had bigger problems than a bit of litter.

"Let's go," I growled, turning away from her and starting down the cracked path ahead of us.

I watched Everly as she methodically packed up her things. Every motion was deliberate, almost ritualistic. She folded her blanket neatly, stowing it away in her pack with care. Her movements were calm, controlled, so different from the chaotic world around us.

She took a moment to stretch, bending and reaching in ways that made me wonder how anyone could be so flexible. She moved with an ease that spoke of years spent in safety and comfort, far removed from the brutal reality we now faced.

After stretching, she pulled out a small tin and a toothbrush. She brushed her teeth, scrubbing away the remnants of sleep and jerky with determined strokes. The sight was almost surreal—a moment of normalcy in a world that had lost all semblance of it.

Next, she pulled out a comb and began brushing her hair. The golden strands shimmered in the morning light as she worked through the tangles with patience. When she was satisfied, she pulled her hair back into a ponytail, securing it with a practiced flick of her wrist.

Meanwhile, the Hellhound watched her intently. Its red eyes glowed with an eerie light, but there was something almost... gentle in its gaze as it followed Everly's every move.

She reached into her pack and pulled out another piece of jerky. "Here you go," she said softly, holding it out to the Hellhound.

The beast sniffed at the offering before taking it from her hand with surprising delicacy. It chewed for a moment before licking her fingers clean. Everly giggled, the sound bright and delighted.

The Hellhound's tail wagged slightly, its eyes closing in contentment as it continued to lick her fingers. The scene was almost comical—this fearsome creature reduced to a contented pet by a piece of dried meat and a gentle touch.

Traitor.

I shook my head, unable to fully grasp what I was seeing. This girl—so naïve and trusting—had somehow managed to tame a Hellhound without even trying. It was absurd, yet there she was, giggling like a child.

"We don't have fucking time for this," I grumbled.

Everly looked up at me, still smiling.

I turned away from them both, feeling an odd mix of frustration and... something else I couldn't quite place. The day was starting whether I liked it or not, and we had work to do.

"Let's move," I said, my voice rougher than intended. "Let's fucking go."

Everly gave one last pat to the Hellhound before standing up and following me down the path. Her stubbornness was starting to wear on me. In this broken world, survival trumped ideals every time.

But even as we walked in tense silence, I couldn't shake her words from my mind: Every action mattered. It was a naïve notion in a place where morality had long since been buried beneath ash and ruin.

But as much as I tried to ignore it, there was a small part of me that couldn't help but be curious about her—this girl who dared to defy a demon's wrath with nothing more than a piece of teriyaki jerky and stubborn determination.

Maybe she'd prove useful after all.

* * *

I lied.

There was no way this girl was useful unless it was to attract anything with a sliver of hearing. She wouldn't shut up.

"Fiona used to tell me that the stars were actually souls," Everly chattered, her voice a constant, grating buzz in my ears. "Can you believe that? But I think that's a beautiful thought, although Zoey didn't think so."

Her words blended into an incessant drone, names and faces I didn't give a damn about. Fiona. Zoey. Nelson. The fact that I even knew these names infuriated me.

I clenched my jaw, forcing myself to focus on the landscape.

The Forsaken stretched out in all directions, a desolate wasteland where hope came to die. Jagged rocks jutted from the cracked earth like skeletal remains of a long-dead world. The sun hung high in the sky now, an unrelenting ball of fire that seared everything it touched.

The heat was oppressive, wrapping around us like a suffocating blanket. Sweat trickled down my back, and each breath felt like inhaling molten air.

Everly's face had turned a bright shade of red under the sun's merciless glare. Part of me hoped she'd burn, that something about her would be marred by this harsh reality.

"I remember Nelson would always—"

"Shut up," I snapped, my patience finally fraying.

Everly paused mid-sentence, looking taken aback. Her wide eyes met mine, and for a moment, silence reigned.

"I'm just trying to keep us distracted from... all this," she said quietly, gesturing to the barren wasteland around us.

I snorted. "Distraction's gonna get you killed out here." A beat. "Idiot."

She pressed her lips together but didn't argue further. We trudged on in silence, the only sounds were our labored breathing and the crunch of our boots against the cracked ground.

A gust of hot wind blew past us, stirring up dust and ash. It clung to our skin, mingling with sweat to form a grimy layer that felt like an additional weight pressing down on us.

The Hellhound trotted alongside Everly, its red eyes glancing at her every now and then as if checking on her well-being. Traitorous beast.

As we continued our trek through the forsaken land, I kept an eye on Everly's reddening face. She wiped at her forehead with the back of her hand, leaving streaks of dirt across her skin.

"Drink," I ordered gruffly. "The last thing I need is you passing out because your dumbass decided to dehydrate."

"The name calling —"

"Is absolutely necessary," I snapped.

She glared, but pulled out a water bottle from her pack, taking careful sips before handing it to me.

I took it without a word and drank deeply, feeling the cool liquid cut through the heat for just a moment.

I didn't think about the fact that she shared it with me.

As we walked in silence, Everly broke it again. "What's the Hellhound's name?"

I kept my eyes forward, ignoring her. Silence was my best weapon right now. I couldn't fucking encourage this shit.

"Shouldn't we name her?" she pressed. "She's been with us for a while now."

"I don't give two goddamn shits about the thing's name," I snapped.

"So, I can name her?" Her tone had that hopeful edge that grated on my nerves. She didn't even give me shit about my swearing.

"Only if you shut up for the rest of the day."

She blew out a breath, clearly frustrated. "You know," she said. "You could ask me nicely."

"Do we have a deal?" I pushed, wanting to end this pointless conversation.

She stuck out her hand. I looked down at it, quirking a brow.

"You have to shake on a deal or it doesn't count," she said matter-of-factly.

Rolling my eyes, I reached out and took her hand. It felt

small and fragile in mine, like a bird's wing I could break without effort. But instead of crushing it, I gave it a firm shake.

"Great!" she exclaimed, pulling her hand back. "Fluffy!"

"Fluffy?" I nearly choked on the word.

She started laughing, the sound like fucking bells ringing in my ears. "You should see your face," she said, putting her hands on her knees to catch her breath. "It's a joke. Of course it's not Fluffy."

My anger flared hotter than the sun above us. She'd tricked me. But as much as I wanted to stay mad at her, it was hard when she was smiling and laughing like that — so genuine and full of life.

Untouched by the jagged edges that made up this place.

Pure. Genuine.

No.

Fuck her.

Fuck all of it.

I turned away from her and kept walking, letting the silence stretch between us once more.

"All right, all right," Everly said, still chuckling. "How about Shadow? Or maybe Midnight? Or—"

"Shut up," I barked, coming to a sudden halt.

Everly almost bumped into me. "What—"

I shot her a look that silenced her immediately. She pressed her lips into a thin line, clearly unhappy but finally silent. Maybe she was learning.

I stiffened, every muscle in my body tensing as I scanned the area. The Hellhound at Everly's side let out a low growl, its ears pricking up.

Then I saw it.

A Bone Gnasher emerged from behind a cluster of jagged rocks, its skeletal frame towering and grotesque. The creature's eyes glowed with an eerie blue light, and its sharp, bony claws clicked against the ground as it moved toward us.

The thing looked like death incarnate, all exposed bones and decaying flesh barely holding together. It was one of those monsters that made Hellhounds look like puppies.

Everly sucked in a breath beside me, but to her credit, she didn't make a sound.

The Bone Gnasher let out a guttural growl, its jaws snapping open to reveal rows of razor-sharp teeth. I could see the venom dripping from its fangs.

"Stay behind me," I ordered through gritted teeth.

She nodded, taking a step back without protest. Good girl.

I reached for the silver blade strapped to my side — one of the few weapons effective against these bastards. The Hellhound positioned itself protectively in front of Everly, its own growl rumbling like distant thunder.

And then it lunged.

CHAPTER 15

Everly

I couldn't breathe, every muscle in my body tensing. This thing was a creature unlike anything I'd ever seen in the bunker's sterile walls or the books we learned from. The thing stood on four muscular legs, its skin stretched taut over an emaciated frame. Its eyes glowed with a predatory hunger, and its maw dripped with saliva that sizzled as it hit the ground.

"What is it?" I whispered.

"Bone Gnasher," D grunted.

My heart pounded against my ribcage, each beat louder than the last. The Bone Gnasher's teeth were long and jagged, like shards of broken glass, ready to tear through flesh and bone alike. Its breath reeked of decay, a putrid stench that turned my stomach.

I wanted to move, to run, but my legs felt rooted to the spot.

The creature took a step closer, its claws digging into the dirt with a sickening crunch. My mind raced, searching for any semblance of a plan. Could I climb a tree? Hide? But those eyes—those awful, hungry eyes—told me it would find me no matter where I went.

I stood frozen, my breath catching in my throat as the Bone Gnasher inched closer. D stepped forward, drawing his blade with a smooth, practiced motion. His eyes never left the creature, his body coiled like a spring ready to snap.

"Stay back," he ordered, his voice low and steady.

The Bone Gnasher attacked, its jaws snapping inches from D's face. He sidestepped with a fluid grace, slashing his blade across the creature's flank. It let out a guttural roar, a sound that reverberated through my bones. D moved with lethal efficiency, each strike precise and controlled.

Out of the corner of my eye, I saw the Hellhound darting towards the fray. Its red eyes gleamed with a fierce determination as it joined the battle.

The Bone Gnasher snarled and turned its attention to the Hellhound. They clashed in a flurry of teeth and claws, each trying to overpower the other. The Hellhound's bites were quick and vicious, aiming for vulnerable spots on the Bone Gnasher's body. It fought with an almost supernatural ferocity, its matted fur bristling with every attack.

D took advantage of the distraction, moving in from behind to deliver a powerful blow to the Bone Gnasher's hind leg. The creature howled in pain, its movements becoming more erratic and desperate. Blood sprayed from its wounds, staining the ground in dark pools.

The Hellhound continued its relentless assault, tearing into the Bone Gnasher's side with razor-sharp teeth. I watched in awe and horror as the two beasts tore at each other, their growls and snarls filling the air.

D circled around, his blade flashing in the dim light as he searched for an opening. He moved with such precision that it was almost like a dance—a deadly dance where one misstep could mean death. The Bone Gnasher lashed out wildly, but D remained just out of reach, his eyes locked onto his target.

The Hellhound delivered a final, brutal bite to the Bone Gnasher's throat. The creature let out a choked gurgle before collapsing to the ground in a heap. Its body twitched once before going still.

D stood over it, panting heavily. His clothes were splattered with blood—some of it his own—but he seemed unfazed by his injuries. The Hellhound stepped back, its eyes still glowing but now with a calmer intensity.

"Is it... dead?" I asked, my voice barely more than a whisper.

"For now," D replied tersely, wiping his blade on his sleeve before sheathing it again.

The beast padded over to me and nudged my hand with her nose. I reached down to pet it, feeling an unexpected sense of gratitude for this strange ally.

Blood smeared D's clothes, some of it his own, but he seemed unfazed by the injuries. The Hellhound, its eyes still glowing but calmer now, stepped back.

D wiped his blade on his sleeve before sheathing it and turned to me. He pulled a knife from his belt and handed it to me. "Ready to skin it?"

"We're... we're going to eat it?" I stammered, feeling my stomach churn.

"We gotta take our food as it comes," he said with a shrug.

I took the knife with trembling hands, staring at the creature's lifeless body. The reality of what I had to do hit me like a punch to the gut. Nothing had prepared me for this—skinning a creature that moments ago was trying to kill us.

I turned away from the Bone Gnasher and retched, my body heaving as I vomited onto the ground. The acrid taste of bile filled my mouth, and tears stung my eyes.

"Fuck me, Bunker rat," he scoffed, shaking his head. "That

thing rots of poison. You think we're going to eat it? And here I didn't think you were as dumb as you looked."

I was too exhausted to even scowl at him. My stomach still churned, and my hands trembled. I wiped my mouth with the back of my hand and forced myself to stand up straight.

"I know that," I snapped, though my voice lacked any real bite. "It's just... I've never heard about that back home."

"That doesn't surprise me," he said, looking down at the creature's lifeless body with disdain. "You about done throwing up? We gotta keep moving. And drink some water too. You need to stop throwing up."

"Trust me, I would if I could," I muttered, still feeling the acidic burn in my throat.

My hands shook as I grabbed my flask from my pack. The cool metal felt reassuring against my skin. I took a sip of water and then offered some to the Hellhound, who lapped it up gratefully.

"I'm almost out," I added, staring at the dwindling supply.

"Not my fucking problem," he replied curtly. "We ain't getting to Ironedge until tomorrow. You better get your shit together, sweetheart. Let's go."

I didn't have the energy to argue with him. The weight of exhaustion settled over me like a heavy blanket, each step feeling like a monumental effort. We set off again, leaving the Bone Gnasher's corpse behind.

The landscape was harsh and unforgiving—craggy rocks and sparse vegetation offering little solace from the elements. Every so often, D would glance back at me, his eyes hard and unreadable. He moved with a purpose that seemed second nature to him while I stumbled along, trying to keep up.

The sun beat down on us relentlessly; the heat radiating off the rocks making it feel like we were walking through an oven. Sweat trickled down my back, soaking my shirt and making it cling to my skin uncomfortably. I couldn't take it anymore.

With a huff, I shrugged off my jacket and tied it around my waist. The sudden relief of cool air on my arms was like a small mercy in this hellish landscape. My skin prickled from the change in temperature, but at least I felt a bit lighter.

"How much further?" I asked, trying to keep the frustration out of my voice.

"No," D grunted, not even bothering to look back at me.

"That's not an answer."

"No," he repeated.

I took a deep breath, trying to steady myself. The exhaustion weighed heavily on me, each step feeling like a monumental effort. But I couldn't afford to show weakness—not here, not now. We had to keep moving if we wanted to reach Ironedge by tomorrow.

The Hellhound trotted beside me, its eyes scanning the surroundings with an alertness that made me feel slightly safer. Its presence was both eerie and comforting—a strange mix that I was still getting used to.

I sighed and wiped the sweat from my forehead. The sun hung low in the sky now, casting long shadows over the rocky terrain. We continued in silence, each lost in our own thoughts. My mind kept drifting back to the Bone Gnasher and the raw terror I felt facing it. Would every day out here be a fight for survival?

The landscape gradually began to change, becoming less harsh and more forgiving. Sparse patches of grass appeared here and there, a welcome sight after miles of barren rock. The sight of green brought a sliver of hope—maybe Ironedge wouldn't be as desolate as I'd feared.

D slowed his pace slightly, allowing me to catch up without completely wearing myself out. He still didn't say much, but his actions spoke volumes. For now, that was enough.

The Hellhound trotted beside me, its presence oddly comforting despite its fearsome appearance. It seemed attuned to my struggles, occasionally nudging me forward when I slowed down too much.

"How far is Ironedge?" I asked after what felt like hours of trudging through the desolate terrain.

"Far enough," D replied without looking back.

I sighed and took another small sip from my flask, savoring each drop like it was liquid gold. The journey ahead loomed large and daunting in my mind, but there was no turning back now. We had to reach Ironedge—whatever awaited us there— if we were going to survive this unforgiving world outside the bunker's walls.

"We'll stop for a few minutes to eat something," D said, finally breaking the silence.

I dropped my pack on the hard dirt; the weight lifting off my shoulders momentarily. My muscles ached from the constant strain, but there was no time to dwell on it. I rummaged through my bag and pulled out some jerky and nuts. It wasn't much, but it was all I had left.

I chewed the jerky slowly, my stomach twisting with each bite. The food felt heavy in my mouth, almost too much to swallow. But I forced it down, knowing I needed the energy. The nuts were a bit easier, their crunch offering a brief distraction from the oppressive heat and fatigue.

D sat across from me, his own pack beside him. He didn't say anything as he ate, his eyes scanning the horizon as if expecting trouble at any moment. His presence was imposing even in this moment of rest, a constant reminder of the dangerous world we were navigating.

The Hellhound lay down beside me, her eyes never leaving him. She seemed to sense my unease, her warm body pressed against my leg in silent reassurance. I reached down and petted her matted fur absentmindedly, grateful for the small comfort she provided.

We ate in silence, neither of us feeling the need to fill the quiet with meaningless chatter. The only sounds were the crunch of our food and the distant call of some unseen bird. My mind wandered back to the Bone Gnasher and how close we had come to becoming its next meal. The thought made my stomach churn again, but I pushed it aside.

It couldn't have been fifteen minutes before D stood up and shouldered his pack again.

"Time's up," he said curtly.

I nodded and quickly gathered my things, stuffing what little remained of my food back into my bag. My body protested as I stood up, but I ignored the discomfort and followed D's lead. We resumed our trek across the barren landscape, each step taking us further from what little safety we had known.

The Hellhound trotted beside me once more. D moved with purpose ahead of me, his eyes always scanning for danger. We walked in silence again, each lost in our thoughts as we pushed forward toward Ironedge.

The landscape blurred together as exhaustion gnawed at my bones. Each step felt heavier than the last, my legs like lead. I could feel myself slowing down, falling further behind D. The sun dipped lower in the sky, casting long shadows and bringing a welcome coolness to the air. But it wasn't enough to revive my failing strength.

I stumbled over a rock, barely catching myself before I hit the ground. My breath came in ragged gasps, my vision swimming with fatigue. D finally turned back, his eyes narrowing as he took in my struggling form.

"Pathetic," he muttered, shaking his head. "Can't even keep up."

Anger flared within me, hot and sudden. "I'm only human!" I snapped, the words escaping before I could stop them. I jerked back, surprised by the intensity of my own anger. It wasn't just frustration or annoyance—he genuinely angered me.

He seemed to know this, too. A smirk tugged at the corner of his mouth as he watched me struggle to compose myself.

"Clearly," he drawled, his tone dripping with condescension. "Keep moving. You're slowing us down."

The words stung more than I wanted to admit. I bit back a retort and forced my legs to move, pushing through the pain and exhaustion. The Hellhound nudged me forward, her presence a small comfort in this harsh world.

We continued in silence, D's figure always just ahead of me, an infuriating reminder of my own weakness. The anger simmered beneath the surface, fueling each step as I struggled to keep pace.

I stumbled and fell, dirt smearing across my face. For a second, I didn't move. My body screamed in protest, every muscle shaking with exhaustion.

Shoot, I thought to myself. *He's right. I am pathetic. This is your first day and you've already collapsed. And if you don't get it together, he's going to leave you. You know he will.*

I tried to push myself up, but my arms and legs felt like jelly, trembling uncontrollably. Tears sprang into my eyes, hot and unbidden.

"Don't even think about it," D's gravelly voice cut through the haze of my despair. "You start blubbering, you dehydrate. Save it."

He lit a cigarette, the small flame flickering in the dimming light.

Anger flared again, igniting something deep within me. I would show him. I forced myself to stand up, my legs shaking beneath me but holding firm.

"I ain't picking you up, Bunker Rat," he said without a trace of sympathy. "And I sure as shit ain't carrying you. You fall behind, you get left behind. You understand me?"

"I understand," I said through clenched teeth, the words tasting bitter in my mouth.

"Good girl," he said, starting to walk again without another glance in my direction.

I had no choice but to follow him. Each step was an exercise in sheer willpower, my body screaming for rest but my mind refusing to give in. The Hellhound trotted beside me faithfully, its presence a small comfort against the vast loneliness of the wasteland.

D moved ahead with relentless determination, never slowing down or looking back. His figure became a dark silhouette against the setting sun.

Every muscle in my body ached, but I kept moving forward. The rocky terrain seemed to stretch on forever, each step feeling like an insurmountable challenge.

The Hellhound nudged me occasionally when I faltered, its red eyes watching me with an intensity that both unnerved and reassured me. I found strength in its unwavering presence and pushed myself harder than I thought possible.

As we trudged on into the night, D's cigarette glowed faintly in the darkness—a tiny beacon that guided us through the unknown landscape ahead. The journey was far from over, but for now, all that mattered was putting one foot in front of the other and surviving another day in this unforgiving world.

CHAPTER 16

Walton

W e trudged through the wasteland, the remnants of the Bone Gnasher battle weighing on us. The girl struggled to keep up, her breath coming in ragged gasps. I didn't slow down. She needed to learn the pace of survival out here.

The sun dipped lower, casting long shadows over the barren terrain. My body ached, each step a reminder of the Bone Gnasher's fury. But I kept moving, focusing on finding a suitable spot to rest. Finally, after another grueling hour, I spotted a cluster of rocks that would provide some cover.

"We'll stop here," I announced.

Everly nearly collapsed, sinking to her knees. She didn't ask for help, and I didn't offer any. Instead, I set about setting up camp.

I scoured the area for dry wood and managed to start a small fire. The flames danced and flickered, casting an orange glow over our makeshift camp. Everly sat slumped against a rock, exhaustion etched into her features.

Ignoring my own fatigue, I rummaged through my pack

for supplies. I pulled out a canteen and took a swig before putting the cap back on.

Everly's eyes got big and hopeful, like a kid catching sight of a candy store. She licked her lips, and it was hard not to stare at the way her tongue darted across her chapped skin.

"What?" I snapped, anger flaring up that she could distract me so easily.

"I... I ran out," she mumbled, her voice barely above a whisper.

"Not my problem," I said, shoving the canteen back into my pack. The girl needed to learn to fend for herself.

I pulled out the last bit of serpent tail I'd saved from earlier. The dried meat wasn't much, but it would keep me going for a while longer. Spearing it on a stick, I started to roast it over the fire. The flames licked at the meat, releasing an aroma that filled the air and made my stomach growl.

Everly watched me with those wide eyes, thirst etched into every line of her face. I ignored her, focusing on turning the meat to get an even roast. Her gaze bore into me, but I wouldn't relent. She needed to understand how things worked out here.

As the serpent tail sizzled and crackled over the fire, Everly shifted uncomfortably on her rock. She pulled her knees to her chest and wrapped her arms around them, trying to conserve warmth. The night air grew colder by the minute, biting at exposed skin and making the fire's heat all the more precious.

"Where did you get that?" she asked finally, breaking the silence that had settled between us like a thick fog.

"Caught it a few days ago," I replied without looking up from the roasting meat.

She hesitated before speaking again. "Could you... teach me? How to catch one?"

I glanced at her, seeing genuine desperation in her eyes.

For a moment, I almost felt sorry for her—almost. But pity wouldn't keep us alive.

"If you're lucky enough to find one," I said flatly. "And if you're strong enough to kill it."

She nodded slowly, understanding my unspoken message: survival didn't come easy out here.

The serpent tail finished cooking, and I tore off a piece with my fingers, savoring its warmth and flavor. Everly watched every bite I took, but didn't ask again. Maybe she was learning after all.

I tore a good chunk of serpent tail from the stick and chewed thoughtfully. The meat's flavor was strong, almost overpowering, but it kept me grounded.

Everly's eyes flickered toward me, but she didn't say anything, just pulled her knees closer to her chest. The fire crackled between us, a fragile barrier against the encroaching darkness.

She shifted slightly, reaching into her pack. From it, she pulled out a piece of jerky and whistled softly. The Hellhound gently took the jerky from her hand.

The Hellhound finished its treat and curled up next to Everly, resting its head on her lap. She absentmindedly stroked its matted fur, lost in thought. I watched them for a moment before deciding it was time to deal with my own wounds.

I rummaged through my pack until I found my sewing kit. The damn Bone Gnasher had managed to catch my arm during our fight earlier. Its poison wouldn't affect me—one of the perks of being a demon—but I still needed to stitch up the gash before it could heal properly.

Rolling up my sleeve, I exposed the jagged wound. Dark blood oozed slowly from it, thick and viscous. Everly glanced over and winced at the sight, but didn't say anything.

I threaded a needle with practiced ease and set to work on my arm. The needle pierced my skin, and I felt the familiar sting of pain, a reminder that despite everything, some things never changed. Each stitch pulled the edges of the wound closer together, closing the gap inch by inch.

Everly watched in silence as I worked. The Hellhound shifted slightly but remained by her side, its presence almost comforting in this desolate place.

Finishing the last stitch, I tied off the thread and cut it with a small knife from my kit. The wound still throbbed dully, but it would heal soon enough. Rolling down my sleeve again, I leaned back against a rock and closed my eyes for a moment.

"Did you get the one on your side?"

I looked at her, not understanding at first.

"The... thing," she clarified, gesturing vaguely. "It got your side."

I blinked, realization dawning. I had forgotten. The adrenaline of the fight must have masked the pain. With a sigh, I slid off my duster and lifted my shirt. A deep gash ran along my side, blood seeping through the torn fabric. The angle made it impossible for me to stitch it up myself.

"Here," she said softly, moving toward me. She got on her knees and held her hands out. "May I?"

I hesitated, the instinct to refuse flaring up. But I knew there was no other option. Nodding curtly, I handed her the needle and thread.

Her fingers trembled slightly as she took them from me, but there was determination in her eyes. She began to work on my wound with a surprising amount of care and precision.

Her fingers worked with a surprising gentleness, each movement deliberate and precise. The needle pierced my skin, threading through with a sensation that was both sharp and oddly comforting. She leaned in close, her breath warm against my side as she focused on her task. I couldn't remember the last time someone had touched me like this—so careful, so... human.

Her fingertips brushed my skin occasionally, sending a shiver through me that I tried to suppress. She didn't flinch at the contact, didn't recoil. It made my mouth go dry, and I found myself clenching my jaw to keep any involuntary reactions at bay. The intimacy of the moment caught me off guard. Her touch was almost reverent, as if she understood the weight of the act itself.

I couldn't recall when anyone had cared like this before... before I changed into this. Most people avoided me, feared me, or simply saw me as a means to an end. But here she was, sewing up my wound with a tenderness that felt foreign and yet achingly familiar. The rhythmic pull of the thread through my flesh became almost soothing, a reminder that maybe, just maybe, some fragments of humanity still lingered in this broken world.

Each stitch tugged at my skin, but I focused on her face, noting how her brow furrowed in concentration.

"You've done this before?" I asked, more to distract myself from the pain than out of curiosity.

"A few times," she replied without looking up. "In the bunker... accidents happened."

She continued working in silence for a while, her movements becoming more confident with each stitch. The fire crackled beside us. The Hellhound lifted its head briefly before settling back down next to Everly.

Finally, she tied off the last stitch and cut the thread with practiced ease. Sitting back on her heels, she wiped her hands on her pants and looked up at me.

"That should hold," she said quietly.

I nodded, rolling down my shirt and putting my duster back on.

She offered a small smile in return before moving back to

her spot by the fire. I watched her for a moment longer before settling down myself, feeling the weight of exhaustion finally catching up with me.

The wasteland stretched out around us, silent and unforgiving as ever. But for now, we had a moment's respite—a small victory in a world that rarely offered any.

I tore a piece of the serpent tail off and tossed it to her. She caught it, her fingers trembling slightly as she held the food.

"Thanks," she murmured, barely audible over the crackle of the fire.

I grunted in response. "Can't have you fainting because you don't have food or water in you," I muttered, trying to mask any hint of concern.

She didn't waste any time. Everly bit into the meat with an eagerness that almost made me laugh, though I kept my expression stern. She had no poker face, and every emotion played out across her features like an open book.

The first taste seemed to surprise her. Her eyes widened, and a look of relief washed over her face as she chewed slowly. She closed her eyes for a moment, savoring the flavor as if it were a gourmet meal instead of charred serpent tail. A faint smile tugged at the corners of her mouth, and she visibly relaxed, sinking deeper against the rock behind her.

Amusement flickered inside me despite my best efforts to squash it. Watching her eat was almost entertaining in its simplicity—her gratitude so genuine it bordered on childlike. She took another bite, chewing thoughtfully this time, and sighed contentedly.

I'd never admit it aloud, but there was something refreshing about her lack of guile. Out here, everyone wore masks; deception was second nature. But Everly? She couldn't hide anything if she tried. Her face betrayed every thought and feeling with unfiltered honesty.

She finished the piece quickly, licking her fingers clean

before looking up at me with a grateful expression that bordered on reverence. I turned my gaze back to the fire, unwilling to acknowledge whatever sentiment she might be hoping for in return.

"You'll need more than that to keep your strength up," I said gruffly, poking at the fire with a stick.

"I know," she replied softly, her voice carrying a hint of determination. "I'll learn."

We lapsed into silence again, the fire's warmth providing some comfort against the chill night air. The wasteland stretched out around us, an unforgiving expanse that cared little for our struggles or triumphs.

Everly shrugged off her jacket and began her stretches, her movements fluid and deliberate. I watched her, noting the way her skin flexed and moved. There was a grace there, a flexibility that spoke of a life where she had the privilege to develop such skills. Not many out here had that luxury.

She bent at the waist, reaching for her toes with an ease that seemed almost effortless. Her fingers brushed the ground before she straightened up again, arms stretching toward the sky. Each movement was precise, almost like a dance, and I found myself unable to look away.

It struck me then—she was more than just some naïve bunker girl. There was strength in her, a resilience that I hadn't given her credit for. But that didn't mean she was ready for what lay ahead.

I tore my gaze away from her, turning my attention to the horizon. The wasteland stretched out endlessly, a barren expanse of desolation and danger. The setting sun cast long shadows across the ground, painting everything in hues of orange and red. It was a stark reminder of the world we now lived in—a world where survival came at a high cost.

Behind me, I heard Everly rummaging through her pack. When I glanced back, she had pulled out a toothbrush. She looked at it for a moment before sighing and running it over her teeth dry. She made do without water, brushing as best she could under the circumstances.

I smirked.

She finished brushing and tucked the toothbrush back into her pack, wiping her mouth with the back of her hand. There was something about her quiet fortitude that struck a chord within me. Maybe it was because it echoed my own struggle to maintain a sense of purpose despite everything that had happened.

We settled into an uneasy silence; the fire crackling softly between us as night fully descended on the wasteland. The Hellhound stirred briefly before curling up again beside Everly, its presence adding an odd sense of comfort to our small camp.

I leaned back against the rock, watching Everly as she stared up at the sky. Her face softened, and her eyes glistened with a mix of wonder and disbelief.

"I never thought it could be real, you know?" she said, her voice barely above a whisper.

"The sky?" I grunted, not quite understanding what she was getting at.

"The stars," she replied, her gaze still fixed upward. "They're so big and bright. Like... like fireflies trapped in a jar, but set free."

I blinked. I'd never thought of it that way. To me, the stars were just there—unreachable, distant. But seeing them through her eyes, it was like they had a new meaning.

"You take first watch," I said instead, pulling myself out of my thoughts. I handed her a gun. "When we get to Ironedge, we'll get you one too. You can't keep borrowing mine anymore, little girl. I'm not always going to be around."

She nodded, taking the gun with a firm grip and settling back onto her perch.

"When do you want me to wake you?" she asked, her voice steady despite the weight of responsibility now resting in her hands.

"A few hours," I remarked, tipping my hat down to shield my eyes from the firelight. The truth was, I was exhausted. Just because the poison wouldn't kill me didn't mean it hadn't taken its toll.

As I lay back and closed my eyes, the pain in my side throbbed dully. Everly's stitches had held well enough for now, but rest was what I needed most. The Hellhound shifted beside her again before settling down with a soft huff.

Everly remained vigilant, scanning the horizon with an intensity that made me feel just a bit more secure in our makeshift camp. She might have been new to this world's harsh realities, but there was no denying her determination to adapt.

Not that I would tell her.

Sleep crept up on me faster than I expected. The last thing I saw before drifting off was Everly's silhouette against the backdrop of the starlit sky—a fragile figure standing guard over our temporary peace.

CHAPTER 17

Everly

"What about Luna? Or maybe Shadow?" I looked over at D, hoping for some kind of reaction. He kept his eyes on the path ahead, not even a flicker of interest. "Midnight could be fitting, given her fur color. Or perhaps Ember, considering those fiery eyes of hers."

The Hellhound padded along beside us, its presence more comforting than I would've expected.

D stayed silent, not even a grunt of acknowledgment.

I frowned but pressed on. "Okay, what about something strong? Like Titan or Fang?"

D turned his head sharply towards me. "Why don't we call her shut the fuck up?"

I didn't flinch. Instead, I tilted my head and replied calmly, "You know, that language—"

"Is very called for," he snapped, cutting me off.

I raised an eyebrow at his tone but kept my voice steady. "Do you have a preference?"

"Silence," he said.

"You want her name to be Silence?" I pursed my lips and

cocked my head to think about it. His eyes narrowed before he blinked and scowled.

"I must have fucked up in my past life if I get you as a traveling guide," he muttered under his breath.

Ignoring the sting of his words, I looked back at the Hellhound and smiled. "Silence it is then."

The Hellhound yipped, a sound that seemed almost cheerful despite the beast's fearsome appearance. I couldn't help but beam back at her, even though every step made my heels scream in protest. The boots I had weren't made for this kind of terrain. I could already feel blisters forming, but the last thing I wanted was for D to know. He already thought I was weak; I didn't need to give him more reasons.

The path stretched endlessly before us, a dusty trail flanked by sparse, scraggly bushes and the occasional twisted tree. It looked the same as it had yesterday, and probably the day before that. The sun hung high in the sky, beating down relentlessly. Sweat trickled down my back, making my shirt stick uncomfortably to my skin. I had put on deodorant, but it felt like a lost cause in this heat.

D marched ahead with purposeful strides, his shoulders set in a way that screamed determination—or maybe it was just sheer stubbornness. Silence, our newly named Hellhound, trotted beside him, her glowing eyes scanning the surroundings as if she were on constant alert.

I tried to hum under my breath to distract myself from the pain in my feet. A tune from an old lullaby my mother used to sing came to mind. The melody was soft and soothing, a stark contrast to our harsh environment.

"Still with us back there?" D called over his shoulder without slowing down.

"Yep," I replied, trying to keep my voice light and free of strain. "Just enjoying the view."

He snorted but didn't comment further.

The landscape seemed indifferent to our struggle—an endless expanse of cracked earth and thorny plants that looked like they'd rather bite you than bloom. Each step sent up little puffs of dust that settled on my already grimy clothes.

Silence barked suddenly, her ears pricking up as she sniffed the air.

D stopped and glanced at her. "What is it, girl?"

I held my breath, waiting for some sign of danger, or maybe just another false alarm. But Silence simply wagged her tail and resumed her steady pace.

I let out a sigh of relief and continued humming, focusing on putting one foot in front of the other. This journey was grueling, but each step forward felt like a small victory.

"Keep up," D growled without looking back.

I rolled my eyes, but quickened my pace slightly. The pain in my heels flared with each step, but I bit down on my lip and pushed through it. I wouldn't give him the satisfaction of seeing me falter.

As we trudged onward under the relentless sun, I found myself wondering how much farther we had to go before we'd find something—anything—that would break the monotony of this barren wasteland.

We stopped briefly for lunch, and I rummaged through my pack, realizing I was down to my last bit of jerky. The sight of it made my stomach twist in hunger, but I knew I had to share. I tore off a small piece and handed it to Silence. She took it gently from my hand, her eyes glowing with gratitude.

"How are your stitches?" I asked D, trying to keep my voice steady despite the dryness in my mouth.

I unscrewed my canteen, feeling the weight of it—so little left. With a sigh, I poured the last few drops into my hand and offered it to Silence. She lapped it up eagerly.

"Fool," D said, his voice sharp. "That's your last bit, isn't it? You managed to find a few more drops since last night?"

"Well," I replied, forcing a smile. "Look at all that fur—"

"She gets most of her hydration from what she eats," he interrupted. "You should have drunk your last bit. We're still miles from Ironedge, give or take." He shook his head, the look on his face somewhere between disgust and disappointment.

I blinked back tears as he continued without me. My feet were killing me, each step a fresh wave of agony that shot up my legs. The blisters had burst, leaving raw skin rubbing against rough leather with every movement.

I struggled to keep up with him; the landscape blurring through the tears that threatened to spill over. My throat tightened as I swallowed hard, fighting back the sobs that clawed at my chest. This wasn't how I imagined the world outside the bunker—cruel and relentless, yes, but not this overwhelming.

Silence walked beside me. I glanced at her and managed a weak smile despite the lump in my throat.

The sun beat down mercilessly as we trudged onward. Every part of me ached—my feet screamed in protest, my muscles burned with exhaustion, and my mind reeled with fear and doubt.

Why did I leave the bunker? The question echoed in my mind, mingling with regret and longing for the safety of home. But there was no turning back now; each step forward was a step closer to answers—to finding Elise.

D's figure grew smaller ahead of me as he pressed on without hesitation or concern for whether I could keep up. Why would he? He didn't care about me. We weren't friends, and assuming anything else was stupid on my end.

My heart pounded in rhythm with my steps—a relentless reminder that I had to keep going, no matter how much it hurt or how scared I felt.

I wiped away the tears that had escaped and focused on

Silence beside me—a small beacon of hope in an unforgiving world.

Each step felt like trudging through molasses. My vision blurred, the world around me turning into a hazy swirl of colors and shapes. My mouth felt like sandpaper, and my tongue seemed to stick to the roof of my mouth. I blinked, trying to clear my head, but the dizziness only worsened.

"Keep going," I whispered to myself, though my voice sounded weak and distant.

The sun's relentless heat bore down on me, sapping what little strength I had left. My skin felt hot to the touch, and beads of sweat trickled down my forehead, only to evaporate almost instantly. My head throbbed with each heartbeat, an incessant pounding that echoed in my ears.

I stumbled, my foot catching on a loose rock. Silence nudged me gently with her snout, her eyes full of concern.

I managed a weak smile and patted her head. "Thanks, girl," I muttered, though it felt like the words were pulled from somewhere far away.

D's figure ahead seemed to waver and flicker in the heat haze. It was getting harder to keep track of him. Every time I tried to focus on his skin and imposing frame, it felt like he slipped further away.

My legs grew heavier with each step until they felt like lead weights dragging me down. The pain in my feet had dulled to a constant ache that blended with the rest of my discomfort. I couldn't remember when we last stopped for a break or how long we'd been walking.

Time seemed to stretch and compress in strange ways. One moment, it felt like hours had passed; the next, mere seconds. I couldn't keep track anymore. All I knew was that I had to keep moving forward.

My throat burned with thirst, every swallow a painful reminder of how dry my mouth was. I glanced at D again, hoping he might slow down or offer some help. But he marched on, not even glancing back.

My vision tunneled briefly, black spots dancing at the edges before expanding and contracting again. Panic fluttered in my chest as I tried to take deeper breaths, but it only made me dizzier.

"Don't pass out," I whispered hoarsely to myself. "You can't afford to pass out. He'll leave you. He'll leave you and won't look back."

Silence stayed close by my side. But even she couldn't ward off the creeping darkness that threatened to overtake me completely.

I forced one foot in front of the other, each step a monumental effort as if walking through quicksand. My limbs felt disconnected from my body like they were moving on their own accord while my mind drifted in and out of focus.

"Just a little further," I thought desperately. "You can make it just a little further."

But deep down, I wasn't sure how much longer I could hold on.

The world around me swam in and out of focus, the edges blurring together in a dizzying haze. My feet dragged through the dust, each step a monumental effort. Silence stayed close, her presence a small comfort against the overwhelming exhaustion. Just as I thought I might collapse, D finally looked back and scowled.

He turned on his heel and stalked back towards me, his eyes blazing with fury. "You're slowing us down," he growled, his voice low and menacing.

I tried to stand straighter, to hide the weakness I felt, but my legs betrayed me. "I'm... I'm trying," I managed to croak out.

"Trying?" His laugh was harsh and bitter. "You think

trying is enough out here? You think you can survive on trying?"

I flinched at the venom in his words, but I refused to back down. "I can... I will," I said, though my voice wavered.

His eyes narrowed as he took a step closer, towering over me. "You're weak," he spat. "Arrogant and naïve. You thought you could just waltz out here and everything would be fine? That you'd find your sister and save the day?"

"I didn't think it would be easy," I whispered, my throat tight with unshed tears.

"You didn't think at all!" He lashed out, his voice rising. "You're a liability. You're going to get us both killed."

I looked down at my blistered feet, feeling the sting of his words as acutely as the pain in my body. "I just... I wanted to help," I said softly.

"Help?" He sneered. "The only thing you're doing is dragging us down."

His words cut deep, each one a blade slicing through my already fragile resolve. But even as tears threatened to spill over, I clenched my fists and met his gaze. "I won't give up," I said, my voice trembling but determined.

D shook his head in disgust. "You're delusional," he muttered. "You should've stayed in your bunker where you belonged." He glared. "You faint, I'm leaving you, you know that, right? Because I sure as shit ain't carrying your bunker ass to Ironedge."

With that final jab, he turned and walked away, leaving me standing there with Silence at my side. The Hellhound whined softly and nuzzled my hand, offering what little comfort she could.

I took a deep breath and forced myself to take another step forward. No matter how cruel D's words were or how much they hurt, I wouldn't let them break me.

As I trudged forward, my vision blurred. Suddenly, I saw

Elise walking beside me. Her figure shimmered, almost like a mirage, but her presence felt real enough to give me pause. It was the heat, I knew, but still. It felt nice not to be so alone anymore.

"Elise?" I whispered, my voice cracking.

"Hey, Ev," she replied, her voice soft and comforting. "You're doing great. Just keep going."

I blinked rapidly, trying to clear my head. "Is it really you?" I asked, doubt creeping in.

She smiled warmly. "In a way. Think of me as your conscience, or maybe just a bit of hope."

Tears welled up in my eyes, blurring her image further. "I miss you so much," I said, my voice breaking.

"I know," she replied gently. "But you're stronger than you think."

I glanced ahead at D's retreating figure and sighed. "He's so cruel, Elise. He doesn't care about anything but himself."

Elise tilted her head slightly, her expression thoughtful. "Cruel people were made cruel by cruelty," she pointed out softly.

I frowned. "What do you mean?"

"Demons aren't monsters, Ev," she explained patiently. "They're humans who were hopeless, who didn't think they were worthy of God. They turned to the devil instead of God."

I looked down at my blistered feet and sighed deeply.

"He's hurting much more than you," Elise continued. "You know God loves you. He doesn't think God even knows his name."

I bit my lip and shook my head. "But that doesn't excuse how he treats me," I argued.

"No," she agreed, her tone firm but gentle. "It doesn't. But understanding his pain might help you find a way to reach him."

I let out a bitter laugh. "Reach him? He's impossible to talk to. And that's when he's talking in the first place."

"Maybe he needs someone to show him that not everyone is against him," she suggested.

I looked at her, frustration bubbling up inside me. "Why should it be me? Why do I have to be the one to help him?"

"Because you have the strength and compassion to do it," she replied simply.

Her words lingered in my mind as we walked in silence for a few moments. Despite the pain and exhaustion weighing me down, something in Elise's presence gave me a renewed sense of determination.

"All right," I said quietly, more to myself than to her. "I'll try."

Elise smiled warmly again and nodded. "That's all anyone can ask for. You're so good-hearted, Everly. Don't let anyone take that away from you. Promise me?"

"I promise," I murmured.

She grinned, her lips moving, but I couldn't hear her words. It was as if the world had swallowed her voice, leaving only the ghost of her message hanging in the air. I strained to catch something—anything—but it was no use.

"Elise?" I called out, my voice barely a whisper. She continued speaking, unaware of my growing panic. Her expression was urgent, her eyes pleading with me to understand.

But I couldn't.

The heat pressed down on me like a suffocating blanket. My vision swam, and the ground seemed to shift beneath my feet. Silence nudged me again, but this time, it wasn't enough to keep me steady.

My legs gave out, and I crumpled to the ground. The last thing I saw was Elise's face, her mouth still moving in silent desperation.

Then everything went black.

CHAPTER 18

Walton

I stomped through the barren wasteland, each step kicking up clouds of dust. The heat radiated from the ground, making the air shimmer like a mirage. My skin itched with the discomfort of a million tiny needles pricking at once. I glanced back, expecting to see Everly trudging along behind me. She wasn't there.

Damn it.

This girl was becoming more of a burden than I had anticipated. She had her uses—her knowledge of runes, for one—but her inexperience with the real world was glaringly obvious. I needed her to get to my target, but every minute she slowed me down gnawed at my patience.

"Girl!" I called out, my voice gravelly and rough from the dry air.

Silence answered me.

I clenched my fists, feeling my nails dig into my palms. Turning back, I retraced my steps, scanning the horizon for any sign of her. My eyes caught a glimpse of her crumpled form on the ground. She lay motionless, her pale face stark against the scorched earth.

"Great," I muttered under my breath.

I knelt beside her, feeling the oppressive heat pressing down on us both. Her chest rose and fell shallowly; at least she was still breathing. The kid wasn't cut out for this world, but she was all I had to work with right now.

I stared at Everly's motionless form, the harsh sun casting long shadows across her face. Part of me wanted to just leave her there. She was dead weight, slowing me down. I had a mission, a goal, and dragging an inexperienced kid through the wasteland wasn't part of it. Every second I wasted on her was a second closer to my target slipping away.

But then, something nagged at me. A small voice in the back of my mind whispered that leaving her would be wrong. She was just some stupid girl, and yet, she had stitched up my wounds with hands that trembled but didn't falter even after I refused to give her any of my water.

I clenched my jaw, torn between pragmatism and... what? Compassion? I couldn't afford to be soft. The world didn't have room for soft anymore. But dammit, there was something about her—something that made it hard to just walk away.

My fingers dug deeper into my palms as I wrestled with the decision. On one hand, she was a liability, someone who needed constant protection and guidance. On the other hand, she had knowledge that could be useful, maybe even vital to my mission. And she was the target's sister. It always came back to that.

A strange sensation began to tickle at my insides—guilt. It felt foreign and unwelcome, like an itch I couldn't scratch away. I tried to ignore it, focusing instead on the practicality of leaving her behind.

"Goddamn it," I muttered under my breath.

My eyes scanned the horizon again before settling back on

Everly. Leaving her would be easy—one less burden to carry. But easy didn't sit right with me, not this time.

I crouched down beside her and placed a hand on her shoulder. The touch felt awkward, unfamiliar.

"Wake up," I growled softly, shaking her gently.

She stirred slightly but didn't open her eyes.

I sighed heavily, feeling the weight of the decision pressing down on me like a ton of bricks. Leaving her might be the smart move, but for reasons I couldn't fully explain or accept, it wasn't one I could make today.

"Fucking hell," I grumbled as I lifted her up. Her body felt fragile in my arms, like holding onto something that might shatter at any moment.

Her eyes fluttered open for a brief second before closing again. She was out cold from the heat. With no other choice, I carried her bridal-style and started walking toward Ironedge.

"Just hold on," I whispered to no one in particular.

I reached the shade and laid her down gently against the cool stone wall. Pulling out a canteen from my pack, I splashed some water onto her face, but she didn't move. Not even when I dribbled a little in her mouth.

"We don't have time for this," I growled to myself. But time was all we had right now if we were going to survive this hellhole and get what we needed.

I glanced down at Everly's pale face. Her chest wasn't moving.

Christ.

Ironedge. I had to get her to Ironedge. There'd be a doctor there, someone who could help. But it was going to cost an arm and a leg. I didn't have many demon shards left, and the ones I had were already spoken for. But I did have two angel feathers. I'd been wanting to save them, maybe even use them as leverage later.

Fuck.

My legs moved faster, the dry earth crunching underfoot as I pushed myself forward. The horizon blurred with heat-waves, but I focused on the distant outline of Ironedge, willing it to come closer with every step.

Her body felt lighter than it should, worry gnawing at my insides like a hungry beast. "Come on, kid," I muttered through gritted teeth, my breath ragged and uneven. "Don't you dare give up on me now."

The sun bore down mercilessly, every step a battle against exhaustion and doubt. The thought of losing her clawed at my mind, but I shoved it aside, focusing on the rhythm of my steps and the distant goal.

I glanced down again. Still no movement from her chest. Panic tried to rise up in me, but I forced it back down where it belonged.

The gates of Ironedge loomed closer now, massive and imposing against the barren landscape. My pace quickened despite the burning in my legs and lungs.

How long was it?

An hour?

Maybe two?

I trudged forward, Everly's weight heavier than I antici-pated. Each step sent sharp jolts of pain through my muscles, but I kept going. Silence trotted beside me, almost like she was worried for Everly just as much as...

The heat beat down relentlessly, sapping my strength with every passing second.

Finally, Ironedge came into view. The fortified walls stood tall and imposing, contrasting to the wasteland surrounding it. Metal and stone intertwined in a haphazard yet sturdy struc-ture. Rusted spikes jutted out at odd angles, and barbed wire coiled like serpents along the top.

Two guards stood posted at the entrance, their eyes narrowing as we approached. Both clutched their weapons tighter, fingers twitching on the triggers. They were rough-looking men, with sunburnt skin and scars crisscrossing their faces. Their eyes widened when they saw me—a demon hauling an unconscious girl.

One of them stepped forward, his rifle raised but not aimed directly at me.

"What do you want, demon?" His voice was gravelly, suspicion dripping from every word.

I shifted Everly's weight in my arms, trying to keep my tone as steady as possible. "The fuck does it look like?" I growled. "She needs a goddamn doctor."

The other guard exchanged a glance with his companion before speaking up. "You know we don't just let anyone in here, abomination."

I took a step closer, feeling Silence's presence beside me like a shadow. She growled. "She's dying," I snapped, letting some of my desperation seep into my voice. "I can pay."

"With what?" the second asked. "Not your fucking soul."

I clenched my teeth together. "I got an angel feather."

That caught their attention. The guard lowered his rifle slightly but kept it ready. "Angel feathers, huh?" He looked me up and down, eyes lingering on my scarred skin.

"Why should we believe you?" the second one asked.

The first guard turned to his companion, his eyes wide with recognition. "Don't you know who that is?"

The second guard furrowed his brow, shaking his head. "No idea."

"That's D," the first one said, his voice barely a whisper.

The second guard's eyes widened as he took a step back. "Wait," he said, the realization dawning on him. "The one with—"

The first one nodded, cutting him off. "Yeah, that D. What the hell is he doing with..." His voice trailed off as he glanced at Everly's unconscious form. "Oh, shit. Is she a Purifier?"

I felt a strange protective instinct kick in, an urge to shield her from their prying eyes and judgmental stares. They didn't need to look at her that closely.

"You fucking her?" the first guard asked, a lewd smirk curling on his lips. "Is she... is she Branded?"

Fury flared up inside me, hot and uncontrollable. My voice dropped to a dangerous growl as I fixed them with a steely gaze. "You gonna let us in, or am I gonna sic my hound on you both?" I asked, feeling Silence tense beside me. "And I guaran-damn-tee you she's faster than the two of you."

Both guards looked at Silence like they hadn't noticed her before. Their eyes widened further as they took in the sight of the Hellhound, her glowing red eyes glaring back at them.

"Is that a Hellhound?" the second guard asked, his voice shaky.

I didn't answer, just kept my gaze locked on them, daring them to make the wrong move.

"All right," he muttered. "But any funny business and you're dead meat."

"Noted," I replied, stepping past him and through the gate into Ironedge.

Inside was a maze of makeshift buildings and stalls, people bustling around despite the oppressive heat. The air was thick with the smell of sweat and metal. But there was life here—a sense of purpose that was missing from the wasteland outside.

I just hoped it was enough to save Everly.

Makeshift shacks and stalls crowded every available space, creating narrow, winding paths that twisted through the heart of the settlement. The structures were a hodgepodge of metal sheets, wood scraps, and scavenged materials, all held together with rusted nails and fraying rope. People moved with purpose, bartering goods and services, their voices blending into a cacophony that echoed off the walls.

I pushed my way through the throng, clutching Everly

tighter to my chest. The heat was still unbearable, but at least there was some shade here. My eyes scanned for any sign of a medical facility—a red cross, a healer's tent, anything that promised aid.

Sweat trickled down my forehead as I navigated the maze-like streets. The smell of cooked meat and burning metal mingled in the air, making it hard to breathe. Merchants hawked their wares—everything from canned goods to weaponry—shouting over one another to catch the attention of passersby.

Finally, I spotted it—a small building with a faded red cross painted above the door. The paint was chipped and peeling, but it was unmistakable. My heart pounded as I approached, kicking up dust with each hurried step.

I didn't bother knocking. Bursting through the door, I found myself in a cramped room filled with shelves lined with jars and bottles of various concoctions. The air was thick with the scent of herbs and antiseptic. A woman stood behind a counter, her gray hair tied back in a messy bun. She looked up from her work, eyes widening at the sight of us.

"Doctor!" I barked, my voice echoing off the walls. "I need a doctor now!"

The woman hurried around the counter, her movements swift despite her age. She gestured for me to follow her deeper into the building.

"Bring her in here," she instructed, leading me to a back room where a makeshift bed had been set up.

I laid Everly down gently on the bed, watching as the woman immediately began to assess her condition. Her hands moved with practiced efficiency, checking Everly's pulse and inspecting her for any visible injuries.

"Heat exhaustion," she muttered to herself before turning to me. "What happened?"

ISADORA BROWN

"We were out in the Forsaken," I replied gruffly. "She collapsed from the heat."

The doctor's hands moved swiftly over Everly, checking her pulse, inspecting for injuries. Her gray eyes narrowed as she worked, focused and precise.

"What's a demon like you want with her?" she asked without looking up.

"You want to know that now?" I snapped, my voice rough. "Fix her!"

The woman glanced at me briefly before turning her attention back to Everly. Her eyes softened, the lines on her face deepening with concern.

"It's going to cost you," she said.

"I understand," I barked, my patience wearing thin.

"You don't," she replied, a note of finality in her voice. "It's not just the treatment. She can't rush off today, so she'll be using a bed. There's food. Water. Shelter. Safety."

I gritted my teeth, feeling the edges grind against each other. This was going to be more complicated than I'd hoped.

"How much?" I asked tightly, trying to keep the anger out of my voice.

The woman moved closer to Everly, brushing a strand of hair away from her face. "We'll discuss it after," she said.

I clenched my fists at my sides, but nodded curtly. There was no point in arguing now; Everly needed help, and this woman was our only option.

The doctor continued her work in silence, her hands deft and experienced. I watched every movement, every flicker of expression on her face. Time seemed to stretch out as I stood there, feeling the weight of the situation pressing down on me.

The doctor began stripping Everly, peeling away layers of grime-encrusted clothing. I growled, a low rumble that caught me off guard. I didn't understand why the sight of the doctor's hands on Everly bothered me so much.

174

"Mind yourself," she said, her voice steady as she pulled off one of Everly's boots. "She can't stay in these clothes. Filled with grime and sweat. Another thing that'll cost you. Washing up. A proper bath." Her eyes landed on Everly again, widening in concern. "Oh, Lord in Heaven. Did you make her walk with these blisters?"

I moved closer to the bed, feeling an uneasy mix of anger and guilt bubbling inside me. The doctor pointed at Everly's feet, and I winced at the sight. Her skin was raw and red, blisters covering her heels and toes. Some had burst open, leaving angry, weeping wounds.

Guilt crept in again, like a shadow I couldn't shake.

"I... I didn't know," I grunted, the words feeling heavy in my mouth.

And it was true; I hadn't noticed the state of her feet. But deep down, I knew it wouldn't have mattered—I'd have made her walk, regardless.

I pushed the guilt away as best as I could, but some of it lingered, gnawing at my insides like a persistent parasite.

Silence snuffed softly and lay down by the foot of the bed, her glowing eyes fixed on the doctor.

"Is that thing going to bite me?" the doctor asked warily as she moved to remove Everly's pants.

"You going to give her a reason to?" I shot back, my voice a low growl.

The doctor glared at me but said nothing more, continuing her work with practiced efficiency.

Minutes passed like hours until finally, she stepped back and looked at me. I didn't watch as she finished undressing the girl, not until she had a hospital gown on her.

"So modest you are, demon," the doctor chided.

I glared at her. "Fuck off."

"She'll need rest," she replied, unperturbed. "Plenty of fluids and shade. She's dehydrated and overheated."

I nodded again. This wasn't part of the plan, but plans rarely survived contact with reality.

"Is she gonna make it?" I asked, trying to keep my voice steady.

The doctor met my gaze squarely. "If we do everything right," she replied simply.

I exhaled slowly, letting some of the tension drain from my shoulders. For now, Everly was in good hands.

The doctor reached for an IV, her eyes never leaving mine. "Now," she said, her tone matter-of-fact, "let's discuss payment, demon."

"I have an angel feather," I replied.

Her eyes flickered to me, but she shook her head. "I don't want it."

My suspicions flared immediately. No one turned down angel feathers. No one. "Then what do you want?" I asked, my voice low and edged with wariness.

"You're that bounty hunter, aren't you?" she asked, hanging a pouch of fluids up before piercing Everly's arm with the IV needle. Everly didn't even flinch. "The one they call Brimstone Stalker?"

I grunted in response. Stupid nicknames never held any weight with me.

She began to clean Everly's feet, methodically and care-fully. The sight of those raw blisters made something twist inside me. The fact that Everly didn't react at all bothered me more than I cared to admit.

"In exchange for everything you need for you and your girl," she said without looking up, "I require usage of your particular set of skills."

My jaw tightened. Her proposal hung in the air between us, heavy and inevitable. There was no way around it; if I wanted Everly to get the care she needed, I had to play along. My mind raced through possibilities as I considered her words.

"What's the job?" I asked finally, my voice gruff.

The doctor finished bandaging Everly's feet before standing up and facing me fully. Her eyes were sharp and calculating, a stark contrast to her otherwise calm demeanor.

"There's a camp just outside the settlement filled with raiders," she said simply. "A threat to this community. We've lost a couple of girls. It's caused travel to go way down. No one can cross over without some kind of attack."

Of course there was. It always came down to killing someone. Or, in this case, a group of someones.

"And in return," she continued, "I'll make sure both of you are taken care of until she's back on her feet."

I weighed my options quickly. Everly's survival hinged on this deal; there was no room for hesitation.

"Fine," I growled reluctantly. "You have a deal."

CHAPTER 19

Everly

I woke up to the sound of silence. For a moment, I thought I was back in my bunker's familiar safety. The air felt wrong, though—too dry, too warm. I opened my eyes and found myself in an unfamiliar room. The walls were a dull gray, marred by scratches and faded stains. A single window let in a sliver of light, casting long shadows that danced across the floor.

Where was I? Panic began to rise in my chest as I tried to make sense of my surroundings. The bed beneath me was lumpy and the sheets coarse against my skin, so different from the ones in my old bunk. I sat up, head spinning, trying to remember how I got here.

And then it hit me. D. Elise. Ironedge so far away. My feet in such pain...

"He... he left me," I whispered to myself, the words barely audible. Tears welled up in my eyes, blurring my vision. "He really left me."

My mind raced back to the moments we had shared—the fight with the Bone Gnasher, the way he handed me the serpent tail when I thought he wouldn't, the small moments

178

of kindness that had made me think he cared. But now, it seemed like all of that had been for nothing.

Stupid.

How could I think he cared?

I couldn't believe I even considered he would want me as his friend. The very idea seemed laughable now, sitting alone in this dim room. He'd warned me time and again not to trust anyone, to keep my guard up. And yet, I had let my guard down around him. Had I really thought he'd wait for me? That he'd stick around out of some newfound sense of loyalty or companionship? It felt absurd, and I hated myself for being so naïve. Trusting him had been a mistake, one I couldn't afford to make again.

I swung my legs over the side of the bed and stood up, wincing as pain shot through my body. My feet ached because of the blisters and my head throbbed from dehydration.

I paused, the room spinning around me. The sharp pain in my feet drew my attention downward. Blisters. They had been bandaged, though the makeshift dressings were rough and hastily applied. As I shifted my gaze to my clothes, I realized I was wearing a nursing gown. Thin, pale blue fabric hung loosely on my frame, a far cry from the sturdy bunker attire I was used to.

Confusion clouded my thoughts as I turned to survey the room. Machines lined the walls, one of them connected to my arm by a thin tube. The sight of it made me feel queasy. I reached out to steady myself against the nearest surface but found nothing but empty air.

My vision began to blur, and a wave of dizziness washed over me. Just as I felt myself beginning to sway, an arm slid around my waist, steadying me.

"Whoa there now, angel."

The voice was familiar, gravelly and rough, like stones grinding together. I turned slowly, finding myself face-to-face with D. His appearance sent a shiver down my spine. His skin was mottled and leathery, stretched taut over his frame. His eyes—sunken deep into their sockets—glimmered amber with an unsettling light. And somehow, he looked...

"Easy," he said, his grip firm yet gentle as he helped me back onto the bed. "You've been through hell."

I stared at him, trying to reconcile the man before me with the one I'd known only in passing.

"Why are you here?" My voice came out hoarse and weak. "You... you were supposed to leave."

"Trying to get rid of me?" he replied with a wry smile that revealed teeth far too white against his decayed complexion. "I'll tell you, darling, you're worse than a welt on the ass, I'll have you know."

I studied his face—every scar and hollow—and saw something there that went beyond the grotesque exterior: a flicker of genuine concern.

"You... you helped me?" The words felt foreign on my tongue.

At that moment, the door creaked open, and a woman stepped inside. She had a kind face framed by loose, wavy, dark hair. Her eyes were a soft grey, radiating warmth and understanding. She wore a white coat that contrasted starkly with the room's gloom, and a stethoscope hung casually around her neck.

"Hello," she said, her voice gentle yet authoritative. "You must be Everly. Your friend was quite worried about you."

I glanced at D, who was still holding me upright.

"Worried ain't the word I'd use," he grunted.

The doctor smiled at his comment before turning her attention back to me. "I'm Wendy," she introduced herself. "You shouldn't be standing. Not yet."

I felt my knees buckle slightly as she guided me back onto the bed.

"W-what happened?" I asked, trying to piece together my fragmented memories.

"You were severely dehydrated and suffering from heat exhaustion," Wendy explained as she adjusted the IV drip attached to my arm. "Your feet were in bad shape too—blisters from walking in improper footwear. You passed out just outside of Ironedge."

D's eyes glinted with annoyance and something else— maybe concern?—as he watched Wendy work.

"How long was I out?" I pressed, trying to gauge how much time I'd lost.

"A day," Wendy replied, checking my vitals with practiced ease. "Your body needed time to recover from the ordeal. You're lucky your friend here brought you in when he did."

I looked at D again, feeling both gratitude and confusion.

Wendy's gentle touch and reassuring presence helped ease the knots in my stomach, but D's gruff demeanor was like a rock in my shoe. I looked up at him, noticing the way his eyes flickered toward the door, restless.

"I'm gonna check on Silence," he muttered, more to himself than to me.

A small smile tugged at my chapped lips. It felt foreign and almost painful after everything.

"What?" he snapped, catching my expression. His tone was sharp, like the edge of a blade.

"You called her Silence," I pointed out softly, my smile widening despite myself.

He scowled, his brows knitting together in irritation. "Don't read too much into it, angel. She's still just a mutt." His voice was harsh, but there was something else lurking beneath it—something softer that he would never admit to.

He turned on his heel and stalked out of the room before I could say anything more. The door closed with a heavy thud, leaving me alone with Wendy once again.

The room seemed quieter without him there, like his presence had filled every corner with tension and energy. Wendy continued her work in silence for a few moments before looking up at me with those kind green eyes.

"He's a tough one," she said gently. "But I think he cares more than he lets on."

I bit my lip, my mind still reeling from the whirlwind of emotions and events that had brought me to this point.

"He carried me all the way here?" I asked, disbelief coloring my voice.

"He did," she murmured. Wendy finished her examination and looked at me kindly. "You need to take it easy for a while. Stay hydrated and rest your feet. You'll be back on your feet soon enough, but don't rush it."

I nodded slowly, absorbing her words. The idea of staying put didn't sit well with me—I had so much to do—but I knew she was right.

"Thank you," I said quietly, meeting Wendy's eyes.

She patted my shoulder reassuringly before turning to leave the room. "I'll check on you later," she promised.

"Wait," I called out, my voice sounding small in the quiet room. "Um, I'm not sure I can afford this. I... I don't have any... what's the currency up here?"

Wendy turned back to me, a gentle smile playing at the corners of her lips. The wrinkles around her eyes deepened, giving her an air of warmth and understanding.

"Your friend already took care of that," she said softly.

With that, she left the room, closing the door behind her with a soft click. I stared at the closed door, my mind racing. Why would D do that? What did he stand to gain from helping me? It didn't add up.

I pursed my lips, trying to make sense of it all. Something felt off about the whole situation. D wasn't the type to go out of his way for anyone, let alone someone like me.

You're really going to question a kind deed? Elise's voice echoed in my head, gentle and chiding. *You should see the best in everyone.*

No, darling, another voice countered, one that sounded eerily like D's gravelly tone. *You question everyone and everything. You shouldn't trust me. Especially not me.*

My head started to throb as the conflicting voices battled within me. I leaned back against the bed, trying to calm the storm raging in my mind. The steady beeping of the machines in the background only seemed to intensify the headache.

I closed my eyes and took a deep breath, focusing on the rise and fall of my chest. The air smelled faintly of antiseptic. The room's dim lighting felt oppressive now, each shadow playing tricks on my already frazzled nerves.

I tried to think about Elise again, hoping her memory would bring some comfort. But instead, it only intensified my longing to find her and understand what had happened.

Why would D help me? The question gnawed at me like a persistent itch I couldn't scratch. So why did he carry me here? Pay for my treatment?

I forced myself to sit up straighter, wincing at the pain in my feet and head. I needed answers.

The door creaked open, and D walked in carrying a burlap sack. He tossed it onto the bed next to me with a grunt. I caught a whiff of something earthy and slightly sweet, but the scent was unfamiliar.

"What's this?" I asked, peering into the bag. Inside were several round, lumpy objects with brown skin. I picked one up, turning it over in my hands. It felt rough and slightly dirty.

"Food," D replied, leaning against the wall with his arms crossed.

I frowned, bringing the object closer to my nose. The smell was stronger now—earthy and musty, with a hint of something almost starchy. I couldn't place it.

"Why are you being so nice to me?" I asked, looking up at him.

He snorted, a smirk playing at the corners of his lips. "I ain't nice," he said, his tone dismissive. "You questioning my good deed, angel? You know those don't go unpunished."

I rolled my eyes. "Aren't you the same guy who says there's no such thing as a good deed anymore?" I asked, pulling out what looked like a smooshed potato from the bag.

He chuckled, shaking his head. "I'm glad you're listening, even when you're yapping," he said. "Don't think anything of it, girl. This is just getting you better so we can get your sister."

His words hit me like a punch to the gut. I stared at him, trying to read his expression, but his face was as inscrutable as ever.

"I ain't being nice," he continued, his voice low and steady. "If I didn't think I needed you to get to her, then I wouldn't be helping you. I'd have left you."

I gave him a long look, trying to decide if he was telling the truth or just trying to mess with my head again. His eyes were hard and unyielding, giving nothing away.

To buy myself some time to think, I took a bite of the food in my hand. The taste was bland and starchy, but not unpleasant. It filled my mouth with a texture that was both soft and slightly grainy.

I stared at the door after D left, chewing slowly on the food. My mind buzzed with questions I didn't dare voice. Why was he so interested in my sister? I knew it couldn't be for a good reason. The thought gnawed at me, a persistent itch I couldn't scratch. If I found out his true intentions, would I still want to travel with him? Could I afford not to?

I had to be smart about this. Right now, he was my best chance of finding Elise, and I was his. Maybe, by some miracle, I could convince him to help out of the goodness of his heart. God's made lesser things possible. Why not this?

"How's Silence?" I asked.

He paused by the door, his face softening ever so slightly as he answered. "By the door, scaring up a storm," he grunted, a ghost of a smile tugging at his lips.

Before I could help it, the words slipped out. "I like when you smile."

His eyes narrowed at me. "You need water," he said brusquely. "Must be seeing things."

"Right," I muttered, looking away and feeling my cheeks flush with embarrassment.

He walked over to the table and picked up a cup, handing it to me roughly. I wrapped my fingers around it awkwardly, taking a long drink. The water was lukewarm, but refreshing nonetheless.

As I drank, D leaned against the wall again, watching me with those inscrutable eyes. His presence filled the room with an unspoken tension that made it hard to think straight.

"Wendy says you paid for... for my treatment?" I asked, still trying to make sense of everything.

"Who the fuck is Wendy?" D looked genuinely perplexed, his brows furrowing.

I blinked. "The doctor," I clarified.

He shrugged, leaning back against the wall. "I took care of it. *Will* take care of it."

"What does that mean?" I pressed, feeling frustration bubbling up inside me.

"You must be getting better, what with all your annoying questions," he muttered, crossing his arms over his chest.

"Tell me," I insisted, setting the cup down on the table. "Please."

D opened his mouth, then closed it, scowling. "I'm doing a job," he finally said. "Getting rid of a problem. It'll cover room and board, food, water, and your treatment."

"But isn't that dangerous?" I asked, concern threading through my voice.

He gave me a long look, one that made me feel like I was missing some crucial piece of information. "I'm a goddamn demon," he replied bluntly. "It'll be fine."

I huffed a sigh, frustrated by his language and the way he seemed to brush off my concerns. But there was also a nagging feeling in the back of my mind, one that hinted at... no, he wasn't going to be fine.

"Why do you do this?" I asked softly, not entirely sure if I wanted to hear the answer.

"Do what?" His eyes bore into mine, challenging me to continue.

"Help people," I replied. "You act like you don't care about anyone or anything."

D snorted, shaking his head. "I ain't helping people," he said. "I'm helping myself. You're just along for the ride."

I couldn't shake the feeling that there was more to it than that, but I knew better than to push him further. Instead, I nodded slowly, accepting his words for now.

"Thank you," I said quietly, my voice barely above a whisper.

He grunted in response and turned towards the door again. "Get some rest," he ordered gruffly, before leaving the room.

"Wait." I chewed my lips. I couldn't believe I was going to ask... I already knew the answer, but I still... I needed...

I sucked in a breath.

"Will you stay with me?"

CHAPTER 20

Walton

T his fucking girl.

I should've said no. It felt dangerous, and I couldn't put my finger on why. My gut twisted in a way I hadn't felt in years. Was I nervous? What the hell would I be nervous about? It didn't add up.

But my feet moved, dragging me to the chair beside her bed, the same chair where she'd mistaken my leaving as abandonment. Where my chest had tightened in a way that caught me off guard because I didn't think it could anymore.

Fuck.

I sat down heavily, the wooden frame creaking under my weight. Her eyes flicked open, and that smile—pure sunlight —hit me like a sledgehammer. I knew I should look away. It was too bright, too hopeful. But I couldn't.

"You should rest," I said again, trying to sound stern but failing miserably.

Her eyes searched mine, and for a moment, it felt like she saw right through the demonic exterior into whatever was left of Walton Cooper.

"Thanks for not leaving me," she said, her voice barely more than a breath.

I wanted to tell her not to thank me. That it was just another job. But the words caught in my throat, tangled up with feelings I didn't want to name. So instead, I nodded and leaned back in the chair, letting silence fill the space between us.

The weight of her gratitude pressed down on me. She had no idea who she was thanking—a demon cursed by his own choices. But maybe it didn't matter to her. Maybe, in this broken world, everyone carried their own demons.

Her eyelids fluttered shut again, and I watched her drift back to sleep. Her chest rose and fell with each breath, fragile yet resilient.

My gaze lingered on her longer than it should have. That damn smile still etched into my mind like a brand. Dangerous? Yeah. But maybe some dangers were worth facing head-on.

The chair groaned as I shifted again, but this time I stayed put.

The door creaked open, and the doctor stepped in, giving me a look that felt like she could see right through me.

"What?" I grunted, trying to sound more irritated than I felt.

She didn't answer right away. Instead, she walked over to Everly, taking her pulse and checking her blood pressure. Her hands moved with practiced efficiency.

"She's fit to move to a room across the way," she finally said, glancing back at me. "At the Old Inne."

"And that's covered?" I asked, already knowing the answer but needing to hear it.

She nodded. "When are you planning to go?"

I sighed, rubbing the back of my neck. "Maybe the day after tomorrow. I want…" My voice trailed off. Damn it.

"You want her to get settled in?" she asked, her eyes narrowing just slightly.

I glared at her, feeling the heat rise in my cheeks. I hated how easily she read me.

"Careful there," she said with a small smirk. "What would happen if people found out you actually cared about some human girl, hmm?"

"I need her," I snapped back, biting my tongue immediately after. What the hell was I doing? Justifying myself to her? No way.

She chuckled softly before turning on her heel and leaving the room; the door clicking shut behind her.

I looked back at Everly, who was still fast asleep. Her face was peaceful, untroubled by the world outside this small room. For a moment, I envied her—envied that oblivion.

Moving across the room to pack up our things felt like an escape from my own thoughts. The doctor's words echoed in my mind: caring about some human girl. I couldn't afford to care. Not now, not ever.

But as I folded our gear and prepared for the move to the Old Inne, I couldn't shake the image of Everly's smile from my mind. That damn smile that had cracked something open inside me.

I sighed again and shook my head. No point dwelling on it now. We had a plan to execute, and lingering here wouldn't help either of us.

And once it was over, that was it.

It was over.

* * *

"D, why are we moving to the Old Inne? Is it safer there? What about food supplies? How long do we stay? And how far is it from here?" Everly fired questions at me as soon as she woke up.

I gritted my teeth, the barrage of questions hitting me like a swarm of angry bees. "Would you shut the fuck up?" I snapped.

She frowned, her face crumpling in confusion. "Why are you so grumpy?" she asked, her voice softer now. "Is it the chair? I bet it was the chair. It doesn't look comfortable, and you were there the whole night."

I grunted, not wanting to admit she was right. The chair had been a torture device disguised as furniture. But that wasn't the point. I didn't want to be reminded that I'd stayed by her side all night.

Before I could respond, the door creaked open, and the doctor walked in with a clipboard in hand. She looked between us, sensing the tension.

"Morning," she said briskly, stepping over to Everly's bedside. "How are you feeling?"

Everly shifted to sit up straighter. "Better, I think. D said we're moving to the Old Inne?"

The doctor nodded. "Yes, that's right. It's a safer location and you'll have more privacy to recover. Plus, we'll need the bed in case someone needs medical assistance."

Everly glanced at me before turning back to the doctor. "Anything I should know before we leave? I don't want to make this worse."

The doctor checked Everly's pulse again, then scribbled something on her clipboard. "First off, rest is crucial. Your body needs time to heal from the heat exhaustion and dehydration."

Everly nodded earnestly. "Okay, what else?"

"Stay hydrated," the doctor continued. "Drink plenty of water and avoid strenuous activities for a few days. That means no walking. And I know water can be hard to come by, but while you're here..." She gave me a pointed look. "Don't shy away from it."

The doctor turned to me then, her eyes narrowing slightly as if daring me to contradict her advice. "And make sure she follows these instructions," she added pointedly.

I gave a curt nod, my jaw tight. The last thing I needed was more reminders that someone was depending on me.

The doctor straightened up and made a few final notes on her clipboard before heading for the door.

"Take care of yourself," she said over her shoulder before leaving us alone again.

Everly looked at me with those bright eyes of hers and gave a small smile despite everything. "Thank you," she said quietly.

I grunted again, turning away to pack up our things for the move to the Old Inne.

The walk took no time at all. The building sat just across the way from the clinic, its weathered sign creaking in the faint breeze. The place looked like it had seen better days, with cracked windows and ivy snaking up its walls. Still, it stood strong amidst the surrounding ruins, a relic of what once was.

As we approached the building, Everly's eyes lit up when she saw Silence bounding towards us. Seeing the joy on Everly's face as Silence leaped at her was a new experience. The massive beast tackled her to the ground, licking her face with enthusiasm.

"Silence! You're such a good girl!" Everly laughed, wrapping her arms around the hellhound's neck and pressing her face into its fur. She didn't seem to mind the dirt or the occasional growl of other creatures lurking nearby. Silence's tail wagged furiously, and she returned Everly's affection with slobbery kisses.

"You don't know where that tongue has been," I pointed

out, my voice gruff but amused. It wasn't often that something brought a smile to my face, but Everly's unfiltered joy had a way of breaking through my hardened exterior.

Everly just ignored me, too wrapped up in showering Silence with affection. "You're such a good girl!" she repeated, scratching behind the hellhound's ears and laughing as Silence licked her cheek again. Watching them together, I felt a strange sense of... something. It wasn't quite peace or contentment, but it was close enough for me.

As we reached the door of the Old Inne, Everly glanced at me, her eyes hopeful. "Can she come in with us?" she asked.

"Not likely," I replied, shaking my head. "Besides, she's making due outside."

She sighed but nodded, accepting my decision. "She does seem to like it here," she admitted, rubbing Silence's head affectionately. The hellhound nuzzled into her touch, its red eyes glowing softly in the dim light.

"And no one would fuck with a Hellhound," I added, though why I was going out of my way to reassure her, I had no fucking clue.

I clicked my tongue against my teeth, and Silence snuffed before trotting off. Everly watcher her go the whole way, lips curved into a frown.

"Come on," I murmured.

We stepped inside, and the scent of old wood and dust filled my nostrils. The lobby was dimly lit, with a few battered chairs and a worn-out rug that had probably been there for decades. A large desk stood at the far end of the room, behind which an older man with a thick moustache glared at us. His eyes narrowed as soon as they landed on me.

His hand drifted behind his desk, fingers brushing something out of sight. My own hand casually found my gun resting there like an old friend.

"Hi," Everly said brightly, breaking the tension. "Dr. Wendy says you're expecting us?"

The man's eyes flicked to her, softening slightly, but still wary. "You with him?" he asked, jerking his chin toward me.

Everly nodded enthusiastically. "Yes."

"You in trouble, girl?" he pressed, his gaze intense.

Everly blinked in confusion. "What? No. I mean, I was dehydrated and collapsed, but D carried me all the way and—"

"That's not what he means," I grunted, cutting her off.

She looked between us, realization dawning slowly in her eyes. "No, of course not," she says. "D's my... he's my friend. We're friends."

I snorted.

She shot me a look.

The man behind the desk relaxed a fraction, but didn't let go of whatever he was holding. "Room's upstairs," he muttered finally, nodding toward a rickety staircase to our right. "Third door on the left." He glanced back at Everly. "You need help, you holler, you hear? Someone will hear you."

Everly opened her mouth to respond to the old man's warning, but I grabbed her wrist and tugged her away before she could get a word out. Her skin felt fragile beneath my calloused grip.

"That's not very nice," she said, looking up at me with wide eyes. "Why does he think I'm in trouble?"

"I am a demon, sugar," I replied as we headed up the creaky steps. The wood groaned under our combined weight, each step a reminder of how far we were from any semblance of safety.

"Well, you're not a typical demon," she said, her voice firm yet soft.

I arched a brow, lips curving into a smirk. "No?"

She shook her head. "I just don't think it's right to judge someone based on what they look like."

"Get used to it," I muttered. "That's how it is up here. For a good reason, too."

We reached the top of the stairs, the hallway dimly lit by a single flickering bulb. The walls were lined with peeling wallpaper and faded photographs of a bygone era. I led her to the third door on the left and pushed it open.

The room was small and sparse, with a single bed against one wall and a battered dresser against the other. A small window offered a view of the decaying world outside, and a thin layer of dust covered everything.

Everly stepped inside, her eyes scanning the room. She didn't seem fazed by its condition; instead, she walked over to the window and peered out.

"It's not much," I said gruffly, leaning against the doorframe.

"It's enough," she replied, turning back to face me. There was something in her eyes—determination mixed with gratitude—that made me uncomfortable.

I glanced around one more time before closing the door behind us. The latch clicked into place with finality.

I set down our stuff, the weight of the bags a welcome relief from my shoulders. The room felt even smaller now with our gear scattered around, but it would do for the night. I glanced over at Everly, who was still standing by the window, her eyes distant as she took in the desolate view.

"There's a tavern a couple of blocks away where the doctor—"

"Wendy," Everly corrected softly.

"Where we can get dinner," I finished, ignoring the interruption.

Everly turned to face me, curling a strand of hair behind her ear. "D," she started, her voice hesitant. "I know you've already done a lot for me, but if I may, I'd like to ask you for another favor."

I narrowed my eyes suspiciously. "What now?"

She cleared her throat, clearly gathering her courage. "Um, I'd like to learn how to... how to defend myself."

"Defend... yourself," I repeated slowly, trying to gauge where she was going with this.

"Yes," she said primly, walking over to the window again. "I know I can't expect you to... to protect me from things or— or people. And there's a good chance you might not even if... Well." She cleared her throat again. "I'd like for this to be more equal." She gestured between the two of us. "A... a partnership. I want to carry my weight. And I think... It's come to my attention I don't know how to do a lot of things—"

"What gave you that idea?" I asked dryly.

She glared at me before continuing. "And you clearly do," she said pointedly. "Anyway. I'd like to know combat. Daggers. Guns. We had some training in the bunker, but I'd like to learn... from you."

I studied her for a moment, weighing her words and sincerity. The determination in her eyes was unmistakable, and despite my better judgment, I felt a flicker of respect for her resolve.

"You think you're up for it?" I asked finally.

Her chin lifted slightly, and she met my gaze head-on. "Yes."

I leaned against the dresser, arms crossed, studying Everly's determined expression. "How are your feet?" I asked, my voice gruff but tinged with genuine concern.

"Better," she replied, shifting her weight from one foot to the other. "They still hurt, but they're much better."

I nodded, feeling a variety of things I hadn't felt in a long time. Relief that she was recovering, irritation at the vulnerability she represented. She needed to toughen up if she was going to survive out here.

I nodded slowly. "All right then. We'll start tomorrow."

A small smile tugged at the corners of her mouth, and she nodded in return. "Thank you," she said softly.

"Don't thank me yet," I muttered, already thinking about what I'd put her through come morning.

But for now, we needed food and rest. The real work would begin soon enough.

CHAPTER 21

Everly

T
he room at the Old Inne felt both familiar and alien. Wooden beams crossed the low ceiling, and rough, hand-hewn planks made up the floor. The walls bore scars from years of use, but they had been polished to a gentle sheen. A single, small window let in just enough light to reveal a sturdy dresser and a washstand with a chipped porcelain basin. It was sparse but functional.

In the center of the room, against one wall, sat a bed—large enough for two, but I didn't want to think about that. Instead, I focused on the bedspread, a faded patchwork quilt that had seen better days. It added a touch of warmth to the otherwise austere surroundings. The scent of lavender hung faintly in the air, likely from sachets hidden in drawers.

"You best get dressed," D said, eyeing me up and down with an unreadable expression. My cheeks warmed under his scrutiny. "You can't go to dinner in scrubs."

I huffed in response, crossing my arms over my chest. "It's not like I had much of a choice," I muttered, more to myself than to him.

He leaned against the doorframe, his gaze steady. "Come

on, little girl. I bet you packed something in that bag of yours. Always prepared, am I right?"

With a sigh, I turned to my bag and unzipped it. I didn't want to admit that he was right, but he was. I was prepared, at least in this respect.

"My uniform?" I asked, turning to him.

"In my bag," he said. "Need to be washed. I don't think it'll ever be pure white again. Nothing up here ever is."

I didn't know what to say to him, so I said nothing. Instead, I moved to the small attached bathroom.

The bathroom was even smaller than the main room. A cracked mirror hung above a rust-stained sink, its porcelain chipped and worn. The shower stall had a flimsy curtain that looked like it might disintegrate if touched too roughly. The tiles on the floor were mismatched, a mosaic of necessity rather than design. A single bare bulb cast a harsh, yellow light, revealing the spiderwebs in the corners and the faint mildew creeping along the grout lines. Despite its condition, it was functional—barely.

I closed the door behind me, grateful for a moment of privacy. My fingers trembled as I peeled off the scrubs, the weight of the last few days pressing down on me like a physical burden. The cold tile underfoot made me shiver as I turned on the tap, letting the water run until it was lukewarm at best.

The shower sputtered to life, and I stepped in, letting the water cascade over me. It wasn't hot enough to relax my muscles or wash away my worries, but it was enough to cleanse my skin of the grime and blood from... well... everything. As I scrubbed at my skin, I tried to shake off the memories of everything that had gone wrong. I didn't want to think about that.

Once I felt somewhat human again, I stepped out and dried off with a thin towel that smelled faintly of detergent and dust. I slipped into clean clothes from my bag—a simple pair of pants and a plain white shirt that was crisp and fresh.

I frowned.

Maybe I shouldn't have brought so much white.

I emerged from the bathroom to find D still leaning against the doorframe, his eyes never leaving me.

"Feel better?" His voice had an edge to it I couldn't quite place.

"A little," I admitted. "What's next?"

"We head downstairs for dinner," he said, pushing off from the wall. "And then sleep."

Sleep. I couldn't help but glance at the single bed. The thought of sharing it with D made my stomach twist in ways I didn't understand. We'd faced a Bone Gnasher together; surely we could handle one bed without it being awkward.

Except... I had never been in a bed with a man before.

Demon, a voice reminded me. *He's a demon.*

I shook off the thought and focused on the next step. Dinner. That was simple enough. And it had to be better than that bat we ate.

We headed downstairs, the wooden steps creaking beneath our weight. The narrow hallway led us past the front desk, where an old ledger lay open, its pages yellowed with age. D's hand came to rest on my back, a light touch that seemed more guiding than controlling. I didn't understand it, but I felt a strange sense of safety with his hand there. It was like an unspoken promise that he'd look out for me.

As we stepped outside, the evening air greeted us with a mix of scents—wood smoke from nearby fires, the earthy aroma of tilled soil, and the faint tang of rust and oil. Ironedge was a settlement cobbled together from remnants of the old world and makeshift constructions. The buildings ranged from pre-war structures still standing through sheer stubbornness to newer shacks built from scavenged materials.

Children played in the dirt streets, their laughter mingling with the clanking sounds of blacksmiths hammering away at metal. People moved about with purpose—trading goods, tending to small gardens, or simply chatting in groups. Despite its rough edges, Ironedge had a sense of community that felt almost tangible.

The settlement sprawled out in an irregular pattern, like it had grown organically rather than through any kind of planning. Wooden signs hung above doorways, hand-painted with symbols indicating what could be found inside—food, tools, clothing. A large central fire pit served as a communal gathering place, where people could share news and stories under the open sky.

I noticed small touches that spoke of attempts to bring beauty into this harsh world—wildflowers planted in rusty cans lined windowsills; wind chimes made from bits of glass and metal tinkled softly in the breeze; murals painted on crumbling walls depicted scenes of hope and resilience.

The air was cooler now that night approached, carrying a freshness that was almost intoxicating after the heat and grime of the day. It felt good to be clean and in fresh clothes. For a moment, I allowed myself to breathe deeply and take it all in— the sights, the sounds, the smells.

"This way," D said, his voice breaking my reverie. His hand remained on my back as he steered me toward a long building near the edge of the settlement. Smoke curled up from its chimney, promising warmth and food within.

I glanced at him as we walked. There were still so many questions swirling in my mind about him—about us—but for now, I focused on putting one foot in front of the other. Dinner first. Answers could come later.

The scent of roasted meat wafted through the air as we approached the building's entrance. My stomach growled in response—a reminder that I hadn't eaten properly in days.

Maybe tonight would bring more than just food.

We reached the tavern, a modest building with a hand-painted sign that read *The Rusty Mug*. It looked inviting, with warm light spilling out from its windows and the sound of laughter and conversation drifting into the street. My stomach growled louder, drawn by the promise of food.

D pushed open the door, and we stepped inside. The interior was cozy, if a bit worn. Wooden tables and benches filled the room, each one scarred and polished by years of use. The walls were adorned with old photographs and faded maps, giving the place a sense of history. A large fireplace crackled at one end of the room, its flames casting a flickering glow over everything.

My eyes went wide as I took it all in. The scent of roasted meat and fresh bread made my mouth water. The warmth from the fire seeped into my bones, chasing away the lingering chill from outside. It was perfect—like stepping into a dream.

I turned to D, unable to contain my excitement. "This is amazing!" I grabbed his hand, practically bouncing on my feet. "Look at this place! It's so... alive!"

For a moment, I expected him to pull away or snap at me for being too enthusiastic. Instead, he scoffed and looked away, but he didn't ridicule me or pull his hand back. His grip was firm, but not unkind.

I decided that was a good sign. Maybe he was coming around. Maybe we could be...

Friends?

Friends? Please. As if a demon would want anything to do with you? And honestly? It's a little blasphemous you'd want it with him, anyway. You are a Daughter of God, aren't you?

The tavern's patrons glanced our way, but quickly returned to their meals and conversations. We found an empty seats at the bar near the fireplace and sat down. The heat from the fire felt wonderful on my skin, and I couldn't help but smile.

D flagged down a server—a young woman with curly hair

tied back in a bandana. She handed us menus printed on yellowed paper, and I scanned it eagerly.

"What's good here?" I asked her, still buzzing with excitement. "I've never been here before. Actually, I've never been to a tavern before, but I'm really excited to be here."

"Here we go," D muttered, keeping his eyes focused on the menu.

She smiled warmly. "The stew's always a favorite," she said. "And we've got fresh bread today."

"Stew sounds perfect," I replied without hesitation.

D nodded in agreement. "Two stews and some bread," he ordered.

The server left to get our food, and I turned back to D, still grinning like an idiot. "Thank you," I said softly.

"I can't let you starve, can I?" he grunted. "And it's not like we're paying for it."

"Oh." I furrowed my brows as two men entered and took seats next to me at the bar. "Are you going to tell me what you agreed to?"

"Why worry your pretty little head over something that doesn't involve you?" He didn't bother hiding his exasperation.

I frowned. "You know, you don't have to be condescending."

He shot me a look that made my stomach twist.

"Anyway," I said, curling a strand of hair behind my ear, "I want this to be equal. Like I said, I've been meaning to ask you. I want to figure out a way to make some money. I want to contribute. What do you suggest?"

"I got a way you can make money," the man next to me said, his voice rough and tinged with something unsavory.

I stiffened and turned slightly to look at him. He was older, with grizzled hair and eyes that seemed too keen on me. The other man with him snickered under his breath.

"And what way is that?" D's tone had a dangerous edge, and he leaned forward, cutting off the man's view of me.

The man shrugged, unfazed by D's posture. "Just sayin', there's always work for a pretty face around here."

My cheeks burned, but before I could respond, D's hand came down hard on the bar.

"You best keep your thoughts to yourself," D growled.

The man raised his hands in mock surrender, a smirk still playing on his lips. "No offense meant, just trying to help."

D's glare could have cut through steel. "Help yourself to another seat."

The man's eyes slid over to me, filled with a lecherous gleam. "You fucking him?" he asked, voice dripping with contempt. "Someone pretty like you? Looking so innocent and pure in that white shirt, really want to get your hands dirty with a demon?"

I recoiled slightly, but before I could respond, the second man leaned in, his breath reeking of alcohol. "How much is he paying you?" His eyes bore into mine. "We'll double it."

"Why don't you crawl back into whatever hole you slithered out of, asshole?" D asked, his voice cold and biting, like shattered glass.

"We wasn't askin' you, Hellspawn," the first man shot back.

"He's not paying me," I said firmly, meeting their eyes with as much courage as I could muster. "He's... he's my partner."

The second man sneered. "Is that what he's making you say?"

"Partner," the first one said. "She said partner."

"I don't understand why you feel the need to be so insulting," I said, trying to keep my voice steady. "Has my friend done anything to offend you?"

"He's a demon," the second man spat. "He's lucky he gets service here. There are plenty of places for his kind."

"Did you say friend?" the first man asked incredulously.

"That's incredibly rude," I retorted, my frustration boiling over. "And yes. He's my friend."

Well, I was his friend.

I trusted him. It might be stupid, and he might have his own reasons, but he brought me here. He saved my life. I could at least give him the benefit of the doubt. And if D didn't like it...

Well. We could talk about it later.

"Oh, I get it," the first man said with a twisted grin. "You are fucking him, aren't you? Demonfucker. You're a demonfucker."

D's growl reverberated through the air like distant thunder. "That's enough." His hand moved lightning-fast, and suddenly his gun was out, safety cocked. The cold metal glinted menacingly under the tavern's dim light.

The men froze, their faces draining of color as they stared at the weapon.

"Get lost before I decide you're worth the trouble of skinning you alive and running your veins through my teeth like goddamn floss," D growled, his eyes locked onto them with a predatory intensity.

Without another word, the men scrambled off their stools and hurried toward the exit, muttering curses under their breath but not daring to look back.

I exhaled shakily, the tension slowly easing from my shoulders as D holstered his gun.

Our server returned with our food—two steaming bowls of stew and a basket of fresh bread. The aroma made my mouth water, momentarily distracting me from the unsettling encounter.

I looked at the men as they hurried away, my heart still pounding in my chest. The tension lingered like a bad aftertaste, and I forced myself to take a deep breath. Our server stood nearby, her eyes wide with concern.

"We don't want any trouble here," she said, her eyes on D.

"Neither do we," D replied, his tone calm but edged with steel. "We don't get any, there won't be any."

The server glanced between us, her eyes settling on me.

I mustered a smile, hoping to convey that everything was under control—though inside, I wasn't so sure.

She nodded once, seeming to accept my forced reassurance, and then turned to leave us to our meal.

I watched her go, the tension in my shoulders slowly easing. Turning back to the food in front of me, I let the warmth and scent of the stew wash over me. It was a small comfort amidst the chaos of our lives.

I tried to settle into my seat, but the tension from the encounter lingered. D sat beside me, eyes narrowed, and I could feel his irritation like a tangible force.

"You made a bigger deal out of that than you should have," he snapped, not bothering to look at me.

"They shouldn't be so insulting to you," I retorted, still feeling the sting of their words.

"They were more insulting to you," he countered, his voice sharp.

"Why do you care?" I asked, genuinely curious. His sudden protectiveness puzzled me.

He huffed, leaning back in his seat. "I don't," he said. "I have a reputation to keep up. Can't have people think I'm fucking you."

His crass language made me flinch, as if he'd struck me. Whether it was from the vulgarity or something deeper, I couldn't tell. I cleared my throat, trying to regain some composure.

"Yes, well," I said quietly, "your vulgar language and taking the Lord's name in vain was also unnecessary."

"Shit, darlin'," he muttered. "When are you going to realize it's always necessary up here?"

His words stung, but they also made me think. The world outside the bunker was harsher than anything I'd imagined.

"Did they really mean what they said?" I asked, leaning forward. "Can you really make money... doing that?"

He arched a brow, an edge to his voice. "Why?"

"Well," I began hesitantly, "I've never had sexual intercourse before, but I'm sure it might be relatively easy to learn, and if it'll make some money—"

"What in the fucking seven hells are you saying?" he interrupted sharply. "Aren't you Purifiers supposed to save yourself for Jesus or something?"

"Our husbands," I corrected quietly. My throat tightened as I thought of Archangel Michael. Would he still want me after all this? Probably not.

"Don't you have a husband?" he asked bluntly.

"No," I admitted softly. "I don't have... anyone."

He grunted in response, his expression unreadable.

"Would you teach me?" The words slipped out before I could stop them.

"You're not doing that," he snapped back immediately. "And I sure as shit ain't touching you."

I opened my mouth to argue, but he cut me off sharply. "Shut your mouth. We're not even discussing it, got it? Now eat before your food gets cold." He tipped his hat down over his eyes as if that ended the conversation.

I stared at him for a moment before turning my attention back to the stew in front of me. The warmth and aroma of the food did little to comfort me now.

I took a bite of the stew. It was hearty and flavorful, each mouthful a reminder that some things in this world still held goodness. We ate in silence for a while, the clinking of our spoons against the bowls blending with the ambient noise of the tavern.

It wasn't perfect. But it was enough for now.

D tore into the bread with his usual brusqueness while I dipped mine into the stew, savoring the rich flavors.

He might not want me doing *that*, but I would find something to do. I wouldn't be helpless. Not anymore.

CHAPTER 22

Walton

I was in trouble.

Fuck.

What the hell was happening to me? I was better than this.

Two men propositioning Everly for sex. The memory burned in my mind, igniting a rage that bubbled just beneath the surface. My fists clenched involuntarily, knuckles whitening as the need to lash out grew stronger. I wanted to kill them. To make them suffer for even thinking they could touch her.

And the fact that she would consider it... for what? To be my equal? Was she really that dense?

Of course she was.

She was raised a Purifier. They were all fucking stupid, but...

Fuck.

I shoved another spoonful of stew into my mouth, forcing myself to focus on the taste of the lukewarm broth and bread instead of the seething anger churning inside me. The food was barely palatable, but it was a distraction, something to ground me in the moment.

She had asked me to teach her.

She was too pure for the likes of me. Too innocent.

I didn't deserve her. My hands were stained with too much blood, too much regret. I'd drag her down, taint her with my corruption. It wasn't right.

"Are you going to finish that?" Her voice pulled me out of my thoughts. She nodded towards the half-eaten loaf of bread on my plate.

I pushed it towards her without a word. She needed it more than I did.

"Thanks," she said—how was she so damn cheery all the time?—tearing off a piece and chewing thoughtfully.

She was nothing to me, or so I tried to convince myself. Just another person in a long line of people I'd crossed paths with. But deep down, I knew better. She was more than that, even if I didn't want to admit it.

I watched as she finished the bread, her eyes never leaving mine. There was a strength there, a resilience that reminded me of... no one else I had met in this godforsaken world.

"What?" she asked, raising an eyebrow at my stare.

"Nothing," I grunted, looking away. "Just thinking."

"About what?"

"Doesn't matter."

She sighed and leaned back in her chair, crossing her arms over her chest. "You know, you're not as brooding as you think."

"Oh, yeah?" I challenged.

"Yeah." She looked at me with a mixture of defiance and something else—something softer. "You think I'm too prissy to get my hands dirty. You don't see me as an equal. And I get that. I'm not strong, not physically. And I don't understand a lot of things up here. Yet. But I'm a fast learner. And I'm willing to learn. I... I want this to work. I know it might be a lot to expect you... you to depend on me. It's silly just saying it. But I promise I'm still going to try."

My jaw tightened at her words, but I stayed silent.

"I'm not going to tell you I can take care of myself," she continued. "I mean, if we were back in my bunker, then yes. I'm incredibly independent, and I, myself, have skills. Did you know I can use Runes?"

"Runes?" I asked sardonically.

She nodded. "You wouldn't like them," she said. "They're dangerous for demons. But I'm pretty good at them. And I still want you to teach me how to shoot. And... and s-stab."

"You can't even say the word," I drawled.

"And fight," she said firmly. "All of it. I don't think I can ever be you. But... but I can be *something*."

"You don't know what you're talking about," I finally said, my voice low and rough.

"Maybe not," she admitted. "But I do know this: we're in this together now. Whether you like it or not."

Her words hung in the air between us, heavy and undeniable. Maybe she was right. Maybe we were stuck together in this twisted fate.

But that didn't mean she deserved to be dragged down by someone like me.

I looked at Everly again—really looked at her—and for a moment, saw a flicker of hope amidst the chaos of our lives.

Teach her to fight, to survive out here in the wasteland. Part of me admired her determination, her grit. But another part—the darker part—resented her naivety. She had no idea what she was asking for, what this world demanded from those who dared to live in it.

As if it was so easy.

The men's laughter echoed in my ears again, and I bit down hard on a piece of gristle, feeling it crunch between my teeth. They had seen her as an easy mark, something to be used and discarded. The thought of it made my blood boil, my vision narrow until all I could see was red.

And then there was Everly herself, sitting across from me, eyes wide with determination and maybe a hint of desperation. She wanted so badly to prove herself, to stand on equal footing with me. But this world didn't care about intentions or ideals; it chewed you up and spit you out without a second thought.

I took another bite of stew, chewing mechanically as I glanced at her from beneath lowered brows. She didn't understand yet – didn't understand what survival really meant out here. It wasn't about fairness or equality; it was about who could outlast the next threat, who could be ruthless when needed.

But then again... maybe she could learn. Maybe there was something in her worth nurturing, despite my instincts screaming otherwise.

As I finished off the last of the stew, I looked up at Everly once more. She met my gaze head-on, unflinching. Damn stubborn girl.

The thing was, I wasn't always going to be around to keep an eye out. And I was positive men up here weren't all that different from men in a bunker. I didn't like the thought of her being so helpless... whether she thought she was or not.

I stood up, my chair scraping against the worn wooden floor. "Come on."

Everly downed her water, a puzzled look crossing her face. "Where are we going?"

Ignoring her question, I reached for the half-eaten loaf of bread and some chunks of meat from my stew, wrapping them in a scrap of cloth. Without another word, I headed for the door, the dim light of the tavern casting long shadows across the room.

She followed close behind, her footsteps quickening to match my stride. The cool night air hit us as we stepped outside, a welcome change from the stuffy atmosphere of the tavern. I didn't slow down, moving purposefully through the narrow streets of Ironedge. The place had its fair share of rough edges and lurking dangers, but it also had potential—a place where skills could be honed and lessons learned.

I walked around the corner, leading Everly through the winding paths of Ironedge. The moon cast an eerie glow over the small row of dog houses lined up against the old, weathered wall. I let out a sharp whistle, and Silence emerged from one of them. Her frame was enormous, almost amusing, as she maneuvered out of the cramped space with surprising grace.

I unwrapped the makeshift bundle of food, tossing it in front of her. She sniffed it once before devouring it eagerly. I couldn't help but reach out and pat her head, feeling the warmth and strength beneath her fur.

Silence's presence had a calming effect on me. I didn't want to get attached, but...

I turned back to find Everly staring at me, a soft smile playing on her lips. Her pale green eyes sparkled in the moonlight, and for a moment, something in my chest tightened uncomfortably. It was as if those eyes could see right through me, past my exterior, to whatever fragments of humanity still remained.

I had to look away.

"I knew it," she murmured, her voice barely above a whisper as she followed me again.

"Shut it," I snapped, my voice harsher than intended.

"You do care about her," she continued, undeterred by my tone.

Silence finished her meal and looked up at me expectantly. I patted her head one last time before turning back to Everly.

Everly's smile widened slightly, as if she saw through my

deflection. She didn't press further, though; she simply nodded and kept walking beside me.

The streets of Ironedge were quieter now, most of its inhabitants either asleep or hiding from whatever dangers lurked in the shadows. I led Everly back towards our room at the inn, Silence padding silently behind us.

I could feel Everly's gaze on me as we walked, but I didn't meet it again. There was too much at stake to get distracted by emotions I had no business feeling.

As we approached the inn's entrance, Silence nuzzled my leg briefly before darting off into the night. I watched her go with a mixture of relief and longing – an odd combination that left me feeling even more unsettled than before.

Everly opened the door to our room without a word. She slipped inside while I lingered for just a moment longer outside, letting the cool night air wash over me.

With one last glance at the moonlit streets, I stepped inside. I kicked the door closed behind me; the sound echoing in the small room. The lanterns flickered dimly, casting long shadows on the walls. I didn't want to leave in the morning without teaching her something useful.

"You ready?" I asked, crossing my arms. "Show me your best fighting stance."

She looked at me, eyes wide and sparkling with excitement. "What are we—? Are you serious?" She squealed, a sound that grated on my nerves as much as it caused inexplicable warmth to trickle in slowly.

"Do I look like I'm joking?" I barked at her, my voice harsh and unyielding. "Get your ass in gear!"

Everly straightened up and took a step back, her enthusiasm replaced with determination. She spread her feet shoulder-width apart and raised her fists awkwardly in front of her face. It was... shit.

213

I sighed, shaking my head as I stepped closer to her. "This is pathetic," I muttered. "First off, your feet are too far apart."

I nudged her right foot with my boot, forcing it closer to the other. She wobbled slightly, but managed to keep her balance.

"Your hands," I continued, grabbing her wrists and adjusting them. "You're not blocking anything like this. Tighten up."

She tried to follow my instructions, but it was clear she had no idea what she was doing. Her stance was stiff and unnatural, like a marionette controlled by an inexperienced puppeteer.

"And your posture," I growled, placing a hand on her lower back and pushing gently. "You're leaning too far forward. Keep your center of gravity low and balanced."

She adjusted herself again, a frown of concentration etched on her face. It was an improvement, but still far from perfect.

"Better," I admitted grudgingly. "But you need to move fluidly. Fighting isn't about rigid stances; it's about adapting."

I stepped back and circled around her, watching as she tried to maintain the stance I'd shown her. Her movements were hesitant, uncertain.

"Loosen up," I snapped. "You're too tense."

Everly took a deep breath and let it out slowly, visibly relaxing some of the tension in her body.

"Good," I said, nodding approvingly for once. "Now let's see if you can keep it together when someone's actually trying to hit you."

I stepped closer to Everly, noting the way her breath hitched as I closed the distance. My fingers brushed against her wrist, guiding her hand into a proper fist. Her skin was warm and smooth, a stark contrast to the rough calluses on my own hands. It had been so long since I'd touched anyone like this, since anyone had let me.

"Keep your thumb outside your fingers," I instructed, my voice gruff but quieter now. "You don't want to break it when you punch."

She nodded, adjusting her grip under my guidance. Her eyes met mine briefly, a flicker of something I couldn't quite place before she focused back on her hand.

I moved behind her, my chest almost brushing against her back. "Now, when you throw a punch, you need to use your whole body," I said, placing my hands on her shoulders to turn her slightly. "Not just your arm."

She shivered slightly under my touch, but didn't pull away. I slid one hand down to her waist, feeling the curve of her hip through the thin fabric of her clothes. "Pivot your hips," I murmured, guiding her through the motion. "Like this."

Her movements were hesitant at first, but she gradually found a rhythm under my direction. My other hand remained on her shoulder, steadying her as she practiced.

"That's it," I said softly, surprised at how natural it felt to guide her like this. My fingers traced the line of her collarbone absentmindedly as I adjusted her stance again. Her pulse quickened under my touch, a reminder of just how fragile and alive she was.

I shook off the thought and focused on the task at hand. "Now try hitting something," I told her, stepping back and holding up an old cushion we'd found in the corner of the room.

She hesitated for a moment before drawing back and throwing a punch at the cushion. It wasn't perfect—far from it—but there was strength behind it.

"Again," I ordered.

She hit the cushion again and again, each time improving

215

---

slightly. With every strike, I couldn't help but notice little things about her—the way a strand of hair fell into her eyes, the determined set of her jaw, the faint scent of lavender clinging to her skin.

"Good," I grunted after several attempts. "You're getting there."

She looked up at me then, sweat glistening on her forehead but a triumphant smile on her lips. It stirred something inside me I hadn't felt in years—something dangerously close to hope.

"Thanks," she breathed out.

I nodded curtly, trying to ignore the way my heart beat faster at our proximity. "We're not done yet. Now hit me." I held out my arms in a defensive stance.

Everly's eyes widened. "No."

"Yes," I countered, stepping closer. "You need to practice on a real target."

"I'm not hitting you," she insisted, crossing her arms defiantly.

"If you're not willing to practice, to put in the work, then I won't teach you anything." My voice grew colder. "This is important muscle memory. You need to train your body simply to react."

She glared at me, the defiance in her eyes almost amusing.

I smirked, leaning in slightly. "What's the matter? Afraid you'll break a nail?"

Her eyes narrowed into slits, and I could see the anger boiling just beneath the surface. She took a deep breath, her chest rising and falling as she prepared herself.

"Fine," she snapped. "But don't say I didn't warn you."

She swung at me; her fist aiming for my face with surprising speed and force. But it wasn't enough. I caught her fist with ease, my grip firm but not painful.

"Not bad," I conceded, loosening my hold on her hand. "But this time, actually hit my face, not my hand."

"You're a butt," she muttered under her breath.

"Language," I chided mockingly.

She squared up again, determination etched on her features. This time, when she swung, there was more purpose behind it—more anger. And that was what I needed to see.

Because out here in the wasteland, hesitation could get you killed.

I watched her get ready, the determined look on her face almost laughable. She had no idea what she was doing. I needed to push her, to break through that naivety and get her to react. It was the only way she'd survive out here.

"Come on," I taunted, my voice dripping with contempt. "Is that the best you've got? No wonder you couldn't even catch lunch back out there. No wonder you fainted."

Her eyes flickered with annoyance, but she kept her composure, fists clenched at her sides.

"You're weak," I continued, stepping closer. "Pathetic. You think you can survive out here with that attitude? You're a liability."

Her jaw tightened, but she didn't rise to the bait. Not yet.

"Your sister must be ashamed of you," I spat, watching for the reaction I knew would come.

Her eyes flashed with anger, and she took a step forward, her composure cracking. *That's it.*

I grabbed her wrist and yanked her towards me, pulling her close until we were pressed together. Her breath hitched, and she glared up at me, fury radiating from every pore.

"There you are," I murmured, my voice low and dangerous. "You little viper."

Heat radiated from her body, and she felt so damn soft against me. My eyes dropped to her lips involuntarily; a primal urge surged within me—an urge to claim her, to consume her completely, to crawl into her skin and live there.

She gasped softly, the sound almost lost in the charged air between us. Realization hit me like a sledgehammer—I was holding her too tightly; we were too close. What the hell was going on with me?

I let go of her wrist abruptly, stepping back as if burned. "Go to bed," I snapped, my voice harsher than intended as I turned towards the door.

"I'm not a dog," she shot back with a frown. "Where are you going?"

"A smoke," I replied without looking at her.

The truth was, I needed space—needed to clear my head before I did something else stupid.

As I stepped outside into the cool night air, I inhaled deeply, trying to shake off the feeling of her softness pressed against me. Damn it all to hell—I couldn't afford distractions like this. Not now.

But no matter how hard I tried, the memory of her anger —her fire—stayed with me long after the cigarette had burned down to ash.

CHAPTER 23
Everly

I stared at the door for... I didn't know how long. Minutes? Hours? The wood seemed to blur as my thoughts spiraled. My breaths came fast and shallow, my chest tight with the remnants of anger and frustration.

I couldn't believe I let D get to me. He was pushing, poking at my vulnerabilities. I prided myself on my temper, on keeping it controlled, on being better than the chaos. But maybe that was the point—my pride.

When he brought up Elise, something inside me snapped. All the training, all the meditation exercises—none of it mattered in that moment. The mention of her name broke through every defense I had built.

I clenched my fists, nails digging into my palms until they left crescent-shaped imprints. Was I really so easy to push? It gnawed at me, the realization that my buttons were so easily pressed.

I should be better than that.

The room felt suffocating, the air thick with my failure. D's lessons echoed in my mind—control your emotions, use them, but don't let them use you. Yet here I was, a mess, because someone knew exactly where to strike.

I took a deep breath, trying to steady myself. The door stood as a silent witness to my turmoil.

But it was more than that.

My eyes dropped to my wrist. Even here, I could see the tiny little fingerprints he left imprinted on my skin. I was almost awed by the sight of them. He didn't even realize what he was doing.

And I... I hadn't been scared.

That was what I didn't understand. How was I not scared? A demon had a hold of me, was dragging me to him so my body pressed into his, and then those amber eyes dropped to my mouth and I gasped...

Not because I was scared, but because...

My cheeks turned pink.

Something was wrong with me.

I grabbed my pack and pulled out my pajamas. At least I didn't have to sleep in my uniform tonight. The pajamas were soft, worn cotton—one of the few comforts from the bunker. The shirt was white and had small lavender flowers scattered across it. The pants matched, loose and comfortable with an elastic waistband that hugged gently without pinching.

As I changed, the fabric felt like a whisper against my skin. It brought a small sense of normalcy, a fleeting reminder of simpler times when the biggest concern was whether the hydroponics system needed tweaking or if there'd be enough fresh vegetables for dinner.

But that world felt like a distant dream now. The reality outside the bunker was harsh and unforgiving. Yet here I stood, untouched by fear when confronted by a demon. It made no sense.

I turned away from the door and caught my reflection in the

mirror hanging on the wall. The woman staring back at me was almost unrecognizable. My once-pristine hair, usually tied neatly, now hung in wild tangles around my face. Dark circles underlined my eyes, shadows of sleepless nights and relentless stress.

The most striking change, though, was in my eyes. They had lost their softness, replaced by a hard edge I never thought possible. A few days on the surface had etched lines of worry and fear onto my face. I looked older, more worn.

How could so much change in such a short time? What would happen if it took longer to find Elise than I initially anticipated? The thought sent a shiver down my spine. What if I lost myself to the Forsaken before I found her? What then? Would I even be allowed to go home? Elise had been forced, taken against her will. But me? I chose to leave. There was a difference.

What if you don't want to go home? a voice inside me whispered.

I banished the thought immediately, shaking my head as if to physically dispel it. That wasn't an option. I couldn't afford to think like that. Home was everything I knew, everything I believed in—despite the betrayals.

I left the mirror behind and headed toward the room where D and I were staying. Each step felt heavier than the last, burdened by uncertainty and self-doubt.

But there was no turning back now.

I stood in the doorway of our room, staring at the single bed. The earlier shock had worn off, replaced by a gnawing discomfort. The room was small, barely enough space for two people to move around without bumping into each other. The bed dominated the room, its worn-out mattress sagging slightly in the middle.

D wasn't back from his smoke break yet. I couldn't just stand around and wait for him. The thought of sharing that bed with him made my stomach churn with a mix of unease and something else I couldn't quite name.

I shifted my weight. What did it mean to share a bed with a demon? Was it an implicit agreement of trust? Or just a necessity dictated by circumstance? My mind swirled with questions, each more unsettling than the last.

Could I trust D? He had saved me from the Bone Gnasher, carried me to safety, and even taught me some self-defense. But there was always that underlying tension, that sense of danger whenever he was near. His amber eyes held secrets, and his smirks hinted at intentions I couldn't decipher.

And he was a demon. Demons were bad. The Purifiers were pretty clear, and as far as I knew, there had been no exceptions to this.

Yet, he hadn't harmed me. He'd had plenty of opportunities, but never took advantage. Was that enough to trust him?

I moved from the doorframe over to the bed, chewing my bottom lip. I ran my fingers over the coarse fabric of the blanket, trying to ground myself in something tangible. Sharing this bed didn't have to mean anything beyond practicality. We were both survivors, thrown together by fate in this unforgiving world. Maybe that was all there was to it.

But then again, there were moments—fleeting but real—when I felt something more than mere survival between us. Like when he looked at me after our fight with the Bone Gnasher, or when he taught me how to throw a punch. Moments where his guard slipped just enough for me to see a hint of vulnerability.

Like he *was* an exception, whether The Purifiers knew of one or not. Like he was different.

Was it possible for a demon to have vulnerabilities? Or was I just projecting my own hopes onto him? My head hurt from all the questions, each one circling back to trust.

I sighed and slowly eased in, careful not to disturb his side of the bed. I lay back on the bed, staring at the cracked ceiling above me. Could I really share this bed with D without losing sleep over it? Did I even have a choice?

My thoughts twisted and turned like a restless serpent as I waited for D to return, knowing that this night would test more than just my comfort—it would test my resolve and judgment in ways I hadn't anticipated.

And maybe that was what scared me most of all.

I had to be stronger, smarter. This world required more than what I'd learned in the bunker. And maybe... maybe it required facing parts of myself I didn't fully understand yet.

The shadows danced across the ceiling from the flickering light outside the window. Tomorrow would bring new challenges—new tests of strength and will.

For now, though, I let myself sink into the comfort of my old pajamas and closed my eyes, hoping for dreams that wouldn't haunt me with questions I couldn't yet answer.

Sleep evaded me, taunting me with the promise of rest just out of reach. I lay there, eyes closed, trying to will myself into slumber. But my mind refused to quiet, thoughts swirling like a storm. Every creak and groan of the old building seemed amplified in the stillness.

Then the door creaked open. I froze, every muscle tensing as the sound echoed in the small room. The door clicked shut softly, and I heard footsteps—measured, deliberate. I recognized them immediately. D's footsteps.

How did I already know the way he walked? It hadn't been that long since we met, but somehow his presence had etched itself into my senses.

The other side of the bed dipped under his weight. One soft thud—a boot hitting the floor—then another. There was a clump of something hitting the ground—his duster, maybe? The sounds were oddly comforting in their familiarity.

He lay down next to me, taking up so much space in the

small bed without touching me. My heart pounded so loudly in my chest that I was sure he could hear it. Surely he could.

But he didn't say anything.

The subtle hint of smoke clung to him, mixed with something else—a scent that was uniquely his. It was earthy, like freshly turned soil after rain, with a faint metallic tang that reminded me of iron. The combination was strangely soothing.

I could feel his warmth radiating next to me, an invisible blanket that chased away the chill in the room. It was a comfort I hadn't expected to find in this forsaken place, from a demon, no less.

Somehow... somehow that warmth was enough to lull me into sleep.

My thoughts slowed, and my breathing steadied as I drifted off, surrendering to the pull of exhaustion. The questions and doubts faded into the background, replaced by the simple reality of shared space and quiet companionship.

* * *

I woke up to the feeling of something heavy across my waist. Groggy, I shifted slightly, only to feel the weight tighten in response.

My brow furrowed.

The pillow beneath my head felt warmer than I expected. A gentle rise and fall moved against my cheek, the rhythm soothing and steady.

It took a moment for my brain to catch up with my senses. I hadn't slept this well in... forever; it seemed. Not even in the bunker had sleep come so easily or felt this restful.

Then it hit me. I had moved in my sleep. My eyes snapped open, and I realized where I was—where *we* were. D's arms were wrapped around me, holding me close. My head rested on his chest, the thud of his heartbeat resonating beneath my ear. One of my legs was draped over his, our limbs tangled together like vines.

I lay still, trying to process the situation without panicking. His arm tightened around my waist as if sensing my thoughts, but he remained asleep, his breathing deep and even.

This was... unexpected.

The pragmatic part of me wanted to untangle myself and put some distance between us. But another part—a part I didn't fully understand—found comfort in this closeness, in the warmth and security of his embrace.

My gaze traveled up to his face, taking in the lines of his jaw and the way he looked so young in sleep. There was a softness to his expression that I hadn't seen before, a vulnerability hidden beneath the hard exterior he always presented.

He was...

I took a slow breath, trying to steady myself. This moment —this strange intimacy—was fleeting, but it felt significant somehow. Maybe it was just the exhaustion finally catching up with me, or maybe it was something more.

But for now, I decided not to overthink it. I closed my eyes again and let myself relax into him, savoring this rare moment of peace before the chaos of the world outside intruded once more.

Was it wrong to feel this way being held by him?

Did that make me a sinner?

I... I didn't know. But surely God couldn't condemn me for... this. Could He? And maybe... maybe it gave D some comfort too?

It was a small respite—a brief escape from the harsh reality we faced—but it was enough to remind me that even in a world as broken as ours, there could still be moments of quiet connection and unexpected solace.

Without warning, D shifted beside me. I stilled, not

wanting him to know I was awake, not wanting him to know I was okay with this in case he wasn't. His arm, which had been a comforting weight around my waist, began to move. My heartbeat pounded in my ears, each thump a reminder of the precariousness of our situation.

Would he catch me pretending to sleep? And if he did...?

He stirred slowly, the movement careful and deliberate. I felt him stiffen as the realization of our position dawned on him. My breath caught in my throat, and I waited for him to pull away abruptly, to sever this fragile connection we had unintentionally formed.

But he didn't.

Instead, his fingertips brushed against my cheek, a light touch that sent shivers down my spine. They traced a path down to my jaw, lingering for just a moment. It was a touch so gentle, so unlike the rough exterior he usually presented.

"Fuck," he whispered, the word barely audible in the quiet room.

Then, with an almost reluctant slowness, he pulled away and stood up. The warmth of his body left me instantly missing his heat. The bed felt emptier, colder without him there.

I kept my eyes closed, maintaining the pretense of sleep as I listened to him move around the room. His footsteps were soft but purposeful, a stark contrast to the turmoil inside me.

What the hell was going on with me?

I didn't know.

I heard D pull on his boots, the soft creak of leather cutting through the stillness. He moved with a quiet efficiency, each step purposeful but not rushed. I kept my eyes closed, feigning sleep as he stepped into the bathroom.

It was still dark outside. I didn't know what time it was, but it felt too early to be awake. The sound of running water reached my ears—he was using the faucet. Brushing his teeth?

Washing his face? I had no idea, and it bothered me more than it should.

The faucet turned off, and he moved back into the room. For a moment, there was silence. What was he doing? I wished I knew. Every fiber of my being wanted to open my eyes and look at him, to see what occupied his attention. But I couldn't bring myself to do it. Instead, I lay there, heart pounding in my chest, waiting.

A low sigh, and then... the creak of the door. The click of it shut.

He was gone, and the room felt emptier than before. A wave of unexpected longing washed over me. Where was he going? What job had they given him here in Ironedge? And more importantly, when would he be back?

I rolled over onto my back and stared up at the ceiling, the darkness pressing in around me. The bed felt vast and cold without him beside me. My thoughts churned with questions and uncertainties.

I sighed softly and closed my eyes again, trying to push those thoughts aside. There would be time for answers later, time to understand what this all meant. For now, I needed to rest, to gather my strength for today. I'd be going to find a couple of jobs... after getting my feet checked out by Wendy. I'd get paid, and I'd show him just how capable I was.

But even as I tried to drift back to sleep, my mind lingered on D—the man who had saved me, fought beside me, and held me through the night without realizing it.

And suddenly, despite everything we faced in this harsh world, I found myself hoping he'd come back soon.

CHAPTER 24

Walton

I stepped out of the inn, my fingers already fumbling for a cigarette. The air was cool, still holding onto the night's chill. I lit up; the flame flickering briefly before it caught. I leaned against the rough wooden wall, taking a deep drag. Dawn was barely breaking, the sky painted in shades of gray and faint orange.

The settlement of Ironedge was silent, wrapped in a heavy stillness that felt almost sacred. No movement except for the slow, deliberate rise of smoke from chimneys. The streets were empty, not even a stray dog nosing around for scraps. It was a rare moment of peace in a world gone to hell.

I needed to get away from Everly, from her warmth that clung to me like an unwanted memory. What had happened back there? Why had I been holding her like... that? My fingers tightened around the cigarette, the ember flaring angrily.

She must not have realized it. Must have sought warmth in her sleep, probably thinking I was just another pillow. The thought made my stomach twist. I didn't want to imagine her reaction when she woke up and found herself in my arms. Best she never even know I'd been in the bed in the first place.

The sky lightened gradually, casting soft shadows across the buildings. A few early risers started to stir within their homes, but it would be a while before anyone stepped outside. It gave me time to think, to try to push down the confusion swirling inside me.

Everly wasn't like anyone I'd met before. Too trusting for her own good, too damn stubborn about doing things right. And yet... there was something about her that made me question everything I'd come to accept about this godforsaken world.

I took another drag, letting the smoke fill my lungs before exhaling slowly. It was best to keep my distance, to stay focused on what mattered: revenge and survival. Getting her sister and getting my damned soul back. Anything else was a distraction I couldn't afford.

But even as I stood there, staring at the growing light in the sky, I couldn't shake the feeling of her warmth against me or the way she had fit so naturally in my arms.

Dammit.

I crushed the cigarette under my boot and turned back towards the inn. It was time to get moving before she woke up and complicated things even more than they already were.

I headed towards the entrance of the settlement, my steps heavy against the dirt. Silence trotted alongside me, her glowing red eyes watching every shadow and corner. I rummaged around in my pack, pulling out a piece of stale jerky. The taste of it had long turned to dust in my mouth, but it would do.

"Stay," I told Silence, holding out the jerky. "Keep an eye on her."

The hellhound sat obediently, her eyes fixed on the inn where Everly still slept. She snorted, almost like she was agreeing to my command.

I straightened up, huffing out a breath. The thought of

leaving Everly behind gnawed at me, but there was no other choice.

I moved to the entrance, already feeling the tension in my shoulders tighten. The guards there were always a pain in the ass. As I approached, one of them straightened and gave me a hard look.

"You going to get the scavengers, Hellspawn?" he asked.

I grunted in response, not feeling up to any small talk or insults this morning.

The second guard smirked. "Maybe you do us a favor and kill them and die there too, hmm? Maybe you leave the girl alone so you can't get your paws on her."

I stopped and looked at him, recognizing him from the tavern last night. My fingers itched towards the hilt of my gun, narrowing my eyes at him. I didn't like leaving Everly behind with an asshole like this hanging around.

"Give me a reason," I said through gritted teeth, fingers wrapping around the handle of my gun.

"Maybe your girl will turn to a real man to comfort her, huh?" The second guard spat on the ground near my feet.

The first guard looked uneasy. "Come on, man," he said to his companion. "He's doing us a favor."

"If he really wanted to do that, he'd die," the second guard sneered. "They're an abomination." He spat again for emphasis.

My grip tightened around my gun's handle. It took everything in me not to pull it out and end this right here and now. But I couldn't afford any distractions or additional enemies— not now.

Not when Everly was there.

"Touch her," I said slowly, "and I'll make it slow."

With a final glare at the guard, I turned away and headed out into the wasteland. Silence would watch over Everly. She'd be safe until I got back.

But that didn't make walking away any easier.

I trudged through the wasteland, the sun already high in the sky. It beat down relentlessly, turning the desert into an unforgiving furnace. The landscape stretched out in every direction, a barren sea of sand and rock, broken only by the occasional dead tree or crumbling ruin.

The air was dry, each breath feeling like I was inhaling dust. Sweat trickled down my back, evaporating almost instantly. The only sound was the crunch of my boots on the cracked earth and the distant howl of wind sweeping across the dunes.

I kept my pace steady, wanting to cover as much ground as possible before the heat became unbearable. The sooner I dealt with this scavenger camp, the sooner I could get back to Ironedge and make sure Everly was safe. Not that I cared about her—no, it was more practical than that.

If anything happened to her, Elise would never willingly come with me. And I needed her cooperation to complete my mission and finally get some semblance of peace. Leaving Everly behind wasn't ideal, but it was a necessary risk. I didn't want anything to happen to her during this job. And I didn't need to owe anymore to Ironedge than I already did.

The landscape remained desolate, each step a reminder of how far humanity had fallen. The sun's rays reflected off the sand, creating mirages that danced on the horizon. I ignored them, focusing on putting one foot in front of the other.

The desert seemed endless, an expanse of nothingness that stretched on forever. Occasionally, I'd spot a rusted-out vehicle half-buried in sand or the skeletal remains of some long-dead creature. Each sighting was a reminder of the harshness of this world and the fragility of life within it.

My thoughts kept drifting back to Everly, despite my efforts to push them away. Her determination and naïveté were a dangerous mix out here. She needed someone to watch her back—someone who knew how to survive in this hellscape. And unfortunately for me, that someone was me.

I glanced up at the sky, noting the sun's position. Half a day had passed since I left Ironedge. Time moved differently out here; each hour felt like an eternity under the relentless sun.

I hoped this raid would be quick and clean—no unnecessary complications. Get in, take them out, get back to Ironedge before nightfall if possible. But things rarely went according to plan in this world.

My grip tightened on my weapon as I pressed on through the desert heat, determined to finish this task and return before any harm could come to Everly or jeopardize my mission any further.

The heat played tricks on my eyes. Ahead, I saw a shimmering oasis—a mirage, I knew, but the sight of water glinting under the sun was tempting. As I got closer, it flickered and vanished, leaving only endless sand.

I cursed under my breath, stopping to take a swig from my canteen. The water was warm, tasting of metal and dust, but it was life out here.

I should've known better than to trust my eyes in this godforsaken place. My throat burned as I swallowed, the liquid doing little to quench my thirst.

You shouldn't be anywhere near that girl, came a voice from my right.

I froze, muscles tensing as if struck by lightning. Slowly, I turned my head.

There she was—Betty. My Betty. Her piercing blue eyes stared at me with an intensity that cut through the heat and the haze.

No. Not anymore.

My jaw clenched so tight it felt like it might shatter. "You,"

I rasped, though there was no one there. Just the desert and the sun playing tricks again.

How long had it been since I'd seen her? One hundred years? It felt like an eternity. She looked exactly as she had back then—determined and unyielding, even like this.

"Why?" I muttered to the empty air, as if she could hear me through time and space. "Why did you do it?"

The question lingered in my mind, heavy and unanswered. Did she feel guilty for betraying me? For taking Emma away from me? After what I did? After what I sacrificed?

The thought of Emma sent a fresh wave of rage coursing through me. My hands trembled as they gripped my weapon tighter.

My anger fueled me, pushing away the ghostly image that taunted me. Betty's form flickered one last time before dissolving into nothingness, just another mirage in this endless desert.

I shook off the remnants of the vision and kept moving forward, each step driven by a fire that would never be quenched until justice—or vengeance—was served.

The desert stretched on before me, unforgiving and eternal. But so was my resolve.

I pressed on through the wasteland, leaving behind memories and ghosts that would not let me rest until every score was settled. My thoughts drifted back to Everly, to the way her hair fanned around her head like some damn halo. The memory of it made my chest tighten, and I clenched my teeth, trying to push it away.

I didn't want to think about her. Not about those dinner plate eyes that looked at me like I wasn't a monster, but just another person. Like I had some semblance of humanity left in me.

Her fierce determination when she fought kept replaying in my mind. The way she threw herself into the fray, unafraid and relentless. The easy way to piss her off had become almost a game—a dangerous one—but a game, nonetheless.

And then there were those little moments that haunted me more than they should. Her drool on my shoulder, her breath warm against my neck as she slept. How I could count the freckles on her cheeks in the dim light of dawn.

Fuck, what was going on with me?

I stopped for a moment, rubbing a hand over my face, feeling the grit and grime of the desert under my fingers. This wasn't who I was. I was supposed to be focused on revenge, on getting my soul back—not getting caught up in whatever this was with Everly.

But no matter how hard I tried to shake it off, she kept creeping back into my thoughts. It made no sense. She was just another job—a means to an end. Yet somehow, she'd wormed her way past all the walls I'd built up over the years.

I shook my head, trying to clear it. I needed to focus on the task at hand—taking out that scavenger camp and getting back before nightfall. Everly could take care of herself for a few hours.

But even as I pressed on through the unforgiving landscape, I couldn't help but wonder what she was doing right now.

Was she still asleep? Had she woken up alone and confused? Had that bastard guard tried anything?

Damn it.

I forced myself to keep moving, one foot in front of the other. There was no room for distractions out here—no room for anything except survival and vengeance.

Yet the thought of Everly stayed with me, gnawing at the edges of my mind like an itch I couldn't scratch.

And that scared me more than any demon ever could.

I spotted the scavenger camp in the distance, a cluster of ramshackle tents and makeshift barricades. It was nestled in a small valley, surrounded by jagged rocks that offered both protection and concealment. Smoke curled lazily from a central fire pit, the scent of burning wood mingling with the acrid tang of sweat and grime.

I crouched behind a boulder, scanning the encampment through narrowed eyes. A few figures moved around—guards, by the looks of it—armed with rusty rifles and makeshift spears. They seemed relaxed, probably not expecting trouble this deep into the wasteland. But that complacency would be their downfall.

I noted the positions of the guards: two at the entrance, one patrolling the perimeter, and another near the central fire. They were spread thin, making it easier to pick them off one by one.

The camp was surrounded by debris—broken crates, rusted barrels, and twisted metal remnants of a time long past. It offered plenty of cover but also potential hazards. I'd have to be careful not to alert them too soon.

My eyes landed on a small tent near the back, slightly apart from the others. That would be where they kept their loot— or perhaps their leader. Either way, it was my main target.

I needed a plan that maximized my strengths: stealth and surprise. Charging in headfirst was suicide; I'd be outnumbered and outgunned. No, I had to play this smart.

First, I'd take out the perimeter guard—quietly. A quick slit to the throat or a silenced shot if necessary. Then I'd move to the entrance guards, taking them down before they could raise an alarm.

With the entrance secured, I'd slip into the camp proper, using the debris for cover. The central guard by the fire would be next—he seemed distracted enough with whatever he was cooking.

Finally, I'd make my way to that isolated tent and deal with whoever or whatever was inside.

It wasn't a foolproof plan—nothing ever was in this world —but it gave me a fighting chance. And right now, that was all I needed.

I checked my gear one last time: knife secured at my belt, gun loaded and ready. Taking a deep breath, I steadied myself.

Time to move.

Keeping low and silent as death itself, I began my approach toward the scavenger camp, every sense on high alert for any sign of trouble.

CHAPTER 25

Everly

I waited until I heard D's footsteps fade down the hallway. The silence that followed seemed to amplify the beat of my heart. I held my breath, hoping he'd come back, but not understanding why. His absence left a void that the walls of this room couldn't fill.

Why did I feel safe in his arms? His warmth, his solid presence—it was all too much and yet not enough. I glanced around the small room in Ironedge, its rough wooden walls and meager furnishings offering no comfort. This was a settlement with humans, people like me, but their presence felt like shadows compared to his.

I didn't even know his real name.

How long was this job going to take? My thoughts spun around that question. He'd left without giving any details, just that I couldn't come because I'd be a liability. The gnawing irritation grew as I realized he never really explained what the job entailed in the first place. Just vague mentions of a raider camp, and now he was off, leaving me to wonder if he'd come back in one piece.

I clenched my fists, feeling the roughness of the bandages

against my palms. He had taken care of me, sewn up my wounds after the Bone Gnasher fight, carried me through the heat when I collapsed. And now he was out there alone.

I threw off the cover and sat up. I knew I needed to check in with my doctor, but then I was going to make some shards. I was going to show D that I could work, that I could earn my place.

I moved to the window, looking out at Ironedge's dusty streets. Settlers went about their business, unaware of the storm churning inside me. A part of me wanted to march out there and find D myself; another part knew I had to stay put and wait.

But waiting had never been my strong suit.

I sighed and sank onto the bed we'd shared—just one bed for both of us, creating a closeness I didn't know how to interpret. My fingers traced the edge of the blanket absentmindedly as memories of waking up in his arms flooded back. It wasn't just safety; it was something more elusive, something that made my chest tighten and thoughts blur.

I sighed, the weight of my thoughts pressing down on me. I couldn't keep waiting around for him, hoping he'd return unscathed. I had to do something—anything to keep myself from going crazy with worry.

I stood and made my way to the restroom. The cold water splashing against my face felt refreshing, a temporary reprieve from the storm inside me. I washed up quickly, determined to keep moving. Staring at my reflection for a moment longer than necessary, I wondered what D saw when he looked at me. Was I just another burden to him?

With a shake of my head, I dismissed the thought and headed downstairs. The inn's common area buzzed with the hum of settlers' conversations and clinking dishes. I crossed through it without pausing, pushing open the door to the clinic across the street.

Silence was there, her sleek black fur catching the sunlight streaming through the windows. As soon as she saw me, her tail started wagging furiously, and she trotted over.

"Hey there," I said, a genuine smile tugging at my lips as I knelt down to pet her. "You're such a good girl." Silence licked my hand in response, her eyes full of warmth and loyalty.

A couple of people looked at Silence and nearly tripped over nothing. One crossed herself while the other screeched.

"She's really quite friendly," I tried to assure them, but they hurried their steps to avoid us.

I pursed my lips as I continued to stroke her fur, turning my attention back to her. "Why didn't D take you with him?" The question hung in the air, unanswered and troubling.

I tried not to worry about him. I didn't know him well, but what I did know suggested he was skilled—he had a reputation that preceded him. Still, the uncertainty gnawed at me.

Silence nuzzled closer, sensing my unease. Her presence was comforting in a way that words couldn't describe. She seemed content just being near me, which was more than I could say for myself at that moment.

Taking a deep breath, I straightened up and gave Silence one last pat on the head before stepping into the clinic.

Silence stayed outside, her sleek black fur glistening in the sunlight as she lay down by the clinic's entrance. I gave her one last look before stepping inside, feeling a pang of guilt for leaving her behind.

The clinic was modest but clean. Sunlight streamed through the windows, casting warm golden patches on the wooden floor. Shelves lined the walls, filled with various medical supplies and books that looked well-used. The scent of antiseptic hung in the air, mingling with the faint aroma of herbs from a small potted plant on a counter.

I took in the details, appreciating the simplicity and functionality of the space. It was a far cry from the sterile, clinical environment of the bunker, yet it felt more welcoming. There was a sense of life here, of people genuinely caring for each other's well-being.

Wendy appeared from behind a curtain, her smile bright and genuine. "Thanks for coming," she said, her voice warm. "I wanted to get a look at your feet before you leave." She glanced around. "Where's your... friend?"

Friend? I wasn't sure D wanted to be my friend, but I wasn't going to correct her. "He's doing the job," I said.

"Oh, yes." Wendy nodded understandingly. "Come on back."

As I followed Wendy into the exam room, curiosity gnawed at me. "What exactly is the job?" I asked.

Wendy led me to a chair and patted its cushioned seat. "He didn't tell you?" she asked, raising an eyebrow as she prepared some instruments.

I shook my head, my ponytail swishing behind me. "No, he didn't."

"Huh," Wendy murmured as she knelt to examine my feet. Her fingers were gentle but firm as she checked for any signs of infection or injury. The cool touch of her hands was soothing against my skin.

The silence between us stretched out as Wendy continued her work, her expression thoughtful. I couldn't help but feel a mix of frustration and concern. Why hadn't D told me more about his plans? What if something went wrong?

Wendy finished her examination and stood up, giving me a reassuring smile. "You're healing well," she said. "Just keep those bandages clean and dry."

"Thank you," I replied, feeling grateful for her care.

She nodded and began tidying up her supplies.

"He's going to take out a raider camp a few miles north of here," Wendy said, her voice matter-of-fact.

"What?" I asked, more sharply than I intended.

Wendy paused, looking me in the eye. "Girls disappear almost constantly, a few times a month at least," she explained. "We never see them again. We think..." She looked away, her expression darkening. "Well, it doesn't matter what we think. He's going to take them out."

"You're just going to let him go alone?" My voice wavered with anger I didn't fully understand. This wasn't like me. I struggled to keep my emotions in check.

She raised an eyebrow. "I don't think you know who you're traveling with," she said, her tone calm but firm. "He's a demon, yes, but he's the Brimstone Stalker. He's the best bounty hunter that belongs to the devil himself."

I flinched at the mention of the devil. It was so easy to forget his existence, but then I inwardly chastised myself for being so naïve.

"He can handle himself," she added before turning back to her paperwork.

"But what if he can't?" The words slipped out before I could stop them, my voice tinged with worry.

She gave me a long, measured look. "Then one less demon in the world," she said coldly.

"How can you say that?" I asked, feeling a surge of indignation. "He's helping you."

"No." Wendy shook her head slowly. "He's helping himself. And you, I suspect. He needs payment. This is how he earns it. You forget, honey, he's a demon. He knowingly and willingly sold his soul to Lucifer. He's not a good man. Hell, he's not a man at all." She paused, her eyes hardening with resolve. "And if I can utilize his skill and get rid of evil, then I'm going to do it to protect this place—these people."

I took in a breath and another, feeling the tension coil tighter inside me. Clenching my teeth, I turned toward the door without another word.

Wendy looked at me with a mix of pity and concern. "I would consider staying."

"I can't do that," I said, my voice firmer than I felt.

"Don't think about going after him," she warned, her eyes narrowing. "It's too dangerous for someone like you even during the day, but especially at night."

I clenched my teeth, frustration boiling beneath my skin. Right. Because I was weak. Pathetic. I kept forgetting how I must look to others—a girl from a bunker, inexperienced and naïve.

"Jobs," I blurted out, needing something to focus on other than my anger and worry for D. "Is there somewhere I can... I don't know... find work? Not the intercourse kind."

Wendy furrowed her brows, considering my question. "Um... well, there's a bulletin board in the middle of the settlement with postings," she said slowly. "You can check there."

"Thank you," I replied politely, standing up and smoothing out my clothes.

The room felt stifling now, filled with unspoken judgments and warnings. Wendy returned to her paperwork without another word, leaving me to navigate this new reality on my own.

As I walked out of the clinic, Silence rose to her feet and walked over to me. "Come on," I muttered, heading down the street with Silence trotting by my side. The air felt heavy with unsaid words and unspoken fears.

I made my way toward the center of Ironedge, feeling the weight of everyone's eyes on me as settlers went about their business. The bulletin board stood near a well-worn path, a cluttered mess of papers and notices pinned haphazardly.

My fingers brushed against a few postings—manual labor, farmhand positions, someone looking for help repairing a roof. Each one seemed mundane but essential in this harsh world.

I read through them carefully, considering which might suit me best while Silence sat by my side.

How could Wendy be so dismissive? Yes, D was a demon now—but there was more to him than that. There had to be.

I stood before the bulletin board, my fingers brushing against the slips of paper. Each one represented a chance to prove myself, to earn my keep. I took a deep breath and picked three that seemed promising: repairing a fence, helping in the fields, and assisting at the blacksmith's forge.

The first job took me to the outskirts of Ironedge, where an elderly man named Harold needed help mending his fence. The wooden posts were weathered and worn, some leaning precariously.

"Morning," Harold greeted me, wiping his brow with a dirty rag. "You're here for the fence?"

I nodded, rolling up my sleeves. "Yes, sir. If you'll have me."

The sun beat down on us as we worked side by side. I dug new holes for the posts while Harold showed me how to properly align and secure them. The rhythm of the work felt soothing—dig, place, hammer—and before long, the fence stood tall and sturdy once more.

Harold handed me a small pouch filled with demon shards. "Thank you, young lady. This should cover your efforts."

"Thank you," I replied, pocketing the shards with a sense of accomplishment.

Next, I made my way to the fields where a group of farmers needed extra hands for harvesting. Rows upon rows of crops stretched out before me—corn, potatoes, and beans swaying gently in the breeze.

"Glad you could join us," a woman named Mara said as she handed me a basket. "We're short on help today."

I got to work, bending and picking until my back ached

and my hands were stained with dirt. The hours passed quickly in the company of others working toward a common goal. We shared stories and laughter amidst the toil.

When we finished for the day, Mara handed me another pouch of demon shards. "You did good work today," she said with a smile.

"Thanks," I replied, feeling pride swell within me.

The final job brought me to the blacksmith's forge, where a burly man named Jebediah awaited my assistance. The heat from the forge was intense as he worked on shaping metal into tools and weapons.

"Ever handled a hammer before?" Jebediah asked with a grin.

"Not like this," I admitted, taking up the heavy tool.

He showed me how to strike the heated metal just right—each blow ringing out like music against the anvil. The physicality of it was challenging but invigorating. Sparks flew as we worked together until sweat dripped down our faces.

When we finished, Jebediah clapped me on the back and handed over another pouch of shards. "Not bad for your first time," he said approvingly.

"Thank you," I replied gratefully.

As I walked back toward the inn with my earnings jingling in my pocket, Silence trotted beside me. Each job had been hard work but rewarding in its own way—a testament that I could contribute and survive in this harsh world on my terms.

The weight of the pouches jingled in my pocket, a small triumph that I couldn't wait to share with D. As I neared the inn, my heart pounded with anticipation. He would be proud —or at least, I hoped he would be.

I pushed open the door and scanned the room. But there was an empty space where he should have been. My excitement wavered, replaced by a growing unease.

"Where is he?" I whispered to myself, glancing around as if he might suddenly materialize from the shadows.

The sun had started its descent, casting long shadows across Ironedge. Dusk was fast approaching, and with it, a sense of urgency gnawed at me. My stomach growled loudly, reminding me that I hadn't eaten since morning.

I headed towards the tavern, hoping that by the time I returned, D would be back. I could almost picture him leaning against the doorframe, arms crossed and a smirk playing on his lips.

Dirty up your dainty hands, angel? he'd ask sardonically.

The tavern was bustling with activity as settlers unwound after a long day's work. I made my way to the counter and ordered a simple meal—stew and bread. The food arrived quickly, but as I sat down to eat, my mind wandered.

I stared at the bowl in front of me, steam curling up in delicate tendrils. I took a bite but tasted nothing. The rich flavors that had delighted me yesterday now seemed muted and distant. Every mouthful felt like an obligation rather than nourishment.

My thoughts kept drifting back to D. What if something had happened? What if he was in trouble? The worry gnawed at me more persistently than hunger ever could.

I forced myself to eat mechanically, each bite a hollow gesture as my mind raced with possibilities. The lively chatter around me faded into background noise—just an indistinct hum that only heightened my sense of isolation.

I glanced at the door every few minutes, hoping against hope that he'd walk through it any moment now. But each time it swung open, it revealed only strangers—people lost in their own worlds of toil and survival.

My heart sank lower with each passing minute. The pouches of demon shards in my pocket felt heavier than ever before, their significance dwindling without someone to share them with.

When I finished eating—or rather, when I couldn't force down another bite—I stood up and made my way back to the inn. Each step felt weighted with worry and dread.

I knelt down and patted Silence on the head. She must have sensed my unease because she licked my hand, her rough tongue a small comfort in the growing twilight. I broke off a piece of the dinner roll that came with my meal and handed it to her. "Here, girl," I murmured, watching as she eagerly devoured it.

Straightening up, I headed towards our room, each step heavier than the last. The inn's wooden floor creaked beneath my boots, echoing the weight of my worries. As I reached the door, I paused for a moment, gathering my thoughts.

"Please, God," I whispered under my breath. "Let him be here. Let him be safe." The words felt like they were being pulled from somewhere deep within me, raw and desperate.

I turned the handle and stepped inside. The room was dimly lit by the last rays of sunlight filtering through the window. My eyes scanned the space quickly, hoping to find D there.

But it was empty.

Tears prickled at the corners of my eyes. It felt like God wasn't listening to me. The emptiness of the room mirrored the emptiness growing inside me.

I had never felt like this.

God had always been with me.

Until I left...

Sucking in a shaky breath, I fought to keep my composure. "If he's not here by dawn," I whispered to myself, "I'll go after him." I had no idea how I'd find him, especially on my own, but I had to try.

I walked to the small bathroom at the back of our room.

The sink was old but functional. Grabbing my toothbrush from my bag, I brushed my teeth mechanically, each stroke a distraction from the gnawing worry in my chest.

I wished for a shower, but knew there wasn't one available. The grime of the day clung to me like a second skin.

After changing into my pajamas, I crawled into bed, making sure to leave room on his side just in case he returned during the night. The bed felt too big without him there, too empty.

"Please," I whispered into the darkness as I lay down, closing my eyes tightly. "Just let him be okay."

I prayed that sleep would come fast and bring some respite from my worries. But that was another prayer that went unanswered as I lay there in silence, staring at the ceiling and waiting for dawn to break.

CHAPTER 26

Walton

I moved like a shadow through the encampment, each step deliberate and measured. The perimeter guard never saw me coming. I wrapped my arm around his neck, clamping my hand over his mouth, and drew my knife across his throat. He gurgled, eyes wide with surprise, before slumping lifelessly in my grip. I lowered him to the ground gently, ensuring no noise betrayed my presence.

One down.

I crept closer to the camp, my senses tuned to every rustle and whisper of the wind. The entrance guards were chatting idly, their attention elsewhere. They never noticed the slight shift in the shadows as I approached.

With a swift motion, I lunged at the first guard, driving my knife into his back. He crumpled without a sound. The second guard turned just in time to see me coming, but not fast enough to react. A single shot from my silenced gun ended him before he could raise an alarm.

Three down.

The central guard by the fire was distracted, poking at whatever sorry excuse for food he was cooking. I slipped through the debris, using broken crates and rusted barrels as cover. When I reached him, he looked up too late—my knife was already buried in his chest.

Four down.

I wiped the blade on my pant leg and made my way toward the isolated tent at the back of the camp. My heart pounded in my chest—not from fear or exertion, but from something else entirely. The thought of getting back to Ironedge by day's end gnawed at me in ways it shouldn't.

Maybe Everly and I would grab stew at the tavern. Maybe I'd teach her more self-defense moves. The thought made something in my chest skip—a feeling I didn't like one bit. I wasn't supposed to look forward to anything anymore.

This girl was changing me in ways I couldn't afford. It was dangerous, this attachment that seemed to be growing despite all reason.

In and out—that was all this should be.

It should be easy.

I reached the tent and paused, listening for any sounds inside. There was movement—a rustling that indicated someone or something was within. Steeling myself, I pulled back the flap and stepped inside, ready for whatever awaited me.

No room for distractions now—just finish the job and get back to Ironedge before nightfall.

But even as I moved with purpose, Everly's face kept creeping into my mind, making me wonder what she was doing right now and hoping she'd be safe until I returned.

I moved silently through the camp, each step a calculated effort to remain undetected. My senses were heightened, my body taut with anticipation. I spotted another guard patrolling near a stack of crates. His posture was relaxed, oblivious to the death that stalked him.

I crept up behind him, my knife at the ready. With a swift,

practiced motion, I clamped my hand over his mouth and drove the blade into his kidney. He gasped, eyes wide with shock and pain, but his struggle was brief. He slumped against me, and I lowered him gently to the ground.

Five down.

I continued deeper into the camp, navigating through the maze of tents and makeshift structures. My objective was clear: eliminate the raiders and return to Ironedge before nightfall. Each kill brought me closer to that goal.

I reached a larger tent at the center of the camp. The fabric walls were patched and worn, and dim light seeped through the gaps. I could hear faint whispers inside—voices hushed in fear.

I pulled back the flap and stepped inside, my knife at the ready. The sight that greeted me made me pause.

Two girls huddled in a corner, their eyes wide with terror. One looked to be in her thirties, her face lined with worry and exhaustion. The other was young—no older than Everly. Early twenties, if that. They clung to each other, trembling.

For a moment, I saw Everly's face superimposed on theirs —scared and vulnerable, tied up for reasons too terrible to contemplate. Anger surged through me like molten lava, burning away my resolve to remain detached.

"D-Don't hurt us," the older woman stammered, her voice shaking.

I gritted my teeth, fighting against the wave of emotions crashing over me. I didn't care about these people—couldn't afford to care. They were just another obstacle in my path.

But something inside me shifted—a crack in the armor I'd built around my heart.

"Go on then," I growled, my voice rougher than usual.

The girls exchanged confused glances, but didn't move. I clenched my fists, hating myself for what I was about to do.

"Now!" I barked, taking a step closer.

I studied the two women, their fear palpable in the dim light of the tent. The older one's eyes were hard, defiant, while the younger one looked like a rabbit caught in a trap.

"You think we're going to risk escaping?" the older one challenged, her voice trembling. "Shelly did just that, and they gutted her. But not before they..." She swallowed hard, tears welling up in her eyes. "They made sure we heard her cries, her begging them to stop. And then... nothing. We're not leaving."

"They're dead," I said, my voice a low growl. "The guards."

"You think just because you're a demon, you can stop them?" The woman's tone was bitter. "You think demons are evil? I've looked into her eyes. Lucifer himself wouldn't want her because she doesn't have a soul. No." She shook her head with finality. "We ain't leaving. Not unless you can show me her head."

Her? I pursed my lips, processing this new information.

"How many are there?" I asked, my patience wearing thin.

"Why do you care, demon?" The younger one sneered, though it was more fearful than intimidating.

"I was sent to do a job," I replied gruffly. "And I'm wasting time chit-chatting with you. I've already taken out six."

"Her?" The older woman's voice wavered with hope and despair intermingled.

I shook my head slowly.

"Then it doesn't matter," she spat, anger and resignation in her eyes.

"How many guards?" I asked again.

The two women exchanged glances, their fear mingling with uncertainty.

"I think... eight," the younger one said hesitantly. "Total."

"Maybe nine," the older one corrected. "We don't know for sure."

I grunted in acknowledgment, weighing my options. Time was slipping away, and every second spent here was a second closer to nightfall—and to whatever hell awaited me if I didn't complete this mission on time.

I turned back to the women, locking eyes with the older one. "Stay here," I commanded, my voice leaving no room for argument. "I'll be back."

With that, I slipped out of the tent and back into the shadows of the camp, my mind already plotting my next move.

The encampment sprawled out before me, a chaotic patchwork of tents and makeshift structures. Smoke curled lazily from fires that dotted the perimeter, carrying the pungent smell of burnt meat and something I couldn't quite place. Shadows danced along the ground, playing tricks on my eyes as I navigated through the maze of twisted metal and crumbling concrete.

The raiders had carved out a domain that was both haphazard and functional. Scavenged items littered the area—rusty barrels, broken furniture, and shards of glass glimmering in the fading light. I noted a cluster of guards near the central fire pit, their laughter echoing through the encampment. They didn't notice that six of their men were dead.

Fucking idiots.

They appeared relaxed, their attention drawn away by their camaraderie. I made a mental note of their numbers: at least three guards were stationed there.

A tent to my left caught my eye—a larger structure draped with tattered fabric that seemed to sway ominously in the breeze. That had to be where their leader operated, likely planning raids or divvying up spoils from unsuspecting travelers. The structure's height gave it an imposing presence; whoever occupied it held power over this disorganized rabble.

I needed to use this environment to my advantage. An ambush wouldn't work. If they caught my face with a bullet, I was dead. And I was so damn close to being... free. I couldn't risk it.

Instead, I decided to create a diversion—something loud enough to draw most of them away from their posts.

I scanned for supplies, spotting a couple of old cans near a discarded crate stacked high with junk. Those could work well enough. With swift precision, I grabbed one and hurled it toward the opposite end of the camp. It clattered loudly against the ground, catching some attention.

As expected, one guard broke away from his group to investigate while another followed closely behind him. The moment was fleeting, but enough to reduce their numbers at the fire pit.

With two less eyes on me, I plotted my next move carefully. The remaining guards would still pose a challenge, but I could exploit their ignorance—distract them further while taking out anyone who stayed behind.

I peered back toward the entrance of the large tent; if I could sneak in while they were preoccupied...

Every muscle in my body thrummed with adrenaline as I prepared for what came next: speed and silence would be my allies tonight as I set about dismantling this encampment piece by piece.

I was ready to move, but I couldn't. My muscles refused to obey, my legs felt like lead. I furrowed my brows, confused, and tried lifting my leg again. It stayed stubbornly rooted to the ground.

"What the fuck?" I grunted out.

"Well, well," a silky, familiar voice drawled. "Look who's fallen into my web."

My teeth clenched at the sound of that voice. Slowly, she stepped around me, her presence unmistakable even before she came into view.

Raven.

She moved with a predatory grace, her dark eyes glinting with amusement as she circled me like a cat playing with a cornered mouse. Her hair was a cascade of jet-black waves that framed her face in a way that made her look both regal and dangerous. A smirk played on her full lips, a cruel twist that hinted at the malice beneath her stunning exterior.

She wore a fitted black leather jacket adorned with various patches and studs that gleamed in the dim light. It hugged her slender frame, accentuating every curve and muscle with a dangerous allure. Her pants were equally tight, tucked into knee-high boots that made her every step echo with authority. Around her neck hung an array of chains and talismans—trophies from past conquests and symbols of her dominance.

"Caught you off guard, did I?" she purred, stopping in front of me and tilting her head slightly, as if examining an interesting specimen. "You're slipping, D."

I couldn't tear my eyes away from her hands, playing with jagged stones—runes. Lines of power crisscrossed her fingers and palms, pulsating like a heartbeat beneath her flawless surface. My stomach twisted as the realization hit me: I had let my guard down, allowing myself to be drawn into her web of deception.

Runes were a rarity—knowledge that only a select few possessed—and those who wielded them were often more dangerous than they appeared.

How the hell had I missed this? The subtle shimmer in the air hinted at the arcane power she held, an arsenal of tricks ready to be unleashed. I cursed under my breath, frustration boiling beneath the surface; I should have sensed something off before stepping into this trap. It was too late now.

"What do you want?" I growled through gritted teeth.

She chuckled softly; the sound sending chills down my spine. "Oh, D," she said with mock sweetness, "you're the one in my encampment. I should be asking you that question. Though... I do have a guess."

I stared at Raven, the tension in the air thick enough to cut.

Her eyes glittered with amusement, the corners of her lips curling up. "Like everyone else, you heard about the kidnapping of Elise Hawthorne. Lucifer sent you on a bounty, didn't he?"

I didn't respond.

"Of course he did," she continued, voice smooth like honey coated in poison. "Why wouldn't the devil want his brother's bride?"

Inside, my thoughts churned. Elise Hawthorne was supposed to marry Archangel Michael? I thought Lucifer said something like that, but I couldn't remember. Couldn't bring myself to care. Did Everly know this? Was that why she was so desperate to find her sister?

I kept my face neutral, but my mind raced.

"So, I take it Skull knows then?" I asked, keeping my tone steady.

"Everyone knows," Raven replied with a casual shrug. "Why do you think we set up camp here? That Purifier Bunker ain't too far. We're hoping to find her... but we don't know what she looks like. Thought we'd take any girl we could find just in case."

"To what end?" I pressed.

"Well, you know as well as I do—girls make good currency," she said with a smirk.

"Skull's in the skin business now?" I sneered. "And here I thought he didn't want to get his hands dirty, like Magnus Rex."

Raven's smirk widened into something more sinister. "If Skull doesn't like what I've found, we'll sell them."

"Such a good lieutenant," I muttered under my breath.

"I remember when you were praising my skills," she said,

sidling closer to me. The proximity stirred something unsettling in my gut.

Dis-fucking-gust.

I grunted in response, trying to shove aside memories of our past. After everything she'd done—after Skull had tried to kill me with her help—I'd washed my hands of her completely.

But now she stood before me again, all charm and cunning. And once I figured out how to free myself from Lucifer's grasp, there would be consequences for those who betrayed me—especially Raven. Hell, I might even smile when I delivered her head to the girls in that tent.

Raven leaned closer, her finger tracing the curve of my cheek like a snake coiling around its prey. "What do you think?" she asked, her voice a seductive whisper. "One last job, for old time's sake?"

I flashed a smile that was all teeth, masking the surge of revulsion clawing at my insides. "I'd sooner slit my wrists and condemn myself to the Seventh Circle than do anything with you."

Her laughter was low and throaty, reverberating through the tension-filled air. "Well, I don't think you have a choice." She leaned back slightly, those sharp eyes glinting with mischief. "Getting my hands on Elise Hawthorne means controlling the devil himself. And you're going to use that skill of yours to help me find her."

"Over my dead fucking body," I spat, each word coated in venom.

"Oh, that'll be arranged," she replied coolly. A finger tapped my cheek lightly, as if we were old friends sharing secrets rather than adversaries in this twisted game. "Luckily, I have an idea of where she's headed."

"How?" I grunted, my curiosity piqued despite myself. "You said you set up camp here to find her."

"And she hasn't been by," Raven replied with a dismissive

wave of her hand. "She was kidnapped. Two of my men returned today with news—a disturbance at the bunker."

My heart sank as she spoke; Everly had told me about Elise before all this chaos erupted. I could feel the weight of Raven's gaze on me as she continued.

"Look." She reached into her pocket and pulled out a ring. The jewel was smashed, but the rose-gold color was hard to mistake. "Someone wanted to get rid of the ring. Why not sell it when it would have identified her as Michael's bride, I don't know. But scavengers have always been idiots. It was found west of the bunker, in the direction of the ocean. I was planning on leaving in the morning to track them down and take her from them." Her smile turned predatory as she added, "And now that I have you... you'll come with me."

"And if I refuse?" I challenged.

Raven's expression turned steely, and her lips curled into a wicked grin. "I don't see how that's possible."

I clenched my teeth.

"I have to get ready," she said nonchalantly, moving away from me. "We have a long trip tomorrow." She glanced over her shoulder as if testing my resolve one last time. "You'll be fine there, won't you? Of course you will."

With deliberate movements, she set down her rune stones —each one glowing faintly—as if mocking me for being unable to touch them. Even if I could move right now, putting my hands on those stones would be like setting myself ablaze.

"I'll see you soon, D," Raven said sweetly, tilting her head slightly like a cat about to pounce. "Unless you'd care to join me? For old time's sake?"

"I wouldn't touch you even if it saved my soul."

Raven flashed that wicked smile, one that twisted something deep in my gut.

"Good night, D," she replied with a casual wave before disappearing into her tent.

I wanted to scream. The darkness closed in around me, a thick blanket of despair and uncertainty. What the hell was I going to do? I needed to get back to Everly—there was no question about it.

But the thought of her alone out there gnawed at me like a ravenous beast. What if she thought I ditched her? She had trusted me after everything we'd been through together, and now this... mess.

Why the fuck do you care what she thinks? the voice in my head growled at me, trying to shake loose the uncomfortable knotting in my chest. But no matter how hard I pushed against it, that weight refused to lift.

It was already dark, shadows creeping through the encampment like phantoms on the prowl. If I didn't come up with something fast—some way to escape this godforsaken camp—I wouldn't have much of a choice but to follow Raven's orders. Those runes she had displayed so carelessly felt like chains around my neck.

I surveyed my surroundings. The dim glow of campfires flickered like distant stars, illuminating the faces of the guards still gathered near their pit—a distraction that could buy me time if I played my cards right.

But how? The runes... they would bind me if I tried to make a move without being cautious. Raven would be waiting for any slip-up on my part; she wouldn't hesitate to exploit it.

Each breath felt heavier than the last as desperation clawed at my insides. Time slipped through my fingers like sand— every moment wasted brought me closer to losing both Everly and Elise for good.

But what could I do? There had to be a way out of this mess without giving Raven the satisfaction of seeing me fall into another one of her traps.

CHAPTER 27

Everly

I stared at the ceiling, sleep a distant dream. My mind raced with thoughts of D. Was he okay? Was I even allowed to wonder that? He was a demon, no question. But why did I find myself missing him? It didn't make sense. He had every reason to harm me, yet he hadn't.

He saved me from that trap, even if he claimed it was for his own reasons. He was helping me find Elise. Selfish motives or not, his actions spoke louder than any words he could say. He let me name the hellhound—even though she submitted to him; he didn't have to do that—and carried me all the way to Ironedge without complaint.

Why?

I squeezed my eyes shut, willing the confusion away. Demons were evil. It was drilled into me since childhood. But D... he complicated things. Maybe demons weren't as black and white as I was taught.

The shame washed over me, but I couldn't shake the thought. Was it wrong to think this way? Would God disapprove?

I blew out a breath, trying to find clarity in the dark room.

No, it couldn't be wrong to save Elise. Even if D was a demon, the Bible had always taught compassion and mercy. Didn't Jesus dine with tax collectors and sinners? Didn't He show love to those society deemed unworthy?

"Blessed are the merciful, for they will be shown mercy," I whispered into the night air.

Wasn't that what this journey was about? Showing mercy and seeking justice? If God commanded love for enemies, how could I justify abandoning someone just because of their nature?

D hadn't done anything to harm me. In fact, he'd gone out of his way to ensure my safety. His actions had shown a side of him that didn't fit the narrative I'd been fed all my life, even if he was a buttface. At times.

I turned onto my side, pulling the thin blanket tighter around me. D was still out there somewhere, and despite everything, I hoped he was okay.

Was it wrong to care about him?

I sighed again, feeling the weight of my internal struggle pressing down on me. But in my heart, I knew what I had to do.

"D," I whispered again, a prayer forming on my lips. "God be with him. Keep him safe."

When dawn began to stretch its fingers across the sky, I rose from the narrow bed. The room's shadows melted away as I washed my face and brushed my teeth, the cool water refreshing against my skin. I moved quietly, not wanting to disturb the silence that enveloped the early morning.

I packed with care, making sure I had enough water and food for the journey ahead. After that, I made sure to have my runes. Just in case. My hands lingered over my Purifier uniform, now worn and frayed from my time outside. I changed into it. This uniform represented so much—my past, my faith, my betrayal. I made a mental note to use some of my shards for new clothes soon.

Everything else stayed behind. I'd be back with D; there was no other option in my mind. The thought of leaving without him was unbearable.

I walked through the inn's dimly lit hallway, my steps light but determined. Passing by the mustachioed man behind the counter, I stopped briefly.

"I will be back tonight, sir," I said firmly, meeting his eyes.

He nodded, frowning in confusion.

"Have a great day!" I exclaimed, forcing a bit of cheer into my voice.

Stepping outside, I was greeted by the gentle embrace of dawn. The sky blushed with hues of pink and gold, casting a soft glow over Ironedge's rugged landscape. The air was crisp and filled with the scent of morning dew on wild grasses. It felt like the world was holding its breath, waiting for something to unfold.

Silence stood there, her sleek form almost blending into the shadows. It was as if she had been waiting for me all along. She padded over to me, her red eyes glowing softly in the dim light.

"Ready to bring him back?" I whispered to her, reaching down to scratch behind her ears.

Her response was a low rumble that vibrated through her body. With one last glance at the inn behind me, I squared my shoulders and started walking toward the gates.

I walked outside Ironedge, the morning light casting long shadows on the dirt path ahead. Silence stayed close to my side, her presence a comforting reminder I wasn't entirely alone.

"You sure you want to go after him?" a guard called out from his post, leaning casually against the wooden frame. "Maybe you should let sleeping dogs lie, hmm?"

I paused, meeting his skeptical gaze. "*Do not neglect to show hospitality to strangers, for by so doing some people have shown hospitality to angels without knowing it,*" I recited softly.

He blinked, momentarily taken aback by my words.

"You can't possibly believe that piece of shit is an angel," he said. "He's a demon, a Satanspawn."

"You're going to get yourself killed, Bunker Rat," a female guard added from her position on the opposite side of the gate. Her voice was sharp, her eyes narrowed with a mixture of pity and disdain.

Forcing a smile, I looked at both of them. "I will be back with my friend," I said firmly. "God will see to it."

The male guard chuckled, shaking his head. "You see God out here?"

Ignoring his question, I continued walking, my steps steady and unwavering. The voices of the guards faded behind me as I moved further away from the safety of Ironedge. I refused to let their doubt seep into my resolve. Not today.

Silence kept pace with me, her presence a silent affirmation of my determination. We moved through the landscape; the sun climbing higher and casting its warmth over us.

Refusing to look back, I pushed forward. Every step was a reminder that faith wasn't about seeing; it was about believing. And right now, belief was all I had to hold onto.

"Can you sniff him out?" I asked Silence.

She yipped and began heading north. At least, I thought it was north. I had never been good at directions.

The desert stretched out before me, an endless expanse of golden sand and rocky outcrops. The early morning light painted the landscape in soft hues, but I knew it wouldn't last. The sun climbed higher with each passing minute, its heat already beginning to press down on me.

Every step felt like a test of my resolve. My boots sank into the shifting sands, making each movement an effort. Silence trotted beside me, her eyes scanning the horizon.

The sky above was a brilliant blue, unmarred by clouds. It seemed to mock my uncertainty. Was I even going the right way? The desert offered no markers, no signs to guide me. Just an unchanging sea of sand and rock.

But fear wasn't an option. I had to be there for D. He'd risked his life for mine. Now it was my turn to return the favor. To show him I would do what it took. I wasn't a scared Bunker Girl. I'd be a trustworthy partner. An equal.

I pressed on; the sun climbing steadily higher, its rays growing harsher. Sweat trickled down my back, my shirt sticking to my skin. Each step seemed harder than the last, but I refused to stop.

Hours passed in a blur of heat and determination. Finally, when the sun hung high overhead and the air shimmered with heat, I allowed myself a break.

I found a small outcrop of rock that offered a sliver of shade and sank down onto it gratefully. Pulling out a piece of jerky from my pack, I chewed slowly, savoring the salty taste. It wasn't much, but it kept me going.

Silence sat beside me, her red eyes watching my every move. I broke off a piece of jerky and held it out to her. She took it gently from my hand before settling down to eat.

I uncapped my water bottle and took a careful sip, letting the cool liquid soothe my parched throat. The relief was short-lived; I had to ration what little water I had left, especially since D might need some.

After a few minutes of rest, I rose to my feet again, feeling the weight of responsibility pressing down on me even more heavily than before.

"Let's go," I said softly to Silence.

She stood up immediately, ready to continue our journey.

With renewed determination, we set out once more across

the unforgiving desert landscape. Each step forward was a step closer to finding D and bringing him back safely—no matter how uncertain the path ahead might be.

The encampment came into view, a cluster of ramshackle tents and makeshift structures huddled together in the middle of the desert. My heart skipped a beat, and I felt a knot of nerves tighten in my stomach.

I slowed my pace, breathing deeply to steady myself. Silence sensed my unease, her ears twitching as she glanced up at me.

"We're almost there," I whispered, more to myself than to her.

Taking a deep breath, I closed my eyes and tried to remember D's lessons on self-defense. His voice echoed in my mind, calm and confident. *"Stay low. Stay quiet. Strike only if you have to."*

My hand instinctively moved to the knife hanging from my waist. The cold metal felt foreign against my palm. Would I really use it? If it came down to saving D or myself, could I take a life?

God looked down on murder, but was self-defense different? My mind churned with questions I had no answers for. Was it justified if it was to save someone? Could I reconcile that with my faith?

"Lord," I whispered under my breath, "give me strength. Help me do what's right."

Silence nudged my leg gently, snapping me back to the present. We moved closer to the encampment, every step making my heart pound louder in my chest.

As we approached the edge of the camp, I crouched low behind a rocky outcrop, peering through the gaps between the stones. The raiders moved about their business, unaware of our presence.

"We need to find him," I murmured to Silence, who

264

seemed to understand. Her ears perked up as she scanned the camp with those glowing red eyes.

I gripped the knife tighter, trying to summon the courage I'd need for whatever lay ahead. The uncertainty gnawed at me, but I couldn't let it paralyze me. D was counting on me.

Silence took a cautious step forward, and I followed her lead. We edged closer to the camp's perimeter, using every bit of cover we could find. The smell of smoke and sweat filled the air, mingling with the faint sounds of conversation and clinking metal.

Each step brought us closer to danger but also closer to D. I had to believe that this was where he was being held—that he was still alive.

As we neared the first tent, I took another deep breath and sent up one final prayer.

"God," I whispered softly, "please guide me."

I moved quietly, each step calculated to avoid detection. Silence followed close behind, her red eyes glowing softly. The camp buzzed with activity, and I could hear voices ahead. I crouched low, pressing myself against the rough surface of a large boulder.

Three scavengers strolled past, their conversation drifting through the still air.

"...found out he slaughtered the damn guards," one said, his voice rough and full of disdain.

"She's skinning him alive," the second one replied, shaking his head in disbelief.

"I thought we was leaving this morning," the third scavenger muttered, sounding frustrated.

"Not until she teaches the demon a lesson," the first one said. "She pushed the whole mission back a day just to torture him."

My eyes widened at their words. Who was she? And why

ISADORA BROWN

would she hurt D? My heart pounded in my chest as I strained to hear more.

"...can't believe we have to skin them and fry it into some kind of jerky," the second scavenger grumbled, his face twisted in disgust.

"Better than collecting the remains for the dogs," the third one said with a shrug.

I clenched my teeth, feeling a surge of anger and desperation. D was being tortured in there, and here I was hiding outside. But there was no way to get in without going through these scavengers.

Silence glanced up at me, her eyes meeting mine. It was as if she understood what needed to be done. Her muscles tensed, ready for action.

I took a deep breath and steadied myself. The stakes were higher than ever, but I couldn't afford to hesitate. D needed me. We had to find a way in without alerting the entire camp.

As the scavengers moved further away, their voices faded into the background noise of the camp. I waited until they were out of sight before slipping out from behind the boulder. Silence followed closely, her steps as silent as her name suggested.

We crept forward, every sense on high alert for any sign of danger or opportunity. The weight of responsibility pressed down on me, but I refused to let it crush my resolve.

D was counting on me—no matter what it took, I would find a way to reach him and get him out of there safely.

I almost reached the largest tent when Silence's growl stopped me cold. My heart hammered as I turned to see one of the scavengers approaching, his eyes narrowing when he spotted me. Silence launched herself at him, her form a blur of black fur and fury.

I ducked behind a nearby stack of crates, my breath shallow and rapid. I hoped Silence could handle him quickly and quietly, but my hope was dashed when another scavenger appeared from around the corner. He was the second one from the earlier conversation, his sneer widening as he saw me.

"You're a pretty thing," he said, stepping closer. "You'll fetch quite a pretty shard—"

"Please," I whispered, desperation seeping into my voice. "Please don't make me hurt you."

He laughed, a harsh sound that grated against my nerves. "You? Hurt me?"

A scream erupted from the direction where Silence had gone, followed by a sickening gurgle. The scavenger's attention flickered toward the noise, just enough distraction for me to remember D's self-defense lesson. I stomped on his foot with all my might.

I bolted, but his hand caught my arm, yanking me back. I fell hard onto my hip, pain shooting through me as I bit down on it to keep from crying out. He lunged, pinning me to the ground with his weight. His fingers wrapped around my throat, squeezing with brutal force.

"The fuck you think you can just leave?" he snarled.

My vision blurred at the edges as his grip tightened. Each breath became a desperate struggle, my lungs burning with the effort to draw in air. The world seemed to close in around me, sounds fading to a distant roar. I clawed at his hands, but his strength far outmatched mine.

Black spots danced in front of my eyes as panic surged through me. My thoughts scrambled for a way out, but every attempt felt futile against the crushing pressure on my windpipe.

My mind screamed for help as darkness began to creep in around the edges of my vision.

My fingers brushed against the knife at my waist. Desperation surged through me as I struggled to draw in breath.

Please, I tried to say, but no sound escaped my lips.

His grip tightened, and I knew if I didn't do something, he was going to kill me.

My fingers wrapped around the blade, feeling its cold, reassuring weight. Without thinking, I pulled it up and jerked the knife clumsily into the man's throat. Blood splattered across my face and chest. My eyes went wide as I watched the life drain from his eyes.

He jerked back, startled, his grip on my throat loosening. He opened his mouth to speak, but only a gurgling sound emerged as blood dribbled out of his mouth. He fell into a heap on the ground, his body twitching before going still.

I gasped for air, coughing and choking as I tried to regain my breath. My hands trembled uncontrollably as I stared at the lifeless body before me. The knife slipped from my grasp, clattering onto the dirt.

Silence appeared at my side, her red eyes glowing with concern, fur matted in blood. She nudged my leg gently, bringing me back to reality. I forced myself to take deep breaths, trying to calm the storm of emotions raging inside me.

"We have to move," I whispered to Silence, wiping the blood from my face with a shaky hand. My stomach turned. I wanted to throw up. I had just — But I couldn't think about it. "We can't stay here."

Pushing myself up on unsteady legs, I retrieved the knife from the ground and wiped it clean on my pants. The weight of what I'd done settled heavily on my shoulders, but there was no time for remorse.

D needed me.

With one last glance at the fallen scavenger, I steeled myself and moved deeper into the camp, Silence by my side. The stakes were higher than ever, but there was no turning back now.

And there was one more scavenger.

Shouting pierced the air, a voice rough and urgent.

"...need some fucking help with the bodies!" someone yelled.

Silence growled low and dangerous beside me. My heart pounded in my chest, but I took a steadying breath. This was the last scavenger. We had to move fast.

"Go," I whispered to Silence.

She sprang into action, her lithe form a blur of fur and fury as she charged toward the source of the voice. I didn't wait to see the outcome; I turned my attention to the big tent in front of me. This had to be where D was held.

I pushed aside the flap and stepped inside, my breath catching at the sight before me. D hung from a wooden stake, stripped of his shirt and duster, his hat on the floor. His arms were skinned, raw and bloody, but miraculously, they seemed to be healing. The sight of him broke something inside me.

"D," I whispered, my voice trembling with a mix of relief and horror.

Without thinking, I rushed over to him. His head lifted weakly, his eyes blinking as he tried to focus on me.

"You..." he murmured, his voice barely audible. "You can't be here."

"I'm here," I said firmly, pushing aside the heat that bloomed in my lower stomach at the sight of him. "I'm going to get you out of here. I promise. And I don't make a promise unless I mean it."

I pulled out my knife, its weight reassuring in my hand as I began cutting at the ropes holding him up. Each slice felt like a small victory against the darkness that had taken hold of this place.

"Stay with me," I urged him softly as the ropes began to give way. "We're getting out of here together."

His eyes locked onto mine, a flicker of determination sparking within their depths despite his weakened state. That flicker was all I needed to keep going. With one final cut, the ropes fell away, and D collapsed into my arms.

"We have to move," I whispered urgently, supporting his weight as best as I could.

"Blood," he murmured.

I didn't have time to figure out what he meant. My focus was on getting him out of this nightmare. I struggled to support his weight, each step a battle against his pain and my own fear.

"Look at this," a silky feminine voice cut through the air, sending a chill down my spine. "Is this an angel come to save your soul, D?"

I turned sharply, my heart racing. A woman stood at the entrance of the tent, her eyes gleaming with a wicked delight. Her presence radiated danger, but what truly caught my attention was the ring on her finger. Elise's ring.

My breath caught in my throat. Anger and dread churned inside me. How did she get that? What had she done to Elise?

"Who are you?" I demanded, trying to keep my voice steady despite the fear clawing at me.

The woman smirked, taking a step closer. "Oh, don't worry about who I am," she said, her tone dripping with mockery. "You should be more concerned about what happens next."

I tightened my grip on D, trying to keep him upright while my mind raced for a way out. Silence had taken care of the other scavenger, but now we faced an even greater threat.

"What do you want?" I asked, desperation creeping into my voice despite my efforts to stay calm.

Her smirk widened into a grin that sent shivers down my spine. "Want? Oh, darling, I'm just here for the fun." She twirled Elise's ring around her finger casually, as if it were a mere trinket and not a symbol of everything I held dear.

"Elise," I breathed out before I could stop myself.

Her eyes narrowed slightly, catching the name I'd whispered. "You know her?" She examined the ring more closely now with an almost predatory interest.

D groaned beside me, his weight becoming harder to bear as he struggled against consciousness and pain. My mind screamed at me to do something—anything—but every option seemed fraught with peril.

"You'll pay for whatever you've done," I said through gritted teeth, though it felt like an empty threat given our current state.

The woman laughed—a cold sound devoid of any real mirth or warmth. "Bold words from someone so powerless. But you... I can use you." She eyed my uniform. "Purifier, eh?" She smirked. "I know just where to take you, little girl. And you're going to hate every second of it."

CHAPTER 28

Walton

T he last thing I expected was to see Everly slipping into the tent, her Purifier uniform drenched in blood. At first, I thought I was dreaming. My heart, that damn rotted organ in my chest I hadn't felt in a long time, lurched at the sight. She shouldn't be here. She should be back at Ironedge. She should be safe.

This had to be a nightmare.

When Raven discovered my trail of bodies, she decided to torture me by using those damned runes and tying me up like some kind of twisted crucifixion. Just because I could heal didn't mean I didn't feel the pain.

And fuck, what Raven did to me hurt like a fucking bitch.

Everly's knife flashed in the dim light, slicing through the ropes that bound me. I crashed to the ground, knees hitting hard dirt. The world spun, and I gasped, trying to draw breath through lungs that felt like they were filled with broken glass.

Her hands were under my arms, hauling me up with strength I didn't think she had. She was yammering on about promises and keeping them, her words a soothing balm to my battered spirit. I almost laughed. Never in a million years did I think I'd miss her talking so much. But hell, I did.

She was real. This wasn't some fever dream cooked up by Raven's torture.

"Look at this," a familiar voice drawled from the shadows. "Has an angel come to rescue you, D?"

Raven stepped into view, her eyes glinting with amusement and something darker. Everly stiffened beside me, but she didn't let go.

I tried to stand on my own, to shield Everly from Raven's gaze, but my legs buckled. Damn it. I could barely move.

Pain seared through my arms, knitting flesh and bone in a slow, agonizing process. The wounds Raven inflicted were healing, but not fast enough. Every inch felt like it was on fire, muscles twitching and spasming uncontrollably. Everly's presence was the only thing grounding me, her grip firm yet gentle.

Everly stiffened beside me but held her ground. Her voice was defiant, though muffled by the roaring in my ears. I felt like I was underwater, every sound distant and distorted.

But it was Raven's ring that caught her eye. Her breath hitched. "Elise," she whispered, barely audible.

Raven's eyes narrowed, a predatory gleam lighting up her face. "You know her?" She examined the ring with a cold curiosity that made my blood run cold.

I groaned beside Everly, trying to warn her without words. If she had any sense, she'd keep her mouth shut. Raven would use her the same way she used me—only with much more cruelty. The thought churned my stomach.

"You'll pay for whatever you've done," Everly said through gritted teeth.

Raven laughed—a sound devoid of any real mirth or warmth. "Bold words from someone so powerless. But you... I can use you." She eyed Everly's uniform with a smirk. "Purifier, eh? I know just where to take you, little girl. And you're going to hate every second of it."

"Don't fucking touch her," I growled, forcing myself to stand despite the agony ripping through my body.

Raven's eyes flicked to me, amusement dancing in their depths. She took a step closer to Everly, almost daring me to stop her.

Everly's hand tightened on mine as if anchoring me to the world of the living. Her courage was a bright flame in the darkness surrounding us.

"You think you can protect her?" Raven mocked, crossing her arms over her chest.

"I'll do more than that," I spat back, blood dribbling down my chin from where I'd bitten my tongue during the struggle to stand.

Raven laughed again and took another step forward.

The room felt like it was closing in on us. The walls of the tent seemed to press inward, and every breath I took felt like inhaling shards of glass.

But Everly stood firm by my side.

And that meant everything.

"How interesting," Raven mused, her voice dripping with mockery. "I thought you hated the Purifiers after what your wife did to you, D. Thought you were going to kill every last one of them after you freed your soul from Lucifer's clutches."

"D would never do that," Everly said firmly.

Why she believed in me, I had no idea. I didn't deserve it. Because I would. I absolutely would.

"Oh, honey, did he use that silver tongue on you too?" Raven asked, looking at Everly with pity. "Though I will say I'm familiar with the Purifiers myself. And for you to be traveling with a demon..." She clicked her tongue. "Naughty girl. Tell me. Did he do the trick with his tongue when he feasted on you, hmm?"

"Shut up," I spat out, my voice a guttural growl that sent fresh waves of pain through my chest.

But Raven's gaze was focused on Everly.

"You know," she said, reaching out to take a lock of blonde hair from Everly and curl it around her finger. "I expect this from someone like you. All good girls want to know what sin really feels like. Just look at Eve. But you." She looked at me, her eyes narrowing. "You care about her. And that... that isn't something I'd ever thought was possible."

"Jealous?" I asked with a smirk I didn't feel.

Raven's scowl deepened.

"I told you not to touch her," I murmured, eyes pointed on Everly's hair wrapped around Raven's finger. "Release her."

"It's not like you can do anything about it," Raven pointed out with a smirk. "I don't think I will."

"Please," Everly said, her voice steady but pleading. "I don't want to hurt you."

Raven laughed, a cold, hollow sound. "As if you could." She yanked on Everly's hair and pulled her forward. "Don't waste my time. Sit down and wait. I'll deal with you later. Not until I finish this. You see, your lover killed five of my men, and I can't let that stand."

She pushed Everly hard, sending her stumbling out of the pentagram Raven had cast that kept me where I was.

The instant Everly crossed the boundary, I felt a searing pain rip through my chest; the runes burning brighter as if mocking my helplessness.

Raven turned back to me with a sneer. "Now, where were we?"

Raven pulled out a wicked-looking tool, something that gleamed menacingly under the dim light. She twirled it between her fingers; her smile sharp and cruel.

"How about that pretty face, hmm?" she taunted,

bringing the tool dangerously close to my eye. "If I take an eyeball, will that heal?"

I didn't flinch. I'd faced worse. But inside, I seethed, my mind racing with ways to end her.

Without warning, Everly knocked into Raven. It wasn't much of a push, but Raven staggered back as if struck by a force far greater. She hit the ground hard, shock plastered across her face.

"I-I warned you," Everly stammered, her voice wavering yet determined. She had her knife in hand and pressed it against Raven's throat. "Please. You're going to let us go."

Raven's eyes narrowed to slits. "I'm not."

"You don't have any guards," Everly insisted. "It's just you. You have no one."

Raven opened her mouth and closed it again, calculating. "You can't possibly tell me you killed three men," she said with disbelief.

No. Everly hadn't done it alone. Maybe one, but Silence had to be with her.

I whistled sharply.

"Please," Everly pleaded again.

Raven's eyes flickered with realization and fear. "You wouldn't," she spat. "You wouldn't fucking dare. You're a Purifier."

In a swift move, Raven jerked her hips, rolling on top of Everly. She raised the tool she had intended for me and brought it down towards Everly's face.

But I was faster.

My hand shot out and grabbed Raven's wrist, twisting it until I heard the satisfying crack of bone breaking. She screamed in pain just as Everly swiped her knife across Raven's face, leaving a deep gash that sent blood pouring down.

Raven's scream echoed through the tent as she clutched her face in agony.

I hauled myself up, using the last remnants of my strength to stand between Everly and Raven. The pain in my body roared back to life, but I ignored it.

We were getting out of here alive.

Everly looked up at me, her eyes wide but resolute.

A low growling sound pierced the silence, vibrating through the air like a warning.

"That's going to leave a scar, you cunt," Raven cried out, clutching her face. "My face!"

"Let's go," Everly said, urgency dripping from her voice.

"I can't," I growled, frustration boiling over.

Everly opened her mouth to ask why, but I jerked my head toward the runes on the floor. She paused, taking in the glowing symbols that still bound me. Her eyes flickered with understanding.

Quickly, she bent down and began picking up the runes.

"What are you—?" I stopped mid-sentence, watching as Everly took the runes and started arranging them around Raven. The woman was too distracted by her injury to concern herself with what Everly was doing.

"There," Everly said, standing back up. "She can't move."

Raven's eyes widened with disbelief. "What? Impossible. Runes only work on demons."

"They don't," Everly replied just as Silence burst through the tent, teeth bared and eyes blazing. She lunged for Raven, but Everly stepped in front of her.

"That's the stupidest decision you've ever made, girl," Raven snapped, holding her injury. "After gashing my face. Because I will get out of this, and I will kill you myself."

"I'm not going to kill you when you can't fight back," Everly said firmly. "That wouldn't be fair." She hesitated before adding softly, "As it is written in Proverbs 21:15: *When justice is done, it brings joy to the righteous but terror to evildoers.*"

"Fuck God and fuck you," Raven spat.

"I'm going to pray for you," Everly said quietly.

I felt the hold of the runes loosen and found I could move again. My body still ached from healing, but there was no pain now—only clarity. Stepping forward, I reached out for Raven's broken wrist. She whimpered as my fingers closed around it.

"Don't touch me!" she snarled through gritted teeth.

Ignoring her protests, I yanked Elise's ring from her finger. I pocketed it before breaking her finger just to hear the bone crunch.

Raven's eyes burned with hatred as she stared at me, powerless and bound by Everly's quick thinking. But for once in this nightmare of a world, we had a small victory.

"You better hope I don't get out of here, D," Raven snarled, her voice dripping with venom as blood continued to coat her face. "Because I will find her. I will do unspeakable things to her. And I'll make you watch."

I considered ending her right then and there. One quick twist of her neck, and all our problems would be over.

But Everly turned to look at me, her big green eyes pleading. Only now did I notice the fingerprints on her throat, dark bruises marring her pale skin. She'd already been through too much.

"Let's go," I grunted.

Relief flooded Everly's eyes, and I had to look away. Her innocence, despite everything, was something I couldn't face right now.

We stepped out of the tent into the harsh light of day. The sun blazed down, making my skin prickle with heat. The smell of blood and burnt flesh lingered in the air, a grim reminder of the battle that had taken place.

Silence trotted alongside us, her hellhound eyes watching for any threats. The world outside felt different—brighter, sharper—as if my senses had been heightened by the ordeal.

Each step I took made me feel more like myself again, the pain in my body subsiding as my demonic healing kicked in.

Everly stayed close to me. Her fingers brushed against mine, a silent promise that we were in this together.

"Are you okay?" she asked softly.

"I'll live," I replied gruffly.

She nodded, biting her lip as if holding back more questions. There was no time for talking now; we needed to put distance between us and Raven's camp.

We made our way out of the tent, the oppressive air lifting slightly with each step. But then I stopped, a thought piercing through the haze of pain and exhaustion. Something gnawed at me, something I had almost forgotten. I scanned the encampment, my eyes narrowing as they landed on a smaller tent off to the side.

Everly furrowed her brows, but, for once, didn't say anything. For that, I was grateful. There wasn't time for questions.

I pushed open the flap and stepped inside. The dim light revealed two girls huddled in the corner, their eyes wide with fear and uncertainty. They were the ones I'd seen earlier, before Raven's ambush.

"Let's go," I ordered, my voice rough but commanding.

"Raven's dead?" the older one asked, her voice trembling.

"She won't hurt you," I said, keeping it simple. No need to dwell on details that would only scare them more.

The girls turned their attention to Everly as she stepped forward, her expression softening. "Hi," she said gently. "I'm Everly. Do you need food, or maybe water?"

She offered her water bottle to them, and I couldn't help but think she was being foolish—wasting resources we might need later. But then again, that's who she was.

The younger girl snatched the bottle from Everly and

ISADORA BROWN

drank greedily. She looked desperate, parched from who knows how long without proper sustenance.

"We're wasting time," I said, trying to keep my impatience in check. Every second we lingered was another chance for trouble to find us.

"You're with him?" the older girl asked Everly, her eyes flicking back to me with a mix of curiosity and fear.

Everly nodded without hesitation.

"He... he doesn't hurt you?" The girl's voice was barely a whisper, loaded with past traumas that needed no elaboration.

"Never," Everly said firmly. Her conviction hit me like a punch to the gut. She spoke of me like I was some kind of good man, and I knew better. I wasn't deserving of this blind faith she had in me. Hell, I wasn't even a man.

"We're burning daylight," I snapped, more to mask my discomfort than anything else.

Everly ignored my tone and turned back to the girls. "Come with us," she urged gently. "I'm sure your families miss you."

The two girls exchanged glances, their expressions torn between hope and fear.

"Okay," the older one said.

We left the encampment, moving quickly and quietly. The two girls stayed close to Everly, their fear palpable but their steps determined. Silence trotted ahead, ever vigilant.

My mind was a storm, rage simmering beneath the surface. I wanted to tear into Everly for risking her life. For what? To find me? Save me? The thought churned in my gut like poison.

I glanced at her, and it hit me like a sledgehammer. There was blood on her hands, staining her uniform. It wasn't just the physical blood; it was the weight of what she'd done, what she'd risked. Yet, in that moment, I couldn't deny how beautiful she looked—resolute, fierce, and alive.

"Everly," I growled, unable to hold back any longer. "What the hell were you thinking?"

She looked at me with those wide green eyes. "I was thinking I couldn't just leave you there."

"You don't know what you're dealing with out here," I snapped, the words harsher than I intended. "You could've gotten yourself killed."

"But I didn't," she shot back, her voice steady despite the quiver in her hands. "And neither did you. I told you, I could hold my own. I'm not some burden."

My fists clenched involuntarily. She didn't understand—couldn't understand—the stakes of this world.

"You can't save everyone," I said through gritted teeth. "Especially not me."

Everly's expression softened, and she reached out to touch my arm. "I know you think you're beyond saving," she said quietly. "But you're not."

Her touch was a balm to my rage, and I felt some of the tension drain from my body. But the anger didn't dissipate entirely; it lingered like a dark cloud.

"God tell you that?" I snapped.

Everly looked away, shaking her head. "I just... I just know."

What the fuck did that even mean?

"Let's just keep moving," I muttered, turning away from her and leading the way through the twisted remnants of civilization.

We walked in silence for a while, the only sounds being our footsteps and the distant cries of scavenging birds. My mind kept circling back to Everly—her bravery, her naivety, her damn stubbornness.

And that look in her eyes when she talked about saving me.

As much as I wanted to push her away, I couldn't ignore

that something inside me had shifted. Everly wasn't just another person needing protection; she was something more —someone who saw through my demonic exterior to whatever humanity remained buried deep within.

But now wasn't the time for these thoughts. We had miles to go before we could rest, and dangers lurked around every corner.

I kept moving forward, Everly at my side, the girls next to her, and Silence watching our backs.

As long as we didn't run into trouble, we should get back to Ironedge by nightfall.

CHAPTER 29

Everly

The desert night wrapped around us like a cold, unwelcoming shroud. The once-blistering sun had given way to an icy chill that seeped through my clothes and into my bones. Stars dotted the inky sky, their distant light doing little to illuminate the vast expanse of sand and rock stretching endlessly before us. The wind had picked up, carrying with it a biting edge that made each step feel like a struggle.

My throat throbbed with each breath, a painful reminder of the hands that had choked the life out of me not too long ago. My body ached in ways I hadn't known it could, each bruise and scrape singing a different note in a symphony of pain. I wanted to move faster, to keep pace with D and the two girls, but my limbs felt like lead. Slowing down wasn't an option, though; I couldn't afford to be a burden.

"You're slow." D's voice broke through the silence, filled with his usual scorn.

"I'm fine," I managed to rasp out, forcing a smile that felt more like a grimace. "Just... need to keep moving."

D nodded but didn't press further. The two girls clung

close to each other, their eyes wide and haunted. They hadn't spoken much since we started walking, and I couldn't blame them. We were all trying to make sense of this new reality.

I swallowed hard, fighting the urge to throw up. The taste of bile lingered at the back of my throat, but I forced it down. There were more pressing things to focus on—like surviving the night.

I couldn't stop thinking about the man I'd killed. His face flashed in my mind's eye every time I blinked, his lifeless body crumpling to the ground replaying over and over like some twisted movie reel. I'd never taken a life before. It felt like something had shifted inside me, something I couldn't quite name but knew I'd never be able to take back.

"You're dragging," D said, his voice dripping with disdain.

"I'm fine," I spat back, though the words tasted like lies. My muscles screamed with each step, but I pushed on.

D narrowed his eyes at me, the firelight casting sharp shadows across his face. "Fine? You're barely keeping up. You're going to get us all killed."

My hands balled into fists at my sides. "I saved your life, didn't I? Or do you not remember that part?"

His face twisted into a sneer. "Saved my life? You mean you put all of us at risk! What were you thinking, running in there like that? You could have gotten yourself killed. Hell, you should have been dead."

I took a step closer, closing the distance between us until we were almost nose to nose. "You think I don't know that? You think I didn't weigh the risks?"

"Then you're stupider than I thought," he growled, eyes flashing with anger and something else—fear?

I couldn't stop the words that poured out of me, fueled by exhaustion and frustration. "Maybe I'm stupid for believing you're worth saving! But someone has to care about you because, clearly, you don't care about yourself!"

His jaw tightened, but he didn't back down. "You don't know anything about me."

"Then enlighten me," I shot back, my voice trembling despite my best efforts to keep it steady. "Tell me why it was wrong to save you!"

D's expression hardened, and for a moment, I saw a flicker of something raw in his eyes—pain, maybe? But it was gone as quickly as it appeared. "You think you're some kind of hero? You're not. You're just a naive girl playing at survival."

The words stung more than I cared to admit. Tears pricked at the corners of my eyes, but I refused to let them fall. "And you're just a coward hiding behind your anger because it's easier than facing your own demons."

Silence hung between us like a heavy shroud, neither of us willing to break eye contact or back down. The two girls huddled together nearby, their eyes darting between us with growing anxiety.

D's eyes gleamed with a predatory glint. He grabbed my chin tightly, forcing me to look up at him. "There it is," he said, a twisted smile creeping across his face. "Little viper. I knew you could get mad. Not always the polite good girl, are you?"

I wrenched my head away from his grip, my skin crawling where his fingers had touched. "What's your problem?" I shot back, my voice trembling. I hated that it trembled. "I just want to help—"

"You can't," he interrupted, his tone dripping with venom. "Why can't you get that through your thick head? You can't help. You're a fucking Purifier."

"I saved you—"

"I didn't ask you to!" he bellowed, his voice echoing in the cold night air.

"You didn't have to," I said, trying to keep my voice steady.

I reached for the words that had always brought me comfort. "The Lord is my shepherd; I shall not want..."

But D's face twisted in disgust before I could finish. "Don't preach to me, little girl," he sneered. "There's no God here."

"Of course there is," I insisted, my voice soft but firm. "He protected me. I could have..."

"And what about the man you killed, huh?" D's words cut through me like a knife. "Why didn't your God protect him? He play favorites?"

My mouth opened, but no words came out. The reality of what I'd done crashed over me like a tidal wave, leaving me gasping for breath. I couldn't answer him because deep down, I didn't know why either.

I took a step back, feeling the bile rise in my throat. The weight of everything—the betrayal, the killing, the constant fear—it all came crashing down at once.

And then I couldn't hold it in any longer. I turned away and threw up into the sand, the taste of bitterness and regret burning my mouth.

D watched me with an unreadable expression, as if waiting for something more.

But all I could do was wipe my mouth and try to steady my trembling hands.

The night around us felt even colder now, and the stars above seemed impossibly distant.

For a moment, neither of us spoke.

The silence between us was louder than any argument ever could be.

The older woman stepped between us, her eyes darting from D to me with a weary but determined look. "We should make camp here," she said, her voice steady despite the tension in the air.

D sneered, shaking his head. "We could have made it back

if we weren't slowed down," he grumbled, but he didn't argue further. Instead, he began setting up camp with quick, practiced movements. He glanced over at me as he unrolled a tattered sleeping bag. "Aren't you going to help? Fucking women are equal to men, ain't you? Time to do something more than running your mouths."

I bit back a retort, focusing instead on helping the older woman and the younger girl. The younger girl looked at me, her voice barely above a whisper. "I can't believe you married a demon," she muttered under her breath. "He's a dick."

My gaze shifted to D. His skin was leathery and pale, pulled taut over sharp cheekbones and a gaunt frame. He reminded me of a beast from the old world's stories—the one locked in a dark castle and kept prisoners.

Anger surged through me—an anger I never expected to feel, an anger I'd never felt before. It burned hot and fierce in my chest, making my hands tremble as I tried to steady myself. Yet despite that anger, I frowned at the thought of anyone calling him names. Because deep down, I knew he was a good man. I just hated that he had to be like this.

"The fuck you staring at?" D's voice snapped me out of my thoughts. "Move your ass, Bunker Rat."

I scowled at him, feeling the heat of my anger rising again.

He smirked as he lit up a fire, his amber eyes glinting with... affection? No. That didn't make sense. It was clear he didn't like me. Didn't want me around.

But maybe... just maybe... there was more...

No.

I couldn't think like that.

Wouldn't.

D turned to Silence, lying quietly by his side. "Go hunt," he commanded.

Silence sprang to her feet, her red eyes glowing in the dim light of the fire. She bounded off into the darkness, her powerful form blending seamlessly with the shadows. The two women jumped at her sudden movement.

"I can't believe she listens to him," the younger one said, her voice tinged with awe and fear.

"He is a demon," the older woman replied, her eyes narrowing as she watched Silence disappear into the night. "Maybe she's bound to him."

D scoffed, a derisive sound that grated on my nerves.

"I don't think that's how it works," I murmured, more to myself than anyone else.

I glanced at them and realized I was being rude. We both were, but I doubted D cared.

"I'm sorry," I said, turning to the other women. I forced a smile. I should be better than this, arguing in front of them. It was rude and they probably felt extremely uncomfortable. I had to be better. "I never caught your names."

The older woman gave a weary smile. "I'm Lydia. This is Callie."

"Nice to meet you both," I replied, offering a small nod as we continued setting up camp.

"We're from Ironedge," Lydia continued. "We were out scavenging when we got caught by those raiders. If your husband hadn't come by..."

D looked at me then, his eyes challenging me to correct Lydia. I lifted my chin, refusing to take the bait.

Callie glanced at D with a mix of curiosity and suspicion. "How'd you wind up married to a demon, being from the bunker? Clearly it's not 'cause of his looks."

"Or his manners," Lydia added, shooting D a sideways glance before focusing on me again. "Is he... is he making you trade things for his protection?"

"No," I said firmly. "Nothing like that. I... He's... he's more than a demon. And even though he has a quick temper... I trust him." My eyes met D's across the fire, and for a moment, everything else faded away. "With my life."

Something akin to surprise flashed across his sculpted face but it disappeared so fast that I thought I was mistaken.

"I think we should check on the hellhound," Lydia said. "Callie, let's see if she needs help."

I opened my mouth to protest, but D cut me off with a glare. The two women disappeared into the darkness.

"What the heck, D?" I asked in a low voice, marching over to him. "It's dangerous out there. What if something happened to them?"

He shrugged.

"You don't care?" I asked, aghast.

"I don't trust 'em," he muttered. "You stay close, you hear me?" His voice left no room for argument.

"You're being ridiculous," I said.

"And you're too damn trusting," he retorted, pulling off his duster and rolling up his sleeve.

"Oh my," I gasped as the firelight illuminated his arm. It was healing, but it still looked bad from where Raven had skinned him. The flesh was raw and red, covered in angry welts and half-formed scabs. Without thinking, I sat down and took his hand in mine. "Do you have water? Maybe I can clean it—"

"The hell are you doing?" D yanked his arm away from me.

"I was just trying to help," I said softly.

"When are you going to get it through your thick skull?" he snapped. "I don't want your fucking help."

I bit my lip, trying to hold back the sting of his words. "You might not want it, but you need it," I replied quietly, reaching for the makeshift bandages in my pack.

D glared at me, but something flickered in his eyes—something that wasn't quite anger. He didn't move as I gently began cleaning the wound with what little water we had left. His skin felt warm under my touch, and for a moment, I forgot about everything else—the danger outside, the distrust between us. It was just him and me and this strange connection that seemed to grow stronger with each passing day.

"You really are stubborn," he muttered after a while, his voice softer now.

I glanced up at him, meeting his gaze head-on. "And you're impossible," I replied with a small smile. "Why won't you just let me help?"

He grunted.

I rolled my eyes. "That's not an actual form of communication, you know."

A ghost of a smile tugged at the corner of his lips before disappearing again.

I took my time wrapping the bandages, my fingers moving with careful precision. The silence between us felt almost comfortable, a stark contrast to the tension that usually simmered just beneath the surface. I'd never been this close to a man since D and I shared a bed. A strange urge to ask if I could sleep near him again bubbled up inside me. Despite what a buttface he was, despite how cruel, there was an odd sense of safety in his presence.

But I didn't want to press my luck.

"What are you doing?" he asked softly.

I blinked, realizing I'd been tracing patterns on his forearm without even thinking. "Sorry." I yanked my hand away, feeling the heat rise in my cheeks.

He stared at the fire; the flames casting flickering shadows across his face. "The ring your sister's?" he asked, nodding toward my hand.

Grateful for the subject change, I looked down at the infinity symbol on my ring finger. "Y-yeah," I said. "She got it when..."

I bit my bottom lip; the words catching in my throat.

"When she was arranged to Archangel Michael?" he asked.

I blinked, looking at him in surprise. "How do you know that?"

"How do you think?" he asked, but his usual edge wasn't in his words. "Everyone up here knows it."

I nodded slowly, processing his words. "She was supposed to be with Michael," I said quietly. "But things didn't go as planned. Not after she was taken."

"And now?" he asked.

"Now?"

"What's going to happen with her gone?" he asked, pulling out a cigarette. "Will another take her place? Or will he try to find her?" He glanced at me. "Not likely, if you left your bunker, hmm?"

I clenched my teeth, staring at the fire.

From my peripheral, I saw D's expression softened ever so slightly, but he didn't press for more details.

"Huh," he said. "And here I thought each life is important to God."

"It is," I said. "The people who run the bunker are just that... people. Not God."

"You have a lot of faith in Him," he muttered.

"Maybe you should have more," I replied.

He leaned back. "Not likely, angel," he said. "I only have faith in things I can touch, things I can see."

"What about love?" I asked.

"What about it?"

"Surely you've been in love," I said. "Raven seemed to imply —"

At that moment, Silence emerged from the shadows, dragging a couple of rabbits in her powerful jaws. Callie and Lydia followed closely behind, their faces alight with a mix of surprise and hunger.

"Real rabbits," Callie said, her voice tinged with awe. "I've never had that before."

D tossed a couple of dull knives at their feet. "Get to skinning," he ordered, his tone leaving no room for argument.

I pulled out my own knife, the same one I'd used to stab the man. My stomach twisted into knots at the memory, but I swallowed hard, pushing the nausea back down where it belonged. D noticed my hesitation and dropped a rabbit by my feet.

"Get your mind off it," he said, his voice softer than I expected. "Skin this."

I didn't argue. Instead, I took the rabbit in my hands and began to work. The fur was soft beneath my fingers, so different to the cold steel of the knife. I focused on the task at hand, letting the repetitive motions soothe my frayed nerves.

As I worked, the world around me seemed to fade away. The only sounds were the crackling of the fire and the occasional murmurs from Callie and Lydia as they struggled with their own rabbits. D watched us with an inscrutable expression, his eyes flickering between each of us, as if assessing our worth.

The rabbit's skin came away more easily than I expected, revealing the pink flesh beneath. My hands moved almost automatically, guided by some long-buried instinct or memory. It felt strange—almost surreal—to be doing something so mundane in such extraordinary circumstances.

Silence lay down next to D, her glowing red eyes fixed on me as if she were judging my every move. I couldn't help but feel a pang of gratitude toward the hellhound for providing us with this unexpected bounty.

Callie looked over at me, her eyes wide with curiosity. "Where'd you learn to do that?" she asked, her voice barely above a whisper.

I glanced up briefly before returning my focus to the rabbit. "Bunker life," I replied simply. "We had to know how to do a lot of things."

Lydia nodded approvingly as she finally managed to peel back a strip of fur from her own rabbit. "Resourcefulness is key out here," she said.

D grunted in agreement but didn't say anything more.

We ate in silence, the crackling fire providing the only sound. The rabbits tasted gamey, but they were filling, and for that, I was grateful. Callie and Lydia picked at their food, their eyes darting between D and me as if waiting for something to happen.

Once we finished, Callie stood up, brushing the crumbs from her lap. "We need to... uh... relieve ourselves," she said, glancing at Lydia.

Lydia nodded and followed her into the darkness, leaving me alone with D.

"You sleep next to me," D said once they were gone.

"You still don't trust them?" I asked, looking up at him.

He didn't say anything, just stared into the fire with that same unreadable expression.

My eyes widened. "Does this mean you trust me?"

"I trust I can knock you on your ass with a flick of my pinky," he said, pulling out his sleeping bag.

I couldn't help but smile at that. Pulling out my own blanket, I looked over at him. "Will you still teach me?"

"You definitely need it," he muttered. "I'll take first watch, hmm?"

I rolled my eyes but didn't argue. Taking off my jacket, I did my stretches before brushing my teeth with a worn toothbrush. The routine helped calm my nerves a bit.

When I was ready for bed, I slid under my blanket. The ground was harder than I'd anticipated and the night air colder than it had been before. The fire crackled nearby, but it did little to chase away the chill that seeped into my bones. I tossed and turned, trying to find a comfortable position, but it was no use. The cold made every muscle tense up, and I couldn't help but shiver.

It was hard to fall asleep.

Every time I did, I saw the man I killed, and fear gripped me.

Not because of him.

But because of me.

Because of what I'd become.

CHAPTER 30

Walton

I sat on a log, watching the fire dim down. Everyone slept, thank God. I didn't need to hear more yapping. The embers glowed faintly, occasionally crackling as they settled into ash. My eyes drifted to Everly. She sat across from me; her face illuminated by the dying light. Her features were delicate, almost otherworldly. She seemed to glow with a soft light that made her look out of place in this harsh, broken world.

God, she was so fucking... ethereal.

A fucking angel.

My eyes skimmed her neck, noticing the bruises forming there. Anger flared up inside me again. If she hadn't killed that scavenger, I would have. Slowly. I would have reveled in making him suffer for daring to touch her.

Everly shifted slightly, wincing as she adjusted her position. The firelight danced on her skin, highlighting every bruise and cut she'd endured. Despite it all, there was a resilience in her eyes that I couldn't ignore. She wasn't just some fragile girl; she had strength buried deep within her.

I noticed her shivering. That flimsy blanket she had

wrapped around herself was practically useless. Did the bunkers not have anything heavier? It was almost comical if it wasn't so damn pathetic. She clung to that thin layer like it could protect her from the world outside.

I leaned back, my eyes tracing the outline of her form. She looked so small, huddled up like that. Vulnerable. It pissed me off more than it should have. I wanted to hate her, really. But damn it, I couldn't bring myself to do it. Not completely.

Everly started tossing and turning, her face contorting with distress. A soft whine escaped her lips, barely audible over the crackling of the fire. She mumbled incoherently, words lost in the fog of her nightmare.

"No... don't... please..."

Her voice trembled, and my heart twisted in my chest. It felt like a vice grip squeezing tighter with every desperate plea she uttered.

My fists clenched involuntarily.

Her breathing quickened, coming out in short, panicked gasps. She flinched violently, as if trying to fend off an invisible attacker.

My instincts screamed at me to wake her up, to pull her out of whatever Hell she was reliving. But I didn't want to get involved, didn't want to open that door any wider than it already was.

Fuck.

This was dangerous territory.

And then she sat up suddenly, eyes snapping open wide with terror. Her chest heaved as she struggled to catch her breath, wild eyes darting around before settling on me. She let out a shaky sob. She scrambled to her feet and moved toward me, throwing her arms around my torso. I sat there, rigid and unprepared for the contact.

"I thought..." she murmured into my chest. "I thought..."

Her grip tightened, as if she feared I'd vanish into the

night. It baffled me why she sought comfort in someone like me, but there she was, clinging on like I was her lifeline.

I should've told her to go back to sleep, that she needed rest, or else she'd be dragging us down tomorrow. The words were right there, but I couldn't bring myself to say them. When the hell had I gotten so soft?

My hands lifted almost involuntarily, hovering over her waist before finally resting there. I waited for the inevitable— her realization that a demon's hands were on her, her shriek of disgust, the shove that would push me away. But it never came. Instead, she curled her fingers in my shirt and tugged me closer, trying to bury her face deeper into my chest.

I didn't pull her closer, but I didn't push her away either.

Damn it, I wanted to breathe her in. I wanted to close my eyes and drag my nose along her throat, inhale the scent of her life mingled with fear and resilience. But I wouldn't. It was too much.

Yet I couldn't deny myself this small moment of connection, either.

Her body trembled against mine, and I felt every shiver pass through me as if it were my own. My hands stayed at her waist, not moving an inch. This was new territory for me— allowing someone this close without pushing them away or using them for some end.

She mumbled something incoherent against my chest, and I felt a pang of something I couldn't name—a mix of protectiveness and something dangerously close to... My heart skipped painfully, like it had forgotten it could do such a thing. Her vulnerability clawed at my hardened exterior, threatening to break through the walls I'd built around myself.

But this wasn't about me. This was about giving Everly what she needed right now—a sense of safety in a world gone mad.

And for some damn reason, I found myself willing to be that for her.

So we sat there by the dying fire, two broken souls finding an unexpected solace in each other's presence, her practically in my lap.

"Nightmare?" I grunted out, my voice gravelly.

She nodded, her head still pressed against my chest. "It was so real," she murmured.

I stayed silent for a moment, contemplating whether to push or let it be. "Wanna talk about it?"

She shook her head, taking a shuddering breath. Her body still trembled against mine, and I felt each tremor as if it were my own.

"He deserved it, you know."

Everly slowly pulled her head back, her eyes searching mine. "How can you say that?" she asked in a low voice. "You don't know what I did to him."

"I know you," I said, my tone firm but not unkind. "A bit. And I know your angelic tendencies wouldn't let you do something unless you had to. I'm glad you did."

Her voice wavered as she asked, "W-why?"

Her eyes were so damn big and green that for a moment, I thought I might drown in them. They held so much emotion; I wanted to yell at her for feeling so damn much. But she was searching for something—maybe reassurance or under-standing.

"Because I would have made it slow," I replied.

We stared at each other, the air between us thick with unspoken words and emotions neither of us was ready to confront.

"Why?" she asked again, her voice barely more than a whisper.

I didn't say anything. Refused to. The reasons were too

complicated, too wrapped up in my own darkness and the remnants of whatever humanity I still clung to.

She swallowed hard, her throat moving with the effort. My gaze dropped to that delicate motion, noticing the way her skin looked almost translucent in the firelight.

The silence stretched on, filled only with the crackling of the dying fire and the soft sounds of our breathing. She didn't push further for answers, maybe sensing that some things were better left unsaid—for now, at least.

Her grip on my shirt loosened slightly, but didn't let go entirely. She stayed close, drawing some comfort from my presence despite the weight of our conversation. And for reasons I couldn't fully explain, I found myself wanting to protect that fragile sense of safety she seemed to find in me.

It was dangerous territory we were treading on, but at that moment, it felt like we had no choice but to navigate it together.

Slowly, I lifted one hand from her waist and gently brushed her chin with my knuckles, tilting her head back. Her skin felt warm under my touch, the pulse in her neck fluttering like a trapped bird. My fingertips dropped to her throat, ghosting over the bruises, wishing I could erase them.

Stupid. Fucking stupid.

But she hadn't pulled away.

I could snap her neck if I wanted, and she would let me. She trusted me so damn much...

"I won't let anyone put their hands on you again," I murmured.

She looked up at me, eyes wide and searching. "You think my nightmare was about him?"

I blinked, caught off guard. "It... it wasn't...?"

She shook her head, taking a shuddering breath. "I..." She looked away. "Just... don't leave me."

Her words hit me like a slap to the face, but somehow, my

grip on her waist tightened. The desperation in her voice clawed at something deep inside me.

"Can I... would it be okay... can I sleep next to you?" she asked. "I know it's almost my turn for watch, but... I just like knowing you're here. That you're... near me. That I'm not..."

Alone. She didn't say it. She didn't have to.

I exhaled slowly, trying to rein in the tumult of emotions swirling inside me. This girl was getting under my skin in ways I hadn't anticipated. But seeing the vulnerability in her eyes, hearing the tremor in her voice...

"Yeah," I finally said, my voice rougher than intended. "You can."

She let out a shaky breath of relief and settled back down beside me, nestling against my side. Her warmth seeped into me, and for a moment, I allowed myself to enjoy the simple comfort of human contact.

We sat there in silence for a while longer, the dying fire casting flickering shadows around us.

"You're so warm," she murmured. "Comfortable."

I didn't know what the hell to say to that. So I didn't say anything.

Her breathing eventually evened out as she drifted back into sleep.

I stayed awake, keeping watch over her fragile form. In that moment, despite everything I'd become and all the darkness that tainted my soul, protecting Everly felt like something worth holding onto.

And for once in what felt like an eternity, I felt cracked open, feeling these dangerous things, like I was worthy of being in this girl's orbit.

But I knew better.

And I hated she gave me these feelings in the first place.

* * *

I woke Everly a couple of hours later, the moon high in the sky, casting an eerie glow over our makeshift camp. I'd let her sleep longer than I should have, but there was something peaceful about watching her. It was hard to look anywhere else. Her face, free of the day's grime and tension, looked almost serene.

And when it was just me, I let myself look.

She clung to me like a lifeline, gravitated towards me as if I were something good. It made me mad because she shouldn't. She had no reason to trust me. But it was becoming more difficult to push her away.

I shook her shoulder gently. "Sweetheart," I murmured. "Time to wake up."

Her eyes fluttered open easily enough, adjusting to the dim light of the fire's embers. She looked up at me with that whole-hearted trust that always threw me off balance.

Always riled me up.

I took off my hat and dropped my duster in her lap. "Can't sleep with it on," I grunted, ignoring the little voice that whispered it was a fucking lie.

She didn't question it, just gave me a small, sleepy smile before pulling the duster around her shoulders like a blanket. The sight of her in my coat sent an unexpected tremor through my heart. She looked so small in it, so vulnerable yet determined.

So fucking beautiful, like the whole world knew she was mine.

She belonged to me.

Except she didn't.

I slid into my sleeping bag right next to her feet, feeling the weight of exhaustion settle over me. The small smile on her face as she nestled into my duster didn't go unnoticed, but I forced myself to ignore it. I had to sleep; we both needed rest if we were going to make it through getting back to Ironedge.

I put my hat over my face and closed my eyes, trying to block out everything else. The warmth from Everly's presence nearby provided an odd comfort I didn't want to admit to needing.

Sleep came quickly, despite the turmoil in my mind. And for a brief moment, in the quiet darkness of our camp, I let myself believe that maybe—just maybe—I wasn't completely lost yet.

* * *

I woke up with the sun, the first light creeping through the trees and casting long shadows across our camp. Everly stood by the firepit, back rigid, Silence at her side. She still wore my duster, looking small but resilient. Her eyes, fixed on the horizon, glistened with tears.

"Why are you crying?" the girl's voice echoed in my mind. What was her name? Carey? Casey?

Everly wiped at her eyes, smiling softly as she stared at the sunrise. "We don't see this... where I'm from," she said quietly. "It's still so... beautiful to me. I like to thank God every time I see it. Not everyone does."

"You believe in God?" Callie asked, innocent and curious.

"Of course I do," Everly answered, turning back to the sunrise.

The colors spread across the sky—fiery oranges and soft pinks blending into deep purples and blues. It was a sight I'd seen countless times, yet watching it through Everly's eyes made it feel different. More... meaningful.

"Come on," the older woman's voice cut through the moment before Everly could respond further. "Let's pee and get ready to move."

I pushed myself up, brushing off the remnants of sleep and stretching out the stiffness in my muscles. The day ahead would be another fight for survival, but for now, I allowed myself to linger on that sunrise—its warmth, its promise of a new day.

Everly turned towards me as I stood up, a small smile playing on her lips. "Good morning," she said softly.

I nodded, returning her smile with one of my own. "Morning," I replied, feeling a strange sense of calm wash over me.

We gathered our things and prepared to move out.

Everly slid out of my duster and handed it to me. "Thank you," she said, her voice soft but steady. "And thank you for... for all of it."

I grunted in response, taking the duster from her.

She beamed at me; her smile like the sun rising all over again. It was too bright, too pure, and I had to look away. I busied myself with breaking down the camp, focusing on the mundane tasks of rolling up bedrolls and dousing the fire.

Everly pulled out some jerky for herself and Silence. She handed a piece to the hellhound, who took it gently from her fingers. She then started her morning stretches, moving with a grace that was hard not to notice. She stretched her arms high above her head, arching her back and then bending forward to touch her toes. Her muscles moved smoothly under her skin, a testament to her determination and resilience.

I turned my attention back to packing up our gear, trying not to get distracted by the sight of her. The world outside was dangerous enough without me losing focus.

After finishing her stretches, Everly brushed her teeth using a small bottle of water and her mini toothbrush. It was a small routine, but it grounded us both in some semblance of normalcy.

When the others finished their morning ritual, we gathered our things and headed out. The desert was quiet, save for the occasional rustle of wind or distant birdcall. The sun had fully risen now, casting long shadows across our path as we walked.

Silence padded along beside Everly, ever vigilant. Despite everything—her naivety about the outside world, her idealism —she moved with purpose and confidence. I found myself respecting that more than I'd like to admit.

As we walked, the sun climbing higher, Everly and Callie fell into a rhythm of annoying questions and answers.

"What was it like in the bunker?" Callie asked, curiosity evident in her voice.

Everly glanced at me before answering. "It was... safe, structured. We had everything we needed—food, water, shelter. But it was also confining. We were told it was for our protection, but there was always this underlying fear."

"Sounds like a cage," Callie muttered.

"In a way, it was," Everly admitted. "What about Ironedge? What's it like living there?"

Callie shrugged. "It's tough. You have to be strong or smart to survive. But there's a sense of community. We look out for each other."

Everly nodded, processing the information. "And the surface? Is it always this harsh?"

Callie sighed. "Yeah, it's not easy. The weather, the creatures... you have to be constantly vigilant. But there's also freedom. No walls keeping you in."

Everly smiled faintly at that. "Freedom sounds nice."

"You know," Callie said suddenly, "I have a brother. He's older too, but he's not a demon. He'd like you."

I narrowed my eyes at that thought, my gut churning with an unfamiliar feeling.

"That's a kind thought," Everly replied quickly, glancing at me before continuing. "But I'm happy where I am." Her fingers brushed mine lightly, and I didn't pull away—neither did she.

"With him?" Callie asked skeptically. "He's kind of mean."

"I'm right here," I grumbled.

"I just... don't you want to be with someone normal?" Callie pressed.

Everly looked at her steadily. "My husband is eclectic, yes," she said softly but firmly. "But I trust him. He takes care of me."

My husband.

That shouldn't sound like anything meaningful.

But fuck if I didn't like the sound of it.

Fucking crazy.

Too long as a demon. That must be it.

"But he's not that attractive," Callie blurted out.

"Callie," Lydia warned from behind us.

"I find him extremely attractive," Everly stated, a light blush coloring her cheeks.

"You do?" both Lydia and Callie asked in disbelief.

I stiffened at her words, my heart doing an odd little flip in my chest.

Everly met their gaze unflinchingly. "Yes," she said softly but clearly. "He's strong and resilient. He's been through so much and yet he still stands tall. There's a depth to him that draws me in. And I like his cheekbones. The collar of his arms. The broad shoulders. He's built to keep someone safe. And I... I'm lucky he chose me to do that for."

I felt my chest tighten with an emotion I hadn't allowed myself to acknowledge.

"More boys for me then," Callie said with a shrug. "Good thing too. You're really pretty. Anyone would want you." She turned her gaze to me then, her eyes challenging. "You know that, don't you?"

"I ain't blind," I snapped back without thinking.

Everly looked up at me in surprise, and I realized I'd

admitted finding her attractive too. There was no taking it back now—not that I wanted to.

She is the most beautiful thing I've seen in a hundred years, bar none.

"Good," Callie said with a nod of satisfaction. "A man should always know their partner can do better."

"You're a real piece of work, ain't ya?" I muttered.

Callie shrugged nonchalantly.

Before anyone could respond further, Ironedge came into view ahead of us, prompting excited exclamations from both Callie and Lydia.

The sight of Ironedge meant we'd soon be among allies again—if only temporarily—and maybe then we could catch our breath and figure out our next steps.

As we walked, Everly never pulled her fingers away from mine... and I didn't either.

CHAPTER 31

Everly

W e trudged back into Ironedge, weary but triumphant. The gates creaked open, and the familiar sights of the settlement welcomed us. The same guard from before eyed me with surprise, his brow furrowing.

"Thought you were a goner," he said, his voice tinged with genuine disbelief.

I managed a tired smile. "I told you I'd be back."

D grunted but kept his eyes forward, not sparing me a glance. His silence gnawed at me, but I pushed it aside. We had more pressing matters.

As we stepped inside, the atmosphere shifted. People started gathering, whispers spreading like wildfire. Callie and Lydia were quickly surrounded by their friends and family. Tears flowed freely as arms wrapped around them in tight embraces.

"Callie! Lydia!" Voices rang out, filled with relief and joy. "We thought you were lost forever!"

The two women clung to their loved ones, their expressions a mix of exhaustion and overwhelming emotion. It was hard not to feel a pang of satisfaction watching them reunited with their community.

I stood to the side, observing the scene unfold. It felt strange to be on the periphery of such raw human connection. My thoughts wandered back to the bunker and the community I had once been part of, but I shook my head to clear those memories.

One of the older women approached me, her face lined with years of hardship but softened by gratitude. She took my hands in hers, squeezing them tightly.

"Thank you," she said simply, her eyes brimming with unspoken emotions.

"It wasn't just me —"

But she was already moving away.

D moved past us without a word, heading toward the heart of Ironedge. I watched him go, feeling an unspoken weight between us.

The crowd began to disperse, people returning to their routines but casting glances our way every so often. Callie and Lydia stayed close to their families, soaking in every moment of their reunion.

For now, we had made it back. And for now, that was enough.

I hurried to catch up with D, Silence padding quietly beside him. He was heading straight for the hotel room without a backward glance. I matched his pace, my excitement bubbling over.

"Can you believe that?" I whispered, my voice filled with wonder. "We helped them. We did that. Look at how happy everyone is."

D grunted, the sound low and almost dismissive. But after all this time, I was starting to pick up on what his grunts meant. This one wasn't annoyance; it was more of a begrudging acknowledgment. He didn't share my enthusiasm, but he didn't dismiss it either.

We reached the stairs, and he began to climb them with long, purposeful strides. Silence waited at the bottom, sitting obediently, as if knowing this part of the journey wasn't for her.

The hotel room loomed ahead as we ascended. The weariness of the past few days settled into my bones, but there was a warmth in my chest that hadn't been there before. The faces of Callie and Lydia flashed in my mind — their tears, their smiles, the overwhelming relief of their families.

D pushed open the door to our room and stepped inside without hesitation. I followed, feeling the cool air hit me as I crossed the threshold.

The room was just as I'd left it: sparse but functional. D dropped his pack onto the floor with a heavy thud and sat on the edge of the bed, his shoulders slumping ever so slightly.

I stood by the door for a moment, watching him. The silence between us stretched, but it wasn't uncomfortable. It was just... there.

"I'm glad you're back," I murmured. I meant the words too, more than I expected.

D glanced up at me, his eyes hard but not unkind. He nodded once before looking away again.

"Oh," I began, breaking the silence. "While you were gone, I actually... Well, I told you I was going to earn my keep. And I —"

"You didn't —"

I cut him off, moving to the drawers with purpose. "I got jobs," I said firmly, yanking open the wooden drawer and pulling out several bags filled with demon shards. "Look. I told you I can be resourceful."

His eyes burned with intensity, a mixture of suspicion and curiosity. "What'd you have to do —"

"Not what you're thinking," I interrupted again, feeling my cheeks warm up. "I helped garden. And I helped with other things."

He arched an eyebrow, clearly skeptical.

"Gardening?" D questioned.

"Yes," I replied, trying to keep the irritation out of my voice. "The hydroponics system here needed maintenance. They were struggling with some nutrient imbalances in their crops. Turns out my background came in handy."

He crossed his arms but didn't say anything, so I continued.

"I also helped repair some of their water filtration systems," I added, feeling a surge of pride in my accomplishments. "They were using outdated methods that were inefficient. With a few adjustments, we managed to improve water quality and save resources."

D still looked unconvinced, so I pressed on.

"And then there was the medical clinic," I said. "They were short-staffed and overwhelmed with patients. Nothing too serious, but lots of minor injuries and illnesses that needed attention."

His expression softened just a fraction as he listened.

"I learned some basic first aid back in the bunker," I explained. "It wasn't much, but it made a difference here. Wendy was grateful for the extra hands."

D let out a slow breath, the tension in his shoulders easing slightly.

"See?" I said softly. "I can pull my weight."

He finally met my gaze again, and for a moment, there was something almost like respect in his eyes.

"You did good," he admitted gruffly.

"We should probably shower," I suggested, glancing at the grime coating our skin. "Not together. I didn't mean... Did you want to go first? I was thinking I could check your bandages —"

"You go first," he cut in curtly. "Now. Before I'm forced to shut your mouth. Damn, girl, can you be silent for a goddamn minute? We just got back."

I huffed, feeling a flicker of irritation. "You don't have to be rude about it," I muttered. "But sure. Fine. I'll take a shower."

I fiddled with the drawer of the dresser, my fingers brushing against the worn wood as I pulled out a towel from the bottom drawer. The fabric was rough but clean, and right now, that was all that mattered.

"What?" he asked, leaning against the headboard. "You're stalling."

"You'll... you'll be here when I get out?" I asked, unable to keep the uncertainty from my voice.

"Where do you think I'm going to go?" he replied snidely.

I let out a breath, deciding not to take his bait. Instead, I headed toward the small bathroom, closing the door behind me with a soft click.

The bathroom was cramped and dimly lit, but it had running water and that was more than enough. I turned on the faucet, waiting for the water to heat up as steam began to fill the room. The mirror fogged over, obscuring my reflection — a small mercy given how worn out I felt.

I stepped under the stream of water, letting it wash away the dirt and sweat from our journey. It wasn't hot, not really, and the pressure wasn't much, but it was a shower, and I needed it. The warmth seeped into my muscles, soothing the aches and pains that had settled in during our trek back to Ironedge. For a moment, I closed my eyes and allowed myself to just be — no worries, no fears, just the sensation of water cascading over me.

As I scrubbed myself clean, my mind wandered back to

D's harsh words. He always had this way of pushing me away with his rough exterior, but there were moments when his guard slipped just enough for me to see the person underneath. It made his rudeness easier to bear somehow.

I finished rinsing off and wrapped myself in the towel, savoring its coarse texture against my clean skin. Stepping out of the shower felt like shedding a layer of weariness along with the grime. I didn't want to pull on my dirty clothes, so I fumbled in my pack and pulled out my pajamas. A little early, but I wanted comfort more than anything. And maybe a nap.

Opening the bathroom door cautiously, I peeked out into our room. D was still there, sitting on the edge of the bed with his head bowed slightly, as if lost in thought.

"Your turn," I said softly, trying not to disturb whatever reverie he was in. "And when you're done, I'll change your bandages."

He glanced up at me briefly before standing up and heading toward the bathroom without a word.

I sat on the edge of the bed, my brush moving mechanically through my tangled hair. Each stroke felt like a ritual, a way to anchor myself in the moment. I took a breath, then another, trying to steady my nerves.

For no reason at all, tears welled up in my eyes. My hands began to shake uncontrollably. I was safe. I was with D. But that man...

Silent tears rolled down my cheeks, each drop a betrayal of the calm facade I tried to maintain. The brush slipped from my grasp, and suddenly, it was gently pulled away.

I opened my eyes to see D in fresh clothes, setting the brush down beside me. He didn't say a word as he knelt down and turned back to me. His brow furrowed slightly as he reached out and wiped away my tears with surprising gentleness.

"I know I talk too much," I blurted out, the words

tumbling out of me unbidden. "I just... I keep seeing his face, the look of shock in his eyes when I dug my knife... And... and I keep trying to feel something — regret? Remorse? Something? I don't know. But I don't... I don't feel anything. I killed someone and I don't feel anything."

D's expression softened, his eyes filled with an understanding that cut through my turmoil. He leaned closer and said softly, "You did what you had to."

His words hit me like a gentle wave, washing over my guilt and confusion. They didn't absolve me of what I'd done, but gave me a frame to understand it.

"Sometimes that's all there is," he added. "You don't owe him that. You don't owe anyone that."

I turned to him, my voice barely above a whisper. "But... but does that make me a monster?" I asked, my heart heavy with the weight of my actions. "Is God going to forgive me? I know he was going to kill me. He was going to... well... he was going to do a lot more than just kill me —"

D clenched his teeth together, his eyes blazing with intensity.

The sight of his anger made me pause, but I pushed on. "But do I have a right to kill him for that?"

He stepped closer, his voice low and firm as he murmured, "Listen to me." His hands gently took hold of my face, and I leaned into his touch, finding comfort in the unexpected tenderness. "You have every right to defend yourself. If you don't fight for the life God gave you, then what does that say about you? And if God didn't forgive you... Well, I'd rather burn in Hell than serve someone who'd rather see you get raped and murdered all for attempting righteousness."

His words hit me hard, and I sucked in a breath, staring at him with wide eyes. For a minute, we said nothing. My heart pitter-pattered in my chest, the weight of our conversation hanging between us.

"I'm glad I met you," I said softly.

He blinked in surprise, his gruff exterior momentarily slipping. "Huh," he grunted. "Me? I'm a monster, darling."

"No," I insisted, taking one of his hands from my face and giving it a squeeze. "You're not."

"The things I've done—"

"You're good," I cut in firmly. "Now." I cleared my throat and shifted gears. "I'd like to check your bandages. Please."

He rolled his eyes but couldn't hide the small smirk tugging at the corner of his mouth. "Stubborn as ever," he muttered as he sat next to me on the bed.

I grabbed my pack and pulled out the med-kit, focusing on the task at hand. The silence between us felt different now —less strained and more understanding. As I worked on his bandages, my fingers moving with practiced precision, I couldn't help but feel a sense of gratitude for having him by my side.

D winced slightly as I peeled back the old bandage, revealing the angry wounds wound underneath. It looked better than before, but still needed attention.

I carefully peeled back the old bandage, revealing the wounds beneath. They were healing, but still angry and raw. I dipped a cloth into antiseptic, gently cleaning around the edges.

"Hold still," I murmured.

"Yeah, yeah," he grumbled, but didn't move an inch.

My fingers moved with practiced precision, wrapping the clean bandage around his arm. As I worked, his scent enveloped me — a mix of earth and sweat, a subtle scent of smoke, with a hint of something metallic. It was oddly comforting, grounding me in the moment.

"There," I whispered, tying a small bow to secure the bandage. I looked up at him.

His eyes were fixed on my neck, where bruises marred my

skin. He reached out, fingers hovering close to the bruises but stopping short. His hand dropped back to his side, and I felt an unexpected pang of disappointment.

"We should probably pack up," he said gruffly. "If we're going to go after your sister, I want to leave early."

"Yes," I agreed, fiddling with the ring on my right finger. "Of course."

I stood up and moved to the dresser again, pulling out my clothes and supplies.

At that moment, a knock echoed through the room. I froze and looked at D. He shook his head but rose to answer the door, his hand instinctively reaching for his gun.

My heart raced as he approached the door.

D opened it, and Callie and Lydia spilled in without invitation, their faces lit up with excitement.

"We didn't interrupt anything, did we?" Callie asked, glancing between us. "I know you two are married and everything."

"We wanted to invite you to a party tonight," Lydia cut in, her voice bubbling with enthusiasm. "As a way to say thank you. To... to celebrate life."

I looked over at D, widening my eyes in a silent plea. I bit my bottom lip, waiting for his reaction. I wouldn't go if he didn't want to. And I was pretty sure he didn't want to.

He gave me a long look before huffing and grunting.

"Really?" I asked, unable to contain my excitement.

"You understood that?" Callie asked, her eyebrows shooting up.

"Great," Lydia said before I could answer. "There's a space on the other side of town. Bonfires. That's where we'll be."

Callie grabbed my wrist, pulling me toward the door.

"The fuck you think you're going with her?" D's voice was gruff and unyielding.

"Whoa," Callie said, holding up her free hand defensively. "I just want to help her get ready. I have clothes—"

"She doesn't need—"

"I'll be all right, D," I said quickly, pulling away from Callie and moving closer to him. "I'll meet you at the party."

"I don't want you out of my sight," he said in a low voice that sent shivers down my spine.

"And here I thought you were sick of my yapping," I teased gently. "Please?"

"She'll be out there in an hour," Callie interjected, rolling her eyes. "Jeez, so protective." She ushered me toward the door.

"I will come for her," D groused, his eyes narrowing at Callie and Lydia. "I'm not afraid to kill an obnoxious teenager if I have to."

"D!" I exclaimed, shocked by his bluntness.

But he didn't waver. His gaze remained fixed on me, his concern palpable even through his rough exterior.

"One hour, cowboy," Callie muttered, before leading me out of the room.

As we walked down the hallway, my heart raced with anticipation for the night ahead.

An actual party. With people. Excitement burned through my blood. I couldn't wait.

CHAPTER 32

Walton

I sat on the edge of the bed, my hands running over my face as if I could scrub away the thoughts crawling through my head. Everly had been gone for all of five minutes, and already I felt antsy. It was ridiculous. She was a grown woman, capable of handling herself. Besides, I didn't need her. She'd been nothing but a thorn in my side.

No, that wasn't true.

Hell, I couldn't even lie to myself anymore.

Fuck, I hated this. I'd been so careful not to get caught up in anything or anyone. And then she showed up in her Purifier uniform, practically a walking billboard of everything I despised. She should have been easy to hate.

But she wasn't.

Goddammit.

I muttered curses under my breath as I kicked off my boots and slid off my duster. The damn thing still smelled like her—vanilla and fucking sunshine. It was maddening. Every breath reminded me of her presence, like she was haunting me even when she wasn't here.

What the hell was I supposed to do for a whole hour without her around?

I paced the small room, trying to shake off the restlessness gnawing at me. The walls seemed to close in, suffocating me with memories of her soft laughter and the way her eyes sparkled when she talked about something she loved. She'd wormed her way into places I thought were long dead and buried.

Dropping back onto the bed, I stared at the ceiling, wishing it would provide some answers. My thoughts were a tangled mess of anger, confusion, and something else—something I didn't want to name because naming it would make it real.

"Get it together," I growled to myself.

But it was no use. The longer she was gone, the more agitated I became. My hands itched to do something—anything—to distract myself from the gnawing feeling inside me. But there was nothing here but the damn smell of vanilla and sunshine.

I ran my fingers through my hair, frustration bubbling up like lava ready to erupt. Why did she have this effect on me? Why did every moment without her feel like an eternity?

I couldn't keep doing this—couldn't keep pretending that she didn't matter when every fiber of my being screamed otherwise.

Damn it all to hell.

What the fuck was wrong with me?

Hell, we shouldn't even be going to this fucking party. Not with Raven on our ass. Not with anger simmering just beneath the surface, ready to explode at any moment.

The image of Everly walking into that tent was seared into my mind—stubborn determination etched on her face, concern in her eyes.

For me.

318

She looked so goddamn beautiful, like a fucking angel come to save my sinning soul.

I needed to be around her, to... Hell, I didn't even know why. Protect her? Especially with Raven intent on getting revenge.

Fuck.

This girl was going to be the death of me.

I had to teach her how to shoot, how to fight. She needed to protect herself. Sure, she had runes, and that was good. But it wasn't enough. Not against what we were up against.

And what happens when you find her sister? a voice whispered in my head. *When she finds out why you're really after the sister, hmm?*

I clenched my teeth so hard I thought they might crack. I didn't want to think about it. But God, it made my chest ache.

"Fuck!" I barked out loud, but even that didn't make me feel better.

I couldn't stand it any longer. I needed air. Grabbing my pack of smokes, I headed out of the room. Everly wasn't here to complain, but hell, the last thing I wanted was her nagging about the smell when she got back.

I stepped outside and struck a match, the flare of it briefly lighting up the darkness. The cigarette caught, and I took a long drag, feeling the smoke curl in my lungs. It wasn't the best habit, but it was mine. And right now, I needed something to steady me.

Silence padded over to me, her eyes glowing red in the dim light. She snuffed at my leg like she disapproved.

"Not you too," I muttered, reaching down to scratch behind her ears. Her fur was rough and warm under my fingers. "Everyone's got an opinion these days."

Silence sat down next to me, her presence a strange comfort as I looked out over Ironedge. The sky was painted with hues of orange and pink, a stark contrast to the ruins below. The sun began its descent, casting long shadows that stretched like fingers over the landscape.

Reminded me of Everly. Fuck, her dinner plate eyes would probably be all big even though she'd already seen a sunset. She'd get that stupidly big smile, and —

Fuck. I needed to fucking stop.

Ironedge wasn't much to look at—a collection of battered buildings and makeshift shelters huddled together against the harsh world outside. But in this moment, bathed in the dying light of day, it almost looked peaceful.

Almost.

I took another drag from my cigarette and exhaled slowly, watching as the smoke drifted up into the evening air. The sky continued its transformation, colors deepening into shades of crimson and violet as the sun dipped lower on the horizon.

It was moments like this that made me remember there was still beauty in this broken world. Moments that made me wonder if there was still something worth fighting for.

Silence nudged me with her nose, breaking my reverie.

"Yeah, yeah," I said softly, petting her head again. "I know."

I stood there for a while longer, watching as day turned to night, each breath of smoke grounding me a little more. Finally, I stubbed out the cigarette on the worn wood railing and flicked it away, watching it skitter across the ground before I turned my steps toward the back of Ironedge. The party was out there, somewhere amidst the bonfires and laughter.

The sun had dipped below the horizon, leaving the sky a deep shade of indigo. Flickering flames from the bonfires cast warm, dancing shadows on the weather-beaten walls and dirt paths. The setup was simple—wooden tables lined with mismatched chairs, a makeshift bar serving who-knows-what in chipped glasses, and clusters of people mingling under the stars. String lights were haphazardly strung between poles, adding a faint twinkle to the rustic scene.

As I approached, a couple of people broke off from a group and made their way toward me. Instinctively, my hand moved to rest on my gun. But their faces lit up with smiles as they neared.

"Hey! You're Everly's husband, right?" one of them called out. "D?"

I gave a slow nod, keeping my guard up.

"We just wanted to thank you," another added, her eyes bright with genuine gratitude. "For bringing Callie and Lydia back."

I blinked, caught off guard. They weren't treating me like a demon or something sinful. Just like another person. It was unsettling.

I grunted.

The first woman leaned in slightly, her voice curious but friendly. "So, where's your wife?"

I opened my mouth to respond, but no words came out. My mind raced for an answer that wouldn't give too much away.

Before I could find one, the second woman chimed in, pointing past me with an easy smile. "Oh, there she is with Callie."

I turned to follow her gaze and spotted Everly standing by one of the bonfires, talking animatedly with Callie. Even from this distance, I could see that stupidly big smile of hers.

I was stunned.

Everly stood by the bonfire, her face illuminated by the flickering flames. She wore a modest green dress that was sleeveless and had a conservative scoop. The fabric cinched at her waist and flared at the hips, accentuating her figure in a way that was both elegant and understated.

For a moment, I couldn't look away.

Her hair, usually pulled back in a practical ponytail, fell loose around her shoulders, catching the firelight and shimmering like gold. She laughed at something Callie said, her eyes crinkling at the corners, and I felt a strange tightening in my chest.

She was the most beautiful thing I had ever seen.

The dress, simple as it was, brought out the color in her eyes—those eyes that seemed to hold an entire world of innocence and stubborn determination. She moved with a grace I hadn't noticed before, her gestures animated as she spoke.

Fuck, I was in trouble.

Every fiber of my being screamed to stay distant, to keep that protective wall up. But watching her now, bathed in the soft glow of the firelight, it felt impossible. She was more than just a companion or a means to an end. She was *everything*.

I took a step forward before I realized what I was doing. The sounds of the party faded into the background, replaced by the steady thrum of my heartbeat in my ears. My feet carried me closer to her without my permission.

As I stood there, my eyes fixed on Everly, she turned and spotted me. Her face lit up with a beam of excitement, eyes sparkling like they'd found something precious.

"D!" she exclaimed, closing the distance between us in a few quick strides. Her hand reached out, and without thinking, I let her take mine. It felt natural, like it had always been meant to be this way.

"Do you know what peach cobbler is?" she asked, her voice bubbling with enthusiasm.

I felt my lips twitch slightly. "What is it, angel?" I said in a gravelly tone.

Everly laughed, the sound light and infectious. She squeezed my hand, her warmth seeping into my skin.

"No," she replied, shaking her head but still smiling wide.

"It's a dessert. A really delicious one. And guess what? They have some here tonight!"

I arched an eyebrow, feigning ignorance while inwardly enjoying her joy. "Peach cobbler, huh? Sounds almost too good to be true."

"It is!" she insisted, tugging me toward the makeshift bar where the dessert was being served. "You have to try it. I waited to try it with you."

As we moved through the crowd, I couldn't help but notice how people stepped aside for us—no wary glances or whispers. Just simple acceptance. It was unnerving, but oddly comforting.

Everly's excitement was contagious. For the first time in what felt like forever, I allowed myself to relax just a little. Maybe tonight wouldn't be so bad after all.

We reached the table laden with food and drink. She picked up a plate with a generous slice of peach cobbler and handed it to me with a grin that could light up the darkest corner of Hellgate Citadel.

"Here," she said, watching intently as I took a bite.

The sweetness exploded on my tongue—rich and tangy, a stark contrast to the usual fare of dried rations and canned goods. I hadn't tasted anything like this in years.

"Well?" Everly prompted, eyes wide with anticipation.

I swallowed and gave her an approving nod. "Not bad. I've had better."

Her face lit up even more, if that were possible. She laughed again, and for a moment, all the tension and anger that had been coiled inside me eased away.

"I knew you'd tasted some before," she said. "My turn."

She took the plate from me, her eyes twinkling with curiosity. She scooped up a piece of the cobbler and brought it to her lips. As soon as she tasted it, a soft moan of pleasure escaped her.

"Oh, goly," she whispered, closing her eyes for a moment to savor the flavor. "How could you think anything is better than this?"

I leaned in closer, my voice dropping to a low rumble. "Trust me, sugar," I said, "there's some pleasure that's much better than that."

Her eyes snapped open, and she swallowed hard. The air between us seemed to crackle with electricity as our gazes locked. Heat passed between us, igniting something deep inside.

"You have something..." I murmured, reaching out to gently dab a bit of crust from the corner of her mouth. Without breaking eye contact, I brought it to my lips and tasted it.

She watched me, her eyes wide and dark with an intensity that sent a shiver down my spine. She swallowed again, visibly affected by the moment.

It was as if the world around us faded away, leaving just the two of us standing there by the bonfire. The taste of peach cobbler lingered on my tongue, but it was nothing compared to the sensation of being this close to Everly.

"Everly," Callie called. "Come here. I want you to meet someone."

I stiffened, eyes narrowing already. Without thinking, I placed a hand on the small of her back and led her to where Callie stood. Luckily, she didn't pull away.

Callie glanced at me with a sigh before looking back at Everly. "This is my brother, Pat—"

"Is that a demon?" the *boy* said, looking at me with a scowl.

He looked like he'd walked out of a damn recruitment poster—square jaw, piercing blue eyes, and a build that screamed he could bench-press half of Ironedge.

"What the fuck is a demon doing here?" He looked at

Everly. "Why is he touching you? Are you okay? Do you need me to kick his ass?"

"Now, son," I began, but Everly cut me off.

"Stop right there, Pat," she said firmly, stepping in front of me like a goddamn shield. "You don't know anything about him, first of all."

Pat's eyes widened in surprise as he took in her fierce stance. "Are you serious?"

"Dead serious," she replied, her voice unwavering. "D has saved my life more times than I can count. He's risked everything to protect me and others in ways you can't even begin to understand."

Pat opened his mouth to argue, but Everly raised a hand to silence him.

"You think just because he looks different, he's the enemy? Let me tell you something—looks can be deceiving. D has more honor and courage in his little finger than most people have in their entire bodies."

Pat's scowl deepened as he glanced between us. "But—"

"No 'buts,'" she interrupted again. "D is not just some random demon wandering around causing trouble. He's my husband."

That declaration hung in the air like a thunderclap. Pat's jaw dropped open, and for once, he was speechless.

"And for the record," Everly continued, her voice softer now but no less determined, "I don't need anyone to kick his ass because there's no reason to. D is my partner in every sense of the word. And it's extremely rude and quite disappointing to say otherwise."

The firelight danced in her eyes as she stared down her brother, leaving no room for doubt or argument.

Pat scowled, his face contorting with disgust. "Demon fucker," he spat.

Without a second thought, I grabbed his shirt and easily

lifted him off the ground. His feet dangled as I held him eye-level. "Now, son," I growled, my voice low and menacing, "she said her peace, and as usual, she rambled, but I'll add mine. You talk about her that way again and I'll rip your head off. Do I make myself clear?"

Everly placed a gentle hand on my forearm. "And quite frankly," she said, her voice steady and calm, "who I'm intimate with is no one's business."

I felt a surge of anger that made me want to do something more to Pat—teach him a lesson he wouldn't forget. But Everly's touch was her way of asking me to put him down.

"Come on," she murmured softly. "You can dance with me."

I dropped Pat to the floor like a sack of potatoes. Callie muttered something to her brother as Everly began pulling me toward the dance floor.

"I don't dance," I grumbled.

She looked up at me with those goddamn big eyes of hers —eyes that could melt the hardest heart. How could I refuse her anything?

"Fuck, fine." I sighed in resignation.

"Do you know how?" Everly asked, a teasing smile playing on her lips. "Do you need me to lead?"

I scowled at her, grabbing her hip with one hand and taking her other hand in mine. "That's insulting," I muttered.

The music played softly around us as we moved together. Her body fit perfectly against mine as if we were made to dance this way. I led her through the steps, my movements surprisingly fluid despite my earlier protestations.

Her laughter was light and infectious as we twirled under the string lights. The flickering flames of the bonfires cast warm shadows over us, creating an intimate cocoon amidst the bustling party.

Everly's eyes sparkled with joy as she looked up at me, our

bodies swaying in sync with the music. Her touch was soft but firm on my shoulder; her fingers interlaced with mine felt like they belonged there.

For a moment, everything else faded away—the dangers outside Ironedge, the betrayals that haunted us both, even the fact that I was no longer human. All that mattered was this dance and the woman in my arms.

We moved together seamlessly, as if we had danced this way a thousand times before. The rhythm of the music guided our steps while our hearts seemed to beat in perfect harmony.

As we danced, I couldn't help but marvel at how natural it felt—how right it felt—to be here with her like this. Despite everything we'd been through or maybe because of it, this moment felt like a small piece of heaven in our hellish world.

And for now—for just this brief moment—I allowed myself to enjoy it.

Another song started playing, but neither of us pulled away. The rhythm shifted, a slower, more intimate tune. I felt Everly's breath hitch slightly against my chest, her hand resting on my shoulder, fingers light but firm.

"Where'd you learn how to dance?" she asked, her voice a soft murmur against the night air.

I glanced down at her, debating whether to answer. Her eyes held an innocent curiosity that tugged at something deep inside me.

"You don't have to tell me," she said quickly, misreading my silence. "Forget I asked."

"My wife," I said finally, the words tasting like ash in my mouth.

"Wife?" Her eyes widened in surprise.

"Before... before the Divine Collapse." I forced the words out. "She insisted I learn. Didn't want me to embarrass her during our first dance."

Everly nodded slowly. "I didn't realize you were married,"

she said. She started to pull away, her face apologetic. "I'm so sorry, I assumed—"

"Not anymore," I interrupted, tightening my grip on her. I didn't want her to pull away. "We're not married anymore."

She searched my face, and damn it, she was making this so hard. I already said too much, already said more than I had to anyone in a hundred goddamn years. I didn't want to talk about this, but it was impossible to say nothing when she looked at me that way.

"It ended badly," I said, the admission heavy on my tongue. "It was a long time ago."

"Is she still...?" Everly began hesitantly.

"I don't know." I shrugged, the movement causing our dance to falter slightly. Couples swayed around us, lost in their own worlds. "Quite frankly, I don't give two good goddamn fucks."

She frowned at my language but didn't say anything.

"The only good thing that came from that was my daughter," I added quietly.

"You have a daughter?" she asked softly.

"I... I don't know," I admitted, the words dragging out like a confession. "I did. But it's been so long..."

We stopped moving entirely then, standing still amidst the dancers who continued to swirl around us. Everly's gaze held mine, filled with a mixture of compassion and sadness that made it hard to breathe.

For a moment, we just stood there in silence, the music playing on as if unaware of the emotional weight pressing down on us both. The warmth of her hand in mine was a small comfort amidst the chaos of memories and regrets that threatened to overwhelm me.

"We should find her," she said, her voice determined yet soft. "We should look for your daughter."

I grunted, shifting uncomfortably. The past wasn't a place I wanted to linger.

"What about you?" I asked, eager to change the subject. "Where'd you learn to dance?"

"The bunker," she replied, her tone lightening as she spoke. She opened her mouth as if to say more, but then stopped herself.

"That's it?" I pressed, sensing there was more to the story.

"Everyone is supposed to learn," she explained. "There are divine occasions that require it."

"Right," I said, nodding slowly. "Like your sister's engagement to Archangel Michael himself."

She looked away, her expression guarded. There was something she wasn't telling me, and it was as clear as day on her face.

"You're hiding something from me, hmm?" I asked, my curiosity piqued.

Her eyes met mine, and she chewed her bottom lip—a telltale sign of her internal struggle.

"Good thing your God doesn't abide liars," I said, my voice carrying a hint of challenge.

"It's complicated," she murmured, her gaze dropping.

"Ain't everything nowadays?" I countered, wanting to push further. For some reason, I needed to know what was going on in that head of hers.

"Yeah," she said simply. Then she stepped forward and rested her head on my chest, swaying gently to the music.

I froze at the intimate contact, my mind racing. It had been so long since anyone had been this close. Since I let anyone this close. My first instinct was to pull away, but the warmth of her body against mine made me hesitate.

Made me crave her even closer.

"D," she murmured, tilting her head up to look at me.

Her lips were only a few inches away. It would be so easy

—so damn easy—to just lean in and kiss her. The thought made my heart pound harder than any battle ever had.

"Do you think you'll ever tell me your real name?" she asked softly, her eyes searching mine for answers.

I looked deep into those eyes—those goddamn big eyes that seemed to see right through me—and opened my mouth to speak when the music abruptly stopped and a call for a speech echoed through the crowd.

The moment shattered like glass hitting the ground. I wasn't sure if I was grateful for the interruption or irritated by it. Probably both.

CHAPTER 33

Everly

Lydia stood on the makeshift stage, her voice clear and strong despite the scars of recent battles. "Callie and I wouldn't be here today if it weren't for D and his wife, Everly." Her eyes met mine briefly before sweeping over the gathered crowd. "They saved me from a fate worse than death."

I shifted my weight, fingers twisting the ring on my right hand—Elise's ring. The smooth metal felt foreign and suffocating against my skin, a constant reminder of everything I had left behind.

"They risked their lives," Lydia continued, her voice trembling slightly. "And they didn't hesitate. Not once."

D's gaze burned into me from beside me. I didn't need to look to know he was watching. His presence was a heavy weight I couldn't ignore, pulling at emotions I didn't want to acknowledge.

Lydia paused, her eyes misting over. "Everly's bravery... her compassion... It's something we all should strive for."

I clenched my jaw, twisting the ring harder. Michael would

discover I'd left soon enough. He always moved on to another chosen one when someone slipped away. That's how it worked.

"And D," Lydia added, her voice growing firmer. "His strength and determination kept us all going. We owe them both our lives."

D's gaze felt like a physical touch now, making my skin prickle. For once, I wished he'd stop looking at me like that—with those eyes that saw too much and made me feel things I had no business feeling.

The crowd erupted in applause as Lydia stepped down from the stage, but the noise was a distant hum in my ears. My fingers stilled on the ring for a moment before resuming their nervous twisting.

For a second, I pretended it was real—that D really was my husband. What would he be like? He had been married before... Would he be tender? Would he be loving? I didn't know.

My gaze drifted to him. He stood beside me, hands relaxed at his sides, eyes scanning the crowd with an alertness that never seemed to leave him. There was a hardness to him, yes, but also a quiet strength. Would he hold me close at night, murmuring soft reassurances when the nightmares came? Would his touch be gentle, his words kind?

I imagined it—his arms around me, offering a sense of security I hadn't felt since before the bunker.

It felt better than pretending to be married to Michael. Instantly, guilt gnawed at me. It was supposed to be an honor—being chosen by Michael—but I couldn't bring myself to feel gratitude.

I glanced down at Elise's ring on my finger. My chest tightened with the weight of my conflicting emotions. Was it so wrong to crave something real, something grounded in mutual respect rather than divine expectation?

D's voice cut through my thoughts. "I can hear you thinking from here, sweetheart." His tone was casual, but there was an undercurrent of concern that made my heart skip a beat.

"Yeah," I replied quickly, forcing a smile. "Just thinking."

He nodded, but his eyes lingered on me for a moment longer before shifting back to the crowd.

I let out a slow breath and tried to focus on the here and now. Lydia had moved off the stage, blending into the throng of survivors who were mingling and sharing stories of hardship and hope. It was supposed to be a celebration of survival, of new beginnings. But all I could think about was the uneasy future that loomed ahead.

I shifted again, feeling D's presence beside me like a solid anchor in the storm of my thoughts.

The thought brought a fleeting sense of peace before reality crashed back in. The world outside our small circle was harsh and unforgiving, filled with dangers both seen and unseen. And Michael... would he come for me?

No.

At least, I didn't think so.

It didn't matter... did it? I would find Elise and bring her back to the bunker. I'd worry about Michael then.

For now, I let myself have this one small fantasy. Just for now.

Lydia appeared through the crowd, balancing three glasses with surprising skill. "I brought you both something," she said, her smile wide as she handed us the drinks.

I took mine immediately, eyeing the pink liquid with curiosity. "Golly, it looks so fun!" I exclaimed. "What's it taste like—"

"Sweetheart," D started, but I was already downing the drink in one gulp.

Lydia's eyes went wide. She shifted her gaze to D. "I didn't think she'd do that," she murmured.

"Goddamn Bunker Rats," he muttered, but there was an unmistakable affection in his voice.

The drink hit me like a wave, rushing to my head in a dizzying whirl of warmth and euphoria. Everything felt brighter, lighter. I felt good—no, amazing—and a giggle bubbled up from my chest.

"Can I get another one?" I asked, my words tumbling out in a rush.

"Absolutely fucking not," D said, his tone firm.

"Boo!" I exclaimed, pouting at him. "You're no fun, D. Come on. We're at a party!"

"Fucking lightweight," he muttered under his breath. His glare shifted to Lydia.

"Don't look at me," she said defensively. "She's your wife."

I giggled again, louder this time. "Yeah," I said, feeling bold and uninhibited. "Yeah, I am." I threw my arm around D's shoulders and leaned in close to him, feeling his warmth against my side. "Come on, sugar. Dance with me again."

"I don't think that's a good idea, darling," he murmured as I swayed against him.

But in that moment, everything felt perfect—like we were the only two people in the world who mattered. The music thrummed through my veins and the room spun in a delightful haze of color and sound. I pulled D closer, determined to make him see how wonderful this moment could be if he just let go for once.

His resistance was softening; I could feel it in the way his arm hesitated before wrapping around my waist. Maybe he was starting to understand that sometimes you just had to live a little—even in a world as broken as ours.

And for tonight, at least, I wanted nothing more than to dance with him until the stars faded from the sky.

The world around me spun in a kaleidoscope of colors, and I clung to D, feeling his solid presence grounding me. "You know," I began, my words tumbling out in a rush, "I've never felt like this before. Everything's always been so serious in the bunker. So many rules and responsibilities. But this"—I gestured wildly around us—"this is freedom."

D huffed, a sound that was part amusement, part exasperation. "Careful there, sweetheart. You're gonna hurt yourself."

I giggled, leaning into him more. "You know what? I used to dream about what it would be like outside the bunker. Imagined all sorts of things—green fields, blue skies, and endless possibilities. But I never imagined I'd meet someone like you."

He raised an eyebrow. "Like me?"

"Yeah," I nodded enthusiastically. "Someone strong and... and kind." My voice softened as I added, "And someone who looks out for me even when I'm being silly."

His grip on my waist tightened slightly, pulling me closer. "You're not silly," he murmured. "A pain in the ass, but not..."

I looked up at him, eyes wide and earnest. "You think so? Because sometimes I feel like I'm just stumbling around out here, trying to figure things out."

He sighed, but there was a hint of a smile playing on his lips. "You're doing just fine, sugar."

"Really?" The word came out more vulnerable than I intended.

"Yeah," he said firmly.

The music changed to a slower tune, and we swayed together. My head rested against his chest, and for the first time in what felt like forever, I allowed myself to relax completely.

"You know," I babbled on, feeling the warmth of the drink and the comfort of his presence loosening my tongue even more, "I've been thinking about Elise a lot lately. Wondering where she is and if she's okay."

He huffed again, but this time it was more of an affectionate sound than anything else.

"I'm lucky I've got you helping me find her," I continued. "That means everything to me."

D didn't respond to my rambling, but I didn't take it personally. His silence was a constant companion, and I had grown used to it. Instead, I let my thoughts drift.

"Do you think it's some kind of honor?" I asked, my voice barely above a whisper. "Being chosen to marry an archangel."

His brow furrowed slightly. "Your sister didn't want it?"

I looked away. "Yeah," I said softly. "My sister... she didn't want it." The silence stretched between us, heavy with unspoken words. I gathered my courage and asked that had been gnawing at me. "Why'd you marry your wife?"

He snorted, a hint of a smile tugging at his lips. "Why anyone gets married, angel. I loved her."

I couldn't help but laugh at that, the absurdity of his comparison breaking through the tension. "What's it like?" I asked, my voice turning serious again. "To be in love?"

He paused, considering his words carefully. "It's... grounding," he began slowly. "Like having an anchor in a storm. It makes everything clearer, simpler." His eyes softened, memories flickering behind them. "It's knowing someone has your back no matter what."

I gave him a long look, absorbing his words and the weight they carried. The way he spoke about love made my chest ache with a longing for something I had never truly experienced.

"I think I could love you," I murmured before I could stop myself.

He didn't respond immediately, his eyes searching mine for something I couldn't quite name.

I opened my mouth to say more, but my stomach rebelled

violently. Before I could stop it, the contents of my dinner spewed out onto the ground. The sharp tang of bile stung my throat, and I heard D mutter a curse under his breath.

"Goddammit."

My head spun, the world tilting dangerously. "I don't feel so good, D," I murmured, my voice weak and shaky.

"Yeah, no shit," he replied, but there was no anger in his tone. He held my hair back from my face with a gentleness that caught me off guard. "I think it's about time we go before—"

Silence chose that exact moment to trot over and start lapping at the vomit.

"Fucking disgusting," D muttered, shaking his head in disbelief.

The sight of Silence made my stomach churn even more. I gagged again, barely managing to hold back another round of sickness.

"Come on, darling," D said softly, sliding his arm around my waist to keep me upright. His touch was steady and reassuring, a lifeline in the midst of my dizziness.

The warmth of his body against mine helped ground me as he guided me away from the mess I'd made. Each step felt like a monumental effort, but with D's support, I managed to stay on my feet.

"Breathe, Evie," he murmured beside me, his voice a soothing anchor. "Just breathe."

I focused on his words, taking slow, deep breaths as we moved away from the crowd and towards a quieter part of the settlement. The noise and lights faded into the background, leaving just the two of us and the cool night air.

We stopped near a small bench under a tree. D helped me sit down gently before crouching beside me, his eyes filled with concern.

"Better?" he asked after a moment.

I nodded weakly. "A little." My head still swam, but the fresh air was helping to clear it somewhat.

He stayed close, not saying much, but his presence was comforting in its own way. Silence sat nearby too, looking up at us with those big, curious eyes that somehow managed to be both innocent and mischievous at once.

I leaned back against the tree trunk and closed my eyes for a moment, trying to steady myself. The night air felt cool against my flushed skin and slowly but surely I felt myself starting to calm down.

D's hand rested on my shoulder—firm but gentle—and I allowed myself to lean into him slightly for support.

"Thanks," I whispered after a while.

"Do you think you'd get married again?" I asked, my voice barely more than a whisper.

"You're still on that?" he snapped, his eyes narrowing.

I looked at him with hooded eyes, trying to read the emotions that flickered across his face. He snorted and shook his head.

"Not likely," he said, a hint of bitterness coloring his words.

"Why not?" I pressed. "Because you still love your wife?"

"Ex-wife," D corrected sharply. "And fuck no, I don't. She's a viper if I ever saw one."

"You call me a viper," I said, frowning. His words stung more than I cared to admit.

"There's a difference," he said, his voice softening slightly. "Betty fucking betrayed me. You..." He let his voice trail off, leaving the sentence unfinished.

"Me?" I asked, my heart pounding in my chest.

"What the fuck are you asking me all these goddamn questions for?" he demanded suddenly, his tone turning harsh again. "We ain't friends, you know that, right? You are a pain in the ass. You are a hindrance. You are an annoyance, like a welt on my ass."

I jerked back as if he had slapped me. "O-oh," I murmured, my voice cracking.

"Now, angel—"

"It's fine." I stood up abruptly and stumbled slightly as my head rushed from the sudden movement. "You, um... you don't have to help me anymore, okay? I don't... I won't be a burden."

"Everly," he said, his voice filled with something that almost sounded like regret.

"Please." My eyes filled with tears that I tried to blink away. "I would like to request some time... alone."

"I can't allow that," he growled, taking a step toward me.

"You don't get to decide that," I said firmly, backing away from him. The weight of his words and the realization of how he truly saw me crushed down on my chest, making it hard to breathe.

He stopped in his tracks, frustration etched across his features. "Everly..."

But I didn't wait for him to finish. Turning on my heel, I walked away as quickly as my shaky legs would allow. The cool night air stung my tear-streaked cheeks as I moved further from him, each step feeling heavier than the last.

All I wanted was some space to clear my head and mend my wounded heart—if that was even possible anymore in this brutal world we lived in.

I stormed through the town, my vision still a bit hazy from the drink. My head spun, and every step felt like I was walking on clouds, but I forced myself to keep moving. I needed to get away from him, away from his biting words and confusing presence.

The buildings blurred together, and I found myself stumbling into one at random. The dim interior and the stale air did little to soothe my frayed nerves.

"We ain't staying there, Evie," D's voice rumbled from behind me.

I turned to face him, my frustration bubbling up. "You don't have to shepherd me—"

"Clearly, I do," he interrupted, his tone brooking no argument.

I clenched my teeth, wishing I could muster more dignity. But it was hard to walk straight when my head was still so bubbly. As I tried to move past him, my foot caught on an uneven floorboard. I tripped forward, expecting to hit the ground.

But I didn't fall.

D's hand snaked around my waist, pulling me flush against his solid frame. My cheeks burned with embarrassment as I breathed in his familiar scent—earthy and slightly smoky.

"You can let me go," I murmured, unable to tear my eyes away from his lips. They were so close. I wondered what it would feel like to kiss them. "I wouldn't want to be a welt on your... your..."

"Ass?" he finished for me, amusement dancing in his eyes. "Can't even say the word, can you?" He smiled that infuriatingly charming smile of his.

"Stop that," I demanded weakly.

"Stop what?" he asked, leaning forward ever so slightly.

"Smiling," I said, feeling a strange flutter in my chest. "It makes me feel... strange."

"Oh, yeah?" He tilted his head to the side, his eyes darkening as they narrowed. My heart skipped a beat at the intensity of his gaze. "How does it make you feel?"

"Like there's a thousand hummingbirds in my stomach," I admitted quietly.

"Is that a good thing?" he asked, his voice softer now.

I bit my lip, unsure of how to answer that question. The sensation was overwhelming but not entirely unpleasant. And as much as I wanted to deny it, there was something about being close to him that made me feel safe—something I hadn't felt in a long time.

D leaned forward, and I knew he was going to kiss me. Despite the remnants of bile in my mouth and the alcohol coursing through my veins, I wanted it. My stomach tumbled, and my heart pounded as his lips drew closer. I should have pulled away, but I couldn't.

Just as our lips were about to meet, my stomach revolted again. I turned abruptly and threw up once more.

"Goddammit," D muttered, his frustration clear.

"I'm sorry," I whispered, my voice small and weak.

"Let's get you to bed," he said gruffly. Without warning, he swooped me up in his arms. "You keep walking, you'll take forever to get back to our room."

I closed my eyes, leaning my head against his chest. His warmth seeped into me, and despite the churning in my stomach, I felt safe.

In what seemed like only moments, we were back in the safety of our room. Too tired to change and so comfortable in D's arms, I didn't protest as he set me gently on the bed.

"Wait," I murmured, eyes half-closed. "Will you... can you hold me? Please? I feel... I feel safe. With you. I'll go right to sleep."

He huffed, but didn't reject me. As soon as my head hit the pillow, I worried he might leave. But then the bed sank under his weight, and I heard one boot fall to the floor, followed by another.

He lay down next to me, and I immediately turned towards him. One of my legs tangled with his, my arm draped around his waist, and my head rested on his chest. His heartbeat was a steady rhythm beneath my ear.

His fingers softly ran through my hair, lulling me into a deeper state of relaxation.

"Walton," he murmured quietly. "My name is Walton."

I wasn't sure if I'd imagined it or if he'd actually said it. But before I could think too much on it, sleep pulled me under completely.

CHAPTER 34

Walton

I didn't sleep. Not for a long time.

She was so warm, so petite in my arms. Her breath came out in soft, steady rhythms against my chest.

It seemed impossible that I had told her my name. The real one. I doubted she'd remember it come morning, especially after the amount she drank. But still...

I'd been such a fool.

I thought I could resist her. I thought I could keep her away from places in me that had been locked up tight for years. The places no one else ever got close to.

But she barreled through, and she wasn't even trying.

And I couldn't fucking deny it anymore.

Everly had a way of doing that—breaking through walls without even realizing they were there. She made me feel things I hadn't felt since before the Divine Collapse, before everything went to hell. It scared the shit out of me, but there it was, clear as day.

I ran a hand gently through her hair, careful not to wake her. Her blonde strands slipped through my fingers like silk. She murmured something unintelligible in her sleep and snuggled closer, making herself comfortable against the hardness of my chest.

This girl... she had no idea what kind of danger she was in, being around me. What kind of monster she'd decided to trust.

A monster who couldn't stop himself from caring about her.

Her scent was intoxicating—partly the soap from the inn's meager supplies, partly something uniquely Everly. It made it hard to think straight, hard to remember why I'd built those walls in the first place.

I thought back to the countless nights I'd spent alone, prowling through the Forsaken with nothing but vengeance to keep me company. Nights when sleep was more an enemy than a necessity, when closing my eyes meant seeing faces I'd rather forget. Betty's betrayal, Emma's being gone—it all came flooding back when I tried to rest.

But tonight... tonight was different.

Everly shifted slightly in my arms, bringing me back to the present. Her vulnerability tugged at something deep inside me, something I'd thought was long dead and buried.

No matter how much I wanted to deny it, this fucking girl had become more than just a job or an ally. She'd somehow managed to worm her way into my cold heart.

And for once, I didn't want to push someone away.

I knew I'd give her anything she asked, do anything for her. Protect her no matter what that entailed. But I could never tell her.

Not that it would matter. She could never...

"I could fall in love with you..." The words she murmured flitted through my mind, but I pushed the thought away. She was drunk. She didn't mean it. The girl probably didn't even know what love was.

And when she found out why I was after her sister, she'd hate me.

I stared at the ceiling, trying to banish the creeping dread. Every fiber of my being wanted to believe she'd understand, but I knew better. The truth had a way of tearing things apart.

Everly shifted again, a soft sigh escaping her lips as she burrowed deeper into my embrace. My chest tightened with an unfamiliar ache. Her trust was a fragile thing, something I had no right to hold onto, but here we were.

It wasn't supposed to be like this. She was just another job, another means to an end. Yet somehow, she'd become so much more.

A quiet knock at the door pulled me from my thoughts. I gently eased Everly off me and slipped out of bed, careful not to wake her. The cool air hit my skin as I moved toward the door, muscles tensing with every step.

I opened it a crack and found myself staring into the wary eyes of the innkeeper. His gaze flicked past me to where Everly lay sleeping.

"Thought you'd want to know," he whispered, "there's been talk of Purifier scouts nearby."

My jaw tightened at the mention of those fanatics. "Thanks," I muttered, shutting the door quietly before turning back to the room.

Everly hadn't stirred. Her steady breathing filled the silence as I sat back down on the edge of the bed, running a hand over my face.

The Purifiers were relentless in their pursuit of those they deemed unworthy. If they found us here... No, if they found *her* here...

I couldn't let that happen.

But how could I protect her from a truth that would inevitably destroy whatever fragile bond we had? How could I explain that Lucifer himself sent me after her sister? That without her sister, I wouldn't have access to my soul.

Everly deserved honesty, but honesty would shatter her world all over again.

And if she was shattered, I didn't know what the hell I was.

I watched her sleep for a moment longer, then leaned back against the headboard, pulling her close once more.

For now, all I could do was hold onto this fleeting moment and hope against hope that when morning came and reality set in, we'd find a way through it together—no matter how impossible it seemed.

* * *

When I woke up, sunlight streamed through the room, casting a golden glow on everything it touched. I didn't think I'd ever slept that deeply before. The night's turmoil had melted away, leaving me with a rare sense of peace.

A groan pulled me from my thoughts. I lifted my head to see Everly stirring beside me; her face scrunched in discomfort. She had one hand pressed against her temple, the other clutching the blanket like it could somehow shield her from the world.

I couldn't help it—I laughed. Really laughed. A deep, hearty sound that echoed off the walls. It felt like ages since I'd laughed this hard, and it was almost as foreign as it was freeing.

She winced at the noise and shot me a pained glare. "It's not... it's not funny," she muttered, her voice rough and barely above a whisper.

I shook my head, trying to suppress another bout of laughter. "Oh, it's funny all right," I said, still grinning like an idiot.

She nuzzled into my side, seeking comfort despite her

hangover-induced misery. Her forehead pressed against my chest, and she let out another pitiful groan. Her hands moved to cradle her head as if she could somehow squeeze the pain away.

"Ugh... what happened?" she moaned, voice muffled against my skin. "Did this come from that pink drink? Why did you let me drink that?"

"Pretty sure you didn't need much encouragement," I replied, running a hand through her hair in a soothing gesture.

She let out a soft hum at the touch but didn't respond further. Instead, she burrowed deeper into my side, her body warm and soft against mine. The intimacy of the moment wasn't lost on me—how easily she'd come to trust me despite everything.

Her hair was tousled from sleep and our shared warmth, strands falling across her face in a disheveled mess that only made her look more endearing. Even with a hangover and all the chaos of our lives, there was something undeniably captivating about Everly.

I sighed softly and leaned back against the headboard, still holding her close. Maybe moments like these were fleeting, but they were real enough to matter. And for now, that was enough.

Everly's groan cut through the morning silence, her hand pressing against her temple. "What do I do to make it go away?" she asked, voice strained and pitiful.

I couldn't help myself. "Well, there's always the classic hangover cure—greasy food, a cold shower, and regretting all your life choices," I quipped, unable to keep the smirk off my face.

She frowned at me, clearly not in the mood for jokes.

"Maybe they have coffee downstairs," I murmured, starting to move away from her.

But she clutched my arm, her fingers digging into my skin.

"Not... not yet," she said softly.

Her touch sent a warmth through me I wasn't ready to admit. Being wanted—needed—by someone like her? It was a feeling I hadn't allowed myself in what felt like forever.

"In the bunker, we had to wake up at six-thirty," she said, almost wistfully. "I don't think I've slept in like this... I don't want to get up yet."

"We have to leave, darling," I said, trying to sound firm but gentle. The last thing I wanted was to scare her with talk of Purifier scouts.

"I know," she replied. "Of course, I know. I just... can I have five more minutes? With you. Like this." Her eyes dropped to the blanket as she continued, "I didn't have a nightmare last night, and... it felt good. I just want to hang onto that for a little longer."

How could I deny her anything?

I grumbled something incoherent and settled back into the bed. "Five more minutes," I muttered, pulling her closer.

I held Everly close, her body warm and relaxed against mine. It was strange, this feeling of comfort. Her head rested on my chest, and I could feel the steady rhythm of her breathing, slow and even. She had her arm draped across my stomach, her fingers lightly clutching the fabric of my shirt as if afraid I'd vanish if she let go.

The room was silent except for the faint sounds of the world waking up outside. Sunlight poured through the window, casting a gentle glow over everything. The bed, which had seemed too small and awkward last night, now felt like a sanctuary—a rare bubble of peace in our chaotic lives.

Everly shifted slightly, her head moving to find a more comfortable spot on my chest. Her hair tickled my skin, but I didn't mind. There was something oddly soothing about it. She let out a contented sigh, the tension melting from her body.

I glanced down at her, taking in the sight of her relaxed face. Even with the remnants of a hangover etched into her features, she looked peaceful. Vulnerable, yet strong in a way that tugged at something deep inside me.

Her fingers brushed against my side as she adjusted herself again, and I couldn't help but smile at how naturally she fit into my arms. It was as if we had always been like this—two pieces of a puzzle that had finally found their place.

"You're really comfortable," she mumbled against my chest, her voice soft and sleepy.

I grunted. "Don't get used to it," I groused. "I ain't your personal pillow."

She hummed in response, her body sinking further into mine. It was clear she didn't want to move just yet. And honestly? I didn't either.

I tightened my hold on her slightly, letting myself enjoy the moment for what it was—a rare slice of normalcy in an otherwise abnormal world. It wasn't something I got often, if ever.

The minutes ticked by in comfortable silence, neither of us feeling the need to fill it with words. The world outside could wait a little longer while we held onto this fragile piece of tranquility.

"What's coffee?" she asked, tilting her face up.

I nearly choked. "You've never heard of coffee?"

She shook her head, looking genuinely puzzled. "We don't have much in terms of drinks in the bunker," she explained. "Wine for holy occasions, water, and juice. But nothing else."

"No wonder you're such a lightweight," I muttered, half-joking but more amazed at her sheltered life.

Everly frowned but didn't argue. She just watched me with those wide eyes, waiting for an explanation.

"Coffee," I began, "is this magical liquid that wakes you up and makes you feel like you can take on the world. It's bitter, hot, and smells like heaven when you're dead tired."

She wrinkled her nose. "Bitter? Doesn't sound too appealing."

"You'd be surprised," I said, reluctantly pulling away from her warmth. This time, she let me go, though she clutched her head with a grimace.

"I'll be back," I told her. "Pack your shit."

Before she could comment on my language, I slammed the door behind me. The hallway outside was quiet except for the faint sounds of morning activity from other rooms.

The stairs creaked under my weight as I descended to the ground floor. The scent of freshly brewed coffee hit me as soon as I entered the common area, and I headed straight for the small kitchen nook where a pot was already half-full.

I grabbed a mug and filled it to the brim, watching the steam rise from the dark liquid. As I took a sip, the bitter taste spread across my tongue, waking me up in a way nothing else could.

Carrying two mugs of coffee back upstairs, I couldn't help but smile at the thought of Everly's reaction to her first sip. She had no idea what she'd been missing out on all these years.

Reaching our room, I nudged the door open with my foot and stepped inside. Everly was still sitting on the bed, one hand pressed against her temple.

"Here," I said, handing her one of the mugs.

I handed Everly the steaming mug of coffee, watching her face as she brought it to her lips. The moment the bitter liquid hit her tongue, she gagged, almost spitting it out. Her eyes widened in shock and disgust.

"What is this?" she sputtered, wiping her mouth with the back of her hand. "Are you trying to poison me?"

I couldn't help but laugh. The sound was deep and genuine, reverberating through the room. "Welcome to the real world," I said, still chuckling. "Looks like your hangover is going to be a bit harder to recover from than you thought."

She glared at me but didn't argue. Instead, she set the mug down on the small table beside the bed, clearly done with her first coffee experience.

"So, then what do I do?" she asked.

I smirked. "You sweat it out," I replied. "Come on, angel. Let's get on the road."

Everly groaned but stood up, stretching her arms above her head before grabbing her pack. She moved with a sluggish grace, still clearly feeling the effects of last night's festivities.

We left the room together, descending the creaky stairs and stepping out into the morning sun. The air was crisp and cool, a stark contrast to the warmth of our room. I took a deep breath, feeling more alive than I had in a long time.

Silence trotted over to us, and I tossed her some jerky.

"Ready?" I asked, looking over at Everly.

She nodded, though there was a hint of reluctance in her eyes. "Yeah," she said softly. "Let's go."

We started walking, our footsteps crunching against the gravel path leading away from Ironedge. The world stretched out before us—wild and untamed—but for now; it was just another day on our journey.

Want to find out when the next book in the **The Of Brimstone & Halos Saga** comes out? Maybe you'd like to jump in on the giveaways, sales, and other fun stuff? Please consider signing up for my newsletter **here**.

Did You Like Ascenscion?

As an author, the best thing a reader can do is leave an honest review. I love gathering feedback because it shows me you care and it helps me be a better writer. If you have the time, I'd greatly appreciate any feedback you can give me. Thank you!

Acknowledgments

First and foremost, to God.

My readers, thank you for your continued support.

My wonderful cover design team, for your beautiful, eye catching covers. I cannot stop staring.

My family - Frank, Kylee, Madisyn, Ely, Avery, Jacob, and Josh. Your love is the best thing that ever happened to me.